A NOTE ON THE AUTHORS

LOTTE AND SØREN HAMMER are siblings from Denmark. Younger sister Lotte worked as a nurse after finishing her training in 1977 and her brother Søren was a trained teacher and a lecturer at the Copenhagen University College of Engineering. After Søren moved into the house where Lotte lived with her family in 2004, they began writing crime novels together. To date they have written eight books in the series of which five have been translated into English. *The Hanging* is the first, *The Girl in the Ice* is the second, *The Vanished* is the third, *The Lake* is the fourth and *The Night Ferry* is the fifth.

hammerhammer.com

THE
LAKE

LOTTE AND SØREN
HAMMER

*Translated from the Danish
by Charlotte Barslund*

BLOOMSBURY
LONDON · OXFORD · NEW YORK · NEW DELHI · SYDNEY

BLOOMSBURY PUBLISHING
Bloomsbury Publishing Plc
50 Bedford Square, London, WC1B 3DP, UK

www.bloomsbury.com

BLOOMSBURY, BLOOMSBURY PUBLISHING and the Diana logo are trademarks
of Bloomsbury Publishing Plc

First published in 2012 in Denmark as *Pigen i Satans Mose* by Gyldendalske in Copenhagen
First published in Great Britain 2017
This paperback edition first published in 2018

British Library Cataloguing-in-Publication Data
A catalogue record for this book is available from the British Library.

ISBN: TPB: 978-1-4088-7067-9
       PB: 978-1-4088-7066-2
       EPUB: 978-1-4088-7069-3

2 4 6 8 10 9 7 5 3 1

Typeset by Integra Software Services Pvt. Ltd.
Printed and bound in Great Britain by CPI Group (UK) Ltd, Croydon CRO 4YY

MIX
Paper from
responsible sources
FSC® C020471

To find out more about our authors and books visit www.bloomsbury.com.
Here you will find extracts, author interviews, details of forthcoming
events and the option to sign up for our newsletters.

'It's clear you're going to get points on your licence, and you should count yourself lucky if that's all that happens. Besides, it's not up for discussion.'

Jan Podowski's voice was calm, the tone almost conversational and devoid of irritation. Not that it was necessary: the balance of power between the two men was already established, and Henrik Krag took his orders without minding very much. He was a young man in his early twenties with unruly, blond hair, blue eyes that encouraged trust, strong limbs and a tarnished criminal record. He also had a steely determination to do well in his new job, learn from his more experienced partner and make a go of things for once. So far it had gone well if you were to ask him, which no one ever did. He said:

'Cool car. How long do we have it?'

'Until the mechanic has fixed our usual one.'

'And when will that be?'

The older man's response was indifferent:

'Tuesday or Wednesday, might be later.'

'I'm in no hurry.'

They drove for a while in silence, before Henrik Krag spoke again:

'So how much would an Audi like this set you back?'

'More than you'll ever learn in a lifetime, so stop dreaming.'

A voice from the back joined in.

'Why shouldn't he? Let him dream, Paw Pojanski. It's good to have dreams, it keeps people motivated. I'm sure you have an unrealistic little wish of your own . . . to live a few more years, for example.'

Laughter pealed out from behind the two men. Jan Podowski bowed his head and said:

'I wish you'd stop calling me that, Benedikte. You know what my name is.'

She laughed again and Henrik Krag laughed with her, against his better judgement; it was hard not to, though he would rather have sided with his partner. He adjusted the rear-view mirror and furtively studied the woman who was in favour of his dreaming, as an oppressive silence descended upon them once more.

Benedikte Lerche-Larsen was attractive in a fresh and straight-forward way. Henrik Krag thought she must be the same age as

CHAPTER 1

The first real day of spring 2008 fell in the middle of March.

A warm, white sun hung over Denmark; it was reflected in that morning's puddles, it tempted the bravest anemones out from the forest floor and chased the chirping lark skywards over stubble fields – it even reached into living rooms where its glare made children's computer screens unreadable and sparked cries of protest.

In Nordsjælland, between the towns of Lillerød and Lynge, a black Audi R8 was eating up the highway. Envious glances followed it whenever it accelerated effortlessly away from the rest of the traffic after pausing for a stop signal or, on one occasion, a pedestrian crossing. Such obstacles now lay behind it, and the road stretched out as far as the eye could see. The driver pressed the accelerator gently and then a little harder, relishing the way the car practically stuck to the road surface as the landscape whizzed past, and youthful exuberance prompted him to release another fraction of the engine's power.

'Drive properly.'

Henrik Krag glanced at the man in the passenger seat, who was leaning back with his eyes half closed as if asleep, only he wasn't. You never really knew with him. Sometimes he would be distant, almost beyond reach, even when he had been dry for a week; at other times he would react with lightning speed, despite having at least ten deep slugs from his ever-present hip flask sloshing around inside his considerable belly. The man's name was Jan Podowski, and Henrik Krag couldn't figure him out, indeed didn't even know if he liked him, although they had now worked together for almost two months.

'But it's clear.'

him, maybe a little younger. She was a redhead and her high, beautifully carved cheekbones and regular features gave her a welcoming expression, cheeky and carefree, as if she were constantly on the verge of breaking into a smile.

She caught him watching her in the mirror and smiled provocatively as she tilted her head from side to side, holding his gaze. Henrik Krag followed her posturing, unable to ignore it, though he could have done without it. Or so he thought. Suddenly she turned on him:

'Stop leering at me. Who do you think you are?'

'Sorry.'

'Let me tell you what my father's cars cost. He has three, and this is the least expensive. The price of this one is about twenty hookers – that is, if they can be bothered to work, and this is where you come in, my gangly friend, because some of them would rather sit on their bony arses and waste the money we've paid for them than do their actual job.'

She tossed her head in the direction of the fourth and final passenger in the car.

'Yes, I'm talking about you, sister. We've gone to the trouble of having you shipped all the way to civilisation, and now suddenly you can't be bothered to keep your half of the bargain. But I'm not going to let you screw over my family, and I can guarantee that very soon you'll find that out for yourself.'

The second girl was also pretty; however, in the current circumstances, she didn't look it. It was hard to guess her age, but not her fear. She was curled up in the back as far away as possible from Benedikte Lerche-Larsen, and when spoken to, the girl pushed herself even further away, despite the fact she didn't understand most of what was being said. No one, apart from her, knew her real name, but here in Denmark she was known as Jessica. All the women in her shipment had been given names starting with the letter 'J' – it was easier that way.

Henrik Krag glanced briefly over his shoulder at her. When they had picked her up an hour ago, she had cried; now she was starting again.

Benedikte Lerche-Larsen studied the girl, before losing interest and leaning forward between the seats.

'Have you told him what's going to happen?'

The question was directed at Jan Podowski, and the answer came reluctantly:

'It's not hard to guess.'

'So you haven't told him that it's her second time either?'

'No.'

She turned to Henrik Krag.

'Wow, this will be interesting. It's your first time, Henrik, but it's Crybaby's second, and you've no idea what you're about to do. A real baptism of fire.'

Henrik Krag said nothing. What was there to say? Whatever he did, she would outwit him. Not to mention everything else that put her out of his reach.

'Now what was her name . . . the last one, who also had to have a second trip before she finally worked out why she'd been imported? No, don't tell me, Jan, I do know it, hold on, hold on . . . Isabella, her name was. Isabella, am I right, Jan?'

'Yes.'

'Hah! I knew I could remember it. Now listen to me carefully, Henrik, do you know what Jan did to her? He used the jump leads from his car, attached one to her tongue and the other . . . Well, you can guess what he attached that to. I'm telling you, she squealed like a pig – and that was long before the power was even turned on.'

The car swerved briefly into the other lane, not much, but enough to reveal that Henrik Krag had flinched at the image seared into his mind. Benedikte Lerche-Larsen loved the effect she was having; she reached out her hand and twisted a lock of Henrik's blond hair around her finger.

'Oh dear, oh dear, that wasn't so hard to figure out, now was it? But you're wrong, sweetheart, that would never do, of course it wouldn't. We mustn't spoil the goods. Who would want to buy . . .'

Jan Podowski interrupted her.

'If you've got any coke on you, now is a good time to throw it out of the window, Benedikte.'

'What are you talking about?'

4

'That little golden antiquity in your handbag needs to be able to withstand close scrutiny, unless you fancy a trip to Hillerød police station.'

Henrik Krag could also see what lay ahead; he slowed down the car as he jerked his hair free from her finger. A few hundred metres ahead a handful of cars had been pulled aside for a random spot check; a police officer was standing in the middle of the road, easily recognisable in his fluorescent vest with white reflective stripes. Benedikte Lerche-Larsen craned her neck and asked, somewhat hesitantly:

'What's going on, Jan?'

'Don't know. Breathalysing, speed or vehicle checks, what do I know?'

'Does it have anything to do with us?'

'No, but it might unless you get your act together.'

Benedikte Lerche-Larsen reached into her handbag and fished out a beautifully engraved gold case, but instead of tipping its contents out of the window, she thrust it at Henrik Krag and commanded him imperiously:

'Hold it.'

Henrik Krag looked quizzically at Jan Podowski. The older man shrugged in resignation, and Henrik Krag stuffed the case in his pocket and then asked:

'What about Jessica? What if she tries to get out?'

'Why would she want to do that?'

'Because of the police, I mean . . . they help people, don't they?'

'It doesn't work like that.'

'What do you mean?'

'I mean, that's not how the system works. If she goes to the cops, she'll be sent back to Nigeria, and there are people in her home country she's considerably more scared of than she is of us.'

'And she knows that?'

'Oh, she does. They all do.'

Jan Podowski was right. The African woman didn't seize the chance to seek any protection from the forces of law and order as they were waved past; instead she started shaking and mumbling incoherently to herself some time later when the car turned off the highway and continued down a smaller one leading through a forest. Henrik Krag managed to steer the car clear of the worst potholes and soon they turned again, this time down a dirt track carved over decades into the heavy clay by countless vehicles. Above them dark conifers shut out the sunlight while, out of consideration for the suspension, Henrik cornered the long bends at a snail's pace. At last they arrived at a small clearing, with an unpretentious log cabin at the far end.

As soon as the car had stopped, Benedikte Lerche-Larsen leaped out and rushed off down the dirt track leading deeper into the forest. The two men stayed in the car. Jan Podowski took a deep slug from his hip flask. Henrik Krag asked:

'Where is she going?'

'To have a pee, I guess.'

'Why is she here? I thought we were doing this on our own.'

'Forget about her, and focus on the job you're paid to do.'

Henrik Krag nodded, but asked:

'Was it true, what she said about that Isabella woman?'

'Only some of it; she was exaggerating, but don't be nervous, we don't use that method any more. It was too difficult to control, and besides, I couldn't start the car afterwards.'

'So what do we use instead?'

He wanted the question to sound casual, as if it was all the same to him whether it was one kind of torture or another. He failed miserably. The older man picked up on his nervous undertone and said quietly:

'Take it easy, it'll be all right, it's not that bad. Come on, let's stretch our legs, we could do with that.'

They got out and stood either side of the car. Henrik Krag noticed how his partner wheezed at the slightest movement; he looked even worse than usual. When Jan Podowski had got his breath back, they carried on the conversation across the roof of the car.

'There's no point in hiding that this is the ugliest part of the job, but it doesn't happen very often, two or three times a year at most, and it gets easier every time. The first time is definitely the worst.'

Henrik Krag nodded, but thought this was small comfort.

'I mean, they all have at least two months' experience from the brothels before we take them over, and they knock the worst of their nonsense out of them there. Besides, the girls who do need disciplining from time to time generally get the message after a few slaps around the head and a bunch of threats. It's rare that we have to resort to this level, and this is her last chance. If today doesn't make a difference, we'll be sending her back.'

'Why?'

'Because violence doesn't fit with our business concept. The vast majority of our business partners don't like this sort of thing.'

'What has she done?'

'The question is what *hasn't* she done. She just lies there like dead meat. There have been several complaints, and we've had to refund seven visits, possibly eight, I don't remember exactly. But this is all new. Up until recently her work has been beyond reproach – nobody knows what has got into her.'

'What does she say about it?'

'Nothing, or nothing that makes any sense.'

'Maybe she doesn't know.' A small glimmer of hope formed in Henrik Krag's mind. Perhaps he could talk to the girl, make her see sense, so to speak. But Jan Podowski extinguished it immediately:

'Well, who knows? We'll find out tonight.'

'She has a client tonight?'

'Of course. By the way, if it's winter or frosty, then it's a good idea to tether them outside for half an hour without any clothes on. It's simple, but it's incredibly effective. I've tried it three times, and all three girls subsequently worked without any problems, even in the summer.'

He laughed as if he had told a joke, and Henrik Krag laughed with him.

'Right, the young lady is back from her stroll. You take Jessica into the cabin, I'll unlock it and get our kit out.'

Henrik Krag turned around; Benedikte Lerche-Larsen was approaching. It was time to get to work.

It was a hunting lodge and very basic: one room, built from heavy logs, with a couple of grimy farmhouse windows on each long side.

At one end of the room two bunk beds had been put up against the wall and a couple of foam mattresses were gathering dust; at the other there was a cast-iron wood-burning stove with a thin chimney pipe leading up through the roof. It was sparsely furnished, just heavy wooden chairs around a long table, which had been nailed to the floor. Nothing else apart from a yellowing steel engraving of a hunter with his dog, and various types of antlers over white skulls with empty eye sockets. The air was stale and dense, beer cans, nicotine and rancid cooking fat from the primitive patio grill competing with regular mould and damp. Henrik Krag scrunched up his nose and considered opening a window, but it remained just a thought.

They told the girl to get undressed, but she refused so they had to strip her naked. Jan Podowski had skilfully trussed her up in a form of torture known as the macaw's perch. He tied her hands, pulled them over her knees and forced a strong stick between them and the backs of her knees. He threw a rope over a cross-beam in the roof, raised his victim about a metre into the air, then casually knotted the end of the rope around the wood-burning stove. She whimpered, not loudly, more pleadingly. Her curly hair hung down towards the floor, while her eyes rolled into the back of her head, leaving only the whites showing. Henrik Krag thought that it was all wrong, and allowed himself to look away for a moment before Jan Podowski handed him the truncheon. It was artfully plaited from electric cable; heavy yet simultaneously flexible. He looked at the girl again. One of her black hairbands had almost slipped off and was clinging to the tip of a lock of hair, like an insect camouflaging itself.

'You need to hit her across her thighs, on her buttocks . . . I mean, her arse, and then her back or her shoulders. Watch you don't damage the kidneys, her neck or genitals.'

Like a good teacher, Jan Podowski indicated the areas without touching the girl. Henrik Krag nodded.

'How many times do I hit her?'

'Until I tell you to stop.'

'And how hard?'

'As hard as you can.'

No more questions were needed, and there was no more reason to delay. Henrik Krag weighed the truncheon in his hand again, and then slammed it forcefully but with control against the girl's back. The girl howled, writhing in agony, and swayed back and forth on her rope. Like a piñata, he thought, and gritted his teeth in order not to cry.

'You can do better than that . . . put your back into it, mate.'

He hit her again in the same place, as hard as he could. The girl wailed pitifully; Benedikte Lerche-Larsen looked away, Jan Podowski nodded wearily. Henrik Krag felt a strange rage well up inside him towards the girl. Perhaps it was her screaming, perhaps because he had had to drag her in here from the car by her ear, and she had refused to take off her clothes so he'd had to pull them off her, or perhaps it was just because she was dangling helplessly in front of him and it was his job to hit her. After that the blows fell more easily, five times, ten times, twenty times; he didn't count, he just carried on hitting to get it over with. The screams merged into one, interrupted only by the occasional gasp for air, and then suddenly, just as everything was going according to plan, Henrik Krag's next blow caught the rope and the loose knot around the wood-burning stove undid itself, sending the girl headlong into the floor. Her neck snapped with a small, ugly sound. Silence fell.

CHAPTER 2

The lake squeezed itself in between two uneven slopes, as if there was only just enough room for it. At the dawn of time, melting ice had carved a valley into the landscape, where deciduous trees now made up a small haven in an otherwise sinister and undisturbed coniferous forest. Along the water's edge, for a full three hundred and sixty degrees, broad borders of reeds, bulrushes and oat grass kept guard, flanked by cotton grass, whose white tufts – also known as the poor man's cotton and the plaything of the May wind – foretold summer.

The lake had no official name; it was too insignificant to merit that and too inaccessible. Locals simply called it 'the pond', and strangers, mostly ornithologists or hunters, had little interest in such insignificant matters. Yet the eastern shore was an exception – old maps referred to this area as Satan's Bog. Myth had it that a platoon of Swedish troops had camped on this very spot in 1658 on their way to Copenhagen during one of Denmark's countless wars with its neighbour. In the evening the strangers had amused themselves with the local farmers' daughters, both willing and unwilling. An orgy that ended with the vicar of Kolleløse Church, no less, being drowned in the lake, when he bravely – armed only with the word of God and his own anger – tried to stop the outrage. The story might play fast and loose with the facts, but the locals hung onto their legends, and it was true that old people around here still believed that if you wanted to cut reeds in Satan's Bog, you had better make the sign of the cross three times, or you risked bad things happening to you before the year was out.

Jan Podowski didn't make the sign of the cross. Partly because he didn't know the legend, and partly because bad things had already happened to him.

He stood by the shore of the lake looking into the undulating reeds, which were as high as a man. Benedikte Lerche-Larsen waited behind him in silence; between them lay a large, coarsely carved granite slab, which had been tethered to a couple of solid, transverse spruce branches with the same rope they had used when punishing the girl. Jan Podowski turned around.

'You did really well, Benedikte.'

He pointed his foot at the granite between them, a milestone with peeling white paint on the section that stood above ground. Despite its weight, she and Henrik Krag had dragged it almost two kilometres, and although she'd lifted considerably less than her partner, her achievement was still impressive. His praise, however, had no effect on her; she acted as if she hadn't heard him. A little later she spoke.

'What will you say to my father?'

'That there was an accident he doesn't want to know about and he has lost an investment, of course.'

'Nothing more than that?'

'That's plenty. Both your parents factor in such setbacks. They've made allowances for it in their budgets.'

'What about me?'

'What about you?'

'Are you going to tell them I was there?'

The older man waited for a bittern, well hidden by the vegetation, to finish its hollow booming.

'I thought you were here today on your mother's orders. To make sure we didn't go easy on the bitch.'

'Stop it, Jan! You know that's a lie.'

He knew perfectly well that her mother hadn't sent her, but he also knew that prying into her ambitions to learn about every aspect of her parents' business wasn't a good idea. Instead he said:

'I presume you're only too aware that your parents can't help you out of this mess. You would get ten years in jail, just like Henrik and me.'

She nodded irritably.

'I am, how did you put it . . . only too aware that all three of us are in deep shit.'

Henrik Krag had managed to lug his burden down the slope to the lake without slipping or falling once. With the dead, naked girl slung over his shoulders, he zigzagged from one tree to the next until he finally found himself level with the other two. He went over to them and kneeled down beside the stone before carefully unloading the dead weight. Jan Podowski asked:

'No one saw you?'

The question was superfluous. If he had met anyone, he would hardly have arrived as calmly as he had, but Jan Podowski knew he had run a big risk by letting Henrik Krag carry the girl in the manner he had. Then again, the alternatives were also risky.

'I don't think so.'

'And the cabin is ready to be torched?'

'Yes.'

Benedikte Lerche-Larsen had turned her back to the body and the two men. Now she asked: 'Why do you want to torch it? That's going to attract attention.'

'Because we have to. We've left dozens of forensic clues in there and they *will* be found, if someone starts looking for them.'

On Jan Podowski's instructions the body of the Nigerian girl was tied to the stone and the branches. It was time-consuming and Henrik Krag feared they might be discovered at any moment. Hailed by a forest ranger or, worse, by a couple of random hunters carrying guns. But nothing happened, and their macabre work progressed steadily and calmly. First they freed the stone from the lattice of branches, then Jan ordered them to dig a number of parallel grooves, each about half a metre long and about five centimetres deep. He drew an outline with a stick, and although they had only their fingers with which to remove the black, damp soil, the two young people did as he had told them without asking why; Henrik Krag in order not to look stupid, Benedikte Lerche-Larsen because she had quickly realised that her best chance of putting the current nightmare behind her was to obey the older man without hesitation.

When they had finished digging, they laid the spruce branches across the small trenches they'd created, then rolled the stone and eased it on top of them Finally they arranged the girl in an obscene position as though she were hugging the stone, with her limp arms and legs hanging down the sides. Jan Podowski and Henrik Krag tied her to it as tightly as they could; Benedikte Lerche-Larsen threading the end of the rope through the grooves they had dug under the stone when necessary. All that remained was to carry the stone and body into the lake, and here all three of them had to help.

Yet again it was Jan Podowski who took the lead.

'We're going to have to take off our clothes and shoes, strip down to our underwear. We can't drive home soaking wet.'

Neither Henrik Krag nor Benedikte Lerche-Larsen protested, so Jan Podowski continued:

'Prepare yourselves . . . this is going to hurt. The water can't be more than five degrees so we can only spend a few minutes in the lake, do you understand?' They nodded and started undressing. Jan

Podowski stopped them: 'No, wait until we've agreed who'll do what. We don't want to be discussing that while we're freezing.'

Soon afterwards the men were in their underpants and Benedikte Lerche-Larsen in her knickers and bra, all still wearing shoes. Henrik Krag was shivering from the cold even before he had tied his shoelaces. A light wind he hadn't noticed until now nipped aggressively at his body

'I'm bloody freezing here.'

Jan Podowski came down hard on him instantly:

'Stop whining, it only makes it worse.'

And Benedikte Lerche-Larsen supported him by snarling:

'You can be warm in prison, or you can be a bit cold out here. Now pick her up.'

Without further ado she stepped into the reeds and waded out until the water reached halfway up her thighs. The men followed her slowly, weighed down by the weight of the girl and the stone between them. Henrik Krag was gasping from the cold, but said nothing. Benedikte Lerche-Larsen had bent the reeds to one side, and step by step the girl and the stone were carried through the vegetation, which soon closed behind them, hiding the shore. When the water reached the men's waists, buoyancy made their work easier, but their numb limbs put a limit on how much further they could walk.

'Another ten steps, then we'll let her go. Come on, Henrik, you can do it. It's just ten more steps, then it'll be over; let's count them together.'

They counted in unison. When they reached ten, the men let go; at that point the water almost reached their necks.

'Take care not to snap those sodding reeds on your way back. We'll walk to the shore just as slowly and carefully as we walked out.'

Henrik Krag heard almost nothing, only the word *back* got through, but Benedikte Lerche-Larsen overtook him and swept back the plants with one hand, while with the other she dragged him to the shore. You didn't need to be a doctor to realise that the cold was about to overpower him, and he needed to warm up very soon. Jan Podowski's fat provided excellent insulation against the drop in temperature and he wasn't so badly affected. He studied the two young people; he would have to sack Henrik Krag, pay him off, tell him to stay away and, most importantly, forget what had happened. It was a shame, he liked the lad, but there was no other option. Then he looked at Benedikte Lerche-Larsen and smiled. For the first time ever he had seen her take after her parents, determined, strong and cynical – sparing neither herself nor anyone else. It was a very different side to what he saw of her most days.

CHAPTER 3

When Henrik Krag and Jan Podowski let go of the stone, the girl sank towards the bottom of the lake, the stone tilting so that she landed on her side, about a metre from where the forest of reeds bordered the open water. Here she lay with her eyes wide open and her mouth gaping, screaming a silent scream into her new world. Her unwitnessed decay began slowly as the low water temperature suppressed biological activity at the bottom of the lake, then progressed faster. At the beginning of April, the effective rasping tongues of the freshwater snails had removed her eyes, and arthropods with long, Latin names had sensed the way to her orifices; when the beech bloomed in May and the aquatic plants swayed above her, luminous green, the process of decay accelerated.

Bacterial gases inflated her from within, and she strained at the ropes in order to rise towards the surface, while small pearl strings of bubbles erupted from her, here, there and everywhere. Towards the early summer the smell of the girl's body attracted many of the lake's vultures: crayfish, larvae and fish of many species and sizes. A group of European eels spent Midsummer and the time that followed inside her, but by the week when the lime trees were in blossom and the short Danish summer began to wane, it was over, she had been reduced to a skeleton, and the fish went away one by one. In August the last sinews and muscles gave way, and her right hand floated off, followed soon afterwards by her left. The duck season opened on the first of September.

The hunter had been in his place on the shore of the lake from dawn. He sat patiently on his folding chair as a faint light seeped into the pearl-grey sky from the east and the landscape around him gained colour. His hunting dog, a three-year-old Irish Setter, which so far in its short lifespan had caused him much irritation and very little joy, was lying next to his chair. The dog's name was Dumbo and he was, quite simply, stupid. The man missed his old dog, which had tragically caught heart and lung worm and, after a dreadful period of illness, had had to leave in his prime. The hunter on his chair reminisced about his old dog as dawn broke, but scratched Dumbo behind the ear nevertheless. The setter couldn't help his lack of intelligence.

The mallard was hit perfectly in mid-flight and fell to earth like a rock; it crashed through the dry reeds and broke the surface of the water with a splash as the shot echoed from the slope. The hunter briefly punched his fist at the heavenly powers above to celebrate his prize shot; Dumbo stuck his tail between his legs and howled. All that remained was to fetch the quarry. Dumbo was ordered into the lake three times, and three times he returned, wagging his tail but with nothing in his jaws, while his owner shook his head and gradually began to accept that if he wanted that bird in the oven, he would have to fetch it himself. Or shoot another duck over dry land. He peered down at his dog and spoke gruffly.

'You should count yourself lucky we don't eat dogs in this country.'

Dumbo perked up and looked happy.

'Come on, I'll give you one more chance . . . now go and get that sodding duck.'

Dumbo disappeared into the vegetation for the fourth time. This time the hunter had to call several times before the dog finally returned, proud as a peacock with his find, though it wasn't the expected mallard.

In his professional life as a press photographer, the hunter had seen many dead bodies, and the skull didn't shock him badly. It was stained and discoloured in shades of black and brown with strands of algae-coloured hair sticking to the scalp and unnaturally white teeth in the upper jaw, while the lower one was completely missing. For a time he held it in front of him like an actor playing Hamlet, until he was convinced that it was the real thing. Then he set it down carefully in the grass, but thought it best not to give Dumbo the opportunity to run off with his discovery. The man picked up the skull and hung it out of the dog's reach on a young birch, with one branch sticking through an eye socket – a disrespectful act that later would cost him over two hours of interviews at Hillerød police station where staff had very little sympathy for Dumbo's lack of manners.

In the days that followed, rain and strong winds drifted in waves across the country from the west, complicating the work of the diving team. The lake might be small, but at its centre it was twelve metres deep, and the shallow water near the shores was tricky to examine because of the vegetation. The returns on the first day were limited to a dead mallard, which partly confirmed the hunter's story, though no one had ever seriously doubted him, his unseemly treatment of the skull notwithstanding. The second day was quite simply a waste of time; however, the findings on the third day justified the investment. In the morning they found the remains of a hand, and shortly afterwards the lower jaw was discovered hidden among a cluster of water lilies. The findings imbued the two divers with renewed energy, now they were sure there was something to look for, and early that afternoon, the skeleton in Satan's Bog was found. The girl and the stone were salvaged on a day almost as cold as the one when her killers had carried her into the lake six months earlier.

Hillerød police took charge of the investigation, but despite a technically excellent piece of police work, it produced no result. The post-mortem report concluded that the body was that of a woman aged between fifteen and twenty, of medium build and approximately 1.68 metres tall. Her death was caused by a fracture of the second cervical vertebra, and she had no other fractures or deformed bones apart from one which was broken, something that might have happened when she was tied to the granite block.

The investigation's biggest problem was that the time the body had lain in the water could only be estimated by a very broad margin. The pathologist put four to seven months as the extreme limits, and this was based on a long list of presumptions that made the dating even more unreliable. In practice, it meant that someone had probably lowered the woman into the lake between February and April of that year. However, the post-mortem did reveal one surprising fact: the woman was of African heritage, which was confirmed triply by the remains of her hair, her skull and her DNA. However, the forensic examination produced little else. The rope used to tie the woman to the granite block was thoroughly analysed, but all that could be ascertained was that it was of a type available in most DIY stores across the country. The granite slab was also scrutinised, but at that point the investigation had already established that the stone had formerly stood on the corner where the gravel road that led into Hanehoved Forest joined the main road. It had been ripped from the ground without anyone being able to say when. The technicians made only one positive contribution: a reconstruction of how the woman would have looked when she was alive. The technique for such recreations had improved dramatically in recent years: the process was now both faster and cheaper, and the results had become more reliable.

The investigators focused on two leads, which unfortunately both culminated in a dead end. One lead was Kolleløse Manor, which owned Hanehoved Forest and thus the lake where the woman had been found. The estate belonged to Adam Blixen-Agerskjold, a forward-thinking and approachable man in his early forties, who could trace his family back for centuries. He was also a chamberlain and would make occasional appearances at the royal palace. Together with his wife and a small handful of staff, he ran a thoroughly industrialised farm on the estate's roughly seven hundred hectares with varying crops of mainly spring barley, winter wheat and wild maize. It was by no means a gold mine, and every krone the landowner made was spent on maintaining his historic buildings. Both he and his wife were conscious of the duty owed to their heritage, even if it was a financially draining commitment appreciated by very few people.

For obvious reasons the police interest was focused on the Chamberlain's forest rather than on his farming. Hanehoved Forest, however, was mostly unexploited. The hunting rights had been leased to a consortium on Frederiksberg, and months would pass without anyone from the estate having reasons to enter the forest. Besides no one, not from the manor or the hunting consortium, had seen an African woman on the estate.

The second lead also turned out to be a dead end. A massive effort ensured that the girl's facial reconstruction was shown not only to the inhabitants of the sparsely populated countryside roundabout, but also to the majority of business owners in the three surrounding towns, Slangerup, Lynge and Ganløse. It was a huge job but all in vain, and the investigation slowly ground to a halt in the absence of any new leads. On the anniversary of the woman's death – an event known only to very few people – no one from the police was really concerned about their lack of progress. Nor was the public terribly worried about her fate.

But that, however, was about to change.

CHAPTER 4

TV-20, Hillerød's local TV station, went on air weekdays at eight o'clock. The channel was run by a team of volunteers on grants from the Ministry of Culture and at times delivered excellent and serious coverage of various activities in the region, from town council meetings to sports events and amateur theatre. A regular feature was the programme *Law and Order in Hillerød*, which went out every other Wednesday, and without sensationalising or skimming the surface, tried to examine crimes in the area. As it did one Wednesday in April 2009 when the programme was due to feature a lengthy interview with Hillerød's chief constable about his recently published review of last year's police efforts. Unfortunately, the chief constable had to pull out just before the programme went on air, and a sergeant was hastily summoned to stand in for his boss.

The sergeant was unprepared of course, but at the same time old and wise enough to admit when he didn't know the answer to a question; besides, the interviewer was skilled at initiating a constructive dialogue on any subjects where the interviewee was well informed. So the first half of the interview was a success, but just as both people concerned had decided that by helping each other, they could sail the programme safely ashore, it all went horribly wrong. The subject matter was the murder investigation in Hanehoved Forest, which couldn't be counted as one of last year's police successes. A fact, however, the sergeant was reluctant to concede. The interviewer pushed him gently.

'But ultimately, wouldn't it be fair to say you haven't made any progress with the investigation?'

The sergeant nodded. It was correct, but at the same time he wanted to defend his investigating colleagues, whom he knew had put in a great deal of effort.

'The thing is, it can be really tricky to work out where those nignogs originally come from.'

The interviewer's jaw dropped and an awkward silence ensued.

'What did you just say?'

'Well, she was from Africa. I mean . . . she could have lived all sorts of places.'

The sergeant had genuinely not meant to cause offence with his language. His own father had used the expression back in the 1970s, referring to migrant workers. The interviewer braced himself and attempted damage limitation.

'When you put it like that, you're not saying that the woman should be treated differently because of the colour of her skin?'

The sergeant frowned, baffled.

'No, of course not. Why should she be?'

However the next days only added fuel to the fire. Hillerød's chief constable was unwise enough both to defend and explain his junior officer's behaviour to the media, with the result that the unfortunate expression was repeated several times on national television and at prime time. The media went into overdrive. Television, radio, national newspapers and several web bloggers picked up on the unfortunate occurrence; linguists held forth about the fatal phrase, sociologists lectured about racism in the Danish police force, and a lively debate flourished about offence versus apology. The clip of the sergeant was shown over and over, while the man himself was put on involuntary gardening leave and sat at home swearing alternately at the Danish media and his new friends from the extreme right.

However, the scandal had one positive outcome. In the wake of the semantic blunder, the discovery of the woman's body was discussed throughout the media, since even the most simple-minded journalist could see that a murder investigation added extra piquancy to the racism debate, while at the same time providing evidence of the police's embarrassing conduct.

The media storm peaked in a news programme on the third day, where the story was served up to viewers under the headline *Pressure mounts on National Police Commissioner*, without it being made clear what the pressure amounted to or what steps the man was being forced to take. Even so his media adviser reacted promptly: that very same evening, she composed a sharp memo that recommended her boss must do something, it didn't matter what, so long as he showed leadership dramatic enough to get through to the man in the street. The National Police Commissioner loathed the man in the street with all his heart, partly because he was always being held up as someone to be won over, and partly because it was exclusively the preserve of media consultants to interpret what that revolting man in the street was thinking. Nevertheless, the Commissioner took her advice. The for all intents and purposes non-existent investigation into the dead woman from the lake was, on his direct and absolute order, removed from Nordsjælland's police and reassigned to the Copenhagen Homicide Department. He couldn't think what else to do.

CHAPTER 5

Detective Superintendent Konrad Simonsen had arrived early for work at Copenhagen Police Headquarters to familiarise himself with the three piles of files on his desk that made up his newly enforced investigation – a resolution which, however, had to be postponed in favour of dealing with an email from the National Police Commissioner who, in extremely vague phrases, ordered him to circulate a memo to every member of the Homicide Department advising them of the appropriate terminology to use in their investigation into the murder of the African woman in Satan's Bog. It was coming up for nine o'clock in the morning, and Konrad Simonsen had yet to comply with his boss's instructions, when Arne Pedersen entered his office. Pedersen was his deputy and closest colleague, a man in his early forties, competent, and usually in a good mood. Today was no exception.

'Hello, Simon. Now this is what I call a great day, I hear we're going on a nice trip to the woods.'

'They're promising rain later on, so I wouldn't bet on it.'

'I detect a certain reluctance to be out and about on this beautiful morning.'

'Shut up and give me a hand with this.'

Arne Pedersen threw his jacket on the desk and positioned himself behind his boss.

'I thought you'd come in early to read up on the "nignog" case.'

'Don't use that word, not ever! I've had an email from the top, and it's not one of the more easily fathomable ones. Several cubic metres of hot air in fact, even worse than usual, but as far as I can gather, he's saying we don't need to break our backs on this new investigation so long as we tell the public we're working hard to solve the case. And no matter what, we must never, *ever* use demeaning terms with racist over- or undertones, not internally or externally, whether speaking, writing, thinking or dreaming.

Something which I'm expected to make crystal clear to every single one of my staff and, ideally, their families.'

'So nig—'

'Shut up!'

'Sorry, boss. But you'll have your work cut out if you want to eliminate that word. Everyone is talking about the case whose name I mustn't mention, using exactly that unmentionable word. You can't prevent it, no matter what you do.'

'Wrong. I can't prevent that, no matter what *you* do.'

Arne Pedersen flung out his arms in a gesture of exasperation.

'You don't mean that?'

'I'm your boss, and what I say means whatever I want it to mean. Use some of our great leader's own phrases, that'll please him, but put them into a meaningful context. Then circulate the result in my name to everyone in Denmark who wears a uniform. I trust you, so I don't need to approve whatever you come up with before you circulate it. Take your time, we're not leaving for another couple of hours. I'll borrow your office meanwhile. Please would you open the door for me?'

Konrad Simonsen was standing ready and waiting with the case files in his arms.

'Not on your nelly. Do it yourself!'

So he did, using his elbow and a couple of fingers, since his subordinate proved so unwilling.

It took Arne Pedersen about an hour to carry out his new mission, and the result was, all things considered, reasonable. After reviewing it a couple of times and making a few tweaks, he decided that it was good to go, and circulated it in the name of Konrad Simonsen, as he had been told. Then he drank the rest of his coffee, which by now was cold rather than lukewarm, and logged onto an online newspaper to get an idea of the last twenty-four hours' news.

He couldn't think of anything else to do now that his own office was occupied. He'd managed a quick scrutiny of three national newspapers before he was interrupted by the Countess, who entered her boss's office, having knocked first as she was supposed to, but without awaiting his reply. She was her mid-forties, skilled and respected, and in a relationship with Konrad Simonsen who had moved into her house in Søllerød about a year ago. Her real name was Nathalie von Rosen, but everyone called her Countess because she was rich and her surname sounded posh. If she was surprised by Arne Pedersen's presence, she didn't show it.

'Hello, Arne. Are you busy?'

'No, I wouldn't say that. The financial crisis and the sports section can wait, but if you're looking for Simon, he's in my office reading reports.'

'Actually I wanted to talk to you too, but why have you switched offices?'

This gave Arne another opportunity to moan about his enforced assignment, though it fell on deaf ears. The Countess shared the general view of the National Police Commissioner.

'I think it's an excellent idea to remind everyone to be sensitive, and you're undoubtedly better at phrasing such things than Simon.'

Her praise was water off a duck's back.

'That's ridiculous. You can't change the way people speak, and it pisses me off that everything always has to be so politically correct. It's become almost impossible to open your mouth these days without the language police going in off the deep end on behalf of some of offended group or other.'

'Nonsense, Arne – and you know it. Of course you can discuss other people respectfully without losing your integrity.'

'You may be right, but surely it's worse if we don't bother solving the case, no matter what we're calling it. That, if anything, would be racist.'

'Surely one doesn't exclude the other. And why wouldn't we bother?'

Again Arne Pedersen explained, and again the Countess sided with the National Police Commissioner, which wasn't always the case. She was known for not flattering anyone either above or below her in rank, which had earned her respect on both sides.

'I'm sure that what he meant was that we should use our resources realistically. Hillerød police carried out an excellent investigation and there's no point in us repeating their work if we haven't anything new to add. This isn't about the dead woman being from Africa. However, we can bring all that speculation to an end by finding the person or persons who killed her.'

The Countess smiled and he smiled back. When she put it like that, how hard could it be?

Arne Pedersen took the opportunity to change the subject and satisfy his curiosity. The whole station knew the Countess had been to a meeting this morning about her personal finances, and there was speculation in every corner as to whether or not the meltdown of the financial markets would send her to the poor house. Although he knew it was none of his business, he asked her directly since it was the only way with her.

'So now what, Countess – has your fortune evaporated? Or are you still filthy rich?'

'My fund manager is an arch-conservative, doom-mongering old fogey, who has never believed in making a quick buck. That would appear to benefit me now . . . but enough about me. I came to talk to you about Pauline – she won't be coming with us after all.'

The subject was a sensitive one, they both knew why. He asked tentatively:

'Why?'

'Because she won't feel safe in a forest. She'd like to, she really would, but it's no good.'

Arne Pedersen nodded without commenting. It was just the way it was.

Pauline Berg was a sergeant in her early thirties and one of Konrad Simonsen's closest colleagues. Two years ago, however, she had endured a traumatic experience when she was kidnapped by a serial killer and imprisoned in an isolated bunker in the middle of a forest. She had witnessed him asphyxiate a fellow female prisoner and had almost lost her own life. Since then she had struggled with a number of things, including entering a forest. Last winter she had finally been given the diagnosis Post-traumatic Stress Syndrome by the doctor who lectured the Homicide Department about the condition, while offering no helpful suggestions as to how they should relate to a colleague whose behaviour was unpredictable, often downright unnerving, and who could no longer do her job properly. Or manage her private life for that matter. In addition to this, Pauline Berg had developed an obsession with the death of a young woman who had died under tragic but natural circumstances.

At times this case – which Pauline consistently referred to as a homicide – was the only part of her job that commanded her attention.

Arne Pedersen asked quietly:

'What does Simon say?'

The Countess lowered her head and studied the carpet, a somewhat vexed expression on her face. Then she straightened up, and answered him briskly.

'The same as you . . . nothing, but that's completely unacceptable. The truth is, Pauline is a massive problem for us, and has been ever since she came back to work, but every time I try to discuss it with you or Simon, all I ever get is evasions and nonsensical answers.'

She jabbed her finger at him accusingly, to reinforce her irritation. He focused on her nails; they were short and the movement made her clear nail polish reflect the light from the window.

'How long do you think this can go on for? Three years . . . four . . . five?'

Arne Pedersen had no answer. Years ago he had had an affair with Pauline Berg, and for a time had been genuinely in love with her, but he hadn't wanted to leave his children and the affair had ended. Today he missed her, as she used to be, but he avoided her whenever he could get away with it, without making it too obvious. He suppressed a sigh.

'What do you want to do – sack her? Which, incidentally, is impossible. There's a memo from the National Police Commissioner saying that no matter how she performs her duties, there can be no employment consequences for her. I know because I got it when I was in charge, and I presume it still applies.'

Arne Pedersen had been acting head of the Homicide Department at the time, while Konrad Simonsen recovered from heart surgery. The Countess brushed this off.

'Of course I'm not going to fire her, what good would that do? But we're going to have to talk to her. It's no use pretending everything is rosy when it's not.'

'Why do you suddenly care about it now? She's been like this for ages. Why don't we talk to Simon about it?'

The Countess shook her head.

'Brilliant idea, genius thinking, Arne, *talk to Simon about it* – how did you come up with that? We'll have plenty of time in the car going to Kolleløse, so please do *talk to Simon about it*. I'm happy to back you, so let's call that a plan.'

He didn't try and protest. What was the use when she was in that mood? He flung out his arms, impotently, and she left. He wondered if someone's back could look arrogant.

CHAPTER 6

They took the Countess's car for the drive from Police Headquarters to Hanehoved Forest. Arne Pedersen ended up behind the wheel without him quite knowing how that had happened, but the Countess herself had got straight into the back and left the driving to one of the three men, not caring which one. Konrad Simonsen also chose the back, and seeing as the fourth member of the group, Klavs Arnold, was still a novice to the streets of Copenhagen and no one wanted to listen to a synthetic Satnav voice, Arne Pedersen was the only option.

He chose the route through the city towards the Hillerød motorway, while he debated with himself whether he should make good on his half promise to the Countess and bring up the Pauline Berg dilemma. However, the Countess beat him to it and lectured the three men on the subject in a lengthy speech, which she made no attempt to hide that she had been saving up for some time. A strained silence ensued until Klavs Arnold leaned forward and peered up through the windscreen at the sky above them.

'I think it's going to rain.'

The provocation was obvious, and the tension in the car worsened when the Jutlander addressed the Countess directly.

'I think we should focus on our investigation for now. Then we can consider your monologue about Pauline at a later, more suitable time.'

Arne Pedersen held up a hand between his face and the rear-view mirror, the Countess snorted, and Konrad Simonsen snapped shut the case file, only too aware that he couldn't avoid being dragged into the dispute. To everyone's surprise, he sided with Klavs Arnold; the problem of Pauline Berg would have to wait.

Even so none of the three men expected the Countess to back down purely because she was outnumbered *and* her boss disagreed with her, and they were proved right. Belligerently, she launched herself at Konrad Simonsen, without adding anything new. The barb about her *monologue* hadn't missed its target entirely and she and Simonsen bickered all the way from Utterslev Mose to Værløse; she sharp and confrontational, he grunting with suppressed ill temper, clearly in a foul mood. As they fought, it began to rain; the drops that fell on the car were scattered and hesitant but soon strong gusts of wind forced Arne Pedersen to reduce speed considerably.

Klavs Arnold's bluntness was brought to bear for a second time.

'The two of you sound like an old married couple.'

The Countess didn't react, but Konrad Simonsen snarled:

'Mind your own business!'

'Now, now, I'm just asking – when is the wedding?'

Konrad Simonsen muttered curses under his breath at the young Jutlander, and the Countess seized her chance to put him down.

'We were married last Saturday,' she announced.

The new bride accepted Klavs Arnold's hasty congratulations and went on to speak at length about the happy event, which had been performed by a registrar from Rudersdal town hall with Konrad Simonsen's daughter, Anna Mia, as the sole guest. A long discussion and many compromises about the size of the wedding had preceded that; Konrad Simonsen had preferred small, the Countess large. Then out of the blue she had changed her mind and agreed with him, without saying why.

'Imagine, we had to ask our neighbour to be our second witness, or it wouldn't have been legal. Isn't that right, Simon?'

Her husband grunted miserably, especially when she added in a loving tone of voice: 'Oh, do cheer up, you look like you've just had root-canal surgery.'

Arne Pedersen was stupid enough to get involved.

'Many congratulations, Simon . . . or rather, to both of you. I must say, you've kept it quiet.'

This was the final straw. Konrad Simonsen practically screamed: 'Will you shut up!'

And they all did for the rest of the journey.

CHAPTER 7

The woman who welcomed the four Copenhagen Homicide investigators was straight out of an old Morten Koch film. Lenette Blixen-Agerskjold was waiting for her guests at the turn-off to the gravel road that led into Hanehoved Forest. Fresh-faced and smiling, still damp from the recent rain, she waved to welcome the car as a rainbow arched across the sky and the sun peeked out from behind the clouds once more.

She was in her mid-thirties, short and sensibly dressed in a Barbour jacket and trousers rolled up at the ankles to suit her short legs. Her square figure bulged in the wrong places and her home-dyed, chestnut-coloured hair was sorely in need of an appointment with a professional hairdresser. Her face was open and not without its charm, her gaze intelligent and humorous.

Once the car had turned off the main road, she guided it down the gravel road. Surprisingly clearly, Arne Pedersen thought, following her instructions. She pointed to the verge where the sloe bushes between the field and the track ended; they could park there. Klavs Arnold seized the opportunity to comment.

'I say, I say, it's her ladyship herself who's receiving us.'

He didn't explain how he knew that, and no one asked. Perhaps he had read a report the others had yet to see. The Countess corrected him:

'She's no more aristocratic than you or I.'

'So what is the wife of a Chamberlain? I thought it was something royal.'

'And, to some extent, it is. If you're in the Queen's good books, she might appoint you.'

'So this woman's not posh, is that what you're saying? She doesn't look it, I must say.'

'There's posh and then there's posh. A Chamberlain is a member of the second class in the order of hierarchy – on a level with bishops, mayors and our dearly beloved National Police Commissioner.'

Klavs Arnold asked with interest:

'How many classes are there?'

It was Konrad Simonsen who replied:

'The scale goes all the way down to class forty, where you will find cheeky police officers from Jutland, along with cartoon characters and cheap Chinese garden gnomes. Let's focus on the job, shall we?'

Konrad Simonsen led the opening pleasantries with Lenette Blixen-Agerskjold. They greeted each other politely, exchanged names and titles, smiling as warmly as the weather. The chief of the Homicide Department thanked her for the welcome, and introduced his team, who shook hands one by one, and then, after a few more remarks about the capricious Danish spring, explained the reason for their visit.

'We're here to get a sense of the area. I don't know if you've spoken to your husband, ma'am?'

'Drop the ma'am, we never use it out here, and yes, I've spoken to Adam. He's very sorry that he couldn't be here to meet you himself; he has a meeting with the bank, so you'll have to settle for me to begin with. But he'll probably be back by the time we get up to the house.'

Her voice was deep, almost sensuous, as though she were flirting when she spoke. Konrad Simonsen laughed lightly, almost by reflex; her good humour was infectious.

'Of course we would like to meet him too, if that's possible. Did he also tell you that none of us has had the time to familiarise ourselves properly with the case, so we may have to . . .'

He hesitated briefly, and she promptly finished the sentence for him.

'I know: ask questions we've already answered. But that's nothing new, it was the same with the officers from Hillerød, so we're used to that. I've planned a route for us. It's just a suggestion, of course, but there's one thing you must see, so perhaps we should start with that.'

Without waiting for a reply, she led them back down the gravel road. She stopped right by the main road, where she pointed to a hole in the ground. They all knew what they were looking at: the granite milestone used to weigh down the body of the African woman in the lake had been taken from here. The officers looked around to form an impression of the scene. Konrad Simonsen asked no one in particular:

'Does anyone remember how heavy it was? I think I read it somewhere, but I've forgotten the exact figure.'

Arne Pedersen said:

'Almost eighty kilos, and it's roughly two kilometres to the lake from here, and that's as the crow flies.'

Their conclusions might vary, but none of the officers volunteered anything. That would have to wait until they were alone. When she sensed that her guests had seen enough, the Chamberlain's wife said, 'I presume you'll want to know how to reach the lake from here.'

She took a map from her Barbour's inside pocket, unfolded it and placed it on the ground in front of her. The offices squatted down in a disciplined semi-circle, while she, using a twig as a pointer, explained.

'Here's the manor house, and there's the lake where the girl was found. You can access it by two different routes. One option is from the main road and down a forest track, but it's very overgrown and barely passable. The other option is continuing down the gravel track and taking a right where a path leads to a hunting lodge; from there you can walk through the spruce forest and down to the lake.

If you go for the latter, you'll reach the lake's northern shore where the girl was found. If you pick the other route, you'll reach the south side of the lake, where there's a platform for buck hunting – I think it's called a deer stand.'

She looked up at her audience, who nodded. Klavs Arnold asked:

'What sort of game do you have here?'

'Red deer, but they're rare, and then there are fallow deer. I'm not entirely sure what the species are called, but Adam knows. I don't like hunting.'

Konrad Simonsen wanted to know if the gravel track they were on led all the way up to the manor house. She shook her head.

'No, it stops a few kilometres further ahead, but then you can walk the rest of the way along a field boundary; it's not terribly difficult, it was how I made my way here.'

'You can't drive it?'

She considered his suggestion critically.

'Possibly in a tractor, but the gravel road here ends in a stone wall. There may be a gap somewhere, there probably is, I don't know.'

'But not in a regular passenger car?'

'It would be difficult, I think, but whether it would be downright impossible . . . Well, why don't you walk with me when we head up to the house, and you can decide for yourselves?'

No one had any further questions, and they walked down the gravel road without saying very much. High up in the sky above their heads, larks sang while the rainbow faded and grey clouds drifted to the east. Arne Pedersen thought that his job had its perks while Klavs Arnold wondered whether the Chamberlain's wife might be just a little too eager to help. Konrad Simonsen and the Countess walked together, without speaking.

The first stop was the hunting lodge. It was new and prefabricated, constructed as a hexagon of vertical, stripped-pine trunks, and each side came with a small farmhouse window. Steps led up to the heavy and cumbersome door. The officers knew that the cabin had been examined meticulously, literally one square centimetre at a time, for potential forensic evidence, all without success. With the scientific expertise available to the Homicide Department, it could be said with almost one hundred per cent certainty that the dead woman had never been inside it.

Lenette Blixen-Agerskjold bent down and produced a key from its hiding place under the doorstep. She opened the door but remained outside herself, as did Konrad Simonsen and the Countess. Klavs Arnold made do with a fleeting glance from the doorway. Only Arne Pedersen went inside. The room was dominated by a hexagonal open fireplace in the centre surrounded by a strong soapstone table, presumably designed so as to retain the heat overnight. Four benches had been erected around the table, and there was a cupboard against one wall. Arne Pedersen sat down on a bench and scanned the room without anything in particular catching his attention. He stayed there dutifully for a couple of minutes, with the same result.

Outside Klavs Arnold asked:

'The lodge is new. When was it built?'

Lenette Blixen-Agerskjold replied promptly:

'A year and a half ago, the old one was so decrepit we really had no other choice.'

'No other choice?'

'We rent out the hunting to a consortium in Copenhagen. They have the right to be here all year round, but in practice they're only here in the autumn; we had the old cabin knocked down in the winter, and put up this new one in its place.'

Konrad Simonsen took over, and said in a neutral voice:

'Your estate bailiff, is that Frode Otto?'

For the first time the Chamberlain's wife showed some irritation. Her voice sharpened.

'Yes, that's right, and I'm perfectly aware that he fell foul of the law when he was younger. But that's over fifteen years ago. Even so he has been interviewed ten times, at least, as if everything he says is automatically assumed to be pure fiction. Surely people can change for the better, or perhaps you don't think so?'

Konrad Simonsen obliged her without hesitation:

'Perhaps they can, and of course it's neither pleasant nor fair to be singled out when you've served your sentence and appear to have kept clean for years. But I'm dealing with a murder investigation, and the truth is I don't care one jot about such sensitivities. I'll interview anyone I like. My many years in the job have made me cynical and destroyed any illusions I may once have had when it comes to mankind's capacity for rehabilitation. That's just the way it is.'

'So a youthful error should be allowed to haunt someone for the rest of their life?'

'I believe there was a single slip recently. Or does my memory fail me?'

Lenette Blixen-Agerskjold looked away. The Countess was surprised. Her husband's tone of voice had been confrontational – too confrontational for her liking. Besides, it didn't seem fair to discuss the estate bailiff's past with his employer. But despite her objections, she did what was expected of her and gently tugged the sleeve of Lenette Blixen-Agerskjold's jacket and led her away. They stepped out of earshot and the men could see that they were talking together. Soon they were laughing, and Konrad Simonsen smiled. Good cop, bad cop – it worked nearly every time.

The party moved through the spruce forest down towards the lake. The trees were scattered and in most places the forest floor was without vegetation. The two women led the way without rushing. They walked some distance in front of the men, chatting about this and that. The Countess asked:

'Did you grow up around here?'

'Almost, I'm from Slangerup. That's not very far away, but as far as the manor is concerned, I might as well have been from Jutland. This isn't the kind of place I would frequent, not before I met Adam.'

'And how did you meet your husband?'

'I was behind the till at a butcher's. Not terribly romantic, is it?'

'Do tell.'

She told her story; the Countess listened and prompted her when necessary.

When they left the conifers behind and entered the deciduous forest, the Countess's friendly overture paid off. Lenette Blixen-Agerskjold said as if at random:

'Four years ago Frode was given a three-month suspended sentence for assault. It was a pub brawl in Copenhagen, and I think both parties were equally culpable. We decided to keep him on, but stressed that it mustn't happen again.'

They had reached a slope. Lenette Blixen-Agerskjold pointed to the post by the lake lying below them and they moved carefully down the slope, half crawling, backing down in single file as they held on to the young beeches growing randomly down most of the hill. A branch swiped back vengefully and cut Arne Pedersen's ear. It bled and stained his light-coloured leather jacket. He swore, Klavs Arnold apologised.

Someone had hammered a post into the soft soil in front of the reeds, which interfered with their view of the lake. A red and white plastic strip stamped with the word 'POLICE' had been tied around the top and finished in a bow. It wasn't difficult to guess what the post indicated. Konrad Simonsen found a pocketknife and cut the plastic free from the post, before scrunching it up and putting it in his pocket. Then he turned and looked further into the wilderness. The others stayed a few paces away in respectful silence, unsure what information he was absorbing as he stood there staring, lost to the world, deep in his own thoughts.

But Konrad Simonsen was absorbing nothing. He was thinking about Kasper Planck, his old boss and friend, who had died last year. He shook his head imperceptibly, surprised at himself, marvelling at the way the mind works; he had headed the Homicide Department for almost a decade without ever giving his predecessor much thought in a professional capacity. There had been exceptions, indeed one major exception, he acknowledged, but overall he had managed the job on his own. And yet now, after the old boy had died, he missed him all the time. Konrad Simonsen wondered what his old friend would have said, had he been here. At first he failed to come up with a convincing answer, then a clear thought swept all other speculation aside. There could be little doubt about Kasper Planck's reaction, if he had been standing next to Simonsen; he could almost hear that dark drawl with its biting honesty, which could so easily turn to sarcasm. Planck would have said:

'What the hell are we doing here?'

CHAPTER 8

Konrad Simonsen, the Countess and the Blixen-Agerskjolds were sitting in the Chamberlain's office in the main building of Kolleløse Manor, enjoying coffee and homemade cake, fresh out of the oven, still warm. The men spoke, the women were silent. The Countess studied the paintings on the walls, which immortalised first the Blixen and later the Blixen-Agerskjold line – well, the male ancestors, at least. They were arranged in a row stretching pretty much around the whole room, from where they watched their living descendants sternly and with the weight of expectation. The Countess was only half listening to the somewhat strained conversation Konrad Simonsen kept going concerning the running of the estate.

Adam Blixen-Agerskjold was a tall, gangly man with a pale, long horsey face, protruding eyes, narrow, bloodless lips and a scruffy goatee on his receding chin. He resembled his many ancestors to an astonishing degree, thought the Countess, who nevertheless found him sympathetic. His voice was deep and his replies to Konrad Simonsen's irrelevant questions were precise and stripped of irritation, though it must be obvious, even to him, that the Detective Superintendent didn't have the slightest interest in the sewage pipes in the boulder foundation or the restoration of copper roofs.

After an extended period of small talk and baked goods, Konrad Simonsen straightened up in his chair and folded his hands across his stomach. The Countess, who recognised the gesture, pricked up her ears. He asked:

'Are you in charge of the estate accounts yourself?'

Adam Blixen-Agerskjold nodded.

'Yes, together with the bank and our accountant.'

'All the accounts?'

'No, not all of them. Our estate bailiff, Frode Otto, prepares the accounts for his own areas of responsibility, but he reports to me, and to the accountant, of course.'

'And his areas of responsibility are?'

'Any activity that doesn't affect the direct management of the estate. At the moment we have only three. There's the hunting, then we have the holiday cottages – we have seven behind the apple orchard for visitors – and we're also currently trying out growing mushrooms in the cellars. But none of this has any major financial impact, sadly. We experiment all the time to find alternative sources of income, but so far without much success.'

'And Frode Otto is in charge of these ventures?'

'Yes, he is. I focus exclusively on agriculture.'

'So how about the accounts, paperwork, budgets, that kind of thing . . . would it be possible for us to have access to that information, possibly take copies of current and past records?'

The Chamberlain smiled.

'Of course, we have nothing to hide. But as for copying historic paperwork, that's going to be a bit tricky.'

Konrad Simonsen's voice sharpened slightly.

'Because?'

The Chamberlain flung a gangly arm in the direction of the bookcases to his left with their rows of tightly crammed leather-bound books, most embossed in faded gold leaf with a year.

'In here we keep the accounts for the second half of the eighteenth century. You can see the profits of the manor house itself and that from tenanted farms as well as forest fees, mill fees and tithes. All measured in bushels. But I'm afraid it will take time to copy that.'

Lenette Blixen-Agerskjold intervened:

'Stop it, Adam. You know perfectly well what he meant.'

Konrad Simonsen's mobile announced loudly that he had received a text message. The Countess frowned; he always turned off his mobile during interviews. She was even more surprised when he checked the message apologetically; it must be important. She took over the interview.

'I regret our somewhat unfortunate choice of words. As I'm sure you can hear we're novices when it comes to accounts. But we have colleagues who are experts in this area. If we ask a couple of our people to come out here, would you be willing to work with them?'

The Chamberlain's answer came without hesitation:

'Absolutely! Like I said, there's nothing here that can't withstand scrutiny. Besides, most information is available online, if you have the right usernames and passwords, and your people can get those from me.'

Konrad Simonsen handed his mobile to the Countess, so that she too could read his text message. It was from Pauline Berg.

Madame says the girl was suspended naked from a tree. Head down and then she was beaten to death. Her clothes were burned in the forest. Madame is very sure of her vision.
P.S. Her husband gives me the creeps!

Despite the macabre contents, the Countess smiled broadly, while she shook her head in despair at her newly acquired husband. So Konrad Simonsen had decided to share one of his most sensitive contacts with Pauline Berg. 'Madame' was a clairvoyant who operated from her home in Høje Taastrup. The Countess herself had had the opportunity to meet her on only one occasion; otherwise she was the preserve of the Homicide chief himself, often without anyone else knowing that he had visited her, let alone what Madame had told him. But in this investigation Pauline Berg would appear to have been awarded that honour. You had to know Konrad Simonsen well to realise how significant a gesture it was, and yet at the same time, it was typical of him not to mention Pauline's visit to the clairvoyant to the others in the car on the way here, but to let them tear strips off him instead. They had been unfair to him, she had to admit that now.

When the Countess had read the text message, Konrad Simonsen asked:

'Would you be willing to give me permission to undertake a more systematic search of Hanehoved Forest?'

The Countess furrowed her brow. Normally Konrad Simonsen didn't attach that much importance to Madame's information. Adam Blixen-Agerskjold replied:

'I'd be happy to. Do you mean the whole forest?'

'Yes, all of it.'

'May I ask what you're looking for?'

'The remains of a fire, possibly of clothing as well.'

'The African woman's clothing?'

'Yes.'

'So her clothes were burned in the forest?'

'They might have been, that's what we hope to find out. My question is whether you'll help us?'

'Oh, I will. You're welcome to use the manor house as your base, if that's practical, and we can also provide you with a couple of volunteers, but that won't get you very far, of course. When were you thinking of starting?'

'I don't know yet, but I soon will. It would be great to work from here; we don't need any volunteers, but it was kind of you to offer.'

They exchanged some practical information, and the officers thanked their hosts for the delicious cake and coffee before they left.

CHAPTER 9

Arne Pedersen and Klavs Arnold inspected Kelleløse Manor and its many outbuildings. They had no specific plan. Whenever they met one of the estate's employees, they would greet them politely and exchange a few casual remarks with them, before strolling on. They hung around the holiday cottages for a while and peered through the windows, then they crossed a lawn diagonally and reached the estate's stud stables, which were no longer in use, but were well tended with ochre-washed walls and small, black-painted metal windows. Klavs Arnold asked:

'That email Simon circulated this morning . . . I mean, what a load of tosh! I tried my very best to understand it, but it makes no bloody sense.'

'I wrote it for him.'

'I know.'

'Oh, you do? Then did you also know that I was ordered to write it?'

'No, but what difference does that make? If there's one thing I'll never get used to, it's these indirect ways of communicating, which you lot over here in the capital use. It would never have happened back home. There we call a spade a spade.'

Back home was the town of Esbjerg. Arne Pedersen thought that it probably always would be for Klavs Arnold, no matter how long he lived in Copenhagen. He and his family had only moved to the capital because his wife had been elected to Folketinget, the Danish Parliament, and they were unlikely to stay, if and when she lost her seat. Arne Pedersen gave the young Jutlander a professorial reply.

'That's because where you come from, you make your living from fishing. It's plain and simple: go to sea, catch the fish, go home, gut them, put them in the oven, get them into your stomach, and you're sated and happy. Over here, however, we're merchants, and that's far more complicated; you often have to go the long way round to secure a good deal. This rubs off on our language; we're more sophisticated, so to speak.'

'If you ever come to Esbjerg, I'll bloody well take you on a fishing boat where you can puke up your condescending remarks into the North Sea!'

'Do you know, I've always wanted to do that . . . not puke, I mean, but go to sea in a fishing boat. Would you really be able to arrange that?'

Klavs Arnold opened his mouth but didn't reply. Arne Pedersen followed the direction in which he was looking. To their left a barn door stood open and a hen slipped out. Klavs Arnold said:

'What's that?'

'*Gallus gallus domesticus*, also known as a hen. You ought to know that, you're the country boy.'

The hen started pecking in between the cobbles in the farm-yard; every now and again it would squint suspiciously at the two officers, as if it knew they were talking about it. Klavs Arnold stayed put even when shortly afterwards the clucking bird waddled off. Suddenly Arne Pedersen could see it too – a brief, white flash of light coming from inside the barn. It lasted barely more than a few seconds, then it was gone. They entered.

The interior was large, and there were agricultural machines everywhere, old and new together, tractors, a combine harvester, sprayers, and several vehicles whose function neither of the officers knew. To the left of the entrance was an old landau carriage; one wheel had been replaced by a wooden post, and decay had eaten its way well into the hood, which was cracked and overgrown with mould. Right next to it was a giant, modern plough, a red-and-green-painted monster with its numerous shiny shears retracted and pointing up at the ceiling.

They zigzagged through the barn, Klavs Arnold leading, Arne Pedersen following a little hesitantly behind, not sure where his colleague was taking them. The flashes of light grew brighter, and a strong smell of ozone found its way to the officers' nostrils. At the back of the room a man stood welding at a small metal table. His face was covered by a helmet and an impressive breathing apparatus that culminated in a big, black hood, which reached down to his shoulders. The welder looked briefly at his uninvited guests, and made a point of carrying on with his work. The two officers watched him for a while, every now and again shielding their eyes or looking away from the bright, bluish light, until Klavs Arnold finally took a few steps forward and turned off the switch on the wall. The man tore off his strong work gloves and, with an irritated gesture, chucked them onto the metal table He pushed up his visor, squinted, took off his helmet and placed it on top of the gloves.

'Frode Otto?'

'Who wants to know?'

Klavs Arnold looked for his ID, but was interrupted.

'Forget it, I know you're cops. And yes, I'm Frode Otto.'

He was a powerful man of about fifty, with heavy features and strong limbs, a body used to physical labour. His face was ruddy, his hair greying and tied together in an unflattering ponytail that flopped about his neck. His eyes were guarded and hostile. Klavs Arnold stared at Frode Otto's hands: they were colossal, even for his size. Working hands, bent, impossible to open fully after decades of toil. His left little finger was missing the two top joints; there was no wedding ring on his ring finger. Klavs Arnold extended his hand but the man refused it with a grunt.

'No, thanks, I don't need your pleasantries. Tell me what you want to know and I'll answer you as best as I can, and try to forget that you've probably asked me the same questions hundreds of times before.'

Klavs Arnold pointed to the metal piece on the work table.

'You're a crap welder.'

The Jutlander's disarming tone of voice made the remark conversational, almost matey. Arne Pedersen smiled, he had seen this before. His partner had excellent people skills in his own down-to-earth fashion. All three men looked; the welding was indeed uneven and knobbly. Klavs Arnold added:

'Though I don't think I could have done a better job myself. It's a lot harder than people think.'

Frode Otto shrugged.

'It's not an altarpiece, it just needs to stick together, that's all. But I've got work to do.'

'Don't worry, we'll be leaving soon. But tell me, have they bothered you a lot, our people from Hillerød, since you're so pissed off?'

The man tilted his head from side to side as if to indicate that it hadn't been that bad. Arne Pedersen broke into the conversation.

'I can sort of see where you're coming from. We have a bad habit of targeting people we've been in contact with before, if I can put it like that.'

The placatory tone of voice succeeded, Frode Otto thawed, and soon they were chatting about this and that. But the mood changed in an instant when Konrad Simonsen and the Countess joined them.

They appeared from behind a tractor, and the moment Frode Otto spotted them, his behaviour changed. At first he froze, almost as if scared, then he quickly slipped on his work gloves and rudely turned his back on the two new arrivals. He restored the power to his welding equipment and donned his helmet. Konrad Simonsen stood on the other side of the work table and watched the bailiff continuously until the dazzling welding light forced him to look away. The Countess decided it was time to go. She turned and left, and the others followed her.

CHAPTER 10

The poker lounge at Casino Hafnia was quivering with dense anticipation; the pot was tonight's highest so far and the winner would become chip leader, securing for themselves the perfect start to reach the very top of the tournament.

Jan Podowski watched the audience, whose attention was focused on the finale table. Those at the back had stood up, and only a few were following the game on the casino's screens, which provided a far superior view; everyone wanted a glimpse of real-live action. Or nearly everyone. He noticed how the three models seized their chance for a brief respite, discarding their smiles and warming their naked shoulders by rubbing their palms up and down their bare skin. They were hired as living posters, almost sexless with their perfect bodies squeezed into flimsy silk dresses, one orange, one green and one red, the colours of Casino Hafnia, indifferent eye candy.

He caught the eyes of Miss Orange, folded his arms across his chest and mimicked her movements, and she rewarded him with a small smile, a genuine one, probably the first since her arrival. The turn card was revealed and apprehension spread briefly throughout the room. He glanced casually up at the screen to his left: the ten of diamonds, which could mean anything. The camera then zoomed in on Benedikte Lerche-Larsen frozen in a pensive pose, one he knew she intended to maintain for what would seem to be an eternity, before she would go all in and lose the hand. It was time for her to pull out; after all, they hadn't come here to win Casino Hafnia's measly 50,000 kroner, though he was the only person in the room apart from her who knew that.

She had played well tonight, most definitely, there could be no doubt that it was one of her finest performances. He already knew her betting style; she was firmly in the category *tight-aggressive*, playing only a few hands and then only when the odds were good. On average she joined in less than thirty per cent of the games, depending on the number of opponents. She was consistent in her raises and re-raises, both before and after the flop, once she got involved. But her strength was that every once in a while she would break her pattern and randomly launch into wild bluffs or semi-bluffs to steal the pot, in some instances two or even three games in a row. It made her unpredictable, hard to read, and matched perfectly her behaviour away from the poker table.

Tonight her strategy had paid off, and she had gone all the way to the final. She had been lucky, of course, that was crucial; in poker luck always beat skill in the short term. Nevertheless, it was no coincidence that she was one of the four remaining players. Jan Podowski reminded himself to praise her when she joined him later, although she would undoubtedly dismiss his appreciation with her usual sarcasm – a form of self-defence she had practised for as long as he could remember, the result of a neglected childhood where nothing she did was ever good enough. It was a mystery why she hadn't turned her back on her parents a long time ago; they had deserved that, as indeed had she. He thought that one day he would ask her. Then he knocked back the rest of his whisky and immediately needed another one.

Benedikte Lerche-Larsen's deliberations were finally concluded. A restrained hush rippled through the lounge when she pushed all her chips into the pot. Her acne-scarred opponent was rewarded with a few seconds' attention from the camera when, without hesitation, he called her. Both players showed their cards, while the television flashed the 2.1-million-kroner stake in the pot across the screen in exaggerated gold letters, Monopoly money with no link to reality. Jan Podowski noted to his satisfaction that she would most probably lose, only a six on the river card could save her, and only two of those were left. As an extra bonus her opponent would get a boost for the hands still to be dealt, which meant they would get the chance to study him further: it was nimbly done. The dealer prolonged the tension as was his job, before he turned over the seven of clubs with his card stick; Jan Podowski gestured to the waiter for another whisky.

It was quite a while before Benedikte joined him; he was about to start looking for her when she showed up, looking surprisingly elated. She waltzed through the room like a queen. People stared after her as she smiled sweetly at everyone and looked absolutely incredible in the dim, yellow light, just as she had done in the sharp, white light over the poker table. A couple of camera flashlights immortalised her, and she turned up the charm an extra notch for the next shot. She was wearing a black skirt, which emphasised her curves as she walked, and a long cashmere cardigan in muted indigo, which matched the precious stones in her large gold earrings. She had left her red hair loose and her make-up was light. She held a silver clutch from Chanel in one hand. Jan Podowski thought that she was becoming a familiar face among the poker players, and tonight could only add to her fame. He had heard whispers that she had even earned herself a nickname: they called her *Ice Queen*, nomenclature she would probably protest loudly against if she ever heard it, though you never could tell with her. She slipped elegantly into the chair next to him, but waited until her admirers had stopped gazing at her before she started talking. Then she nodded in the direction of his whisky glass.

'Are you drunk?'

'No more than usual.'

'So you're drunk – as usual. Well, I won't be driving you home, or indeed anywhere else, you can take a cab.'

Jan Podowski was known to keep his private life private; on those occasions when she had given him a lift, he had always demanded to be dropped off at Roskilde Station, then he could manage the rest of the way himself. He said, 'I'm perfectly capable of making my own way home. Tell me, what was that performance all about? It's not like you.'

'I bumped into a girlfriend. She's sitting at the bar making eyes at absolutely everybody. I decided to show her the difference between good and bad style. I can't stand her.'

'Why do you have friends you can't stand?'

'None of your business. Maybe because they're the only friends I can be bothered with. Get me a pomegranate and elderflower soda with ice, and tell me what you think about that boy. Are we staying here or are we going home?'

Jan Podowski snapped his fingers for the waiter, before answering pensively.

'I think he has potential, but I'm not sure. His playing style is quite disjointed, so he's hard to read. What do you think?'

'The same as you: flaky, unschooled. On the other hand, he's sharp as a pin, no doubt about it. But Svend has followed him online or we wouldn't be sitting here. What does he say?'

Svend was her father. It was only in recent years that she had started to refer to him by his first name, and it still grated on Jan Podowski's ears when she did so. The habit revealed better than anything her distance from her father, and she knew it; indeed she probably enjoyed it and savoured the casual ease with which she uttered the name. As if he had never been known as anything else as far as she was concerned . . . It was borderline frightening. However, Jan Podowski had no particular desire to discuss his boss with her; it was a minefield.

'I'm not really sure how much your father has had a look at his hand to check him out – I mean, literally, ha-ha . . . You'll have to talk to him about that yourself.'

The joke fell flat as she simply ignored it. Jan Podowski continued:

'Do you think he'll win?'

He stressed his question with a gesture at the TV screen, which was showing a close-up of the young man deep in thought. His exposure had risen noticeably since Benedikte Lerche-Larsen had left the table. She glanced up indifferently at his face, but was surprisingly precise in her assessment.

'No, not unless he's exceptionally lucky. That country boy is too strong, he'll eat him up at the end. But he might get to second place.'

'Second place is still good.'

'Second place makes you a loser, and you'll have to talk to him alone. He's been slavering over me for hours, I can't stand him.'

The waiter came over and Jan Podowski ordered her drink on her behalf. It gave him time to think. Then he got straight to the point.

'OK, we'll have a chat with him when he's done. We'll give him five grand and set him a couple of the usual web challenges, as well as book him on an online course, which he must pass. If he completes those within a reasonable time – let's say two months – we'll keep him on, otherwise we'll drop him. And I'll make it clear that you're not part of the deal. Do you agree?'

She nodded half-heartedly, as if it had nothing to do with her.

'I guess so.'

The waiter brought her drink, which she immediately sent back; the bartender had forgotten to add ice. The room filled with scattered applause; the country boy had dispatched the third finalist with a gutshot straight. Jan Podowski remembered his earlier decision to praise her and said casually:

'You played really well, by the way, you're getting good.'

She turned to him, instantly on guard.

'If you're making a crass pitch for my prize money, I intend to keep it all for myself, just so you know. I'll give you a grand, if you keep your mouth shut to Svend, but that's it. All you've been doing this evening is knock back the booze.'

Her prize money hadn't even crossed his mind; in fact, he had forgotten all about it, but she was right, the money rightfully belonged to her father, and he would undoubtedly lay claim to it if he ever found out. Not because of the amount, he wouldn't care less about that, it was the principle that counted. Svend Lerche paid their wages; Podowski had no idea how much Benedikte earned, but she was on the payroll, and so her father was entitled to any profits she generated during working hours.

'That's for you to sort out. I won't say a word, unless he asks me directly. But he can easily find out for himself by checking Casino Hafnia's homepage tomorrow.'

'I don't think so, a regrettable error will occur. My name won't feature.'

'Oh, is that what took you so long?'

'Yes, it took a little time to arrange.'

'So your trashy girlfriend was just a cover story?'

Benedikte Lerche-Larsen shrugged. The waiter placed her drink in front of her, this time with ice. He tried a light-hearted remark, she blanked him. Then, without warning, she placed one hand on Jan Podowski's arm. Her voice grew more intense.

'Did you see the news yesterday?'

'Yes, some of it. What did you have in mind?'

'That Homicide chief, I don't remember his name, but he has taken over the investigation into . . . well, you know what I mean.'

More than a year had passed since the incident in Hanehoved Forest, and it was the first time she'd referred to it to him.

'His name is Konrad Simonsen, and he's a Detective Superintendent in Copenhagen. What about him?'

'Nothing special. Just . . . well, I don't like it.'

'Are you scared?'

She nodded and then said quietly, 'Yes, I'm scared. Aren't you?'

'Nah, not particularly, not any more. I was nervous immediately afterwards, but now I don't think there's much to be scared about. However, I do know it's not a subject we should be discussing here. Not under any circumstances.'

'No, of course not, you're right. What about Henrik? Are the two of you in touch?'

'No, we're not and we won't ever be, so stop it, Benedikte. You can drive me to Roskilde after all when we're done here. We can talk in the car.'

She agreed reluctantly to his suggestion.

They followed the poker game for a while in silence. The final result dragged. The two combatants had a roughly equal number of chips, and it had been like that for a long time. Jan Podowski was bored rigid and Benedikte Lerche-Larsen's mind was elsewhere. He interrupted her thoughts.

'I'm going outside for a fag.'

She sized him up critically from head to foot as he struggled to his feet.

'If drinking doesn't kill you, obesity will . . . unless cancer gets you first. What does your girlfriend say? Has she started looking for a replacement?'

He had seen it before and wasn't hurt. She had opened up ever so slightly, revealed a tiny bit of herself, and this bitterness invariably followed soon afterwards. She was like that, poor girl.

CHAPTER 11

The Easter weather was showing its best side, but the man who was walking down the residential road in Rungsted that Saturday morning had little interest. His quick steps echoed on the pavement and only an occasional, fleeting glance at the neighbourhood's road signs revealed that he wasn't local but had memorised his route from a map.

The regular sound of his footsteps briefly made a postman look up from his letters, and then an angrily barking dog pursued him for as long as its territory extended; apart from that no one took any notice of him. He got the distinct impression that this was an area where people minded their own business and didn't poke their noses into other people's affairs, and he concluded matter-of-factly that the residents in this neighbourhood were the decent sort. He himself was a man who preferred to live in the shadows and curiosity made him uncomfortable, even when he was just a visitor. Being too visible meant big problems, if not now, then later. He stamped his boot extra hard to underscore his thoughts; this was his philosophy, and he had stuck to it his whole life. But those who confused his reticent nature with weakness and a lack of resourcefulness were mistaken; Bjarne Fabricius was not someone whose hands would ever tremble under pressure. He was a danger-ous man and over the years many people had learned that lesson the hard way.

Less than ten minutes later he reached his destination. He stopped for a moment in front of the garden gate and carefully assessed his surroundings. The detached house lay well back from the road, the red brickwork in good condition under the green, salt-glazed roof tiles; the house was neatly built into a sloping hillside and staggered across three levels. Two panoramic windows faced a white-painted terrace, the garden looked expensive but dull, and in the rendered-brick garage he had just passed were two cars; one a white Porsche, the other a black Audi. The water of the Øresund sparkled behind the house in the sunshine, blue and lazy with its miniature container ships industriously following their courses; from a distance they looked immobile, as if anchored. Beyond them the Swedish coastline lay on the horizon.

He opened the gate and entered. Yellow and white daffodils paraded in even clusters along the garden path up to the front door, and on impulse he bent down and picked one. He sniffed the yellow flower, but realised to his disappointment that it was unscented, and placed it next to the others. He rang the doorbell. Benedikte Lerche-Larsen opened the door; Bjarne Fabricius's smile was broad and possibly genuine.

'Benedikte, good to see you. I was hoping you would be in.'

He embraced her before she had the chance to get away. She let her hand glide across his shoulders and concluded that he was fit and healthy, despite being fifty. His muscles were hard and well developed.

'My father is on his way, he had an accident this morning that required a trip to Casualty.'

Bjarne Fabricius furrowed his brow; coincidences always made him suspicious.

'An accident – what happened?'

She took him by the arm and led him alongside the house while she told him.

'Nothing serious, he slipped in the bath and hurt his foot, there was a lot of fuss involving an ambulance. Forget it, it doesn't matter. By the way, my mother asked me to show you round the house, she'll be here shortly, but don't worry, I said no.'

'Thank you. So tell me, do you like your new home?'

She shrugged.

'It's OK, but then Klampenborg was OK too. Let's sit in the back garden and admire the sea view, or you can have a look at Svend's orchid collection – it's his and the gardener's latest hobby.' She gestured towards two greenhouses diagonally to their right and added: 'But I'll be staying outside, orchids stink, don't say I didn't warn you.'

Bjarne Fabricius mulled it over, then opted for the greenhouses. He took an interest in flowers. She added:

'If you want anything, I'll call Jan.'

'Good old Jan Podowski, so he's still alive and kicking, eh? Well, the devil doesn't come for his own while they're still green. Do you think he could get me a glass of iced tea?'

'I was rather thinking, while we're wandering around, a bottle of beer or a soft drink? A glass is too much hassle, you can have iced tea later. I believe my mother is about to organise a spontaneous display of refreshments on the terrace.'

'Oh, God. In that case, I'll wait. Incidentally, will Jan be there to review the accounts?'

'Some of the accounts, and the same goes for the accountant. But neither of them will be present for everything.'

'As opposed to you?'

'For the first time, yes. That's the plan, but who knows if Svend might change it at the last minute? It's happened before.'

'Or I might.'

The remark didn't provoke her. She replied with a smile, 'Yes, or perhaps you might.'

Bjarne Fabricius thought that it was very difficult not to like her, in stark contrast to her father. When they reached the greenhouses, she let him go ahead and continued on her own. He looked after her, and then called her back.

'Benedikte, show me those orchids.'

CHAPTER 12

The greenhouse was hot and suffocating, and Bjarne Fabricius realised that his hostess hadn't exaggerated the unpleasant smell. They wandered slowly down the centre aisle, Bjarne walking ahead as he studied the flowers around him. He stopped in front of an extra-large specimen, hanging from a branch and form-ing a star with its five pink petals.

'Do you know anything about orchids?' he asked the girl.

'Bugger all.'

He slowly turned his head towards her and said in a chilly voice:

'I don't like it when people swear at me.'

Benedikte smiled disarmingly and corrected herself imme-diately:

'I'm sorry, I didn't mean to. But no, I know nothing about orchids, except that there are thousands of species, and that those hanging from trees are called epiphytes, I believe. And I also know that if you pick one to put in your hair, Svend will blow his top.'

'Hmm, in that case I'd better not. Tell me, how are your studies going?'

'Slowly. I'm in my fourth term, and I should be in my fifth. And I need to sit an exam very soon.'

'Why are you not in the fifth term? Is it difficult?'

'Not particularly, but don't forget, I work almost full-time for you. And then Svend keeps sending me on all sorts of extra courses, which take up time.'

'I didn't know that. What kind of courses?'

'Well, I'm studying business administration and I spend most of my time at Copenhagen Business School, but I guess you already know that. The extra exams my father wants me to pass are a mixed bag, it's almost as if he's making it up as he goes along. Accountancy, IT courses – lots of them, he was completely obsessed by them for a while – advanced image- and sound-processing was another one. At the moment I'm doing corporate law at the Faculty of Law, and he has also mentioned that I ought to be able to speak French, but so far he has only talked about it. It's beyond me how speak-ing French benefits your business. But perhaps you can give me a sensible explanation, given that Svend won't – after all, you pay half my wages.'

'I thought he was only interested in your knowing probability calculation and statistics.'

'I already know those. That was pretty much all I did in sixth form. He taught me himself, way beyond sixth-form level. It wasn't much fun, but I admit that it was effective. Besides, those subjects form a core part of my degree.'

'So you can take over the day he no longer wants to run everything?'

Benedikte Lerche-Larsen hesitated; she sensed a very slight change in his tone of voice. The question wasn't nearly as casual as it sounded. She deflected it carefully.

'I can handle a fair bit, but I'm sure I've much to learn.'

'Such as loyalty.'

If he had hoped to shock her, he was disappointed. She looked him straight in the eye and said with a smile:

'Yes, that too. But it will be very hard.'

'How many girls do you and your mother run on the side?'

'Four, and we're thinking of expanding to six or seven during the year.'

He couldn't help but admire her. The reply had come without hesitation and without any hint of fear. He knew very few people could master that art. After all, she was stealing from him as well as her father. He turned and walked a few more steps as he resumed his study of the flowers. He could hear that she followed him and smell her perfume among all the other olfactory traces in the room. Without turning around, he said quietly:

'Do you know what happens to little girls who get too greedy?'

'The same thing that happens to big men who obsess about the small stuff. They fall apart.'

He laughed and then discarded all politeness.

'You were on the cover of *Poker Player*, mentioned by name and everything. You were all tarted up, so you must have known where the paparazzi would point their cameras. Tell me, what the hell were you thinking?'

'I know, I'm sorry. It was a mistake. And Svend completely agrees with you. It's not much fun being yelled at for half an hour. I hope you're not going to yell at me too.'

He was impressed by the way she managed not to lie, while at the same time giving the impression that her father had reprimanded her. But he hadn't seen the magazine, not yet, though Bjarne would make sure that happened very soon. He hated publicity, most of all in print, no matter how insignificant the poker magazine was in the overall media scheme of things.

'No, yelling isn't my style. That girl they found in the woodland lake, the one who has caused so much commotion, was she one of yours?'

He already knew the answer to that too; he was merely interested in whether she would lie about it. In which case she was more stupid than he had taken her for.

'It was an accident.'

'Of course it was an accident. Did you help kill her?'

'Yes, I did. Do you want the whole story?'

He nodded, and she told him, matter-of-factly and pragmatically, without making excuses. He had turned to face her and was watching her while she spoke. When she had finished, he asked in a neutral tone:

'And what's your conclusion?'

She shrugged her shoulders, not sure what he wanted from her. Yet his cold, direct gaze demanded an answer, and she said tentatively, 'My conclusion is that I'm scared. And that I'm alone. Svend would never lift a finger to help me; my mother is too stupid, even if she wanted to, which incidentally I highly doubt.'

'And is that all you have learned?'

'No, I've also learned that poker and women are each a brilliant idea when run separately, but not together, and that much more discretion is needed. We ought to drop the hookers and concentrate on the Poker Academy. There are plenty of customers for that sort of money-laundering operation, if it's managed efficiently, and ours is. Very useful to you, I would imagine.'

She echoed what he himself had believed for years, but there was no way she could know that. He asked without emotion:

'What do you know about my other activities?'

'Absolutely nothing except that they're extensive and that my parents' little corner shop is only a small part of your operation. Nor do I want to know anything, I'm not that stupid.'

He abandoned the subject, pleased with her answer.

'But your father disagrees with your business strategy?'

'Yes, unfortunately. And he's in charge, not me. Which is how it'll stay. Unless *you* force him, of course.'

Bjarne Fabricius shook his head, slowly but firmly. 'How could Svend help you with your little accident? That is, if he wanted to.'

Again he had changed the conversation, and again she answered without hesitation:

'By convincing you to get rid of Henrik and Jan, of course.'

'Henrik Krag and Jan Podowski?'

He narrowed his eyes and pondered her suggestion only to shoot down the idea.

'You're consistent in your train of thought, I grant you that, but no. It could very easily end up backfiring, and we would be facing two problems rather than just the one. Or more accurately – I would be facing two problems, whereas you just have one.'

'If a killing is linked to us, we might have to shut up shop, or at least be forced to undertake a major restructuring. Surely that's also your problem?'

Bjarne Fabricius answered pensively:

'Perhaps we should carry on this conversation another day when we have more time. It might be of mutual benefit.'

'Is that an invitation?'

She smiled slightly and caught his eye in a mischievous gaze, which he did not return.

'Think of it like that if you wish. Is that a yes?'

Her voice was cheeky:

'What would your daughters say if you started dating someone their age?'

The remark was an error, stupid and crass. Yet his reaction took her completely by surprise. He stepped forward and spun her around, brutally forced her arm behind her back and twisted it upwards, until she whimpered. He yanked her head back by the hair, so her right ear pressed against his mouth. He hissed in a low voice:

'So you don't like orchids?'

Her response was more a sound than a 'no', his grip hurt. It got worse when he shoved her head in front of a random flower without releasing his hold on her arm. She gritted her teeth, but still emitted a short gasp of pain.

'This is *Cattleya* "Barbara Belle", and that one is . . .'

He turned her head in a brusque jerk to the next flower.

'. . . *Paphiopedilum lathanianum*. The species is easy to recognise from its lady slipper below.'

Again he forced her ear close to his mouth. He snarled:

'If you ever speak to me like that again, I'll make you learn the names of every single flower in here, and those you get wrong, I'll make you eat. And don't think this is an empty threat, I mean it, quite literally. Do you understand?'

He threw her forward without waiting for her answer. She tripped and scraped her knee against a terracotta pot. As if nothing had happened, he said:

'Your father will struggle to keep both species alive in the same greenhouse. They demand different winter temperatures, but he'll find that out for himself in due course. Why don't we go down to the terrace? I think I've seen enough orchids for one day.'

She got up. A drop of blood trickled down her shin; he offered her his handkerchief. The cut wasn't bad. She wiped off the blood with a brusque movement and folded the handkerchief around the stain.

'Five, Benedikte, no more than five.'

He held up a hand with splayed fingers and his palm facing her.

'Five hookers on the side for you and your mother. That'll have to do. And if your father finds out, don't you dare claim that I sanctioned your extra-curricular activities.'

'He won't, but five it is.'

She placed the handkerchief in his hand and slowly closed his fingers around it.

'So when will we meet?'

He smiled icily and withdrew his hand.

'I'll let you know.'

CHAPTER 13

The terrace was Karina Larsen's pride and joy. It was made up of an artful circle of Swedish granite cobblestones worn until they shone; every single stone had been carefully chosen and only the smoothest had found favour with their new owner. The rest had been returned to the supplier. It had cost a fortune, but that was nothing compared to the one-and-a-half-metre retaining wall built from medieval bricks, which Mrs Larsen personally, with much difficulty and by consistently evading conservation rules, had sourced from a dismantled cemetery wall on Falster. Now the regular black- and red-hued bricks, neatly reconstructed in a Gothic bond, shielded the house from the east wind.

Jan Podowski leaned heavily on the wall. His gaze swept across the Øresund, which lay languid and shimmering beneath him with the blue-grey Swedish coastline on the far horizon. He felt unwell and wondered whether to sneak off for a swig of his usual medication, but decided against it. Today was not a day to risk excess alcohol consumption. Karina Larsen was sitting in an armchair with her back to him; even so it seemed she could read his thoughts when she said:

'You'd better stay sober, Jan.'

He made a half-hearted promise and thought that he could, not unreasonably, ask her to do the same. While they had been waiting, she had drunk two glasses of white wine and was halfway through her third, a clear sign that she was nervous. Another sign was the display of snacks; she had frantically ordered the maid around all morning. The result was the table in front of her, which was groaning with far too much food: tapas, French brie, chorizo, tapenade, Parma ham and melon, olives, grapes, marinated garlic and guacamole, which had to be made three times before she felt they had captured the original Mexican flavour she remembered from the twenty-four hours the cruise ship had docked in Veracruz. It had to be perfect, as always with Karina, and if she was aware that people laughed at her behind her back, she never let on.

'There he is.'

Her voice was excited and the information superfluous. You had to be blind not to see Benedikte Lerche-Larsen and Bjarne Fabricius stroll up the garden path. A little too intimate together, Jan Podowski thought, although he was unable to put his finger on the nature of that intimacy. Maybe it was all in his mind.

Bjarne Fabricius pulled out a chair for Benedikte Lerche-Larsen and sat down next to her. Karina Larsen grabbed the white wine and asked nervously:

'A glass, Bjarne? It's a Christwein, the grapes were picked on Christmas Eve.'

Benedikte Lerche-Larsen added:

'By the mouths of blind Corsican nuns.'

There was no humour in her voice, merely contempt for her mother's snobbery. Bjarne Fabricius ignored her and politely declined the wine while praising the terrace and the food. Karina Larsen beamed. Benedikte Lerche-Larsen sulked and poured herself a glass, then flung out her arm to indicate the impressive garden and said:

'And to think that all this started with just one hooker and one gambler.'

Jan Podowski hushed her.

'Give it a rest, Benedikte. What would you like to drink, Bjarne?'

'Some iced tea, if you have it, would be great. If not, then a glass of water.'

He pointed to the carafe, but Karina Larsen wouldn't hear of it. She chirped on.

'Yes, of course we have iced tea. I'm sure we do. Don't we, Jan?'

Jan Podowski got up wearily, took a step backwards, then sat down with a bump. He had had cirrhosis of the liver for years caused by his excessive alcohol intake, and his doctor had told him over and over that he had to quit drinking if he wanted to live. And on this lovely April day in Rungsted his doctor was finally proved right.

A varicose vein burst in his throat, haematemesis, the doctor would have called it, or a haemorrhage as it was more commonly known. Bloody vomit projected from him and across the table displaying the hostess's munificent light lunch. Then he flopped sideways and collapsed heavily onto the ground. Karina Larsen screamed, long hysterical squeals, with her glass in one hand and the other pressed against her temple. Bjarne Fabricius rolled the sick man onto his side and called 112 from his mobile. Benedikte Lerche-Larsen threw her white wine at her mother's face, then squatted down on her haunches and held Jan Podowski's head.

By then he was already dead.

CHAPTER 14

The National Police Commissioner was speaking. He had been doing so for almost fifteen minutes, but without anyone understanding a single word.

The Homicide Department – along with everyone else from Police Headquarters – were on a course to learn how to implement the new values of the police force. The course was mandatory and it was essential that everyone participated. For months senior police officers and a firm of consultants had worked to identify the five adjectives that from now on would be the lodestars for every single officer across the country, and today these adjectives would be unveiled. Tivoli Congress Centre had been booked, no one could excuse themself, the new values applied to everyone, and at the end of the course every single employee would be given a coffee mug listing those five values. It was time-wasting on a monumental scale.

Konrad Simonsen sighed, then elbowed Klavs Arnold, who was sitting on the chair next to him, fast asleep. The Jutlander woke up, squinted and started clapping loudly and noisily with his big hands. A few people around the room followed suit, but not when he stood up and continued his applause, now with his hands raised above his head. Konrad Simonsen yanked him back down.

'Go back to sleep, I'll wake you up when they have a break. Or if you start snoring again.'

Later that afternoon every imaginable word about the police force's new values had been uttered so many times that even the dimmest line manager couldn't think of anything to add. This was followed by sessions where smaller groups of participants would offer their take on what those values meant to them personally in their daily work. Konrad Simonsen, Arne Pedersen and Klavs Arnold gathered in meeting room 22A, where coffee and cake had been set out, and where a list of forty questions – purely for inspiration, if they couldn't come up with anything themselves – were waiting for them. They were surprised to see each other because all the other groups were bigger and made up of staff taken randomly from across departments. Arne Pedersen was impressed.

'How on earth did you wangle that, Simon?'

Konrad Simonsen looked baffled, he hadn't wangled anything. The explanation arrived soon afterwards when the Countess joined them.

'I fixed it so we could spend at least some of today being productive. I presume we're dropping the official agenda?'

She looked at Konrad Simonsen, but it was Klavs Arnold who replied:

'We are, or I'm going home. I simply can't handle any more waffle.'

Arne Pedersen grinned. 'You'll forfeit your mug. But tell me, where is Pauline?'

Konrad Simonsen took a small piece of cake and informed him gravely:

'She let fly at one of the consultants during lunch, and then she stormed off. I caught her in the car park. She was going to go to Frederiksværk, but I talked out of it by promising that one of us will go there with her next weekend.'

Klavs Arnold volunteered, which was surprising. Of all of them he knew her the least well.

'If we can make it the Saturday, then all right. I'm presuming it's the case you call the "Juli-non-case" she wants to investigate.'

Konrad Simonsen nodded, and the Jutlander added:

'I had a mate who was in Afghanistan. He came home with PTSD, so I know why she suffers from uncontrollable outbursts of crying, anxiety attacks and outbreaks of rage.'

The Countess mimicked his tone of voice:

'You don't know the half of it.'

Klavs Arnold continued:

'If we reject her, she has nothing left. We're the ones who have to shoulder the heavy load, that's just how it is. But let's do something worthwhile now, I'm in need of that.'

Konrad Simonsen stood next to the whiteboard with a marker pen in his hand, ready to brainstorm the 'nignog' investigation, as he must remember never, ever to refer to it.

'What angles have we got? Let's list them and discuss them individually.'

'Well, that shouldn't take us long,' Arne Pedersen quipped.

'Would you rather be discussing values?'

No one wanted to do that, and they agreed on three strategies: *A thorough search of Hanehoved Forest*, *Potential witnesses* and the estate bailiff at Kolleløse Manor, *Frode Otto*. Konrad Simonsen numbered the three points, and underlined each with a red dry-wipe marker pen. Then he put the cap back on the pen, tossed it onto a table next to the whiteboard and said what everyone was thinking:

'That's pathetic.'

'As far as the lake is concerned,' the Countess remarked, 'we'll just have to wait and see. We can always hope that we find her clothes, but I don't suppose we'll get that lucky. We have to assume that the killer or killers removed them and disposed of them later. Doing anything else would be almost too idiotic. But, like I said, we'll know more next week.'

Konrad Simonsen added:

'As you know, I'm in charge of organising the search, and it's going to be a major operation. There'll be about a hundred men from the Territorial Army, and we're doing it over three days. But you're right, Countess, the likelihood of us finding anything interesting isn't great. However, it's worth a try. Besides, it's no secret that this is also about us showing initiative for the benefit of the top brass. And ideally an initiative that will earn us press coverage. That's the reality of the situation. Unfortunately.'

The Homicide chief's closest staff accepted these facts, before Arne Pedersen speculated for five minutes on the next item: the witnesses. He had nothing new to add, and was mainly speaking because he thought it was his turn. He summarised what everyone knew, which was that any potential witnesses would be found amongst hunters and ornithologists, and that option had long since been explored to no avail. But Konrad Simonsen could add something that wasn't entirely pointless.

'I would like one of you to check members of all registered hunting or ornithology clubs on Sjælland, to see if one of them had a female African member in 2008 who isn't a member today. It should have been done before, but as far as I can see from the file it hasn't happened. Would that be something for you, Klavs?'

Klavs Arnold accepted. It reeked of two dull, fruitless days spent on the phone, but he agreed with his boss that it was worth a shot.

All that remained was Frode Otto, the estate bailiff, who had reacted as if he had been stung by a wasp when he saw Konrad Simonsen. This was undoubtedly the Homicide Department's most interesting lead, despite the fact that absolutely nothing linked Otto to the murder of the woman. Their interest was purely sparked by his strangely negative reaction to the sight of Konrad Simonsen, which must have some grounds, although the Countess, who was allocated that job, couldn't contribute anything new.

'Together with a few colleagues, I've reviewed every single investigation in which Simon has been involved since he started working in the Homicide Department. We haven't quite finished yet but almost, and I'm afraid that so far we haven't come across the name Frode Otto.'

Nor did Konrad Simonsen himself have any suggestions that might explain the estate bailiff's behaviour.

'I'm almost certain I haven't met him before. It's rare for me to forget a face, and . . . yes, as I said, I don't know Frode Otto.'

Arne Pedersen said tentatively:

'Perhaps we should try a reconstruction of the episode? We have plenty of time, and we might have overlooked something. Another idea would be to call and ask Frode Otto himself. There might be a natural explanation, we can't rule that out.'

They opted for a reconstruction. Tables and chairs were reorganised based on the surprisingly accurate sketch Arne Pedersen drew on the whiteboard. Klavs Arnold played Frode Otto, Arne Pedersen talked them through the incident.

'Klavs and I are talking to him. At that point he has mellowed and our conversation is almost pleasant. Then you appear from behind some agricultural machinery . . . we haven't heard you arrive.'

Konrad Simonsen walked up to the table representing the agricultural machine, but the Countess didn't follow him; instead she interrupted the Jutlander.

'Maybe he was reacting to me.'

The three men were enthusiastic; there was good reasoning in that observation.

'However, I don't fancy reading through all my own cases. They bring back memories I could really do without.'

Arne Pedersen volunteered to take charge of the review, and the reconstruction continued. Klavs Arnold said:

'The moment he spots you, he turns and switches on the power for the welding apparatus. Or, no, hang on . . . the first thing he does is put on his welding gloves. Then he turns on the power, then he puts on his helmet and lowers the visor.'

Klavs Arnold mimicked Frode Otto's actions as accurately as he could. He looked ridiculous, but no one laughed. Konrad Simonsen said thoughtfully:

'If he didn't want the Countess or me to recognise him, why on earth didn't he put his helmet on first? That would have made more sense. But he put on his gloves instead.'

'Because he didn't want you to see that he only has nine fingers. That's why.'

It was Arne Pedersen who spotted the logic. Konrad Simonsen nodded his approval.

'You're right, I hadn't thought of that. But why does it matter to him? As far as I remember, I've never . . .'

The Countess interrupted again:

'Is he missing his left little finger?'

Arne Pedersen and Klavs Arnold nodded and the Countess continued in a grave tone:

'Nordjylland, the summer of 1992, sexual assault on a fifteen-year-old German girl. It was unusually violent and cruel, undoubtedly one of the worst cases I've ever seen. We worked like maniacs for several months, but we never found the perpetrator.'

Konrad Simonsen asked her:

'But you had his fingerprints, I gather?'

'Yes and no, sadly. We had nine distinct bruises on the girl's buttocks and hips from nine fingers pinning her down.'

CHAPTER 15

Hanehoved Forest was searched with military precision.

The logistics were undertaken by the Territorial Army, along with nine dogs and their handlers on loan from Hillerød police. In a long row, with each man roughly four metres apart from the next, they moved slowly through one section of the forest after another. The dogs ran on ahead in high spirits, enjoying their work. The men followed behind attentively, everyone using a stick to turn over branches or plants.

The organisation was skilfully handled by a middle-aged platoon commander, who seemed able to be in several places at once. Every time an area had been examined, he carefully crossed it off his map, rearranged his men and ordered them to start on the next section. During breaks he was taciturn and stayed on the fringes of the group, often sitting up against a tree trunk reading a book. Konrad Simonsen thought he was worth his weight in gold. It meant he himself was freed from the practical responsibility of leading the operation, a task the Homicide chief was only too pleased to delegate when it was handled as competently as it was now. So instead of leading from the front, Simonsen plodded behind the column, enjoying the walk. For two of the days he walked alongside Adam Blixen-Agerskjold, who thought it only natural that he was present, though he had no specific role to play. As far as Konrad Simonsen could gauge, it was a matter of honour for the Chamberlain. A young woman had been found dead on his land, and the least he could do was take an interest. Besides, Adam Blixen-Agerskjold had personally paid for sandwiches for the men during the lunch break on every single day of the three-day operation, plus a cold beer at the end of the working day for anyone who fancied one.

In return he was rewarded with two findings that sent him almost into ecstasy: a flint axe head, beautifully polished and almost intact, and on the second day, a belt buckle, which without hesitation he classed as being from the Germanic Iron Age, and which would need to be logged with the National Museum, if he wanted to keep it legally.

But in terms of the investigation, the result was poor. Apart from a fair amount of rubbish, especially where the forest bordered the road, the miserable reward for all their efforts amounted to a rotting umbrella, a cardboard box containing three wheel caps, which baffled everyone, an ancient mobile phone that quickly proved to be of no relevance, and a wine bottle, an elastic hairband and a condom, all found in the same place.

As usual Konrad Simonsen was walking with Adam Blixen-Agerskjold, a dozen metres behind the men searching the very last stretch, which was the deciduous forest in the south-western corner towards the manor house. The forest undulated in regular waves approximately five metres apart. Adam Blixen-Agerskjold explained:

'We're walking on ancient farmland – this is how Danish fields used to look. The level fields we know now are a modern phenomenon from the start of the nineteenth century. Since the introduction of the plough thousands of years ago, we would plough our fields in waves, so that they would drain more effectively.'

Konrad Simonsen had learned quite a lot of Danish history from the Chamberlain in recent days. Now he changed the subject and ventured carefully:

'Your estate bailiff, Frode Otto.'

The Chamberlain froze, the amicable mood instantly evaporating.

'Yes, what about him?'

'I would like you to tell me about him. His work, his family, his background, his habits. Perhaps when we're done here, if you have the time.'

Adam Blixen-Agerskjold didn't reply immediately and Konrad Simonsen didn't press him. It was clear that Frode Otto was more than just a hired hand to the Chamberlain. They'd crossed another three waves before Simonsen got an answer.

'I'm uncomfortable discussing Frode behind his back.'

'I completely understand and respect that. But I'm investigating a murder, so personal loyalty no longer counts. Deep down I think you know that.'

The Chamberlain swiped his stick angrily across a cluster of tender stinging nettles, before he gave in.

'Dine with us tonight, we can talk afterwards. Lenette needs to be there when you interrogate me.'

'Interrogate is a strong word, but thank you for the invitation.'

Adam Blixen-Agerskjold felled another cluster of stinging nettles, then hurled his stick into the distance. Konrad Simonsen let himself fall a few steps behind. But soon afterwards they were walking side by side again, Simonsen could tell from his voice that the Chamberlain had composed himself:

'Perhaps you could do me a favour in return?'

'That's not quite how it works, but go on. What is it?'

Adam Blixen-Agerskjold was silent for several minutes.

'You seem like an agreeable man, Konrad. The kind of person one would like as a friend. Except when you're being a detective superintendent, then you're arrogant and often unpleasant. Don't worry about the favour, forget it.'

Konrad Simonsen was hurt and had to restrain himself from snapping back. The situation was getting to him. The last three days with the Chamberlain had been pleasant, despite the fruitless search of the forest. He said quietly:

'I don't know the name of the dead African woman, where she came from, let alone why she was killed and ended up in your lake. But I do know that she's the only one who really matters to me. Because she has no one else. And it's Simon, not Konrad. Now tell me about that favour, Adam.'

Adam Blixen-Agerskjold told him. It concerned his grand-mother, Victoria Blixen-Agerskjold, a woman in her late-eighties who lived in a care home in Holbæk, and who was convinced that she had important information about the murder investigation, information she absolutely refused to tell her grandson as he didn't have the relevant security clearance.

'My grandmother suffers from dementia, she gets the past and the present mixed up. She was in the Second World War as a young woman. Worked for the Special Operations Executive, the British intelligence service, and from 1941 to 1943 she was a radio operator in France, a high-risk job only very few survived. She was awarded the George Cross by Winston Churchill in 1952 during his second term as Prime Minister. Only five women have ever been awarded that distinction.'

'Impressive.'

They straddled some wild raspberry bushes. The Chamberlain stomped on the plants whenever he got the chance. Suddenly he sounded outraged.

'In the Paris Metro there are still seats reserved for war veterans. Young men, who have sacrificed their limbs for France, should at least be able to . . .'

He didn't complete his sentence, but returned to the subject a few steps later.

'Here in Denmark we don't know how to look after our injured soldiers properly, when they come home. They're made to queue up for help like every other disabled person. And the waiting lists themselves are a disgrace, but to make young people, who have sacrificed their health for Denmark, wait for years . . .'

Again his indignation simmered. Konrad Simonsen asked:

'What exactly can I do for your grandmother?'

'Do you read French?'

'No, but my wife does.'

'I want to lend you a book about what my grandmother and other SOE women achieved during the war. But what you can do is accompany me to Holbæk and have the privilege of meeting a woman like her.'

'That's a deal.'

'In uniform?'

'Definitely in uniform.'

CHAPTER 16

The three days spent in Hanehoved Forest turned out not to be quite as fruitless as Konrad Simonsen had initially feared. The forensic examination of the hairband that was found along with the wine bottle and the condom proved that it had belonged to the murdered woman.

The other items were older and irrelevant, but two tiny hairs from the elastic matched the victim's DNA. The hairband was black and tangled up, with fraying ends sticking out everywhere, and looked like a cheap supermarket purchase. With the evidence contained in a small plastic bag, Konrad Simonsen handed it to Pauline Berg in the corridor outside his office, where he had bumped into her and Klavs Arnold on their way to the canteen for lunch.

'Please would you find out where it was made, which shops sell it, and so on?'

Pauline Berg nodded briefly. Then she pulled the hairband out of the plastic bag, gathered her hair with much difficulty into a small ponytail, wrapped the band around it a couple of times and left. The plastic bag she stuffed into her pocket. Konrad Simonsen was left speechless. Klavs Arnold said irritably:

'I'll handle it, but seriously, couldn't you have asked anyone else but her?'

It was then that the penny finally dropped for the Homicide chief. He muttered curses under his breath and apologised.

When Pauline Berg had been kidnapped, she had lost most of her hair under the most distressing circumstances – being forced to pull it out so as not to fuel the obsession of the man who had captured her. It had never regained its former fullness. Simonsen had forgotten about this when he gave her the hairband, and could see now that he had screwed up. He apologised again and felt like an idiot, while the Jutlander, as usual, merely shrugged and raced after Pauline Berg. Why the hell did everything have to be so complicated with her? It wasn't like he was a doctor or psychologist.

Klavs Arnold struggled to keep his word and 'handle it', as he sat facing Pauline Berg at a table in the canteen. He tried several times:

'Take out that hairband and return it to the bag. It's evidence, Pauline, and you know it.'

She raked one hand through a strand of hair until it slipped out of the band and then repeated the movement, while smiling invitingly at him. She managed to eat with her other hand, using her fork to cut her sandwich into bite-size pieces. He wondered if she had always been like this.

'So you're coming with me on Saturday? I've a three o'clock appointment in Asserbo with the forester who found her.'

'Her' was the young woman whom Pauline Berg was adamant had been murdered. Klavs Arnold realised that he couldn't even remember the victim's name.

'Yes, I'm coming with you. We were talking about the hairband, Pauline. Now take it out and put it into the bag where it belongs.'

'Afterwards we can drive home to my place and have dinner.'

'That's kind, but no thanks.'

'Do you think my hair looks nice? It's getting long again, isn't it? What about my eyes? I have contact lenses at home ... do you think I'd be better-looking with brown eyes? Or green? A lot of men prefer me with green eyes.'

He started getting annoyed then and knew that was her intention, she was trying to rile him. But he was saved when the

Countess sat down next to them with her tray. She held out one hand, knocked on the table with the other in front of Pauline Berg, who mutely gave her the hairband and then the plastic bag. The Countess put the hairband into the bag and pressed it shut.

Pauline Berg pointed at Klavs Arnold and said in a thick voice, with tears in her eyes: 'The Jutlander won't go out with me.'

'The Jutlander is spending five hours of his weekend on you, and you can come back to my place Saturday evening so we can talk. Simon is out so we'll have the house to ourselves.'

Klavs Arnold felt annoyed at the way this dinner invitation between the two women was settled, without quite knowing why.

CHAPTER 17

The walls in Svend Lerche's office were covered with steel engravings from the beginning of the nineteenth century. He was a collector, but he didn't collect just anything. The subject must be 'naughty' was the way he explained it to any guest expressing an interest; he would then wink and his audience would struggle not to smile.

Svend Lerche was sitting behind his desk reading a memo. In his early fifties, with silver hair, a firm chin, alert blue eyes and exquisite manners, he could often be charming and inspire trust, but he also had a violent temper, which in certain situations would boil over and cause problems. He glanced up. Across the desk Benedikte Lerche-Larsen waited impatiently for him to finish. She was sitting back to front on a chair, with the back of it facing him, while she studied the wall behind him with disapproval. Her father thought it did the girl no harm to wait.

Finally he was done. He put the memo away, then from his top desk drawer he took out a magazine, which he slid in front of her. It was entitled *Poker Player*, and the entire front page was taken up by a picture of his daughter. Benedikte Lerche-Larsen dismissed it with a sneer. She showed no other reaction; he tried to suppress his rage when he said:

'What the hell were you thinking?'

'I have no control over who photographs me in public places, or what pictures are shown in the newspapers. We have a free press in this country.'

'Did you have to be tarted up like that?'

'*Tarted up*? Excuse me. We were at a casino, I couldn't very well be dressed like a librarian. I had to make some effort to blend in.'

'And pose for the cameras, did you have to do that too? You're aware that your name is mentioned inside the magazine?'

Benedikte flapped her hand indifferently and he carried on.

'Our business success is founded on discretion. I didn't think I had to tell you that.'

'It's the foundation for *your* business success.'

'Oh, really, so who pays your bills?'

She got up, turned the chair around and sat down again. Then replied to him sharply:

'Are you, of all people, going to lecture me on discretion? I'm not the one with an injunction against them, preventing them from turning up at the town hall. So how discreet does that make you, Svend?'

She had identified his Achilles heel, and it needled him. A month ago he had lost his temper with some bureaucratic nobody in the tax office, screamed and shouted, and unfortunately also made personal threats against her. It was a massive faux-pas. Especially given the negligible amount of tax he had to pay – a trifle really. Besides he hated it when Benedikte addressed him as 'Svend' rather than Dad, which she pretty much always did. He changed the subject:

'What were you and Bjarne Fabricius talking about last Saturday? Your mother tells me you spent a long time together in the greenhouse.'

'If ten minutes is a long time, then Mum is right. We talked about orchids.'

'About which you know nothing.'

'And about which Bjarne knows a lot. All I had to do was listen.'

'*Bjarne*, is it, so you're on first-name terms now?'

'So it appears.'

'Are you deliberately trying to provoke me, Benedikte? Because if you are, you're being remarkably successful.'

She backed off, as she always did when he got angry. At first she straightened her dress unnecessarily by pulling it a few extra centimetres neatly over her knees, then she burst out laughing, revealing rows of pearly white teeth and throwing back her head apparently spontaneously. He thought with dismay that no one else in all the world could turn on and switch off their moods like she could.

'Dad, we spoke about orchids. And I'm perfectly aware that any information Bjarne Fabricius needs about our business must come from you. Besides, I don't think he would listen to me moaning about you, if that's what you're worried about. He would merely brand me disloyal.'

'So him calling me, lecturing me on how you'll soon be ready for more responsibility, is just a coincidence?'

'I'd no idea that he'd called. But you can do what you like. You're the boss.'

They both knew this wasn't true. The reality was his business depended on a successful partnership with Bjarne Fabricius. He said in a deadpan voice:

'Of course I am.'

'So how about it? Will I be given more responsibility?'

He never knew where he was with her. On the one hand, it might be better if she moved out, learned to stand on her own two feet and got a regular job. It would benefit all parties in many ways, and he wouldn't mind helping her get a flat and giving her a monthly allowance. On the other hand, she knew a lot about his activities, and though they disagreed profoundly about his business strategy, she contributed considerably to its daily management. She was especially strong when it came to finances, and though he had yet to give her full financial insight, she relieved him of many hours of work every week. He paid her generously for this, but it would be difficult, not to say impossible, to replace her while he also had to train a replacement for Jan Podowski.

'Yes, possibly. Let's return to that later. But that wasn't the reason I wanted to talk to you.'

If she was disappointed, she didn't show it. On the contrary, she was dutifulness personified.

'So what do you want, Dad?'

'For you to stay away from Jan's funeral.'

'Fine, I wasn't going to go anyway. But why?'

'Because about a year ago Jan was involved in an incident where one of our African employees got hurt.'

'And what does that have to do with me?'

'Nothing, Benedikte. And that's how I would like it to stay.'

She met his eye, but looked away after a second. Then she said:

'If I take on more responsibility, I want a pay rise.'

CHAPTER 18

Svend Lerche's business consisted of two elements: one part prostitution, the other poker.

Almost forty women worked for him, and the number had steadily risen as he and his wife, Karina Larsen, found new, suitable host families. The women all came from Africa, and had officially been brought to Denmark to work as au pairs. They each lived with the family that had hired them – they had nice rooms with their own entrance and separate lavatory and bathroom, which was one of many conditions that must be met in order for the family to be approved. Another condition was that the women could only do hoovering, cleaning and other domestic work for a maximum of one hour a day, and must otherwise be free during the daytime and every single weekend. Apart from their real work, of course, which was to service clients, but never more than one man a day.

Svend Lerche believed in quality rather than quantity. The profits were split equally between him and the host family. However, the host family had to pay their 'au pair' three thousand kroner each month, plus provide board and lodging; to this extent the legislation concerning the au pair arrangement was fully complied with. Other conditions were ignored when Svend Lerche's contacts in the Integration Ministry approved the family's applications. The girls were replaced at least once a year.

The second part of Svend Lerche's business was poker playing. He had hired about fifty poker players, the majority single young men, who, four times a week, played online for him. And for themselves. That was the deal. On a working night they played for six hours: three for themselves and three for Svend Lerche. Whichever session proved to be the most lucrative was then regarded as work, whereupon the winnings – or, on rare occasions, losses – were neatly entered into the business's accounts. Losses for private gaming, however, were covered with an envelope of cash on the first of every month. If a player made a profit playing privately one evening, he could keep the winnings. The result was that Svend Lerche was free to launder much of the money he and his sleeping partner, Bjarne Fabricius, earned from prostitution.

Svend Lerche's garage was large with space for three cars. It was located as far from the house as possible in the eastern corner of the plot, right up against the neighbouring property. An extension of around forty square metres had been added to the back of the garage, where three men who worked for him hung out – that was when they weren't out delivering cash to the poker players or collecting money from the au pairs' night-time work.

The room was neatly decorated with wall-to-wall carpet, designer furniture and two workstations kitted out with computers and telephones. Right inside the door was a coffee machine and a fizzy drinks vending machine. A small table had been squeezed in between the two machines with plastic cups, cream, sugar, teaspoons and a bowl with tokens for the vending machine.

Benedikte Lerche-Larsen visited only rarely. Partly because she had no dealings with the men, and partly because she didn't like how they spoke to each other. Lowlife types, poorly educated, with limited interests and the vocabulary of a Neanderthal.

However, this Tuesday she had left university early and was back in Rungsted after lunch, where she had gone straight to the office to get to grips with Jan Podowski's computer.

After a few days' pause for reflection, her father had finally made up his mind and, as she had expected, taken Bjarne Fabricius's advice and given Benedikte a more central role in the business. As a part of this expanded role, Jan Podowski's computer was a good place to start. She could gain a better financial insight while tidying up his files, transferring anything that needed hiding onto a USB stick, and deleting other information once she had familiarised herself with its contents. It was a good idea – it had been her father's – but the reality proved to be different.

She had spent her first hour looking for Jan Podowski's password in his desk and in his files in order to unlock the computer. She finally found what she was looking for in the form of a scrap of paper glued to the back of the mouse pad. The password was *sesamesesame*, as unoriginal as the man himself. After the word he had carefully drawn a small recycling logo with three arrows pointing at each other. She didn't know what they meant. She turned on the computer, accessed the files and decided to help herself to a cup of coffee before she got stuck in.

The coffee machine was playing up or, rather, produced no coffee no matter which button she pressed. A red display at the top confirmed the problem by flashing capital letters summing up the issue with the information *NO DRINK*. She swore irritably and turned to the only other person in the room – a man in his thirties, sitting at the desk behind her, listening to music on his iPod. He had put up his feet on another chair, and his eyes were half closed. He was a skinny rake of a man with filthy tattoos on both arms and long, unwashed hair scattered with dandruff. She shouted at him:

'Can you fix this crap?'

He took out his earplugs, and she repeated her request. He answered her slowly, as if speaking was a great effort for him:

'You need to empty the bottom tray. It's probably full.'

'Wrong. *You* need to empty the bottom tray, and then fix me a mocha.'

To her surprise, he didn't stir, merely flashed her a smarmy grin.

'Do it yourself, you're the one who wants coffee.'

She glowered at him.

'Tell me, just who do you think you are?'

'I'm the guy whose last day of work is this Friday, and you're the one who'll empty the tray, if you want coffee.'

He grinned again; she decided to go up to her own flat.

The letter was waiting for her in the hall along with a pile of junk mail. It was in a white envelope with her name and address drawn ruler-straight, the letters reminding her a little of runic writing. The postmark was 3660 Ganløse, no sender was listed. She opened it with a knife from the kitchen; it contained a smaller envelope as well as two pieces of A4 paper. She recognised the first. It was the cover of the most recent issue of *Poker Player*, where she was smiling invitingly at the photographer. The other was a colour printout of a photograph, grainy but recognisable. Most of the picture showed a forest, but two people could be seen among the trees. She herself was clearly visible at the front; at the back – where you could really only see hands and a little bit of the arms – was Henrik Krag. Between them, tied to two spruce branches, they carried a stone. She opened the enclosed envelope, tearing it open with her finger, although the knife was lying right next to her. It contained a piece of cardboard with a SIM card taped to it. On the cardboard it said in the same runic letters as before *24.04, 10.00*, nothing more.

She sat down at her desk and carefully reviewed what she had been sent, the papers, the envelopes and the cardboard separately, before she calmly returned everything to the big envelope and locked it in her desk drawer.

She was soon back in the office. Her lazy, dandruff-laden friend from before was sitting where she had left him. She yanked out his ear plugs and, as he spun around angrily to confront her, showed him a banknote.

'I need your help.'

The man stared greedily at the five hundred kroner she was holding between her fingers.

'What do you want me to do? By the way, my name is Jørgen.'

He offered her his hand, she ignored it.

'That's great, Jørgen. Were you around back when Henrik worked here?'

'Henrik Krag? Yes, I was, but only for a week, then he stopped coming.'

'Do you know him?'

'Not really, why?'

'I need his address or his phone number.'

'And for that you'll give me five hundred?'

'Almost. I also want you to carry Jan's computer upstairs to my flat and plug it in. I'll show you where it goes.'

'Sure, what do you want me to do first?'

'The address and telephone number.'

'You'll find that on Jan's computer in the Human Resources folder. But I don't think that phone number works any more. There's an access file, but the password for that is the same as when you log on.'

'Sesamesesame.'

'That's right.'

'Why the hell didn't you say so sooner? I've wasted over an hour looking for it.'

He threw up his hands in an apologetic gesture, then asked:

'Do you want the computer taken to your flat now?'

'Yes, but first I have another question.'

She showed him the scrap of paper on which Jan Podowski had written his password and pointed to the recycling logo.

'What does that mean?'

'There are two hard drives. If you want to access the D drive, you need to spell the password in reverse.'

'And what's on the D drive, which is so secret, that it would take someone almost ten minutes to guess how to access it?'

He smiled half-heartedly before replying.

'Jan's pension pot. That's what he used to call it, but he never got round to cashing it in.'

Dry laughter followed the observation.

'And what's in that pot?'

He extended his fingers and bumped the forefinger and thumb together to simulate a vagina, accompanying the obscene gesture with a leer. Benedikte Lerche-Larsen looked daggers at him. Then she let the banknote drop to the floor. He followed it with his eyes without commenting on the humiliation.

'In Danish, if you can manage it?'

'Video footage of a lot of important white men getting a lot of good, black pussy.'

CHAPTER 19

The car was quiet, only the muffled cries of the girl in the boot, whimpering and heart-breaking, at times panicky, would some-times reach the men. Frode Otto turned on the radio and found a station he liked. Then he checked his watch.

'When is kick-off?'

It was 1992 and that night Denmark was playing the Netherlands in the European championship semi-final. Jan Podowski didn't reply, instead he asked:

'What the hell are you going to do with her?'

'Just give her a kiss, it won't do her any harm, bloody German. You heard for yourself how she dissed us in the shop.'

They had stopped outside some shop earlier, Jan Podowski couldn't remember the name of the village, nor did it matter. Frode Otto had pushed in front of her to pay for their stuff. Six lagers and two packets of Prince cigarettes, not that that mattered either. The girl had taken offence, which was odd, really – she could barely be more than fifteen. The shop assistant had served the girl first, and Frode Otto lost his rag. They had drunk a beer each in the car before driving on; a few kilometres outside the village they came across the girl again. She was cycling with her groceries and ignored Frode Otto's shouting as he slowly drove up alongside her and called to her. Eventually she had stuck out her tongue. That made him see red, and now she was lying in the boot. Jan Podowski turned down the music, it irritated him.

'What do you have against the Germans?'

'I hate all foreigners who come up here and don't know how to behave themselves properly.'

'You don't know what she said to you, you don't speak bloody German!'

'That's her problem, not mine.'

Frode Otto laughed at his own joke, while struggling to remove the signet ring from the ring finger of his right hand. It was stuck; he spat on his finger and tried again without success. Eventually it came off, and he slipped it in his pocket.

Jan Podowski considered the situation. He had taken the wheel when Frode Otto attacked the girl, although he was fairly drunk. They passed a junction, and he had time to read a road sign: Hald 3 kilometres. Hald . . . please let that be some sort of town. From there he could call a taxi and get back to the hotel; after all he had plenty of money. He finished his deliberations and stopped the car. The girl whimpered behind them. He shouldn't have hit the brakes so hard, he thought, and said:

'I don't want to get involved with this crap, Frode. Either you let her go or I'm off.'

'You would walk?'

'Yes, anything but this.'

'How are you going to get home? You've no idea where you are.'

Jan Podowski took the four remaining beers, which were in a carrier with a paper handle. Then he got out.

'I'm in Jutland, and they speak Danish. I'll find my way home.'

'OK, see you tonight.'

'Make sure she gets some air.'

'She has plenty of air. This old rust bucket is full of holes.'

Frode Otto edged across to the driver's seat.

'Can I count on you not to tell?'

He didn't get a reply, only a headshake that could mean anything.

CHAPTER 20

The Countess spoke, slowly and gravely.

'She had turned fifteen two days before, poor girl. Hannelore Müller was her name, and she and her parents were on a camping holiday in Jutland. They lived in Altendorf, a suburb of Essen, ordinary people, her father was a bricklayer, her mother a lab assistant, I remember. They were staying at Erikstrup campsite between Viborg and Hobro.'

Konrad Simonsen, Arne Pedersen and Klavs Arnold were stony-faced. Even Malte Borup, the department's student intern and computer genius, narrowed his eyes and tightened his lips. Only Pauline Berg appeared unmoved, and Konrad Simonsen decided that he would tell her to go to hell if she started acting up. They were sitting in the Countess's office around her desk. Space was tight, and the only one sitting comfortably was the Countess herself, with the rest huddled together as best they could. She passed around a photograph, the first in a pile on the desk in front of her.

The girl was naked and lying on her stomach, she had a bandage on her left hand. Her slim back was covered in bruises, the right side worse than the left. At the top of each buttock were two bruises the size of a thumb. Each officer looked, looked away and passed on the photograph in silence. When they had finished, the Countess asked:

'Do you want to see more?'

Given what they had seen in the first picture, the question sounded almost like a threat. Everyone shook their head.

'It's the worst sexual assault case I've ever investigated. He broke two of her fingers, presumably out of pure sadism. Her jaw was also broken, as was her left cheekbone. Her right eardrum had burst, and she was in just as bad a state on her front as you've seen on her back, indeed almost worse. She was penetrated orally, anally and vaginally, and he took his time. Afterwards he or they threw her in the water and scoured her from top to bottom with seaweed.'

Arne Pedersen asked darkly:

'Semen traces?'

'No, sadly, nor any other DNA evidence.'

'Did he use a condom?'

'No, he pulled out before he ejaculated.'

Konrad Simonsen grunted.

'Can we have the whole story?'

The Countess continued:

'It was very difficult to interview the girl. She was in shock, so her statement cast only sporadic light on the assault. But we've established that she was attacked and forced into a car around one o'clock in the afternoon on a main road two kilometres north-west of Vammen, as she rode her bicycle back to the campsite with groceries she had bought at the local village store. In the shop she'd had a row with two Danish men in their thirties, and they may have been the ones who kidnapped her. Most of us believe that. Unfortunately, the shop assistant was old and short-sighted, so his description of the men was inadequate, to say the least.

'The girl herself couldn't remember whether she was attacked by one or two men, only that she was thrown into the boot of a car. Nor was she sure about the colour of the vehicle. The next thing we know for certain is that she was found at nine o'clock that same evening on a forest path in Lundø, a peninsula that sticks out into Skive Fjord, by a man out walking his dog. She was naked and deeply traumatised. We don't know exactly where the rape took place, only that at times during the assault he forced her across the bonnet of the car, and that it happened close to water, possibly Limfjorden, but we can't even be sure about that. We never found her clothes. I travelled to Essen eighteen months later to talk to her. We thought she might be able to remember more once some time had passed since the event, but . . .'

Pauline Berg interrupted her angrily.

'*Event*? You make it sound like a birthday, why don't you say the *rape*? I recognise that I use cowardly paraphrases myself, but—'

The Countess refused to let herself be derailed.

'My apologies, you're right, of course. The bottom line was that Hannelore Müller remembered barely anything about her rape. The doctor I spoke to thought her mind was suppressing it. Mentally she has paid a huge price, and I don't think that she'll ever fully recover, but of course I'm no psychiatrist. Perhaps she has learned to live with the assault, in spite of everything, as the years have passed.

'As I'm sure you can imagine, every resource was deployed to find the perpetrator or perpetrators, and I was summoned from Copenhagen to assist Viborg police. The case attracted considerable media interest, as you would expect, and I was on the front page of the local newspapers on several occasions where I was hailed as the expert from Copenhagen and in charge of the investigation. Both of which were untrue.'

'So that's how Frode Otto might have seen your face.'

Malte Borup wanted to be quite sure that he had grasped the connection.

The Countess nodded affirmatively.

'The only useful description we had of the perpetrator was that he was either missing the little finger on his left hand, or that he might have damaged or broken it, possibly during the attack on the girl. Of course we searched high and low, especially the campsite where the Müller family had stayed, but we found nothing, and eventually the investigation petered out and the case was shelved.'

'Do we know where Frode Otto was on 22 June 1992?' Klavs Arnold asked the Countess.

'No, but we know where he was three days earlier, because he and a mate robbed a savings bank in Struer, seventy kilometres as the crow flies from Erikstrup campsite. They got away with just under two hundred thousand kroner. They threatened a cashier with a toy gun, and Frode Otto left a clear print of his middle finger on the counter next to the till. However, he wasn't caught until almost two years later, when he was arrested following a simple break-in of a corner shop. He was sentenced to three and a half years in Ringe State Prison, but he never gave up his mate – or accomplice, if you prefer.'

Konrad Simonsen wondered out loud:

'Surely someone, as a matter of routine over the years, must have checked if any men with nine fingers have been added to our registers? The sexual assault case is still unsolved.'

The Countess pulled out a photocopy from a file behind her. It was awkward, Klavs Arnold was in the way and had nowhere to move to. He had to stand up, holding his chair. It looked ridiculous, but no one was laughing. The Countess tossed the photocopy on the desk with an irritated gesture. Everyone recognised the traditional fingerprint form. All of the ten squares had been filled out, but if they looked closely, the left little fingerprint deviated strongly from the norm. The Countess explained.

'Some total imbecile from Odense police used the joint that remained on Frode Otto's little finger for the print, and the Central Bureau added it to the database without questioning it.'

Arne Pedersen rapped a knuckle against his temple to show his opinion of that. Then he made the obvious suggestion

'Why don't we head to Simon's office? This is making me claustrophobic, and when Malte brings up Frode Otto's records,' he pointed to the laptop, which the intern was balancing on his lap, 'it'll be impossible for all of us to look at them at the same time.'

The Countess looked around as if she hadn't noticed how tightly they were squeezed in until now, then she smiled.

'Of course we can. And perhaps we could break for five minutes, I want a cup of coffee and some fruit.'

As is often the case, a five-minute break in Denmark meant just under half an hour. Konrad Simonsen was the last to arrive, a bad habit he had acquired over the years, based on the egotistical, but usually correct, assumption that meetings wouldn't start until he turned up, and then he was saved the hassle of waiting for others. Malte Borup was sitting on the chief's usual chair at the end of the conference table, as he was leading the presentation. Nonetheless he started by apologising. Konrad Simonsen seized the opportunity to wrong-foot him. Malte studied computer science at university and had a tendency to blind them with techspeak.

'Perhaps you could give us the short version, then we can read the long one later on in our own time?'

The student intern accepted the suggestion; after all he had no real choice, as Pauline Berg archly remarked. She was ignored as she usually was when she was rude, and Malte Borup hurried to start.

Frode Otto was born in 1960 in Næstved, where he also grew up. After leaving school he was apprenticed to a blacksmith, and qualified in 1982, the same year he moved to Sydhavnen in Copenhagen. He never had a regular job as a blacksmith, and during the next ten years lived in several different towns in Denmark, including Odense, Køge and Copenhagen. During that time he got involved in various petty criminal activities, swindling, fencing stolen goods, a couple of break-ins, some stolen cars, but apart from the bank robbery in Struer, nothing major as far as the police were aware.

From 1993 to 1995 he was in prison, and in 1997 he was convicted of assault after he carried out a nasty attack in Assens. In 2000 he was employed at Kolleløse Manor, and didn't appear to have done anything unlawful since then, apart from taking part in a pub brawl in 2005, which resulted in a three months' suspended sentence. His only known hobby was wrestling, and he had been a member of several wrestling clubs across Denmark, depending on where he lived. In 1987 he reached the final of the Danish championship in his class.

Konrad Simonsen added:

'I spoke about him to Adam Blixen-Agerskjold and his wife ...'

Pauline Berg interrupted:

'His wife is called Lenette, Lenette Blixen-Agerskjold. You spoke to Lenette Blixen-Agerskjold and her husband about Frode Otto.'

The Countess grinned and sided with her.

'She has a point, Simon.'

Klavs Arnold and Arne Pedersen rolled their eyes at each other. Simonsen flapped his hand as if dismissing a fly, and started over as he slowly and formally stated both names, and pointed out that the sequence had been chosen at random. Then he continued:

'Frode Otto regularly spends the first weekend in odd months, that is January, March, May and so on, in Copenhagen. Or rather, he says he does. He claims to be visiting his sister. The problem is, he doesn't have one. He leaves Saturday afternoon or early evening, and returns to the estate approximately twenty-four hours later. It has been going on for as long as Lenette Blixen-Agerskjold and her husband can remember. I would like to know where he goes and what he does, so we'll watch him the next time he goes visiting his *sister . . .*'

He made quotation marks in the air with his fingers and carried on:

'. . . which will be in eight days, if my maths is up to scratch. Who wants to handle that?'

Klavs Arnold thought about it quickly. His Saturday with Pauline Berg had been cancelled, the forester wasn't free that day after all, so the trip had been postponed to 2 May, the very day Frode Otto was due to drive to Copenhagen. But one was in the morning, and the other towards the evening, so he should be able to do both without any problems. He volunteered, and interjected at the same time:

'Rapists don't usually stop at one victim unless they're caught, so could there have been more?'

'Good point. You, Countess, look into that. Review all unsolved sexual assault cases from when Otto was eighteen, that is from 1978. Also try to check out his holidays if you can. I have an email from Adam Blixen-Agerskjold listing any foreign trips he remembers Frode Otto taking, but it's probably incomplete. Pauline, you can assist, if you like.'

'And what if I don't?'

'Then help Arne when he tries to dig up something from Frode Otto's old cellmates, or Klavs when he checks out any information we might get from the wrestling clubs.'

'Can't I get my own area of responsibility?'

'No! Incidentally that hairband, Countess, did you get anywhere?'

'Yes, I learned a lot, but nothing useful. It was made in China, imported by Fair Fashion in Ballerup and distributed to thousands of shops across the country. I made a file note, if you're interested in the details.'

Konrad Simonsen clearly wasn't; he rounded off the briefing.

'Frode Otto is obviously our priority right now, if only because we have no other sensible leads. If there is any way we can get him for the rape, we will, of course, but at the same time, it's worth bearing in mind that he may well have nothing to do with the murder of the African woman. If he did kill her, there are lots of things I can't currently explain. You probably feel the same, but let's hang on in there until we know more.'

No one objected to that.

Konrad Simonsen was lying on the sofa at home in Søllerød, relaxing after dinner; the Countess sat in an armchair so close to his head that she could stroke his thinning hair. A book, *Femmes en guerre*, was resting on her lap. She opened it, but changed her mind and laid it over the armrest, ready to be picked up once she got off her chest something that had been troubling her since the meeting at Police Headquarters. She carefully asked:

'If Frode Otto has information about our murder inquiry, will you do a deal with him regarding the rape?'

Konrad Simonsen looked genuinely surprised. He sat up.

'This isn't America, we don't do deals, you know that better than anyone.'

'Except that we do. We're just more subtle about it. We work a little less hard on one investigation and put our backs into another. Besides, it's highly unlikely we can get him for the rape of Hannelore Müller. Not without physical evidence. We can't even be sure that it's him.'

'Where are you going with this? Frode Otto might know nothing useful, or he may be the killer; surely it's way too early to tell. Not to mention doing deals, as you call it.'

'Stop pretending the thought hasn't crossed your mind. I know you too well, Simon.'

He mulled it over; she gave him time by flicking through her book. Eventually he said:

'As a last resort, I'll go to Germany and talk to the girl. If that doesn't give me anything, I see nothing wrong in using the rape to pressure him for information, if we can, and if he has any in the first place. Are you satisfied?'

She wasn't, she merely pretended to be. Then she reached out and poured herself a cup of coffee, opened her book again and started telling him about France.

CHAPTER 21

'Benedikte!'

Henrik Krag's jaw dropped when he opened his front door and recognised his visitor. Benedikte Lerche-Larsen smiled tight-lipped and ran her hand through her hair to shake off the raindrops. She said in a business-like tone:

'We need to talk.'

The flat was small enough for her to take it in quickly. A narrow hallway with a kitchen at one end and a living room at the other; opposite the front door a lavatory and a bedroom. Classic 1970s brutalist social housing where the architecture was secondary to manufacturing neat concrete modules. The living room was furnished with a small dining table right inside the door, and dominated by a sofa and armchair, which faced the television at the other end. A door to the balcony and a panoramic window with a view of the next high-rise block took up half the end wall, and the floppy beige curtains either side of the window were in dire need of washing. As was the window.

Benedikte Lerche-Larsen entered the living room. A woman her own age was sitting on the sofa, glowering at her. Cheap clothing, rhinestone on one canine, metallic eyeliner and white eyeshadow, peeling nail polish and bleached yellow hair with dark roots.

'What are you looking at?'

Benedikte Lerche-Larsen ignored her and turned to Henrik Krag.

'Perhaps your girlfriend could go for a walk so we can talk in private.'

Without awaiting his response, Benedikte opened the sliding door and stepped out onto the balcony. Grey storm clouds rushed westwards, blowing an occasional gust of wind heavy with fine droplets. She wiped the moisture from her forehead with her sleeve, zipped her jacket up to her neck and shuddered. It was a short, black leather jacket with a diagonal zip and quilted collar, offering little protection against the elements. Shortly afterwards Henrik Krag opened the door for her, his girlfriend had gone.

She went inside and flopped onto an armchair, having first taken off and thrown her jacket over the armrest. Then she took an envelope from her bag, pulled out the printout of the picture from Hanehoved Forest, and placed it on the coffee table between them. Henrik Krag bent over it as though it were poisonous. He said hesitantly:

'Someone took a picture of you when we carried that stone.'

'Someone took a picture of *us* when we carried that stone,' she corrected him.

'But how did that happen? And who sent it?'

She explained the situation and answered, to the best of her ability, his subsequent questions. Until he started to repeat himself.

'I don't know what we can do. It's the third time you've asked me. And I guess we can't do much apart from wait for him to call and then we'll find out what he wants from us.

'April the twenty-fourth at ten a.m. . . . that's this Friday?'

Benedikte Lerche-Larsen nodded.

'I'll be at work then.'

'No, you won't. You'll be with me when I take that call.'

Her eyes flashed at him and he gave up protesting. Of course he would be there.

'What does Jan say?'

'If you're referring to Jan Podowski, then he's not saying anything. He's dead.'

Henrik Krag was shocked, and Benedikte Lerche-Larsen had to explain all over again. However, he eventually returned to their present dilemma. He pointed to the printout still lying on the coffee table between them.

'Her death was an accident. We didn't mean to kill her.'

'I'm sure she appreciates that.'

'No, what I'm saying is, it can't cost us that much. Prison time, I mean.'

He had begun sweating around the bridge of his nose and wiped it off with his sleeve. She shook her head without putting him straight.

'What about you?' he said. 'There's no need to drag you into it. We can say that you stayed in the car.'

'And how long do you think you can keep lying to Denmark's most professional lead interrogators? One hour, two hours, ten hours? But I appreciate the thought. Any chance of some coffee?'

While Henrik Krag made the coffee, Benedikte Lerche-Larsen sniffed around the living room, taking it in. The laptop was an older model, a Dell, at least six years old. However, the television looked new. His furniture was ugly and threadbare, the carpet stained and the cable from the ceiling to the lamp over the dining table was shortened with a loop and held in place with a pen. On the windowsill she spotted the little gold box in which she used to keep coke, but she was done with that crap, at least for now, so he could keep it. Then she checked his DVDs, and discovered they were all Danish. She looked around for books, but found none.

When he brought the coffee, she was back in the armchair. He placed a mug in front of her, she thanked him and declined his offer of milk and sugar before taking off her boots, tucking her legs up under her on the seat and pointing to his DVDs.

'Do you only watch Danish films?'

His gaze flitted to the shelf as he replied.

'I prefer them.'

She took a sip of her coffee, screwed up her lips in disgust and said: 'You can't read, can you?' She nodded as she made the statement, and then abandoned the subject.

'Why don't you answer your phone? I've called you a million times.'

'My mobile was stolen.'

'Then buy or steal another, I need to be able to get hold of you.'

At that point her own mobile rang. She took it out of her bag, was about to press *Ignore*, then saw the name on the display and changed her mind. Bjarne Fabricius wasn't a man you avoided if he wanted to talk to you. She took the call and asked him to wait a moment, putting her other hand over the mobile.

'It's about an appointment I have tomorrow, but I would prefer to discuss it in private.'

This time it was Henrik Krag's turn to head for the balcony. It was more than ten minutes before she summoned him by tapping on the window. They sat down as before. He picked up the conversation where they had left off without commenting on the interruption and promised he would get himself a new mobile. Only it would have to wait until the end of the month when he got paid. She shook her head in despair. A lock of red hair tumbled over her forehead, which she brushed aside. She found her purse, chucked a business card onto the table, followed by three five-hundred-kroner notes. Henrik Krag protested.

'That's way too much, I only need five hundred max.'

'Then buy yourself some decent coffee as well. Besides, it's a loan.'

She sounded weary rather than sarcastic, as if her thoughts were elsewhere after the telephone call. He had an eye and an ear for such things – her voice was flatter than before and she was less animated. She glanced at her watch, a gold vintage Cartier. It was after nine and growing dark outside. She reached for her boots.

'Time for me to go. I have an exam tomorrow that I'd like to pass.'

'In April? I didn't think . . .'

'It's a resit, I was ill the last time.'

Her voice had suddenly turned sharp. He stood up, flapping around her pointlessly as she put on her boots, and talked nonsense about how seeing her had been nice. She made no reply until her hand was on the front door in order to let herself out, then she said casually:

'You don't happen to know a man called Frode Otto, do you?'

He grabbed her shoulder quickly, almost brutally. It was pure reflex in response to the name, there was no thought behind it. Nor when he spun her around and grabbed her again.

'Don't go out with him! He's dangerous, and I know it's none of my business, but I don't care . . . just don't do it. Never, ever.'

Her reaction was surprisingly understated. She placed her free hand on top of his on her arm and let it rest there for a long second, as if warming the lid of a jar with the palm of her hand before untwisting it. Then she removed it, without anger, almost gently, and let him have it back.

He stressed again: she was to stay away from Frode Otto, and it wasn't up for discussion. With one hand on his chest, she pushed him back into the living room, and they sat down. She massaged her shoulder, but didn't comment on his grabbing her.

'If it'll calm you down, I've no idea who Frode Otto is. Except that he appears to have contacted both my parents and . . . tell me, do you know who Bjarne Fabricius is?'

'Yes, he's the big boss. He owns your father. And lots of other people, Jan told me. But I've never met him.'

'Count yourself lucky. So this Frode Otto – whoever the hell he is, but perhaps you can explain that to me – would appear to have called and threatened Bjarne as well as my parents, as far as I can work out, which is pretty much the dumbest thing he could have done, but that's his problem. Unfortunately, it sounds as if Mr Otto knows more than he ought to know, and I gather you can tell me a little about what that is.'

'He and Jan were mates, they went way back. They did each other favours.'

'What kind of favours?'

'Frode Otto let Jan use his hunting lodge in the off season. I mean, he didn't own it, but he was the caretaker at the manor house that owned the hunting lodge, and . . .'

'Go on.'

'And every other month, by way of payment, Frode got a free . . . well, a free fuck. But there was a problem. Jan himself told me it was messed up. Really badly messed up.'

Henrik ground to a halt again. Benedikte's voice rose an octave.

'Messed up how? Do I have to drag every single word out of you?'

Henrik explained.

'He was rough with the women, often very rough. Usually he only got those we were getting rid of anyway.'

'What makes him contact us, especially Bjarne Fabricius whom he shouldn't even know? He says we owe him money, can that be right? And he demands that his visiting arrangement, or whatever we call it, continue.'

'I know nothing about the money, but I wonder if he fixed the cabin? Jan torched it, you probably remember that. But you need to stay away from him, Benedikte. I've seen a video of how he . . . behaves when he's with the girls. He's a pervert and he's dangerous.'

Benedikte Lerche-Larsen thought about it for a long time. Henrik Krag sat in silence, looking at her quizzically, until she finally reached a conclusion.

'Frode Otto might be dangerous, but he's pissing off someone who is even more dangerous, and if he took that photograph of us, we'll kill him.'

Henrik Krag shook his head firmly.

'Forget it. I'm not killing anyone.'

'You already have, that's why we're here now.'

CHAPTER 22

'B plus.'
Benedikte Lerche-Larsen smiled as her tutor reviewed her exam, and she shook his hand and thanked him like a schoolgirl. He took her by the elbow with his other hand, and her smile broadened. Everything was as it should be; there was a chance he would be teaching her next term, if her father insisted on her taking more legal modules. Eventually he let go, and she marched off without caring about her two fellow students sitting behind her, waiting to know how they had done.

The morning traffic through Copenhagen moved without noticeable hold-ups. The sky was dark and rain was on the way. She drove north along Strandvejen but stopped near Trianglen, where she was lucky to find a parking space in a side street. That morning she had found and copied three video clips stored in a folder named *Frode Otto* on Jan Podowski's computer, but she hadn't yet had time to view them. She might as well do that now, while enjoying an espresso and a well-earned break.

With her Mac under her arm, she crossed the street diagonally, and avoided being caught on camera just in time when she spotted a group of Japanese tourists who, with an excess of smiles, bows and gestures, took turns photographing each other in front of a sausage stall. She watched the event while she waited for the light to turn green at the next junction. With undeterminable guttural sounds the owner of the sausage stall handed one grilled sausage with mustard and ketchup after the other across the counter, and would appear to have given up communicating with his customers at a more sophisticated level, although most of his delicacies were dumped in a bin after a few seconds, having served their purpose as props. Here commerce, balance of payments and the health of the Japanese population all benefited at the same time.

The café was half empty. She fetched her espresso and a small slice of cake from the counter and took a seat by the window. It had started to drizzle outside, and soon it was pouring down. She looked out while she ate. The drops bounced off the gleaming road surface where the reflection of the traffic lights produced red, green and amber patterns, continually spoiled by the tyres of passing cars, only to reform immediately in new configurations. A flash of lightning rent the sky and briefly bathed the street scene in brilliant light. The pressure wave from the thunder caused the windowpane in front of her to vibrate, and she flinched away from it. It wasn't until the storm had eased off that she opened her Mac and clicked on one of the films.

Her espresso grew cold. Three films of three African women being assaulted. She had to turn down the volume, though it was already very low. The picture quality was poor, barely more than five frames per second, which made the viewing even more terrifying. Jerky, almost unreal, the girls were subjected to punches from all angles, sexual degradation and unadulterated sadism. Frode Otto was a strong man. And a persistent one.

CHAPTER 23

When Benedikte Lerche-Larsen arrived home in Rungsted, she went straight to see her father, who was out in the garden. He was on his knees in the herbaceous border, busy pulling up gout weed, a stress-relieving occupation he was reluctant to leave to the gardener. He didn't notice his daughter until she blocked out the sun, which was now starting to peep out between the clouds. He plunged the garden trowel into the ground and stuffed the weeds into a bucket next to him, before turning his attention to her.

'How did it go?'

'I didn't fail, so that's all right. I got an E.'

'That's bad, what happened?'

She knew that the low grade would irritate him, especially if she dismissed it as unimportant. On the surface she had to be perfect, nothing less would do. Her real feelings were of no interest to him.

'Nothing went wrong, I'm just not that good.'

He tried prising it out of her. She replied evasively or with a shrug, until he gave up and changed the subject.

'That idiot who called yesterday, have you managed to find out anything about him?'

'Frode Otto?'

'Yes, that was his name.'

'Forget him. I'm handling it.'

'He also called Bjarne Fabricius. That's not good. Bjarne was angry, you know what he's like if he gets dragged into anything.'

'No, I don't, but you do. Like I said: I'm handling it. You don't have to worry.'

'What are you going to do? Give him money and a free pass to our services as he demands? I don't like being blackmailed.'

'No free passes. He wrecks the women and that would make it far too expensive in the long run. Why can't you just accept that I'm dealing with it?'

It was as if he hadn't understood what she was saying until now. He narrowed his eyes and looked at her for a long time, then he nodded. She would take charge and that was to his advantage, of course, there was nothing more to discuss. He asked in a lighter tone of voice:

'Will you be going with your mother this afternoon? There is a fresh delivery arriving from Nigeria, and we need to replace seven or eight of our existing staff. She seems to think that the two of you are going together.'

'Yes, I'll go with her.'

'And then there's some data from the three poker players, which I would like you to look at tonight. It's urgent.'

'That may be so, but it'll have to wait until tomorrow. I have plans for tonight.'

'Who with?'

'A man, and the rest is none of your business, Svend. If it really is that terribly urgent, then do it yourself rather than waste time on this donkey work.'

She pointed an accusatory finger at the border without considering that she behaved in exactly the same way, only with her the displacement activity was lawn mowing. Then she turned on her heel and left.

CHAPTER 24

Karina Larsen loved a good deal. She always felt the thrill of anticipation when she chased a bargain. The system was the same wherever you went: antiques from Portobello Road in London, steel engravings for her husband's study from Porte de Clignancourt in Paris or African women from a cheap hotel on

Vesterbro in Copenhagen – it was all about buying low and selling high. Methodically, without rushing, she scanned the goods as she made notes on the pad lying on her lap.

The room where they were up for inspection wasn't much bigger than an ordinary living room, and yet the hotel had the cheek to call it a suite. Along one wall, facing the street, sixteen Nigerian women were lined up, some sitting on chairs, others standing, with a single one seated on the windowsill. At the far end their mamma was sitting in an armchair watching the women with cold eyes. She spoke Hausa and Yoruba as well as perfect English, the official language of Nigeria. Benedikte Lerche-Larsen and her mother, two buyers from Aarhus – one African and one Dane – were sitting opposite the women. The Danish man had a cold, he kept sniffling. It was wearying to listen to and eventually Karina Larsen handed him a packet of paper tissues from her handbag. He accepted her gift politely and carried on sniffling.

Benedikte Lerche-Larsen glanced at her mother's notes, then she leaned closer and whispered into her ear:

'I don't think the girl to the left of the window has been broken in.'

She nodded in the direction of the girl, whose eyes were moist. She had clearly been crying earlier. Mamma was vigilant. Though she couldn't possibly have heard what Benedikte Lerche-Larsen whispered, she said in a sharp voice:

'All my girls have come here of their own free will.'

Benedikte Lerche-Larsen replied to her in the same language. Karina Larsen, whose English was average, asked:

'What did you say to her?'

'I said that of course they've come here of their own free will. And if they haven't, they'll get a beating until they understand what free will means in Danish.'

'Why do you put it like that? It's essential that they're here of their own accord. Otherwise many of our customers won't want them.'

'Because I'm so fed up with the hypocrisy, but all right, let's go with that: right from when they were very young, each and every one of them dreamed of coming here to our legendary welfare state to be screwed by ten to twelve men a day, until they're so old and sagging that no one would pay fifty kroner for them. Their Danish

95

dream has come true, look how they smile at us! Let's just buy the ones we need so we can get out of here.'

Benedikte Lerche-Larsen spoke the truth. Every single one of the sixteen volunteers was beaming as if her life depended on it, each of them sincerely hoping they would find favour with Karina Larsen. They were just a few of many, many thousands of sex slaves exported to Europe each year from Africa, primarily from countries such as Niger, Chad and Nigeria, known as the Triangle of Shame. Human trafficking was the polite term for this – organised rape would have been more accurate.

All the women were trying to appear sexy and eager to work to the older, blonde woman sitting at the opposite end of the room, scrutinising them. Rumours had long since spread among them: if Karina Larsen owned you, you would only have to service one client a day. It sounded incredible, but it was the truth. And what luxury it would be – just one customer a day! In the land of the blind, the one-eyed man is king.

At length Benedikte Lerche-Larsen and her mother agreed on five applicants – that was Karina Larsen's term for them – whom they would examine more closely. Mamma handed over the girls' passports, and the chosen ones followed the two women from the suite into an adjacent hotel room. A young man was waiting here. He got up when they arrived and greeted the women nervously. It was his first time doing this kind of work, and he wasn't sure whether he was involved in anything illegal, but the money was good, and he was being paid in cash, to avoid troubling the taxman. He dried his sweaty palm on his trouser leg before he offered it politely to the two Danish women. He had put his doctor's bag on the bed.

'Take off your clothes, please,' Karina Larsen ordered the girls in her best school English.

Benedikte Lerche-Larsen nodded to the young man and remarked to her mother:

'You usually pick a woman doctor.'

'He was the only one available, not that it matters. Blacks have no modesty. They're primitive, nudity is natural to them.'

Karina Larsen found a pair of latex gloves in her pocket and put them on; then, like an experienced horse trader, she carried out a thorough examination of the women, one after the other. She opened their mouths, ruffled their hair, widened their eyes, lifted up their feet and checked the soles. Then she compared them to their passport photos. On paper they had to be at least eighteen years old before she would buy them; how old, or rather how young, they really were, was of no interest to her.

Two women were rejected, one due to saggy breasts and limp, drooping labia. Probably the result of having a kid along the way, a kid she might even be hiding somewhere over here. It had been known to happen. The other was rejected due to her teeth, which would be too expensive to fix, triggering a discussion between mother and daughter. Benedikte Lerche-Larsen used all the accountancy skills she had learned at Copenhagen Business School. Investment, depreciation, net profit – after a quick estimate, the numbers proved that the dental treatment would quickly pay for itself. However, her mother's experience and gut feeling said no, and that was the end of that.

Then it was time for the doctor to carry out essential medical check-ups. Years ago Karina Larsen had been tricked when she had bought a woman who later turned out to be pregnant, and only after great difficulties had they convinced her to abort the baby. That could never happen again. Karina Larsen now demanded to have the goods checked for venereal diseases, pregnancy and other such inconveniences before the deal could proceed.

All that was now left was to decide the price. Mamma and Karina Larsen withdrew; to her immense irritation Benedikte Lerche-Larsen wasn't allowed to join in. As always, the negotiations were animated. The two women haggled and argued, their language a Tower of Babel mix of Danish, English and non-verbal communication, the numbers in Euro, international, easy to understand.

Karina Larsen had three women to return – barely used, as good as new – which formed part of the deal and should be offset to reach a reasonable price. This complicated the bargaining, but finally they reached an agreement. However, with one proviso.

'On strict condition they don't have any hidden diseases. Half now, the other half when the doctor reports back.'

'Sure, Madam, sure.'

They shook hands, and the women were sold.

CHAPTER 25

Princess Blå on inner Nørrebro overlooking Lake Peblinge was one of many Copenhagen restaurants to open on the strength of a Nordic kitchen and an innovative food culture. Visionary and brilliant craftsmanship had attracted international gastronomists and at the last assessment it had earned a rising star recommendation in the Michelin guide – an indication of a future star, if the high standard continued.

Benedikte Lerche-Larsen had made an effort with her appearance prior to her dinner engagement with Bjarne Fabricius. Apart from the venue itself encouraging it, this evening – should the opportunity arise to talk business – might be of great importance to her. She had chosen a black, sleeveless, knee-length dress cut simply, apart from the back, which from her neck down to her waist consisted of black, see-through lace. She had applied discreet make-up.

Bjarne Fabricius received her gallantly with kisses on both cheeks Continental-style, complimented her on her appearance and escorted her to their table, which was in a bay, almost a separate room, at the back of the restaurant. Benedikte Lerche-Larsen looked around. There was space for at least another two tables. Bjarne Fabricius pulled out a chair for her so that she could sit down, and said as if he had read her mind:

'I've arranged things so that we can talk undisturbed. I thought that was for the best. But let's eat first. I've ordered for both of us, I hope that's all right with you?'

She nodded, it was fine with her. He held up one finger and a young waiter in a white dinner jacket and black trousers with silk stripes along the outside seam materialised and reviewed their menu nervously. Benedikte Lerche-Larsen asked about a couple of the dishes, the man replied as if he was being examined, correctly but stiffly. When he had left, she asked:

'Tell me, do you own this place?'

Bjarne Fabricius poured wine for both of them before he replied.

'That's one of the things I like about you, Benedikte. You notice the details and draw the right conclusions.'

Benedikte Lerche-Larsen ate quickly and finished before him. At his invitation she told him about herself and her studies, but when he moved to top up her glass, she held her hand over it. Slowly he poured wine over her fingers, until she removed her hand. The waiter appeared immediately. Bjarne Fabricius demanded a fresh tablecloth and: 'A warm, wet towel for my young friend.' She washed and dried her hands, while the waiter and a second man replaced the tablecloth with impressive speed.

'Are you trying to get me drunk?'

His laughter was dry, bordering on hostile.

'Not on Chablis Les Clos 2002, that would be a waste of good wine.'

'So why humiliate me? To show me that you can? Because there's no need, we both already know that.'

Bjarne Fabricius bowed his head and scratched his neck with one finger, pausing for a moment in this slightly awkward position apparently unconcerned by her watching him. At length he said:

'You're beautiful, Benedikte, no doubt about it, and you have style. Besides, you have a brilliant mind. The gods have blessed you.'

It wasn't a compliment, only a statement of fact, a starting point that couldn't be contradicted. She didn't reply, simply shrugged, this time without smiling.

'Are you scared of me?'

'Only when you laugh.'

'Answer me properly.'

99

She made eye contact.

'Of course I am. Or rather: I'm scared of getting on the wrong side of you. Only a fool wouldn't be.'

During the next course the mood lightened as if by magic. He talked about the old days when he and her father were young. She listened with interest and laughed in all the right places. And again when he told her the story her parents had always refused to tell her of how they met. Her father had won the pools, sixty thousand kroner, most of which was blown on a three-day bender. She accepted Bjarne Fabricius's conclusion: if AGF hadn't equalised against KB following some incomprehensible penalty in extra time, she would never have been born. She shook her head and her red hair undulated in slow motion. *A toast to crap Danish referees!* They clinked glasses, he continued telling her anecdotes from his youth and the waiter arrived discreetly with another bottle of wine. At one point she interjected:

'I have to drink some water now. I don't want to be tipsy in case I get the opportunity tonight to tell you how we ought to expand my father's businesses. I've come prepared, and I want to do it properly.'

Bjarne grinned.

'You won't be presenting anything. It would be a waste of time and way too boring. You underestimate me, Benedikte, that's why I poured fine wine all over you. I think.'

He then reviewed her plan, without unnecessary discussion, paring it down to the bare bones. The poker business should be set up internationally, still legally – or rather as legally as possible – but with two to three players in each of fifteen to twenty different countries. Money-laundering transactions would happen in the same way as the one used by traditional internet swindlers, by going through a long line of international financial institutions, banks in San Marino, the Ukraine, El Salvador, Lebanon and so on, with each player given his own individual sequence, which should be changed regularly. The hooker business should be closed down, as it was sheer foolishness to run it using the same structure as the Poker Academy. The brothel business was doing well, but it must be kept at arm's length from the card games.

If Benedikte Lerche-Larsen was surprised at his review, she didn't show it; she was too practised at the poker table for that. When he fell silent, she quizzed him.

'From Jan Podowski?'

He confirmed that Jan Podowski had passed on her ideas long ago, which didn't make them any less interesting.

'But you have a problem. What about Karina and Svend? What am I going to do with them? Or perhaps I should ask you: what are *you* going to do with them?'

She shrugged. It was irrelevant. These ideas were just her thoughts about the future. There was nothing that could be set in motion right now.

'Is that right? So Jan was wrong when he told me that your business plan runs to over twenty pages and is ready to be rolled out? It's nothing but fancy business-school theory, nothing that could ever be put to the test?'

His irony stung, but she didn't try to duck the question.

'As you quite rightly point out my parents are a problem, which I can't solve. I'm perfectly aware of that. So for the time being, my business model is just a theory. But I'm not the only one of us with a problem.'

'If you're thinking that I'm in need of a competent replacement for Jan to keep an eye on your parents, then I'm hoping that problem will be solved tonight.'

'And what do I get in return?'

'What do you want?'

'Your goodwill, money in a personal account, the right to screw up from time to time.'

'Smart girl.'

It grew late and they were both quite drunk by the time they left the restaurant. The night smelled of spring and petrol from Østerbrogade, the neon lights gleamed enticingly around them, the stars above. Benedikte Lerche-Larsen grabbed him and laughed.

'You have to support me, my legs are like jelly and it's your fault. What do we do now?'

He put his arm around her; she rested her head on his shoulder.

'We walk around the lake and enjoy the evening. Then we find a bar where we drink a cheap whisky or two, and afterwards I put you in a taxi and send you home.'

He removed his hand from her neck, took her by her shoulders and revolved her ninety degrees so that she was facing the lake. Then he added:

'Unless you get too amorous, then I'll put you in a taxi right away. You're perfectly capable of walking on your own.'

They agreed a compromise whereby she looped her arm through his as they followed the path along the lake. He was whistling quietly but with remarkable skill 'My Heart Will Go On'. She was surprised.

'You're good at that. Do you do requests?'

'You would have fitted right in on the *Titanic*. Perhaps you were born a century too late.'

'Perhaps, who knows? Let me think about a melody for you.'

He never found out which tune she thought would be right for him.

Suddenly a small gang of drunk, aggressive teenagers blocked their path. *Hey, a fucking pensioner and a lousy whore, how about you give me some money, you rich bastard?* A knife flashed in the street lamps, while a girl shouted out a few metres ahead of them that she didn't want any fucking hassle and the boys should come with her now. Bjarne Fabricius handed over his wallet with a short, stiff nod, and never took his eyes off the knife as he firmly pushed Benedikte Lerche-Larsen in front of him, past the other two boys. A few steps further ahead, he put his arm around her neck. Behind them, they heard a commotion, some blows and a couple of muffled cries; Fabricius would appear to have had some of his men with him, discreet and at a distance – she hadn't noticed them. She wanted to turn her head, but could feel his fingers holding it firm.

'What a shame, I was looking forward to my melody, but the moment has passed. I want you to think about something else instead. Frode Otto. That was the name of the moron who rang me up and threatened me, wasn't it?'

Quick footsteps reached them. She glanced at him, still unable to see what was going on behind them, but she noticed him reach out his free hand and return his wallet to his inside pocket. With no words, as if his shoelace had come undone and he had tied it again, no big deal.

'Yes, his name is Frode Otto. What you want me to think about?'

'How you'll solve the problem, something I understand you've told your father that you'll handle. I presume you'll need my help?'

'Yes, that was what I had in mind.'

'Let's say you have free rein. I want to see what you can do.'

He released his hold on her head; she caught his hand and pulled it around her waist.

'Free rein sounds like a dream.'

'Then start dreaming.'

CHAPTER 26

Many little rituals were associated with a Homicide Department investigation, some created by Konrad Simonsen, others inherited. Thus it was the custom that pictures relating to an investigation, including those of witnesses and suspects, were displayed on a large noticeboard in his office to the left of the door. Also that blue or red cotton string would be used to illustrate connections between people on the board, red for a proven connection, blue for an uncertain one still to be proved.

In a major case it could be a complicated jigsaw puzzle to arrange people and their individual relationships as meaningfully as possible so that the noticeboard gave the viewer the best possible overview, and the board would often have to be reorganised in the course of an investigation – a job which was the preserve of the chief of the Homicide Department and no one else unless they fancied a major bollocking. When the Countess and Arne Pedersen entered his office, Konrad Simonsen was standing with a picture of Frode Otto in one hand and a small plastic box of pins in the other. The Countess pointed to the photograph in his hand.

'We were just coming to talk to you about him.'

They sat down at the desk at the far end of the room. The Countess began.

'We've now been able to establish without a doubt that Frode Otto was in Nordjylland in June 1992 when Hannelore Müller was sexually assaulted.'

Konrad Simonsen's inner alarm bells started ringing. Their somewhat formal behaviour and their determined manner, which left little room for chit-chat, combined with the fact that there were two of them ... they wanted to talk him into something. Something he didn't want to do. He interrupted them.

'We were able to confirm that a week ago.'

The Countess refused to be railroaded.

'Indeed we could.'

She made this sound significant. Then she showed him a couple of pictures from a plastic folder, both of Frode Otto as a younger man. One computer-animated where he had been made to look years younger than he was today, the other a grainy black-and-white one, reproduced from a newspaper page.

'*Frederiksværk Weekly News*, popularly known as the doormat, the sports section from third of February 1993, when Frode Otto won the Sjælland Wrestling Championship eighty-four-kilo class. At that point he was a member of AK Heroes, the local wrestling club.'

The picture was in profile and not all that useful for identification purposes; the other was better, but there was always the risk that the picture of the wrong man had been put in the paper by mistake. Konrad Simonsen studied it briefly and nodded without knowing why; Arne Pedersen took over.

'Hannelore Müller, the girl he raped ...'

'... is alleged to have raped.'

'She lives in Wandsbek today; it's a Hamburg suburb.'

Konrad Simonsen got the message.

'You want me to go to Hamburg, is that it?'

Simonsen had an old friend in Germany, Bastian Jancker was his name, who had retired in 2008. Prior to that he had been the *Polizeivizepräsident*, the second-in-command of Hamburg police, and much earlier a CID detective in Flensburg, where he was born and brought up as a part of the Danish minority living in Schleswig. As a result he spoke very good Danish and had excellent connections within the German police. Konrad Simonsen gave it some thought.

'What's wrong with Interpol or an official request to Germany? Their administrative systems work very well, I'll have you know, in case you had any doubts.'

They all three knew that a short, personal trip to Hamburg would be much quicker and probably also more effective, despite the excellent, official German police systems. The Countess, who knew Simonsen better than anyone, could see that he had already made up his mind. She smiled.

'As I recall, you've already promised me that you would go. I've packed your suitcase, it's in the back of the car, Arne will organise a train ticket for you, you leave Copenhagen Central Station in two hours.'

'What amazing efficiency, my staff are truly skilled. But how about I start by calling Bastian to make sure that he's at home?'

He wanted to sound ironic, but he failed. The Countess got up.

'I did that yesterday. He'll have *Currywurst mit Pommes* ready at seven o'clock, and you're staying with him; he wouldn't hear talk of a hotel room.'

Konrad Simonsen's next remark about how he had been looking forward to a trip that same evening to the Reeperbahn also fell flat. She waved as she left, wishing him a pleasant journey and *don't forget to call, Simon*. Arne Pedersen hurried out at her heels.

Three days later Konrad Simonsen let himself in through his front door in Søllerød. It was early evening but not dark yet, the days were getting longer. The Countess welcomed him with a warm embrace. She felt guilty for not having picked him up at Copenhagen Central Station, but *Operation X* was on the television, a documentary she was obsessed with, so he had been left to take a taxi.

She didn't ask about Hamburg until Konrad Simonsen had eaten. They had spoken on the telephone while he was away, but only touched upon his work sporadically; there were other more personal considerations that took priority and the case could wait until he came back. The Countess asked darkly:

'So no luck with Hannelore?'

'Yes and no, mostly no. The poor woman's life is ruined. She's suffering from the full spectrum of PTSD: memory and concentration problems, trouble sleeping and nightmares, depression, anxiety, shame, you name it, she's just like . . . well, you know.'

He was referring to Pauline Berg, and yes, his wife *did* know. She nodded, and thought it must be almost the worst thing that could happen to you. Afterwards people you knew and perhaps counted on eventually began to distance themselves from you because the repercussions were too stressful also for them. Her husband continued speaking.

'I hate rape cases, and now I feel just like you. I would love nothing more than to put him away for what he has done – Frode Otto, I mean.'

'But we can't?'

'No, that was always unlikely. There's no chance of Hannelore Müller giving evidence in a Danish court. She didn't want to, nor would she be able to.'

Before she was shown pictures of Frode Otto, her brother, a doctor, had been called. He had shut down the interview immediately when Hannelore had a serious panic attack the moment she glanced at the first picture and couldn't breathe. Konrad Simonsen said:

'I have it on video, it's horrible to watch, but as evidence, it's useless.'

'Did she recognise him?'

'She nods fiercely on the video, but like I said, she couldn't breathe, so any defence lawyer would be able to show reasonable doubt about her reaction. Her brother called me later to confirm that she had recognised Frode Otto as her attacker, and I have his signature on a solemn document on official letterhead from Hamburg Police with stamps and italics and the whole caboodle, but it's still only hearsay, so it counts for pretty much zilch. And she can't sign it herself because she quite simply can't cope with hearing about the case. Possibly one day in the future, but it's highly unlikely. So all in all, it was relatively depressing, although it was good to see Bastian.'

The Countess spent fifteen minutes reading Konrad Simonsen's document and watching the video of the interview with Hannelore Müller. When she finished, she had made up her mind.

'I'll visit Big Bertha tomorrow if she'll agree to see me. If we're very lucky, we might get a warrant for his phone records.'

Her husband was sceptical.

'No one is ever *lucky* with Big Bertha. That's how she got the name in the first place.'

CHAPTER 27

Bertha Steenholt, commonly known as Big Bertha when she was out of earshot, was the Public Prosecutor for Copenhagen and Bornholm.

Despite her sixty-four years, she was a truly impressive sight with her grey curls and a heavy face reminiscent of a cross between Simone Signoret and Leonid Brezhnev; she exuded an air of power in an almost primal form. She lived in a sinister house on Frederiksberg with her daughter and an unknown but considerable number of cats, and rumour had it that you should never visit because you would not get out alive but would be put down and turned into cat food. Her daughter was a defence lawyer and boasted the third-best law exam result ever achieved at the University of Copenhagen, exceeded only by the legendary left-wing lawyer Carl Madsen and her own mother. When mother and daughter clashed in court, as they did from time to time, it was standing room only.

The Countess wasn't a woman who scared easily, but Big Bertha was the exception that proved the rule. Especially when the Countess didn't have her legal argument fully in place, something which the Public Prosecutor rarely failed to pick up on. But still, she had to try.

The office of the Public Prosecutor was in Jens Kofods Gade, a side street to Store Kongensgade. The Countess walked from Police Headquarters in the lovely spring weather, arrived a few minutes before the appointed time, and was shown in immediately. *She's expecting you, please go straight through.* The secretary had pointed to a closed door, the Countess preferred to knock first.

Bertha Steenholt listened without interrupting, and together they watched the video of Hannelore Müller's breakdown. When it was evident that the Countess had no further information to show her, the Public Prosecutor said:

'I hope you don't expect me to charge him. If so, you can get lost.'

'No, I want a warrant to access his phone records.'

'Get out of here, they're long gone.'

'And I want it with no restrictions.'

The Public Prosecutor mulled this over. The Countess herself was normally an expert at obtaining telephone records, but only from major providers. Frode Otto's mobile was provided by the relatively young telecommunications company NewTalkInTown, where the Countess had no contacts. She waited expectantly.

'Is this about the "nignog" case?'

The Countess nodded.

'And did he also kill that poor girl in the lake?'

'Unlikely, but he's our only lead.'

'Hmm, tell me, why did you come to me? This could easily have been dealt with elsewhere.'

Elsewhere was clearly further down the system, so why bother her? The Countess answered truthfully.

'Because I only stand a chance with that warrant if the request comes from you.'

She deliberately avoided getting tangled up in any form of flattery, Bertha Steenholt loathed that sort of thing. The Public Prosecutor nodded briefly again.

'No, it's not enough. Bring me more, then I'll try.'

It was disappointing, but the Countess accepted it. She made no attempt to persuade the woman to change her mind, knowing it would have been futile. She got up, thanked her for her time and left the office.

CHAPTER 28

The Countess and Konrad Simonsen couldn't remember when they were last in uniform at the same time, if indeed it had ever happened, and they watched each other, smiling, unable to shake off a carnival feeling at being in matching outfits. But it didn't matter because Victoria Blixen-Agerskjold was clearly delighted when she saw the two officers, which was the whole point.

The old woman was sitting in an armchair by the window with a knitted blanket covering her legs; the others were seated around her. In addition to the two officers, Adam and Lenette Blixen-Agerskjold were there. It was a tight squeeze, and the mood was somewhat awkward as Victoria Blixen-Agerskjold was able to sustain a normal conversation only for short segments of time. Occasionally she would appear to doze off for a minute or two, and when she woke up, it was as if she experienced the situation from the beginning. Then she would cheer up again. Besides, she was alternating between Danish and French, sometimes halfway through a sentence, which meant that Konrad Simonsen and Lenette Blixen-Agerskjold understood only half of what was going on. Simonsen thought it probably didn't matter. Yet he was determined to stay there for as long as the old lady was enjoying herself, which was to the Countess's credit. As she had read aloud to him, in Danish, selected extracts from *Femmes en guerre*, he had developed a considerable amount of respect, bordering on awe, for the old lady.

Victoria Blixen-Agerskjold scolded the Countess:

'Your French is bad, your accent gives you away. You must be careful. We won't protect you.'

The warning was underlined by a crooked finger pointing at the ceiling. The Countess promised to be careful.

'*Mieux vaut perdre une bête plutôt que de voir tout le troupeau dévoré.*'

The Countess looked quizzically at the Chamberlain, there were limits to her French. He translated.

'Better to lose one animal than see the whole herd eaten.'

She had a point; the Countess smiled obligingly and was sharply admonished by the old lady. This was no laughing matter, this was serious. It was the little details that gave you away.

'That's how Juliet was caught, and Josephine and . . . Now what was her name, the one with the freckles? You remember, Hans-Henrik? The one they caught at Saint-Augustin, where I managed to get away?'

'I'm Adam, Grannie. Hans-Henrik is dead, don't you remember? I thought that girl was called Émilie?'

He could have saved himself the trouble, his grandmother was dozing off again. Lenette Blixen-Agerskjold looked sideways at her husband, warning him that they couldn't very well take up much more of the two officers' time. He nodded and got up. As did his wife and Simonsen. The Countess remain sitting. She caught the Chamberlain's eye and asked: 'Saint-Augustin?'

'Do you have time for this?'

The Countess nodded firmly, Konrad Simonsen sat down again, the other two followed suit. Adam Blixen-Agerskjold told them the story.

It was in Paris in May 1943. Victoria and Émilie were wanted by the Germans, and had been betrayed. Suddenly Saint-Augustin, the Metro station where they had just got off, was teeming with Gestapo officers. The women split up and Victoria headed towards the Boulevard Haussmann exit. On her way up the steps, she had grabbed her pistol, wrapped her scarf around it to conceal it and tied the ends around her neck as if her right arm were injured and had to be supported in a sling.

The exit at street level was guarded by two German soldiers armed with pistols. They made sure that no one came up or went down. Below her, on the platform, the Gestapo was systematically checking everyone, which at some point would include her, which would mean the end. The Germans keeping guard at street level were from the regular occupying forces, young people like her, sons of peasants from Saxony-Anhalt and Thuringia, now stationed in the French capital. She started chatting to them in her respectable German, asked where they were from, learned about their families, had charmed them, taken her time, laughed with them. Then she had clumsily fished out her lipstick and a compact mirror from her handbag. One German soldier had gallantly offered to hold the mirror, while she touched up her lips, bright red, as was the fashion at the time. She adjusted the mirror, once, several times, laughing until they found the right angle. Meanwhile, the other soldier held her handbag. Then she shot both of them, picked up her bag and left. Adam Blixen-Agerskjold added:

'She once told me how one second she was looking at her own reflection in the mirror, and the next she was staring right at the face of a young man who had been shot through the eye. She was twenty years old at the time.'

The Countess asked quietly:

'I bought a copy of *Femmes en guerre* from an antiquarian bookseller. Do you think she might sign it? Is she able to?'

The Chamberlain never had time to reply because suddenly the old lady burst out:

'That estate bailiff claimed he had been in Norway, but they don't have the Euro in Norway, he was lying ... he was! I want you to know that, Detective Superintendent, he killed the nignog, the bastard.'

The words were spoken clearly, though the old woman's eyes were closed. But when Konrad Simonsen asked about her allegation, she didn't reply. Instead she snarled irritably:

'*Il a tué le nignog, le salaud!*'

Konrad Simonsen looked at Adam Blixen-Agerskjold, who shrugged this off, it meant nothing to him. But it clearly did to his wife.

'Bloody hell, Victoria is right, he *is* lying.'

Everyone's jaw dropped, the Chamberlain's because he hadn't heard his wife swear for years.

They borrowed the care home manager's office where they had to wait for Lenette Blixen-Agerskjold, who went looking for something. When she finally returned, she held a box in her hand. It was transparent and rectangular, about a finger-width tall and about as long as a hand. It contained five miniature bottles of perfume, each shaped as one of Salvador Dalí's surreal figures. She apologised to them.

'I'm sorry to keep you waiting. It's Mrs Jørgensen, she loves those little bottles, and steals them from Victoria whenever she gets a chance. Normally she doesn't mind giving them back, but her daughter was visiting, and . . . Well, it took a little longer. Now, listen.'

She told them that the estate had employed a kitchen assistant a couple of years ago. Frode Otto had flirted with her regularly, but she showed little interest in him. After a holiday, a ten-day hiking trip to Guldbrandsdalen in Norway, he claimed to have bought the perfumes for her as a gift. However, she didn't like them, or she didn't like him, so she passed on the present to Victoria Blixen-Agerskjold, who at that point was still living at the manor. Lenette Blixen-Agerskjold said:

'Now there could be many explanations for it, but I remember Frode talking about his holiday in detail when he came back, and I was surprised because normally he never does.'

The expression on her husband's face confirmed this. His bombastic declaration to Konrad Simonsen in Hanehoved Forest about getting Frode Otto the best defence lawyer money could buy would appear to have been forgotten.

The Countess picked up the box with the perfume bottles. It was unopened, still with the original plastic wrapping on. It would appear to be the beautifully coloured bottles, rather than the contents, which attracted Mrs Jørgensen. The price sticker stating €25 was intact. It had been stuck on top of another label. She carefully eased off the price tag with a fingernail, and a logo appeared. *Tallink Silja Line*, it said.

'When was he away?'

Lenette Blixen-Agerskjold replied without hesitation.

'Two thousand and seven, the last two weeks of June.'

The Countess punched the air.

'Yes!'

CHAPTER 29

Henrik Krag had mixed feelings as he turned his motorbike into the car park in front of Jægersborg Library in Gentofte. Benedikte Lerche-Larsen had ordered him to meet her there that Friday, 24 April, the date stipulated by the anonymous letter writer. He parked near the library, a long two-storey brick building whose many windows bore witness to a time when energy prices were much lower than they were today. He removed his crash helmet and scratched his scalp vigorously, before he unzipped his biker jacket halfway to cool down. He was sweating.

Benedikte Lerche-Larsen was already there when he stepped through the automatic sliding doors to the library. She was reading a poster on a noticeboard to the right of the entrance, but turned her head when she heard the doors open. She was wearing a honey-coloured trench coat, tight jeans and boots.

'Did you come here on your bike?'

He nodded. She glanced quickly at her watch.

'Show it to me.'

They left together, and she studied it for some time.

'It's a Harley-Davidson?'

The question was superfluous as the brand name was clearly stated on the tank.

'A Sportster Forty-eight, twelve hundred cc.'

'It's nice.'

He thanked her and felt foolish.

Benedikte Lerche-Larsen walked up to the counter with Henrik Krag in tow. A librarian in his thirties was reading a magazine. He glanced up vacantly, then handed her a key, which he had already placed in front of him on his desk. She led them through the library, then down a short flight of stairs and unlocked a door at the foot of them.

The room they entered was almost empty. In the middle stood a table with a computer connected to a machine Henrik Krag didn't recognise. In front of the keyboard were three small cardboard boxes stacked on top of each other, as if whoever had put them there had wanted to make sure they would not be overlooked. Two rickety chairs with peeling, laminated teak backs had been pushed under the table.

Henrik Krag watched Benedikte Lerche-Larsen as she took out her MacBook from her bag, turned it on and clicked on a couple of programs he had never seen before connecting her mobile to the laptop. When she was done, she checked the clock on her mobile.

'We have twenty minutes. If he calls us on time, that is. Did you bring your mobile like I told you to?'

He had. She pointed to the door at the back of the room.

'Go outside and call me, so I can test this.'

'Test what? Please tell me what's going on first? What's that?'

He pointed to the machine to the right on the table.

'And why are we here, and not at my place . . . Or yours?'

'We're here because Ishøj isn't really my kind of place, and that contraption over there is a machine used for viewing microfiche, old-fashioned rolls of film of, say, newspapers. I've requested back issues of *Jyllands-Posten* and *Dagbladet* from January and February 1955, and you're welcome to read them when we're done.'

'You know I can't read, there's no need to mock me. Is this so we can use the room?'

She nodded, and tossed her head imperiously at the door. He stayed put.

'What are we testing?'

'OK, my mistake. I forgot, of course, that you haven't worked it out.' She exhaled through her nose and reviewed her set-up. 'I've connected my mobile so that you and I can both hear and speak at the same time, while everything will be recorded. And that can only be done using a computer. I want to test it, and the reason I want you to go outside is that otherwise everything in here starts to howl, due to a phenomenon called positive feedback.'

The door led to another basement passage. He half closed it, and rang her. When she picked up, he reeled off the months of the year, he couldn't think of anything else to say. She interrupted him before he got to July. When he came back, she was busy replacing the SIM card on her mobile.

'Stop taking the piss out of me the whole time.'

At first she made no reply to this and he thought she hadn't heard him. Then she mimicked him cruelly:

'"Stop taking the piss out of me." Ah, poor you! Then get your shit together and wise up!'

'And I want to be there when you meet Frode Otto. Otherwise you can sort all this crap out yourself.'

He had blurted it without thinking, as if the words were coming from someone else. She looked up at him with renewed interest then smiled widely, from earring to earring. She placed one hand on his forearm.

'Well, then, you'd better join me. Now sit down, Henrik.'

He sat, strangely happy to hear her say his name. She went on:

'You can be really sweet sometimes.'

Their shared laughter was interrupted by Benedikte Lerche-Larsen's hoarse voice, sexy and ill-suited to the occasion, saying: *ding dong, ding dong*, the ringtone she had recorded on her mobile.

She spoke her name and they heard keystrokes before a synthetic female voice could be heard coming from the computer's speakers:

'*State your name again, your first name and your surname.*'

She obeyed and again she heard keystrokes, then the voice came back:

'*Why is there an echo?*'

'There are two of us on speakerphone.'

The keystrokes were hit faster, and the volume of the voice was turned up:

'*Just you! Will call again in two minutes. Just you!*'

The call was ended.

She swore, then pulled the cable from her mobile. Henrik Krag said optimistically:

'Doesn't matter, you can always tell me what happened afterwards.'

'I can still record it, that's not the problem. But now he knows you're here and he's bound to ask me about you. However, that can't be helped.'

Henrik Krag couldn't really see that much harm had been done; he mumbled something about the two of them already being in it up to their necks. She didn't answer him, but moved to the far end of the room where he couldn't hear anything. Shortly afterwards, she began talking. He studied her in detail after which he concluded realistically that a guy like him would never get a girl like her. Strangely this conclusion didn't hurt; on the contrary, it only spurred him on.

When she returned, she was pale and didn't say anything. She reconnected her mobile with a cable, activated a program on the computer, after which sound poured out of the speakers:

'*Are you alone now?*'

'Yes.'

'*Where are you?*'

'Jægersborg Library, a basement room I've borrowed.'

'*State the name, address and age of the person who was listening in before.*'

'Henrik Krag, twenty-four years, I don't have the address.'

'*That was lie number one, there won't be a second one unless you want the police waiting for you when you get home.*'

'Number four three one, Ishøj Fælledvej.'

'*Is he the man you killed the Nigerian girl with?*'

'Yes.'

'*Your email address.*'

'lerchelarsen@gmail.com, lerchelarsen no hyphen.'

'*You will donate a hundred thousand kroner to the CNN Freedom Project. For your information, the project works to fight sexual slavery. You will make the payment on Tuesday, I will email you the details.*'

'We don't have a hundred thousand kroner.'

'*Watch it!*'

'Give us until Friday. We need more time.'

'*Friday is fine. Secondly, you will each be given two tasks, which you must – repeat must – execute. They are your just punishment.*'

'What tasks?'

'*You will be told later.*'

'Why do we have to do them?'

'*Because you deserve it.*'

With every sentence they heard keystrokes, and when the voice said *watch it*, the sound was turned up so much that the words distorted and became hard to make out. Benedikte Lerche-Larsen had sat down on a chair, apparently drained of energy, but after the second playing she got up and started pacing round in aimless circles. *Just punishment* ... she shook her head impotently, vigorously, so her red hair billowed around her, another three paces, then again: *Your just punishment*.

She stopped by the wall. It was ages since it had last been painted, the paint was peeling, exposing the plaster in several places. She picked out such a spot and kicked the tip of her boot into it to worsen the damage, while she kept repeating the words.

'*Your just punishment* – that psycho can force us to do anything now, and there's fuck all we can do about it.'

'Perhaps it won't be that bad, we'll just have to wait and see how she's going to punish us.'

'It's not a woman. Don't you get it, it was a man? It was a synthetic voice.'

'Yes, of course I do, but it was just because it was Ida, and then ... then ... It doesn't matter.'

She looked at him, baffled.

'No, go on, tell me. Who is Ida?'

'There's Ida and Carsten and Per. There is also Mette, but she was too expensive ... way too expensive for my school. And then there's Emily and Mary in English.'

The silence that ensued oppressed him, and it was almost a relief when she asked:

'Tell me, have you had a stroke or something?'

He explained that the special educational needs co-ordinator at his school had lent him a laptop and what was known as a scanner pen, which he used to trace over a text, whereupon a computerised voice would read the text aloud to him. The different voices had names, and Ida was one of them.

'She was my favourite. And she was the one we used the most.'

Benedikte nodded without commenting and pointed to the back door.

'Please would you get us a couple of beers from the shop across the road? Do you have any money?'

He did, he left and she started packing up.

They sat outside on the steps to the basement. Henrik Krag opened their beers, and Benedikte Lerche-Larsen lit a cigarette.

'I didn't think you smoked.'

'Once in a blue moon.'

She looked at the cigarette, took another drag then flicked it away.

'I don't like the sound of those tasks he was threatening us with.'

She took a deep swig of her beer, and he did the same.

'If it's too bad, we can always turn ourselves in. Perhaps the judge will realise it was an accident. Sometimes they can be really nice, you know.'

She turned her head and her green eyes flashed.

'I know that you would fit in just fine with the other inmates. For you it would be one long, free holiday. But I'm not wasting five precious years of my life with a bunch of losers who can't tell the difference between a bin bag and Louis Vuitton, or lowlife ghetto types whose vocabulary only exceeds a hundred if you count *fuck* fifteen times. Forget it.'

They sat for a while without speaking, then she said:

'We have to find out who it is. We must.'

'But how will you . . . will we do that? And what about the money, can you get it?'

'I can get half. What are you going to do?'

'I don't have fifty thousand.'

'Oh, yes, you do.'

She told him the obvious answer, the thought he hadn't dared form for himself. He drained his beer, almost in a trance, and another long silence ensued. Then she reached out a hand, pinched his chin gently and turned his head.

It was hard to tell whether it was the damp weather or if he had tears in his eyes.

'Are you crying about your motorbike?'

He shrugged. There was no other way out, and he knew it. She patted his knee and said pensively:

'I understand that this is bad for you, but you really should have thought about that before you dropped that nignog on the floor like a sack of potatoes.'

CHAPTER 30

Tallink Silja Line sails between Stockholm and Helsinki. The ferry departs from Sweden in the early evening and docks in Finland the following morning, when it is cleaned, ready to depart the same night in the reverse direction. Two ferries serviced the route.

23 June 2007 was a Saturday, and the weather in Stockholm was pleasant, warm and calm when early that afternoon a group of young people gathered in Ringen, a circular area between the ground and first floors of Stockholm Central Station. They knew one another from the internet site www.vimusiker.se.

Randi Hansson was nineteen years old and came from Jämtland in central Sweden. Early that morning she had driven to the capital in high spirits, excited because she rarely went out. The young-sters didn't know one another well, but the mood was high and the beer flowed freely. When they embarked on the ferry, Randi Hansson was already drunk, a state which gradually worsened as the evening progressed, and which culminated in her throwing up in the lavatory strategically placed right outside the onboard club. A female security guard strongly recommended that she went to bed, a piece of advice she followed as she staggered away.

The rape was brutal and sadistic. It took place in her cabin and lasted several hours. Two ribs and four fingers were broken, chunks of her hair torn out, and the remote control from the cabin's television had been inserted into her anus as a final humiliating gesture by her attacker.

Both the Finnish and the Swedish police gave the assault high priority, partly because the attack was unusually brutal, and partly because something similar had happened before. About three years earlier, a seventeen-year-old Finnish girl had been raped on the same ferry under similar circumstances, a crime that had yet to be solved. But the odds of solving the rape of Randi Hansson were small: almost seven hundred people had been on the ferry during the crossing, but most of them were unregistered as no passport checks were required. Furthermore Randi Hansson had been blinded, as once he had gagged her, her attacker had sprinkled pepper in her eyes; six months later the investigation petered out and was shelved.

Swedish and Finnish media covered the attack extensively, but the Countess knew of it purely by chance: in the autumn of 2007 she was contacted by a Swedish colleague and friend, who asked to borrow her summerhouse for a couple of weeks to get away from it all. Her friend had been granted two months' much-needed leave. The Countess's summerhouse was near Blokhus on the North Sea coastline, and en route from Stockholm to Nordjylland, the friend stayed with her in Søllerød where she told her about Randi Hansson's terrible fate on the Tallink Silja Line ferry. The Countess had never been able to forget it.

As soon as the Countess arrived for work the morning after visiting Victoria Blixen-Agerskjold, she contacted her friend and explained the situation. Then she sent her Frode Otto's fingerprints, waited thirty tense minutes and bounced a couple of centimetres in her chair when the call from Sweden came in. It was a match. She was elated. Not because the match unequivocally linked the estate bailiff to the sexual assault on the ferry, because it didn't, but because she now had the additional information on him needed for the Public Prosecutor to grant a warrant to access the man's telephone records. She hoped. She took great care with her report and sent it to Big Bertha personally. Five minutes later she received a short, *OK, I'll try* by way of reply. Her mood was therefore superlative when she discussed the case with Arne Pedersen later that afternoon.

'I'm one hundred per cent sure that Frode Otto can't stand up to scrutiny. Something or other will crawl out of the woodwork, just you wait and see.'

Arne Pedersen agreed, but only partly. He said tentatively: 'Maybe he did kill the African girl, but I don't think he dumped her in the lake. Or rather, helped dump her in the lake, because that would have taken more than one person. He would have had many better options for disposing of the body, the most simple of which would be to bury her deep in Hanehoved Forest.'

'Or cut her up into little pieces and feed her to the pigs. It's incredibly effective, they'll eat everything.'

This from Malte Borup; he was sitting with his back to them struggling with a printer problem on Arne Pedersen's computer. The Countess said dryly:

'You watch too many movies and you'd make a hopeless killer, Malte. Stick to computing. Besides, they don't keep pigs on the estate.'

The intern changed the subject:

'I hate printers. Why can't you write it out by hand, Arne?'

Arne Pedersen ignored him and spent the next two minutes convincing the Countess that the people who had concealed the African girl in the lake had done so because they didn't have a spade – an argument which the Countess had long since accepted, so she patiently allowed herself to be convinced a second time. Arne Pedersen rounded off:

'Has Simon decided when we'll be interviewing Frode Otto?'

'Yes, Monday afternoon.'

'Has he made up his mind who will do it?'

'Yes, you and Simon himself.'

'And who will be watching him tomorrow? Klavs volunteered, didn't he?'

The Countess couldn't remember; he would have to ask Konrad Simonsen. However, there was no need: Malte Borup's fingers flew across the keyboard.

'He did, I believe. He has booked a civilian car for the weekend.'

The two older officers exchanged looks. The information society was terrifying; the student intern regularly breached pretty much every single security precaution the Department used to protect its databases.

CHAPTER 31

Melby Common is an abandoned army exercise area over-looking the waters of the Kattegat between Asserbo and Hundested, a conservation area and part of the Kongernes Nordsjælland National Park.

A young woman died there on 10 July 2008. Her name was Juli Denissen and she was a twenty-four-year-old technical college student from Frederiksværk. Her death was caused by a massive haemorrhage to her brain membrane and so it was a natural, albeit rare, occurrence. It had happened during tragic circumstances as the woman wasn't found until the sobbing of her three-year-old daughter alerted a forester in a plantation further inside the national park. Shortly after the woman's death, her family and friends had developed a conspiracy theory that her death was the result of criminal activity. They had formed a pressure group that tried to convince the police of their outrageous theories, but the only person the group had managed to persuade before it was dissolved was Pauline Berg. The death of Juli Denissen had become an obsession with her, one that should probably be viewed in the light of her own mental-health issues. There was also the fact that the woman had been an important police witness when Pauline Berg was kidnapped. Amongst her colleagues the death, which didn't merit a criminal investigation, was known as the 'Juli-non-case', usually said with a knowing grin or a roll of the eyes.

On Saturday, 2 May, a sunny but cool morning, Pauline Berg and Klavs Arnold were waiting in the car park adjacent to Melby Common. They were alone, with no other cars or people in sight. Pauline Berg had a ten o'clock appointment with the forester who had found the woman and the child, but it was becoming increasingly clear that the man wasn't going to show. Klavs Arnold took the situation in his stride. Firstly, because he found it difficult to see why she would even bother with the forester. Secondly, because he hadn't come along for investigative reasons as, despite the forester, there was nothing to investigate. The day before he had borrowed a Skoda Octavia from Police Headquarters, and this morning at eight o'clock, bright-eyed and bushy-tailed, and bringing along a bag of fresh bread rolls, he had picked up Pauline Berg from her home in Rødovre.

She frowned out at the landscape and asked in a surly voice: 'Why are you even here?'

'Because it's my turn. For one thing.'

He explained this to her, although she would appear to have understood him immediately. From time to time she became a burden, whom everyone in the department avoided if possible. However, a tacit agreement had been reached among her closest colleagues that they would take turns to look after her, outside work. And today it was his turn.

She didn't say anything, simply processed the information and abandoned the subject.

'Let's take a look at the place where she was killed.'

She pointed to a path winding its way through the dunes. They walked, she in front to show the way, she claimed, a superfluous action as there was only one path. When they had walked for some time, she asked without turning around:

'What was the other reason? You said, for one thing, so there has to be more.'

Klavs Arnold looked about calmly and saw heather, lyme grass and wild roses. Then he said slowly: 'Because I once knew someone like you, but that's private.'

She started to cry. Noiselessly, the tears trickled from her eyes as she looked at him. She was like that, hot and cold from one second to the next, and often without any sensible rationale for her actions, which just happened.

He embraced her, stood for a while pressing her head into his shoulder while he carefully stroked it. Then he turned her gently and led her onwards down the path with his arm around her waist. After a while, she said quietly:

'I thought it was because you liked me.'

He didn't reply, not even when she sniffled: 'I really did.'

They sat down on a dune sheltered by a slightly bigger one behind, and she stopped crying. The sun warmed them, and they both enjoyed it. He told her softly that he had had a friend once, a really good friend, someone who was always there when you needed them, someone who would always be there for you your whole life. She nodded. She had never had someone like that, sadly. She had thought that she had, but after she became . . . ill, it turned out that she didn't.

'Did you let him down?' she asked.

'Yes, I did. So did the whole country, including me.'

She took his hand, held it, almost squeezing it in her lap. Then she pointed to the hollow between the dunes down below in front of them.

'She died down there.'

He squeezed her hand by way of reply, which could mean anything. He didn't know what to say.

'I've been here sixteen times already, this is my seventeenth visit. One visit was with Simon, by the way. I often dream about Juli. It's as if she won't let me go, and no matter what everyone else says, I'm convinced that she was killed.'

'Yes, I know, we all do. And you also know that we laugh at you behind your back, and that everyone but you is convinced she died of natural causes, including crime technicians and pathologists.'

'Perhaps she's my friend and I am hers.'

He dismissed this.

'No, Pauline, you can't be friends with the dead.'

At her request they undertook an experiment. She walked to a clearing in the forest, which was about five hundred metres inland, exactly how far was difficult for him to estimate by looking. Once she reached the clearing, she held up her hands as a sign, whereupon he sat down in the hollow where Juli Denissen had died, and screamed at the top of his lungs. He got up, received another sign and repeated the process. They tried four times, before she was satisfied. When she came back, she was shaking her head: yes, she had been able to hear something, but it had been very faint.

'I've also tried tying my Dictaphone to a branch and doing the screaming myself, but when I played back the recording, I couldn't hear anything at all.'

'Which means what?'

'That the forester is lying when he says he was working *in* the forest when he suddenly heard a baby crying, and that was how he discovered her – or them, if you like. A kid can't possibly scream that loud, I just don't believe it.'

Klavs Arnold estimated the distance, now vaguely intrigued. He said reluctantly:

'A *child* crying, not a baby, a three-year-old child isn't a baby. I don't know ... evolution has ensured that children hit certain sensitive frequencies, something you'll discover when you have children of your own, but ... sound is complicated, determined by many factors. Do you know how far it is?'

'About six hundred metres, according to Google Earth.'

He evaluated the distance again, critically. Then he shook his head.

'No, it's too far, you're probably right, but it still doesn't make any sense. Why don't we call it a day now, Pauline? Let's go back to my place and have some lunch, then you can help me watch Frode Otto later. That makes more sense. What do you say? Are you free?'

She agreed, somewhat taken aback. It was rare for anyone to talk to her like that these days.

CHAPTER 32

The surveillance of Frode Otto was a total disaster.

Klavs Arnold and Pauline Berg had already learned from Adam Blixen-Agerskjold that when he set off on his Saturday trip every two months, the estate bailiff tended to leave between five and six in the afternoon, and they were in place in plenty of time. At four-thirty they were parked on a side road to the main entrance to Kolleløse Manor, well hidden behind a closed down petrol station. From here, they saw the estate bailiff's car, an easily recognisable green Golf, drive past around six o'clock. Klavs Arnold settled a hundred metres behind him and had remarked to Pauline Berg that Frode Otto was probably going to Copenhagen, when the car turned left and headed east around Hanehoved Forest. They passed the missing milestone and everything was going according to plan when their engine cut out. They rolled along in neutral for a little while before coming to a halt.

'What just happened?'

Pauline Berg asked:

'Did you put petrol in it?'

Of course he had, he wasn't a total amateur. He got out and opened the bonnet, and eventually identified the problem: the cam belt had snapped. He called Falck for breakdown assistance, and muttered grim curses at the waiting time: *within two hours, was that really the best they could do?* Then he called Konrad Simonsen and explained the situation. His boss took the news well, not that he had much choice, and asked Klavs to give his best to Pauline, which he did.

They sat in the car for a while chatting, before Pauline Berg pointed in the direction of the lake.

'How long does it take to walk the lake where she was found?'

Her voice was shaking, and he immediately guessed why.

'About three-quarters of an hour, do you want to give it a go? We can always turn back, if you get scared.'

'Do we have enough time before it gets dark?'

'Absolutely, we have ages.'

'There must be daylight all the time, or I'm not doing it.'

'All right, let's just walk down to the hunting lodge and back again, then you can be sure it will be light all the time. I'll keep an eye on you, and it'll give you a chance to see the lodge you've spent so much time researching.'

She hesitated. Absurd scenarios sprouted in her mind. What if Klavs Arnold abandoned her in the forest? Or if they were attacked inside it? She decided to stay put, but by then he had already got out of the car.

The track down alongside the forest was good for her; it was a forest, and at the same time, it wasn't. She could feel fear, but also that she could control it. They walked close together, that helped too, but when the road continued inside the forest itself, she stopped. It was enough for now, and yet it wasn't. Possibly because he wasn't pressuring her; she tried a few more steps, stopped again, proud of herself, walked a short stretch, and then a long one. They soon reached the clearing containing the hunting lodge. She was sweating, her heart was pounding like crazy, but she had done it, and the open area – roughly the size of a football pitch – gradually calmed her down.

She walked up to and around the lodge.

'It was built, or rather assembled, in December 2007. That's at least one month before the earliest date the African woman can have been dumped in the lake, so it was here when she was killed. But the technicians found no trace of her, not one.'

Klavs Arnold nodded, though he was already familiar with the information. Pauline Berg looked through a window while he squatted down on his haunches and examined one of the six staddle stones that supported the lodge. She said:

'Frode Otto put them in place; he was sent a template from the construction company of all the things that must be done before they dispatched the lorry. It's standard.'

'How much was the shack by the way?'

'Only twenty thousand kroner, he got it cheap, well below half-price, because the company had used it for a couple of years for display purposes. Otherwise it would have broken the two thousand and seven budget. Frode Otto has free rein when it comes to those activities he's in charge of, but Adam Blixen-Agerskjold prefers each annual set of accounts to show a profit, even though the lodge is regarded as capital expenditure, which should be written off over time.' She glanced anxiously up at the sky and said: 'Shouldn't we be getting back to the car?'

'Yes, we should. But first tell me how the lodge was put together, if you know.'

She did, and the story was quickly told. The parts which made it up arrived on a truck along with three men, who assembled them as each section was hoisted off the back of the truck by its crane. The job could be done in a day. He confirmed this as if he wasn't the one who had originally asked, but she the one who wanted to hear if she had understood the process correctly. Then he pointed to the clearing in front of them.

'And it was put up towards the end of 2007 – do you remember the exact date?'

She couldn't, but it was between Christmas and the New Year.

'Yes, that's also what I recall from your report. But that can't be right. Come over here, let me show you something.'

He took a few steps into the area. It was overgrown with grass and weeds, clearly kept down from time to time with a scythe or something similar. Klavs Arnold squatted down on his haunches again. Pauline Berg said in an anxious, pleading voice:

'Please tell me what's going on. I can feel I'm getting scared. Don't act weird, because ... please don't.'

He got up and put his arm around her, although she tried to get away from him.

'There, there, I'm not being weird. It's the tyre tracks, Pauline, you can see them yourself in the grass. See how the truck drove right up to the pine tree over there and then reversed up to where the lodge is now. Twin wheels, it's clear.'

She looked and could see that he was right. It calmed her down, she didn't know why, but it did.

'Come on, let's walk back to the car.'

It wasn't until they had left the forest and turned onto the track alongside it, that he explained.

'In December 2007, between Christmas and the New Year, it was hard frost, down to minus twelve. Overall the month had been grey and rainy, but on Boxing Day the weather changed, and it froze until the thirtieth, don't you remember?'

'Not really, and why does that matter?'

'Those tyre tracks were left in soft soil, there can be no doubt about it. Spring or autumn, would be my guess, but definitely not while the ground was frozen solid, it's quite simply impossible. The tracks were between five and ten centimetres deep, and the lodge wouldn't have been that heavy. In terms of loading the truck that would have been regarded as a light load. So the ground must have been soft.'

He let her draw her own conclusion. It didn't take her long.

'So the lodge was constructed at another time, is that what you're saying?'

'Yes, I bet you it was.'

She laughed, naturally, for the first time in years, it felt like. Then she nudged him with her hip.

'Wow, we make an awesome team.'

CHAPTER 33

Early in the evening of Saturday, 2 May, Benedikte Lerche-Larsen and Henrik Krag were sitting in a basement in a house on Parkovsvej in Charlottenlund, one of Copenhagen's most desirable northern suburbs. The room they were in was about twenty square metres and dominated by a bed, which took up roughly half the floor space. Apart from the bed, there was little else in the room except for a wardrobe and a bureau with a small television on top. The room had two doors, one leading to the hallway, the other to a cramped lavatory and bathroom. They were sitting at opposite ends of the bed. Henrik Krag pointed to the bathroom door, and asked a little nervously:

'Who is he?'

When he had arrived a little earlier, Benedikte Lerche-Larsen had been sitting with a man he didn't know. The man was in his forties, of small build, with drooping eyelids and an inscrutable expression in his eyes. He wore a suit and black, highly polished shoes, and he didn't return the greeting when Henrik Krag, rather tentatively, had said hello. Instead he got up and went into the bathroom, leaving the door slightly ajar. Benedikte Lerche-Larsen replied dismissively:

'Someone you want to forget about.'

'Is he foreign?'

'Polish, I think, stop asking questions.'

'All right, if you say so. What about the girl, where's she?'

'No idea. My mother has taken care of it, so I guess she has the night off. Why, does it matter? By the way, do you know if this is one of those places where Jan installed a camera?'

She spoke in a low voice, almost a whisper; there was no need to involve the Pole in the bathroom in that discussion. That is if he even spoke enough Danish to understand what she was talking about. Henrik Krag shook his head, not so far as he could recall. He had another look around. There wasn't much to see. No, he was sure there wasn't a camera.

'So we're not being recorded?'

'Jan would use clocks or teddy bears, those American nanny cams you can buy online, and there are no clocks or teddy bears here, so we aren't being filmed.'

The answer seemed to satisfy her, because she asked:

'Do you miss your motorbike?'

He gave a light shrug, reluctant to show her how upset he was at having had to part with it to raise his share of the money. It was the same when last week they had paid the hundred thousand kroner to the CNN Freedom Project at Købmagergade Post Office, as their anonymous blackmailer had demanded. She had needled him about his motorbike then. He asked:

'Has he sent you your first task?'

She forgot all about the motorbike and concentrated on herself. Her face was almost ugly when she sneered:

'We have to find out who that evil bastard is.'

She looked like she had sucked a lemon.

'So what do you have to do? You promised to call me when you got your email.'

'I have to volunteer for a fortnight at some soup kitchen for losers in Stengade on Nørrebro. Volunteer! There's no volunteering about it.'

'That doesn't sound too bad.'

Her eyes flashed and he apologised without meaning to, her reaction was so strong. He thought that their anonymous tormentor must know her well, since he had sentenced her to this particular punishment. He changed the subject.

'What's the plan once he gets here?'

'The plan is that you do as you're told, and don't ask stupid questions.'

He heaved a sigh. He knew what such plans involved, but he was the one who had insisted on being here, so he could hardly complain.

They were alerted when Frode Otto's green Golf parked in front of the basement window and blocked out most of the already sparse light. A car door slammed and two legs walked past. Henrik Krag took out a knuckle-duster and slipped it on his right hand, but had to remove it again when Benedikte Lerche-Larsen hissed at him and made it clear that it was *overkill*.

Soon afterwards, the estate bailiff marched into the room without knocking, as if he owned the place. When he saw the couple on the bed, he froze, then checked out Benedikte Lerche-Larsen for a few seconds, before addressing Henrik Krag.

'OK, she's a fine catch, but I want her for free as well. I don't care if she normally costs extra, and I don't want any hassle if there's a bit of wear and tear afterwards. So get lost. But tell your boss, I'm still waiting for his reply, and my patience is running out.'

He made a bee-line for Benedikte Lerche-Larsen and grabbed her by the arm.

'Right, doll face, I've been looking forward to this.'

Henrik Krag leaped to his feet and punched the man in the shoulder as hard as he could.

'Get your filthy hands off her, she's not a tart.'

At first Frode Otto looked stunned, as if his brain couldn't quite take in what was going on; he didn't react to the pain from the blow. Then he lunged with surprising speed at Henrik Krag and floored him without much effort, landing on top of the younger man. Henrik Krag felt his elbow being twisted to breaking point in an arm lock, but he could do nothing except hammer a few clumsy and ineffective blows at his opponent's chest. He screamed, which initially seemed pointless, but then he felt Frode Otto slacken his grip on him and go limp. He leaned back his head. The Pole in the suit was standing silently over him, pointing a pistol with a silencer at Frode Otto's forehead, smiling faintly. Upstairs, on the ground floor of the house, two voices began a loud row over who had burned the gravy.

Henrik Krag got up and massaged his sore elbow, while the Pole took out a couple of strong, black cable ties from his inside pocket with his free hand. He gave them to Henrik Krag, never once taking his eyes off the man on the floor. Frode Otto scowled up at the barrel of the silencer, but he didn't move. Benedikte Lerche-Larsen commanded calmly:

'Put them around his wrists and tighten them, so that his hands are fixed. Tie them in front, and don't get between him and the pistol. Afterwards find his jacket, it's probably in the hallway, where you'll also find his car keys. Bring his jacket in here, then go outside and start the car.'

Henrik Krag obeyed orders and enjoyed tightening the cable ties until Frode Otto winced.

CHAPTER 34

'Where are we going?'

Henrik Krag had just turned off the Hillerød motorway at the Farum exit and was now continuing left down Slangerupvejen. Benedikte Lerche-Larsen, sitting next to him on the passenger seat, didn't reply, and he didn't ask again. He studied the landscape to get his bearings, without it making much difference. They had to be somewhere in Nordsjælland, that was pretty much all he could work out.

When they approached Frederikssund, Benedikte Lerche-Larsen's instructions became more frequent. *Right here, next left.* They reached a cluster of buildings he thought must be a hospital. He didn't have time to read the signs, but noticed the Red Cross logo in front of the letters. She told him to drive all the way around the building and down a relatively narrow lane between two houses. He did as he was told, and pulled up in front of an entrance. She pointed to the end of one of the houses. Frode Otto started protesting, straining as hard as he could against his plastic ties with no other effect than inflicting some nasty-looking stripes on his wrists. Henrik Krag and the Pole had to drag him out of the car. A difficult job as the man was kicking and squirming despite the pistol being pointed at him. He screamed at the top of his lungs when they pushed him through the open door of the building. The Pole hit him hard in one kidney, and that made him calm down a bit. Henrik Krag asked Benedikte:

'What did the sign say?'

'Crematorium. And he can scream all he likes. There's no one here at weekends.'

The room they had entered was light and inviting, furnished with a couple of chairs along one wall. Another was decorated with a black crucifix, neither too big nor too small. A conveyor belt with metal rollers led from the door diagonally across the room up to a hatch to the oven. Next to this a row of buttons was mounted below some dials. There was a beige curtain which could be closed, but wasn't. On the conveyor belt, as close to the hatch as possible, was a good-quality, glossy white coffin.

Frode Otto started screaming again when he saw the coffin, which seriously annoyed the Pole. He thrust a hand between the estate bailiff's legs and squeezed his testicles while with his other hand he tapped his ear: *quiet, please.* It worked. From then on Frode Otto kept his mouth shut. The Pole took out a mobile from his inside pocket, dialled a number and grunted a short, incomprehensible word when the caller answered. Henrik Krag could feel the heat from the oven, even though he was some distance away and the hatch to the fire was closed. He put two and two together and asked, shocked:

'Are you going to burn him alive? You can't do that. You just can't.'

Benedikte Lerche-Larsen replied angrily.

'Will you stop asking questions? Just wait and see what happens.'

A few minutes later two men entered the room. One was Bjarne Fabricius, the other a crematorium employee. Bjarne Fabricius greeted Benedikte Lerche-Larsen in a friendly manner and thanked her gallantly for the pleasure of her company the other night. Then he took a seat on one of the chairs alongside the wall. The message was clear: this wasn't his show, he was only here to watch. Nor did the crematorium employee want to get more involved than absolutely necessary.

He handed a Phillips screwdriver to Benedikte Lerche-Larsen, who immediately passed it on to Henrik Krag, who thanked her, though he had no idea what to do with it. The crematorium guy went up to the oven, pressed a button; the hatch slid up and the heat billowed into the room like a burning wall. Then he pressed another button and the hatch was lowered until it slotted in place with a clunk that echoed heavily between the walls.

'Red button up, green button down. Don't touch my settings. It's at the correct temperature.'

He repeated this in a lecturing voice, then he left. As he passed Frode Otto, he held up his palms to him as if to say, regrettably, these things happen, better luck in your next life, mate.

Benedikte Lerche-Larsen commanded Henrik Krag:

'Give me one of your socks.'

He did as he was told; balancing on his right foot, he twisted off his left trainer and pulled off the sock in one swift movement. He held it out to her, but she had second thoughts and didn't take it.

'No, that was stupid, hold it yourself.' She turned to Frode Otto and said harshly: 'Open your mouth!'

He obeyed her, ashen-faced and terrified. His viciousness had evaporated, fear had taken over. Henrik Krag scrunched up his sock and stuffed it into Frode Otto's mouth. Frode Otto snorted, he was struggling to breathe.

Benedikte Lerche-Larsen gestured to Henrik Krag to unscrew the coffin lid, then she walked right up to Frode Otto. She stroked his cheek.

'What a pity, I would have liked to hear you scream, but unfortunately we're in a hurry.'

The statement was illogical, but no one appeared to notice. She walked the few steps to the coffin and opened it.

'And who do we have here? Oh dear, you're nothing but skin and bones, I think it's about time that you left this earth. Tell me, would you mind some company on your journey?'

She walked back to Frode Otto and informed him cheerfully:

'Mrs Skin and Bones doesn't mind. There's room for two, but what do you say? Can you *live* with it as well?'

She was the only one who laughed, a short, dry cackle at her own witticism, while she squeezed shut his nostrils with her thumb and forefinger. Frode Otto emitted various strangled sounds. His face grew scarlet, his eyes bulged in their sockets. Finally she released him.

'Right, then we're agreed.' She turned around. 'Let's get him inside. Face down, so he can get to know his hostess before he goes to hell.'

Frode Otto wriggled and kicked as best he could, so the Pole and Henrik Krag had to employ maximum force to execute her order. Bjarne Fabricius watched Benedikte Lerche-Larsen as the men struggled with the estate bailiff. When she became aware of his gaze, she smiled at him. He didn't smile back.

After Henrik Krag had screwed the coffin lid back on, he asked, almost pleadingly:

'Please can I go?'

Benedikte Lerche-Larsen shook her head firmly.

'Roll him along the conveyor belt and count to ten. Then you can take him out.'

The Pole smiled with approval. This was a first, he hadn't seen this one before.

Frode Otto had grown old from his trip in the coffin. The darkness, the fear, the heat, his close contact with the dead body, had aged him, turning his skin grey. On Benedikte Lerche-Larsen's command, Henrik Krag relieved the man of both his handcuffs and the sock in his mouth. Nevertheless, the terrified estate bailiff kept pressing himself up against the wall, his lips quivering and his eyes wet. He was broken.

Benedikte Lerche-Larsen yelled at him:

'Bloody hell. Did you shit yourself? Fuck me, it stinks.'

She pinched her nostrils as she dived into her handbag and found a small, white plastic jar with a screw lid. She opened it and rubbed some lotion under her nose, then handed it to the Pole, who copied her.

'Listen, you stupid bastard, these are the rules. If I think you're lying to me, you're going straight in the oven, and next time it'll be for real. If I think you're *not* lying, I might let you live. Do you understand?'

Frode Otto nodded. Yes, yes, he understood, no lying. He struggled to utter the words, stammering and cowed, and it was difficult to tell whether he actually understood, or whether he was just saying what she wanted to hear, ready to do whatever she wanted. Benedikte Lerche-Larsen would appear to have her doubts too. She spoke slowly, as if emphasising something very difficult.

'So this isn't about whether *you* lie. It's about *me* thinking you might be lying. There's a difference.'

He assured her that everything he had said was the truth.

'I haven't asked you anything yet, you moron.'

He reached beseechingly for her hands, he would tell the truth, for pity's sake, he would. And then, without prompting, he started talking in a disjointed manner, but not without making some sense.

It was as Benedikte Lerche-Larsen had suspected. Frode Otto had been an old friend of Jan Podowski, whose silence had kept him out of prison, and so Frode Otto had let him have the use of the hunting lodge in return for a free hooker every two months. He had also made sure that a replacement cabin was built when the old one was torched. When Jan Podowski died, Frode Otto had called his friend's bosses, he couldn't remember their names, and tried to extort money in return for keeping his mouth shut about the dead girl in the lake. But he would never, ever say anything, she had to believe him, not a word. He was due to be interviewed by the police in Copenhagen the following Monday, but they wouldn't get anything out of him. Or about that business in Jutland, because they couldn't prove anything.

Benedikte Lerche-Larsen interrupted him sharply.

'What business in Jutland?'

Well, he had raped a girl, a German, but Jan Podowski hadn't been involved, he would rather watch the football. Otherwise Frode Otto had restricted his activities to his holidays abroad, six girls in total, but no one suspected him.

It took some time before Benedikte Lerche-Larsen could make head or tail of his story, and initially she didn't comment on it. She was more interested in other subjects.

'Did Jan ever talk to you about card games? Some kind of card club?'

He denied it, heart-breaking in his pleas for her to believe him.

'Does the name *Svend* mean anything to you?'

Yes, that was the name of Jan Podowski's boss.

'What about *Ida*?'

No, he didn't know an Ida. She furrowed her brow. *Now think carefully*. He pleaded his case again, swore that he didn't know anyone called Ida. It was clear that he was telling the truth: he didn't know any Ida, nor was he Ida. She tried *Bjarne*, yes, he was also his friend's boss, the ringleader Frode Otto thought, and he would never phone him again, ever.

Benedikte Lerche-Larsen thought about it briefly, then she went over to Bjarne Fabricius and spoke to him for a while without the others being able to hear what was said. The conversation ended with Bjarne Fabricius stepping into the centre of the room and taking over. He said in a conversational tone of voice to Frode Otto:

'This is where we find out if you're really going in the oven. No, don't speak, just listen. You see, I'm in two minds; on the one hand, I don't want you to go home and carry on with your life as if nothing had happened. On the other hand, torching you will probably create more problems than it would solve, so I've decided on a middle way.'

He explained his middle way in detail; Frode Otto accepted without protest. Bjarne Fabricius concluded:

'In that way we'll know where you are, but don't make the mistake of thinking that we can't get at you in prison, because nothing could be easier, even if you choose solitary confinement. It'll make it a little more difficult, but we'll get you in the end.'

The estate bailiff nodded. Bjarne Fabricius continued:

'There's another option for you, and that's almost more entertaining. You could try to do a runner, abroad or some village on Bornholm, the opportunities are endless. And it would give you a chance, no doubt about it. Now you don't look like a man I can discuss percentages and probabilities with, so let's just say that your chances are small. Sooner or later we'll sink our executioners' claws into you again, and then we'll take a second trip up here. But next time you won't be screaming when we drag you inside, and do you know why?'

Frode Otto shook his head miserably.

'Because we'll start by ripping out your tongue.'

CHAPTER 35

I f the aim was to taunt her, Benedikte Lerche-Larsen's voluntary assistance in Kirkens Korshær's soup kitchen in Stengade on Nørrebro represented a success in every possible way.

She was forced to contribute her services for two weeks, and after her first evening, she wanted to scream. Henrik Krag had to put up with her discontent when, after her shift, she drove straight to Ishøj to pay him an unannounced but very urgent visit. Presumably because she had no one else to moan to, he thought, while he pretended to share her opinions about this and that. He was getting used to her habit of coming and going as she pleased. This was her third unannounced visit. She waved her hands about like a ringmaster in a circus and dramatised her experiences to the maximum the moment they entered the living room.

'I'm telling you, I feel as if I reek of those ... *people*. Each more scruffy and greasy than the one before, mega gross, the vast majority of them. Black people, East Europeans, Danes and Greenlanders, of course ... bottom of the barrel, no use to anyone. I didn't even know people like that had a place of their own, and you really must be deeply socially responsible or a religious nutter to waste your life helping them. Why we don't just send them back to where they came from and hand out free meth to the rest, so we can get rid of them quickly, is beyond me.'

She went on and on, and he tried nodding in the right places though it didn't really matter, she was too deeply immersed in her own troubles. When he finally saw a chance to get a word in edge-ways, he asked:

'Would you like a cup of coffee? I've bought proper coffee, but you already know that.'

She would, he went into the kitchen, she followed – still talking. She was now slightly more relaxed.

'People donate the weirdest things. Today we got a crate of avocados from a greengrocer, and some CEO turned up with five surplus gateaux from Bella Conference Centre, and I've cut and brushed the hair of an old crone so riddled with lice you'd think she bred them commercially. I much preferred peeling potatoes. You probably won't believe me when I tell you that many of the other volunteers are on benefits, and they're top dog in that cesspit.'

Eventually she ran out of words.

'So what about tomorrow, are you going to go?'

'Of course I'm going to go, it's not that bad, although ... I'm doing the nightshift tomorrow, and I bet that's even worse.'

'Haven't you anything positive to say?'

'Nope, what would that be? Oh, yes, the food was halfway decent. We served pork meat loaf for lunch; I haven't had that for years.'

'Did you see anyone who could be our blackmailer?'

'No, but then again, I spent most of my time back in the kitchen where the riff-raff aren't allowed. It's one of the few rules they have in that place. And also that you aren't allowed to drink alcohol, so the dossers politely hand over their bottles to us on arrival, and we put little labels on them and stick them in the fridge. Incredible, isn't it? OK, no more about that, I don't want it taking up that much space in my life.'

She flopped onto the sofa, acting as if she were at home. Henrik Krag briefly considered squeezing himself into the other end of the sofa between her feet and the armrest, but dropped the idea when she flung her arms over her head and with a long, lazy yawn stretched out from head to foot, claiming the rest of the space. He sat down in the armchair opposite her, not knowing how to handle her new mood; he found her impossible to understand. Perhaps it would be best if she left.

Benedikte Lerche-Larsen put one hand under her head and looked at him with a curving smile. It was hard to believe this was the same girl who had for half an hour, almost maniacally, entertained him with her antipathies and prejudices.

Her voice was deep and considerably slower when she spoke again.

'That cheap cow who was here the first time I came ... the Goth princess with the stupid eyes and the overly developed secondary sexual organs ...'

She led the sentence hang in the air without finishing it.

'Do you mean Lone?'

'Lone, Line, Lene, whatever, who cares? What's the situation between you and her?'

'I didn't know that ... that you were going to visit me. She doesn't matter.'

'No, of course she doesn't matter, she was born not mattering. Tell me, are you two an item, or what?'

140

CHAPTER 36

Frode Otto was a strong man. He was on the short side but broad-chested, with long, muscular arms that gave him an ape-like appearance. His face was broad and lethargic, any trace of animation, except for the coarsest kind, submerged in its folds of flesh. His eyes were colourless, reptilian, giving nothing back and constantly scanning their surroundings, slowly and methodically, without pause.

Pauline Berg was overcome by a suffocating feeling of helplessness when she saw him. Her cheeks and neck started to quiver, fine tremors that might be the forewarning of a panic attack or which might fade and settle instead into a harsh muscular contraction in her stomach. She never knew in advance, so she took a pill from her handbag and kept it in her hand, just in case. She was sitting, ready to observe the interview, which had yet to begin, through the large one-way mirror. To her right sat the Countess, to her left Klavs Arnold and two other officers attached to the investigation. At the far end, close to the door, in the worst seat, was Public Prosecutor Bertha Steenholt. She was the last to arrive, and it took some time before the others noticed her presence.

'He gives me the creeps. Have you seen his arms and hands? He looks like a gorilla,' Pauline Berg said.

'He's a former wrestler, and you need to watch yourself around them. Once they get hold of you, they'll tear you to pieces, no matter how strong or quick you are. You must always keep your distance, attack quick as lightning, strike at their weak spot and then retreat,' Klavs Arnold replied.

'Be quiet.'

The Jutlander peered down the row of spectators, then looked quizzically at the Countess; he didn't recognise the woman by the door. The Countess whispered something in his ear. Pauline Berg, too, had noticed Klavs Arnold's confusion, and said out loud:

'That's Big Bertha. You'd better shut up, Klavs, or you'll be torn to pieces in more than ways than one.'

In the interview room Konrad Simonsen and Arne Pedersen had been through the preliminaries. They had expected Frode Otto to arrive with a legal representative of some kind, but the man had come alone. And this gave the officers greater scope in their questioning.

Konrad Simonsen had decided to open with the sexual assault cases. Firstly, because they were of such a serious nature that the interview could hardly allow them to be reduced to a minor point. Secondly, because he was hoping that Frode Otto, having been confronted with such serious charges, would be more motivated to admit his presumably less serious offences relating to the dead African girl. This argument was based on the theory that he didn't kill the girl, because Konrad Simonsen didn't think he had, and in this opinion he was backed by all of his close colleagues. He started the interview.

'Are you interested in football?'

If Frode Otto was surprised at the question, he didn't show it.

'Not in the least.'

'I thought not. The twenty-second of June nineteen ninety-two was a Monday, and I can help you with the sporting details: Denmark played the Netherlands during the European Championship in Sweden.'

'Right.'

'I'm not terribly interested in sport either. But I am interested in crime, or more precisely, in making sure that people who commit crimes are held accountable.'

Konrad Simonsen fell silent, as was Frode Otto: strictly speaking, he hadn't been asked a question, and the Homicide chief's announcement wasn't exactly earth-shattering. Arne Pedersen took over.

'As am I, and I don't really mind whether they're committed in Denmark, Sweden or Finland. As long as it's a country with a decent legal system, where vermin like you get a fair trial, well, that's all right with me.'

Frode Otto jumped slightly when Arne Pedersen spoke up. The Countess frowned behind the mirror; she was surprised, she would have expected it to take much more to rattle the estate bailiff, but this boded well.

Konrad Simonsen took a photograph from the pile of papers in front of him, turned it over and slid it across the table. It was a colour picture showing a smiling Hannelore Müller. It was taken diagonally from the side, with her holding up a medal she wore around her neck; in the background you could make out PE equipment, including a vaulting horse with two girls on top of it, waving.

'Her name is Hannelore Müller, and she's a German national. On the twenty-second of June nineteen ninety-two, you beat her up and sexually assaulted her. She had just turned fifteen.'

'Yes.'

It was exceptionally rare for Konrad Simonsen to be wrong-footed during an interview, especially on his own turf at Police Headquarters, but it happened now. He was almost dumbstruck when he asked:

'I beg your pardon, what did you just say?'

'I said that I raped her. It's true.'

Frode Otto sounded almost bored, and nothing made sense. Konrad Simonsen looked at Arne Pedersen, but he was gawping and no use at all. Then he quickly, almost feverishly, took out another two photographs. They also showed young women. He placed the pictures in front of Frode Otto and said, while pointing:

'Susanna Laine, she's Finnish, and you raped her on Tuesday the third of August two thousand and four. Randi Hansson, who is Swedish, you raped on Saturday the twenty-third of June two thousand and seven. Both assaults were carried out on the Tallink Silja Line ferries that sail between Stockholm and Helsinki.'

Frode Otto briefly studied the girls' pictures, then said:

'No, not them, just her.'

He placed his hand on Hannelore Müller and stroked her portrait with his fingers, while he looked at her with a smile. His behaviour was deeply offensive, and Konrad Simonsen had to stop himself from snatching the picture away.

'Then let's focus on her to begin with. Arne, please would you?'

Arne Pedersen took over and for the next half hour Frode Otto told him sullenly, but quite willingly, how he had met the German girl in a shop in Vammen in Jutland, and later overpowered her on the road and forced her into the boot of his car. He also accounted for the subsequent rape and abuse, and though he was speaking in short sentences, and often needed cues or probing questions from Arne Pedersen, it was clear that he enjoyed recalling the event. He showed no remorse for his own perverted actions, rather the opposite, which was revolting to witness, but in the circumstances made the interrogation much easier.

His confession was lacking in only two particulars. Firstly, he refused to give up the name of the man whom Arne Pedersen already knew he had worked with when he robbed a savings bank in Struer three days before the sexual assault. Frode Otto simply denied that there even was an accomplice, which was illogical but effective. The other point where his confession was unsatisfactory came when Frode Otto was unable to describe in detail the location where he had committed the rape. He claimed that he had no idea, which probably was true. Nevertheless, the description of the act itself was so detailed – including on crucial points that had been kept from the public by the police – that the estate bailiff in all likelihood would be convicted, whether or not he later withdrew his confession.

When Arne Pedersen had finished, he looked quizzically at Konrad Simonsen, who shook his head. Arne Pedersen got up and his attitude changed. Up until now, his behaviour had been controlled and proper, now he snarled maliciously:

'You obviously think that your crime is . . .'

He got no further. Konrad Simonsen harshly interrupted him, and then, sounding almost conciliatory, spoke to the estate bailiff:

'You've done your homework, which is your right, of course, and your crime falls under the statute of limitation, which I regret naturally, but that's the law, and you know it better than anyone. The statute of limitation for rape is ten years, plus another five if the circumstances are particularly brutal, and they are here, there can be no doubt about it, but we're unfortunately still a few years late to charge you. I suggest we break for an hour, and I'll make sure you get a lawyer whether or not you want one. Afterwards, we'll take a written statement and we need you to sign it, so you should expect to be here most of the day. Let's say that we'll see you again at twelve-thirty.'

In the room next door Pauline Berg practically screamed:

'Simon's letting him go? He can't do that. Shit!'

She looked beseechingly at Bertha Steenholt, and Klavs Arnold agreed with her. What the hell was going on? It couldn't be true. Besides, their boss was wrong. They could add one year to the statute of limitation for each year under eighteen that Hannelore Müller was when she was raped, so Frode Otto's crime *wasn't* covered by the ordinary statute of limitation. The Public Prosecutor hardly deigned to look at him, but grunted in her deep bass:

'Listen and learn.'

In the interview room Frode Otto was almost as agitated. He stared at Konrad Simonsen.

'You're releasing me?'

'You're not even under arrest. Pull yourself together, man.'

'But I'm free to go?'

'I don't make the laws in this country. But I appreciate your confession, it could mean a lot to Hannelore. I was in Germany last week and she's still in hell, after what you did . . .'

The estate bailiff interrupted him, clearly uninterested in the German woman's condition.

'Can I serve my time for these in Denmark?'

He pointed to the pictures of his Swedish and Finnish victims. Konrad Simonsen flung out his arms as if the matter wasn't terribly interesting to him.

'You won't go to prison for something you didn't do.'

'But if I did do it, can I do my time in Denmark?'

'I really don't know. I believe the ruling on cross-border criminal activity is quite complicated, and we're not lawyers. I can always ask, should I happen to bump into a lawyer, and give you a call if I remember, but this isn't the Citizens Advice Bureau, if that's what you're thinking. Right, let's finish for now, I'm bored with looking at you.'

Frode Otto gave up. He put his hands on the pictures of the two other girls.

'All right, they were mine too.'

'Yours? How were they yours?'

'I raped them, both of them.'

Arne Pedersen had sat down again; he had finally cottoned on to Konrad Simonsen's strategy. He assumed the same indifferent attitude as his boss, as if the whole thing was of little importance, merely an incidental the Homicide Department could barely be bothered to waste its time on. He asked wearily:

'Why would we believe you now, when you've been lying to us the whole time?'

'I stuffed a remote control up the arse of that Swedish bitch . . .'

He pointed to the picture of Randi Hansson.

'. . . and I bit the Finn with a set of false teeth . . .'

He grinned horribly, then continued:

'. . . all over her tits, her nose, her cheeks, her stomach and her toes. And no one except me and the cops know that, so I'm not lying.'

CHAPTER 37

It took most of the week before Frode Otto's confessions had been written down and investigated properly.

The Homicide Department was ably aided by both the Swedish and the Finnish police, who both dispatched staff to Copenhagen, and everyone was delighted when the cases were finalised on Thursday afternoon, ready to be submitted to the Public Prosecutor. The Deputy Commissioner herself made an appearance. She had a tendency to turn up whenever she got a whiff of success, and a case where the Public Prosecutor was involved, well, need she say more? Bertha Steenholt ignored the Deputy Commissioner's exaggerated veneration of her, but as usual took the time to study the woman's outfit. The Deputy Commissioner was famous for her individual and appalling dress sense. Like a colourful, almost festive insect, Big Bertha thought to herself, and apart from that took no notice of her.

Konrad Simonsen, however, did take notice of the Deputy Commissioner. Firstly, she was his immediate superior, and secondly, he liked her, although he preferred her to stay in her office. On the other hand, she didn't interfere in his investigations; she demanded only to be kept informed and was utterly grateful when she was, almost irrespective of what he told her. The Deputy Commissioner said:

'You don't look happy, Simon. And I thought everything was going so well.'

'No, when it comes to the Hanehoved case, he clams up like an oyster.'

It was the truth. Frode Otto refused consistently to discuss anything other than the three rapes. By now Konrad Simonsen was persuaded by Klavs Arnold's argument that the hunting lodge in Hanehoved Forest hadn't been built at the time the estate bailiff had claimed. That had prompted several valid questions, all of which remained unanswered. Nor would the man talk about his Saturday trips, which took place every two months, nor was he willing to help them with the telephone numbers he had called or the calls he had received in recent years. And then they mustn't forget the greatest mystery of them all: why had Frode Otto confessed to the rapes now? No one had any constructive suggestions about this, although everyone, possibly with the exception of the Countess, would regularly launch into more or less credible speculations.

The estate bailiff himself said nothing, but smiled unpleasantly and claimed he wanted to unburden his conscience, nothing more, and he wasn't even prepared to listen to follow-up questions.

'Has he worked out yet that you tricked him?' the Deputy Commissioner asked.

Konrad Simonsen shrugged his shoulders, he didn't know. She was referring to the very first interview where Konrad Simonsen had realised that, for some inexplicable reason, Frode Otto wanted to be found guilty of something, and didn't really mind what. Simonsen had therefore let the estate bailiff think that the statute of limitation for his rape of Hannelore Müller had expired, which it hadn't, whereupon the man, almost out of desperation, had confessed to a further two crimes since he believed he could no longer be punished for the one he had committed in Denmark.

'But it's quite something that Big Bertha is running the case herself,' Konrad Simonsen said to the Deputy Commissioner: 'Usually, she only takes on difficult and complicated cases. I think it's because you and she work so well together.'

'Do you really think so?'

The Deputy Commissioner beamed and blushed like a young girl, the soft shade of pink in her cheeks matching that of her blouse.

'I'm sure of it. Oh, by the way, I may end up needing a little more money than we agreed for this investigation. I haven't been able to make all that many savings once I had to factor in the international perspective.'

'No, of course not, I'm sure we can work something out, don't you worry about that. Tell me, did she *say* something about working with me?'

'That was my impression, and I wasn't the only one, definitely not.'

CHAPTER 38

From the Kolleløse Manor accounts as well as those of Store Heddinge Holiday Homes LLP, a company based in Køge and specialising in the transport and construction of smaller log cabins, they learned that the hunting lodge in Hanehoved Forest had been delivered, erected and paid for in Christmas 2007.

However, there was evidence to suggest that the invoice had been predated, and that the actual time of construction was the week of 20 March 2008. During that time Frode Otto had had seven telephone conversations with the company, and weather-wise it would also fit neatly with Klavs Arnold's tyre-track theory. If he was correct, then his theory was interesting because 20 March was within the time window estimated by the forensic pathologist for the African woman's death.

Konrad Simonsen and Klavs Arnold drove to Køge to interview the managing director and sole proprietor of Store Heddinge Holiday Homes. Here they hit a wall.

Predating an invoice wasn't a major crime; it happened often if the customer wanted the invoice included in last year's budget. Konrad Simonsen expressed his understanding of this, but to no avail. The managing director insisted he hadn't predated anything at all, and he had better things to do than talk to them. At this point, the two officers had barely sat down. Nevertheless, Klavs Arnold carried on the conciliatory line:

'Listen. We're not from the Revenue, and we don't care about a bit of cash changing hands on the side.'

The managing director was in his late twenties, articulate and utterly unmoved.

'No one gets bribed here, friend. Anything else?'

'Come on, please. We're investigating a murder.'

'And I'm running a business, or at least I was until you barged in.'

Konrad Simonsen tried the stick rather than the carrot: Customs and Exercise, the Revenue, a labour inspection or health and safety issues on the premises, and he wondered out loud if the managing director's 4x4, which was listed as a business vehicle, had ever been seen in Køge Marina? What could it possibly be doing there? Oh dear, oh dear, that could be expensive.

The managing director was unperturbed.

'You don't like the authorities?' Konrad Simonsen asked. 'Is that why you won't help us?'

It was clear from the expression on the man's face that he had hit the nail on the head. Nevertheless, all he said was: 'I've answered your questions, do you have any more?'

They did.

'Who built the hunting lodge?'

'It's hard to say after all this time. We've no records, and if you're going to interview my staff, I would appreciate it happening outside working hours.'

'Fortunately that's my decision, and I don't care what you would appreciate. But another thing: last March you spoke six times on the phone to a man named Frode Otto. He's the estate bailiff at Kolleløse Manor. What did you talk about?'

Konrad Simonsen placed a piece of paper with Frode Otto's telephone records in front of the managing director, who instantly pushed it back.

'No idea, I speak to twenty people every day. Are we done?'

Klavs Arnold asked his boss:

'Please let me beat him up?'

The managing director, however, refused to be intimidated or provoked.

'Get out, and the next time, if there *is* a next time, which I hope there won't be, then call in advance, so I have time to contact my lawyer.'

The breakthrough came just under a week later in Northern Ireland, of all places, more precisely on the road between Derryvara and Monea Castle in County Fermagh. The Næstved Retired People's Association were on their annual trip abroad, and this year their destination was Northern Ireland, where they set off on a hiking trip. While they enjoyed the landscape, they chatted to each other about this and that. For example, a seventy-one-year-old woman told her friend about her grandson, who had been threatened with the sack at his job with Store Heddinge Holiday Homes if he ever told the police anything about a particular job he had carried out for a member of the aristocracy. *The police, imagine, he's not even allowed to talk to the police, it's outrageous.* Her friend agreed, it *was* outrageous. Outrageous enough to be repeated in a slightly embellished version when she spoke on the phone to her daughter later that night. Her daughter in turn added a little extra and passed on the story to her son when he casually asked how Granny was getting on. Her son was a bricklayer and currently working alongside a young man on a major roof renovation of a property in Mitchellsgade in Copenhagen. The young man's name was Oliver Malinowski. The bricklayer shouted from his scaffolding:

'Oi, Oliver, isn't your father-in-law a top cop?'

Oliver Malinowski was standing on the roof of the property, busy replacing the zinc bottom of a gutter pipe.

'Calling him my father-in-law is pushing it, but yes. Why?'

'Three guys down in Køge have been threatened with beatings and the sack if they talk to him. But they know who killed that nignog girl from Nordsjælland. Only they're too scared to say anything because some bigwig is involved. And it's definitely true, I heard it from someone who knows them well.'

Oliver Malinowski wasn't a stupid man. He was perfectly aware that the story might not be one hundred per cent true, but the word *Køge* rang a bell. Through his girlfriend, Konrad Simonsen's daughter Anna Mia, he had heard the other side of the story. Some moron of a managing director was obstructing the investigation the Homicide Department was currently working on, or something like that, he had been tired and missed a few details.

But perhaps his girlfriend's father would appreciate the information the bricklayer had just given him. From where he was standing, he could look down at Police Headquarters, and he thought it might be fun to nip over there during his lunch break to see if Konrad Simonsen was in. His information might be important, and he would get to see the building from the inside, something he had wanted to do for a while. The outcome was that the duty officer called Konrad Simonsen's office just under an hour later and giggled as he told the Homicide chief that *there's a Russian downstairs claiming to be living with your daughter*. Konrad Simonsen had his guest brought up to his office where Oliver Malinowski who, despite his foreign-sounding surname, was Danish born and bred, repeated the story he had just heard. Arne Pedersen was told to investigate, while Konrad Simonsen invited the young man to lunch in the canteen. He liked him and, more importantly, Anna Mia did. The Countess, who knew about these things, even claimed that his daughter had become happier since moving in with her boyfriend.

Arne Pedersen cursed under his breath. He had better things to do than chase rumours, he thought. Yet he did as he was told and via telephone call after telephone call, he followed Oliver Malinowski's story back to its starting point, which, completely against his expectations, turned out to be worthwhile. A temp working in the reception at Store Heddinge Holiday Homes insisted that a few weeks earlier he had overheard the company's director in strong terms forbid three employees ever to mention the construction of the hunting lodge in Hanehoved Forest to a living soul, including the police.

Arne Pedersen got the name of the three employees and then had a flash of inspiration. He asked to be transferred to their shop steward, and the two men had a nice long chat, which resulted in him being called less than thirty minutes later from Stockholm by an agitated union secretary from the Swedish Transport Workers' Union. Arne Pedersen struggled to understand what the man was saying and had to ask him to slow down. That helped. The union secretary wanted to know if it was true that a big-headed Danish director of some tinpot business calling itself Store Heddinge Holiday Homes was obstructing the investigation into the Helsinki ferry rape. Arne Pedersen confirmed it shamelessly, while grinning from ear to ear. Over three-quarters of the cabins Store Heddinge Holiday Homes sold in Denmark were bought in Sweden and transported directly to customers there. Of course it might now become difficult to find someone to transport them.

Konrad Simonsen politely ushered the managing director to a chair on his arrival, and offered him a cup of coffee. He felt no need to gloat, he just wanted the truth. The managing director poured coffee for himself and mumbled half-heartedly that he regretted his previous unhelpful attitude and was now ready to co-operate. The hunting lodge in Hanehoved Forest had indeed been put up in March 2008, rather than December the previous year. The work had been carried out on Sunday, 23 March, and the day before the customer, a man called Frode Otto, had picked up six staddle stones and a template for their location. The managing director himself had taken part in the construction of the lodge, as had the customer, along with two of the company's employees. Konrad Simonsen showed him a photograph of Frode Otto; the managing director confirmed that he was the customer.

'Do you normally help put up log cabins yourself?'

'It happens, but not often. In this case, it was because it was the weekend, and I couldn't get an extra man at such short notice, and also because I was offered fifty thousand kroner in cash to keep quiet once the lodge was finished.' He spoke with a sigh, but without remorse. 'Does your offer not to call the Revenue still stand?'

'Yes, I would think so, but let's wait and see. Tell me how the arrangement came about.'

It was straightforward: Frode Otto had called him, made him an offer and he had accepted. At that time he had financial problems, so the extra money came in very handy.

'If you spend more than you earn, you run into trouble, no matter how much money you make. Do you want the details? It's nothing illegal, apart from a bit of cash in hand here and there.'

'What happened to the old hunting lodge, did you take it away?'

'No, I think it had been torched.'

'Tell me more, this is extremely important to me.'

'I could smell smoke, I'm sure of it. But I saw no remains; I guess they had been chucked into the forest.'

He was mistaken about that, the theory had been eliminated after the police's meticulous search of the area, but he had no way of knowing that, of course.

'I presume it's possible to disassemble the lodge, so our people can examine the ground, and then put it back up again when we're done?'

'Of course.'

'And you'd be willing to do this at your own expense?'

'Absolutely, I'd be more than happy to help. But you need to know that Otto threatened me and my family if I ever spoke about the case. The bastard even knew the name of my wife, it was terrifying.'

This information didn't surprise Konrad Simonsen; he had already surmised something to that effect.

'That bastard won't be bothering anyone for the next ten years, so you don't need to be scared.'

The police only had to dig down a spade's length before the charred remains of the old hunting lodge appeared. The job was then handed over to forensic technicians and it took them four days. Konrad Simonsen went there every day, where he would watch their activities impatiently for half an hour. He felt they were progressing far too slowly but he watched from a suitable distance and didn't interfere. Nevertheless, on the second day he received some interesting information. A female forensic technician explained.

'The lodge was torched in two stages. First with petrol as the accelerant, the second time with paraffin. Any wood that survived the first fire was sawn into smaller pieces with a chainsaw, before being burned again.'

The third day also offered up a surprise. When Konrad Simonsen arrived for his daily visit, he bumped into Bertha Steenholt. Puzzled, he asked her:

'What on earth are you doing here?'

'Taking an interest, no law against that, is there?'

'Would you please give me a proper reply? After all, you're interfering in my investigation.'

The Public Prosecutor watched the forensic technicians for a while before answering:

'The hysteria about the "nignog" name really got my goat. If anyone refers to an African girl in politically incorrect terms, the country goes crazy and the media bubbles over with outrage, but hardly anyone cares that countless African women are trafficked here every year to work as sex slaves. It makes me sick. That was my reaction when the case originally blew up in the media and my disgust returned when your wife contacted me.'

'You think the victim was a prostitute?'

'Yes, don't you? Who else can you kill without them being reported missing? Surely that thought has crossed your mind – but you should go over there, they've found something for you.'

All of the metal had been separated out: the wood-burning stove and other large objects were lying on a plastic sheet on the grass, smaller pieces had been laid out on a long table as they were found. So far they had all been nails, screws, fittings and equally uninteresting objects from the old lodge. But this was the exception.

Konrad Simonsen held up the jeans button to the light, and a pleasant sensation of clarity washed over him, a moment of insight and meaning; he could describe it in no other terms. It had been *hers*, he was sure of it. LEVI STRAUSS & CO., it read, and he said quietly into the air:

'You wore jeans and this is where you were killed.'

Shortly afterwards a technician came over and placed a belt buckle on the table. She told him in no uncertain terms to keep his fingers off it.

CHAPTER 39

The air over Læderstræde in the centre of Copenhagen was a mix of noise and spring warmth, which couldn't quite get a foothold.

Benedikte Lerche-Larsen had sat outdoors at one of the many cafés for thirty much-needed minutes of peace and quiet. She sipped her espresso and shivered. Perhaps she should go inside, it was a little too chilly out here, she thought, but left it at that, reluctant to do anything other than stay where she was and just empty her head of worries for half an hour. On the pedestrian street in front of her people rushed past in different directions, on constant collision courses and swearing at anyone who stopped or moved diagonally. A van drove slowly through the pedestrians, who slammed angry hands on its bonnet if it got too close. One called out, 'It's a bloody pedestrian street, you halfwit,' but the driver didn't react, just sat staring wearily into the distance as he patiently inched forward. Benedikte Lerche-Larsen looked around. Not many people were sitting outside, most tables were vacant. Scrawny pigeons with nodding heads wandered in between them on an eternal hunt for a few dropped crumbs. She kicked lazily out at one that was being a little too intrusive.

As if spirited out of the clear spring air, a young man sat down at her table. He had an open, cheerful face and attractive eyes, and when he spoke, it was with exactly that touch of insecurity she liked. He had spotted her from across the street and thought she looked lovely. Was it OK if he bought her a cup of coffee? She told him to get lost and smiled at his back, when he slunk off with his tail between his legs. The episode had brightened her mood.

The problem was she was too busy, she was simply unable to juggle everything. There were the poker statistics, which she was always behind with; her mother would regularly trouble her for help with the hookers; there was her studies, which had been pretty much a joke in the last fortnight; and on top of everything, as if that wasn't enough, there were her daily shifts in the soup kitchen, and Henrik Krag, whom she couldn't make a low priority either.

She took out her mobile, called Bjarne Fabricius and got through to him immediately. That was rare. While she sipped her coffee, she delivered her weekly report on what was going on in her father's business, short and matter-of-fact, as her recipient liked it. Nothing sensational had happened, it was pure routine: the hookers made money, the poker players laundered most of it. The absence of anything newsworthy, however, didn't seem to bother Bjarne Fabricius. He listened, interjected a question every now and then, and thanked her when she had finished. Then he praised her briefly for her handling of the weekend trip, as he called it, to Frederikssund with Frode Otto. It was the second time he had done so, but it made her just as happy as the first, as she knew that he only very rarely showed his approval.

When she had finished the conversation, she called her mother, knowing full well that she was about to become highly unpopular, but she was lucky and got her mother's voicemail. Benedikte left a short message regretfully cancelling her participation this afternoon; something had come up at the university that couldn't be put off. She had promised her mother and three of her Nigerian prostitutes to go shopping with them in Lyngby Storcenter. Karina Larsen placed great emphasis on her employees' clothes, and her otherwise miserly side, when it came to anyone but herself, was suspended during these shopping trips. *When you pay five thousand kroner for a night with a hooker, you're entitled to expect a certain standard.* Besides, she loved these power shopping trips, as did the African women and her daughter, or so she thought. It was welcome respite from work whether your work involved sitting up or lying down, a day out with the girls. That was how Karina Larsen viewed it.

Benedikte Lerche-Larsen drank her espresso, quickly checked her handbag to make sure that she had remembered the money, which she knew perfectly well she had, then got up and half ran to her car. She was in a hurry.

It was almost 11.30 at night when she got to Henrik Krag's flat. She had been held up at the soup kitchen; they had been understaffed, two of the full-time workers were off sick. Henrik Krag washed up, she half-heartedly helped him dry. Sometimes she would drop a piece of crockery back into the washing-up bowl without looking at it, just for the sake of it. He didn't protest, only washed it even more carefully; she tried the same cup three times, and he never complained. They discussed her favourite subject: the identity of their anonymous tormentor, and as usual it was futile, but she persisted nevertheless. Mostly to change the subject, Henrik Krag said:

'You'll soon be done in Stengade, isn't that great?'

'Yes, of course. Yes, it is. However, I've volunteered for some extra shifts.'

He nearly dropped the washing-up brush.

'You did what?'

'I know it sounds ridiculous, and I haven't got the time, but it's – now don't laugh – it's the first real job I've ever had. Even if I don't get paid. A job that isn't working for my father, and . . . well, I've already promised them. After all, they need to eat too, and we're really busy at the moment. But enough about me. You want to buy yourself a dishwasher.'

'I did have one, but you scared her off.'

She elbowed him. Hard. He winced and grinned. She elbowed him again.

'We'll have to go back to the lake one day, Henrik. Even though it'll be unpleasant. I need to know where that picture was taken.'

'Yes, you've told me so eight times. I'll come with you. Have you been given your next task?'

'I get it in a week; the psycho emailed me this morning.'

'Will you promise to call me?'

'Yes, I'll call you. Now get a move on, it's nearly midnight.'

'Do you have to leave at midnight?'

'No, I should have been home hours ago. But I have a present for you, and I want to give it to you while it's still your birthday. And don't look so surprised, I saw it in your diary and on Jan's computer. Hasn't anyone wished you happy birthday yet? Haven't you got any presents?'

He turned his head and replied evasively. Yes, he had gone to his mum's for coffee and cake. Unfortunately Benedikte Lerche-Larsen pressed him and this time he told her the truth.

'She was drunk and had forgotten all about it. It doesn't matter, and I'm really touched that you have a present for me . . . that's much nicer.'

She chucked the tea towel over his shoulder and stroked him briefly between the shoulder blades, then quickly withdrew her hand as if she had done something wrong.

'Come on then, you big baby, let's go down to the car park.'

He followed her down the stairs, excited and mystified. He hoped it wasn't something that would humiliate him. He wouldn't be able to handle that, not now, not today. He braced himself for the worst . . . and crossed his fingers. Walking in front of him, she said:

'One is just a loan for the time being. We'll have to wait and see. The other is your real present.'

When he saw his motorbike, he couldn't hold back the tears. He couldn't remember the last time he had felt so happy. Joyously he turned around and reached out for her, and she pushed him away.

'Control yourself. And it's not a present, it's my property. But you get to borrow it because you were so keen to protect me the other day in Gentofte. That was really sweet, although you're crap at fighting.'

He struggled to pay attention to her; she gave him the keys.

'Aren't you excited to know what your real present is?'

'Yes . . . yes, of course. Really, Benedikte, this is the best . . .'

She interrupted him.

'Go on then, ask me what it is, you idiot.'

'All right. What is it?'

'A date with me. But you have to think of something we can do that I haven't tried before.'

She kissed her forefinger and trailed it down his nose. Then she turned on her heel and walked to her car.

CHAPTER 40

Svend Lerche spoke in a hectoring tone.

'If you believe, you'll find confirmation everywhere you look. Only the person who doubts will see the truth.'

Benedikte Lerche-Larsen knew the words in her sleep; she had been force-fed them ever since she was a child, though she had yet to discover from which book he had stolen the quote.

She looked at her father, exasperated, and concluded she couldn't be bothered to give him an answer. In order to wind him up, she pointed to his erotic etchings and snarled:

'When you die, that trashy porn will be one of the first things I sell.'

Svend Lerche refused to let himself be provoked, and warmed to his theme: she had promised him a report on two poker players and she had failed to deliver. Now she was saying that she *thought* they were good enough to be moved up to the five-dollar table. Thought! Since when did they make decisions based on *belief*? He spat out the word. He wanted statistics, tables, graphs and game theory probability distribution based on relevant and valid data.

She protested half-heartedly, knowing full well it would make no difference.

'That report is on my desk by tomorrow evening, or I'll dock your June salary by twenty per cent. By the way, where are you spending your evenings? You're never here.'

'That's none of your business.'

'When you don't do your job, then it becomes my business.'

'I was getting rid of that blackmailer, it took time.'

'And I'm happy that you did, but I'm not happy that you won't tell me how you did it. That makes me angry, and while we're on the subject of things making me angry – did you know that Jan videoed our customers when they used our services? Your mother had to go round and personally take down over twenty hidden cameras.'

'Yes, I was perfectly aware of that.'

Svend Lerche spluttered through clenched teeth.

'And you never thought to tell me!'

'What am I? Human Resources? It's your job to keep the staff in check. I can't be doing everything around here.'

'Do you know where he kept the footage?'

'On his computer, the one I took over, but I'm guessing he kept a copy on a USB stick; that's what I would have done. That footage will turn up on the internet one day, just you wait and see, and when it does, you'll be leaving skid marks as you run from Bjarne.'

She saw how a vein bulged on his forehead, she had hit a bull's-eye with her reference to Bjarne Fabricius. Her father spoke with ice in his voice.

'Go to your room and do your job.'

She left the door to his study open on her way out. She knew it would irritate him even more than if she had slammed it.

Back in her own flat Benedikte Lerche-Larsen did what her father had told her. She didn't want him to dock her pay, though financially it made little difference. She received considerably more money from the prostitutes that she and her mother ran on the side without Svend Lerche's knowledge. Rather it was the principle. She fetched herself a fizzy drink and activated the programs on her laptop, which she used to watch a poker player: an application which caused her own computer constantly to change IP addresses so external monitoring from the authorities was impossible, a program that connected to the poker player's computer and would regularly show her his screen picture, and finally a Skype connection, which electronically distorted her voice, so the player wouldn't know who he was talking to. The poker player said hello and they made small talk for a few minutes.

She watched him for two hours, then she got bored. It was monotonous work. After each game she completed a report that was added to the Poker Academy's considerable database of over ten thousand games. This database was her father's pride and joy. It was his concept, he had developed most of it himself, and it was an excellent tool for assessing a poker player's skill and whether it would be profitable to move him up to a more expensive table. Finally she logged on as an ordinary player and played against him aggressively; she had the benefit of being able to see his cards, a not inconsiderable advantage for a poker player. He handled himself well and read her right a couple of times, after which he folded though he had a good hand. She made a note in a different register, then closed down all her applications except Skype.

'According to our statistics, you could make eleven thousand kroner a week, if you went solo. Is that something you've thought about?'

The subject wasn't off limits, some of the Poker Academy's players quit to go it alone, but many later returned.

It took a little time before the answer came but Benedikte Lerche-Larsen didn't pressure him. She knew that he was still busy playing.

'Yes, I'm saving up, but it'll be six months at least. More possibly.'

'Could you recommend someone to replace you?'

'No, not really.'

'Think about it. And one more thing: would you like to earn a little extra money?'

Of course he would. She explained. She needed information on some people and it would most probably be available on the internet. Was he a hacker? He confirmed that he was – as she had expected – they had touched on the subject before, but never directly. She told him what she wanted to know.

'I'll send you five thousand extra the next time you get paid.'

'Why not ten?'

'OK, seven and a half. You have two weeks.'

'Where do I send the information? Do you have an email address?'

'I'll call you and ask for it, after which you'll forget all about it. The latter is important, otherwise we have a problem.'

'That sounds almost like a threat. I don't want to get mixed up in anything.'

'And that's exactly why you'll forget all about it. And yes, that *is* a threat.'

CHAPTER 41

Henrik Krag peered impatiently out of the window at the car park below, hoping that Benedikte Lerche-Larsen hadn't forgotten their date. She was late and he had his mobile in his hand, ready to call her, when her car pulled up. Soon afterwards he opened his front door, and got a quick squeeze of the hand; this was new, almost intimate. She was a vision of loveliness.

'I've been looking forward to this. Where are we going?' she asked him.

'It's a secret. Wait and see.'

'I hope we're going on my motorbike.'

He nodded.

'Ever ridden a motorbike before?'

'Never.'

He found a jacket, some gloves and a helmet for her. She sniffed the jacket, it was leather and well-worn. 'It reeks of smoke. Who wore it before me?' she asked, disapprovingly.

'Lots of different people. Once we get going, you won't smell anything.'

She accepted his argument, and they got kitted up.

The weather, though chilly, was perfect for this time of year. The May sun beamed down on them, the sky was clear except for a glowing band of cloud to the east, and there was barely a breath of wind. They stood in front of the motorbike; Benedikte Lerche-Larsen studied it warily.

'Up close that's quite a beast. How fast does it go?'

'Quite fast, but we won't hit maximum speed today.'

'Because I'm a newbie?'

'Among other things.'

'Any special instructions?'

'Yes, don't let go.'

Just before they reached Solrød Strand, he left the motorway and they continued down a number of smaller roads until he turned off and onto a path. Henrik Krag reduced his speed considerably. Benedikte Lerche-Larsen loosened her arms around him and held onto his hips instead; eventually she let go of him completely. There was no one else on the path except for a runner, who yelled at them though they overtook him with care. The path soon ended in a badly maintained cart track. The view to their left was blocked by hazel bushes, tangles of bramble, ground elder, and couch grass; to their right a herd of cows chewed languidly on meadow grass. They stopped at the end of the track. Benedikte Lerche-Larsen took off her crash helmet and gave it to Henrik, eyeing her surroundings suspiciously, while he secured their helmets and locked the motorbike.

'That was a great ride, but where are we, Henrik?'

He jumped effortlessly across a fraying fence to the meadow, where grasses and stinging nettles grew knee-high.

'Come on, we're nearly there.'

She scaled the fence, though not as elegantly, leaving a long, green algae stain on her trousers from her knee downwards.

'Now look what you've done. Do I look like a milkmaid or a field biologist? And I'm telling you right now that if this involves horses, then forget it, I can't stand them . . . Henrik, I'm not walking another step until you tell me . . . dammit!'

She was talking to his back, which was heading along a well-trodden trail winding its way up a short, steep hill. She threw up her hands in a gesture of frustration and hurried after him. The heels of her boots kept sinking into the soft earth, but she managed to catch up and grab hold of his leather jacket, which he had unzipped.

'Don't you dare walk away from me.'

He took her hand by way of reply, and she let him.

On the other side of the hill the vegetation was shorter and sparser. Henrik Krag stopped before they reached the bottom. Then, without warning, he threw back his head and squawked out loud while pumping his cheeks like a faulty siren. Benedikte Lerche-Larsen gaped at him in astonishment, bordering on fear. He repeated the process, louder this time. And then for a third time, after which he got a response.

A turkey strutted out from behind a bush a dozen metres ahead. Its tail feathers were extended as if to signal they were intruding on its territory. It stared them suspiciously with one eye, then scratched the soil with its strong talons as it threw back its head and again emitted its babbling call, the warts on its ugly, scarlet face quivering.

Henrik Krag smiled proudly and said:

'Give it a go, it's not hard.'

Benedikte Lerche-Larsen ignored his invitation. She furiously took his hand from hers, her eyes flashing.

'Tell me, did you drag me out here, to the back of beyond, so that you could scream like an idiot at some stupid bird?'

'Its name is E.'

'You named it? No, no, don't answer that, Henrik.'

'Only letters.'

'*Only* letters.'

She angrily mimicked his call, but spun around, almost frightened, when a turkey behind her responded with a similar sound.

'That's B.'

'Yes, of course it is. Hello, B. And where are A, C and D, and the rest of the alphabet? I'm guessing I'm about to meet them too. You're such an idiot.'

He said quietly:

'They only go to F, and C is dead. I think he was slaughtered and eaten.'

'Good heavens, what a tragedy, how about a minute's silence for C, before we fuck off? Of all the people in the world, how did I end up with you? Is this where you take all your loser girlfriends?'

'No, this is a first. Usually I just come here alone.'

'To practise the alpha—'

She stopped herself.

'No, I didn't mean that, I'm sorry. But this is a total train wreck of a date.'

Yet she threw back her head like Henrik Krag and the turkey had taught her, and called at the top of her voice. She received three responses. Henrik praised her.

'Good God . . . I've discovered my true vocation. Talking to turkeys. No, wait, it's my turn again! They're used to you, they deserve some variety.'

She pushed him hard so his call failed. A few tears trickled down her cheeks without her showing any signs of wiping them away and, for a moment, he thought she was upset. Then he realised that she was laughing. He laughed with her, it was impossible not to.

She cracked up during her fourth call. She convulsed with laughter, her hands clutching her stomach, slumping helplessly to her knees. He glanced anxiously at her trousers, stained from the moist, black soil. She might get annoyed about it when she recovered, and blame him. She followed his gaze, appearing to guess his thoughts, and she laughed at them as well. Then she dragged him down to where she was, and both of them howled with laughter, forehead against forehead. The turkeys wandered off to mind their own business; but the pair didn't even notice. It took a long time before they regained some level of control, and then only because they avoided looking at each other, knowing full well that the tiniest giggle would trigger a new fit in the other. Benedikte Lerche-Larsen wheezed:

'Bloody hell, Henrik, you could pull even Aphrodite with this stunt.'

He struggled to get out the words.

'I don't know her.'

'No, you don't, and that's her loss. This was a stroke of genius.'

They got up and didn't let go of each other until they were back at the fence. He offered her a hand, which she declined with a smile. On the other side of the fence she stood for a few moments, lost in thought.

'All right, Henrik, one good turn deserves another. If you have plans for tonight, then cancel them because I'm staying with you. We need to stop at a DVD store on the way home, and if you can find a place where we can get a couple of half-decent pizzas, that would be perfect.'

In the video store she picked their movie, while Henrik Krag collected crisps, a six-pack of Coke and some chocolate. She held up her choice, *Inglourious Basterds*.

'Do you know it?'

He tried his hardest, but to no avail. The first word of the title was incomprehensible. He couldn't even see whether or not it was Danish. She came to his rescue.

'*Inglourious* is a completely impossible word and it's deliberately misspelled. A decent Danish translation would be *Skændige møg-svin*, not that it matters.'

'Benedikte, I can't read the subtitles, and you know it. If you're just doing this to humiliate me, you might as well piss off home now.'

The nearest customers glanced in their direction. Benedikte Lerche-Larsen dismissed them with a glare. Then she smiled.

'Easy now. I'll read them aloud to you, of course. That's the whole point.'

They made themselves comfortable at home in Henrik Krag's flat. The snacks were lined up, and the armchair moved to make more space in front of the television. He fetched his mattress, she arranged the sofa cushions for back support.

'What about the pizza? Aren't you hungry?'

'That's for the breaks. We'll have to pause every now and again. Now shut up and watch. It's actually a really cool film. Not a masterpiece like some of his other stuff, but definitely worth seeing. You'll love it.'

She was right. Moreover, as the film progressed, and she read the subtitles out loud for him, the miracle happened: he forgot about the food and about her, and enjoyed the experience, just like a little kid being read to. During breaks he was impatient, almost pestering her to start again. Benedikte Lerche-Larsen said:

'Did you notice how that Nazi colonel is portrayed as an educated person, and that he drinks milk?'

'Yes, yes, now please can we watch some more?'

'I need some food and to rest my voice for a while.'

'But you just have.'

They watched some more, and he loved every minute.

CHAPTER 42

Klavs Arnold was in high spirits when he turned up for work at Copenhagen Police Headquarters just after nine o'clock that morning. No one could tell from looking at him that he had already spent nearly three hours making packed lunches, getting his children dressed and taking them to their respective nurseries and schools.

His wife had gone to Paris with one of her Folketinget committees – he couldn't remember which one – on a five-day study trip, so he was currently working overtime for the sake of democracy, as he loudly announced when chatting to his next-door neighbour over the hedge. The pressure on the home front meant he found it almost relaxing to be at his paid place of work where, for the next seven hours, all he was expected to do was to solve a crime or two. This explained his good mood, that and the fact he was a naturally happy person. Besides, he had actually solved something – if not a whole crime, then a not insignificant detail. He walked to his boss's office with a small pile of papers in his hand.

Konrad Simonsen and the Countess were sitting in the room adjacent to Simonsen's office watching breakfast television. They had achieved nothing since turning up for work that morning. A mutual acquaintance of theirs was about to be interviewed in the studio with his five dogs, a wire-haired fox terrier bitch and her four cute puppies. They didn't want to miss that, so Denmark's criminals would just have to roam free a little longer. Klavs Arnold sat down on the sofa between them, the feature with the puppies came on, was watched and duly commented on, after which the working day could start. The Jutlander suggested that they should sit down around the conference table in Konrad Simonsen's office, which they did. He started:

'It doesn't take much to make people happy – a good hobby, for instance.'

No one could disagree with that observation. The Countess guessed where it was leading.

'Is this about your ornithologists?'

It was. Over the last few days he had contacted several bird lovers, who had forwarded his request to dozens of their fellows. If anyone had taken pictures in and around Hanehoved Forest in the period 16–25 March 2008, the police would very much like copies, regardless of the birds depicted in the picture. The request had paid off; he had been sent almost two hundred images. As was to be expected, some still fell outside the time frame, but not all.

Konrad Simonsen, who had a meeting in twenty minutes, asked impatiently:

'Which resulted in?'

The Jutlander took his time. He hated being rushed, and was generally of the opinion that things moved too fast in the capital compared to Esbjerg, his home town, where people took the time to talk about things properly.

'Well, to begin with, I can say that I now know a great deal about the birdlife in Hanehoved Forest. There are black woodpeckers in November and common goldeneyes breed there, and if you're lucky, you can see green sandpipers in the alder bog on the south side of Satan's Bog, along with bearded tits in many places. Or it could have been some other kind of tit, I can't quite remember. And then there's this.'

He placed a photograph in front of his audience. It showed a falcon perching on a fence post with a mouse in its beak.

'What is it?' Konrad Simonsen grunted.

'It's a very rare Angry Bird, but the bird doesn't matter. However, look at the date and the plume of smoke to the left across the forest.'

At this point Konrad Simonsen's and the Countess's interest perked up. They bent their heads and looked closely: the Jutlander was right. A distinct column of dark grey smoke was rising almost vertically above the treetops. Klavs Arnold explained that the ornithologist who had taken the picture had shown him that very fence post yesterday afternoon.

'The angle and distance are right, but whether it's the first or the second torching of the lodge we're looking at, I don't know.'

The Countess concluded: 'Nineteenth of March fits perfectly with the pathologist's time estimate.'

'Yes, and there's more. The ornithologist remembered the date clearly because she was fined during a vehicle inspection check that was taking place that day a few kilometres north of Lynge. It was an operation carried out by Hillerød police, and I got the duty officer to email his colleagues to see if anyone remembered attending the spot check and, of course, if they had seen anything that might be relevant to our inquiry. I didn't get my hopes up either, but I was proved wrong. A traffic police officer will visit us on Friday when he's back from his holiday. I've already spoken to him on the phone, and what he remembers isn't earth-shattering, only that there was an African woman in someone's car, but that's reason enough for us to talk to him.'

Klavs Arnold wasn't the only one with results on this Tuesday, when Lady Luck really seemed to smile on the Homicide Department. The forensic report on the spruce branches tied to the stone and the African woman in the lake had finally arrived. It was one of the few issues from their initial investigation that had yet to be resolved.

The report had taken weeks – an unacceptable amount of time, but nothing could be done. Arne Pedersen knew only too well that if you rushed the technicians, let alone chided them for their sluggishness, you would run into a wall of incomprehensible science, and could be absolutely sure that the next report would take twice as long to be completed. He sat in the canteen at Police Headquarters, eating his leek and potato soup, while working his way through the report one line at a time. It was almost three pages long and unnecessarily convoluted, in his opinion, but its conclusion was far from uninteresting.

Both spruce branches showed traces of four-stomach ruminants of the Cervida family. Arne Pedersen shook his head and went online on his laptop, which he had taken with him to lunch. As he had expected, the Latin nonsense turned out to mean a *deer*. A call to the treasurer of Fredriksberg Hunting Club shortly afterwards confirmed that there had been a pile of spruce branches used for transporting red deer stashed behind the old hunting lodge. A stag could easily weigh over two hundred kilos and you didn't just pick up a chap like that. No, Arne could see that. The treasurer was insufferably pedantic and it took Arne ten minutes to get rid of him. He wondered if the African girl had been transported from the hunting lodge and down to the lake in the same way as a deer, with her hands and ankles tied together and a spruce branch threaded in between, so two men could lift her. Then he went to his boss's office to report.

Pauline Berg's investigation also bore fruit that day. She had been tasked with tracing the jeans button and belt buckle found among the remains of the old hunting lodge. The button, like the hairband they had found when the forest was searched, she was forced to give up on. Thousands of both items had been sold in hundreds of shops in Denmark; the button, of course, as part of a pair of Levi's. The belt buckle, however, was another matter. The belt was made from nickel-free steel and shaped like a snake coiled around itself in a stylised pattern, evocative of the engravings on the tenth-century Jelling Stone or an old-fashioned carpet beater. The technicians had also found three studs used for fixing the buckle to the belt.

She started with the big supermarkets and caught a lucky break with Co-op Denmark's warehouse in Brøndby, where a purchasing manager remembered the buckle.

'We discovered seven crates of belts in our warehouse. They had been missing ... that's to say, from our system. It happens sometimes. They must have been sitting around here for years. We offloaded them to Kvickly supermarket in Lyngby Shopping Centre for a song, just to get rid of them. That was two years ago. Try the Lyngby Shopping Centre, they might be able to help. I can give you a copy of the product number, date, that kind of thing.'

She thanked him.

In Kvickly in Lyngby Shopping Centre, the store manager referred to the belts as retro crap, which had been impossible to shift. Eventually they had flogged them for twenty kroner each and the owner of Mode & Trend in Lyngby Hovedgade had snapped up the lot.

This was where the trail went cold. Mode & Trend in Lyngby Hovedgade didn't have the same superb logistics records as Co-op Denmark, and all credit-card information had long since been deleted. The owner threw up her hands apologetically. However, she did have a belt herself, at home in her wardrobe, and she never wore it so Pauline Berg was welcome to it, if she was interested. Pauline Berg was disappointed, but thought, despite the ultimate dead end, that she had a decent result to present the next day.

Konrad Simonsen listened to her, without interruption, and smiled broadly when she showed him the new belt. It was made from black leather, produced at the Guangzhou factories in the Guangdong province in China. The buckle was from nickel-free steel and ...

He listened, thinking that he must remember to praise her when she had finished, a thought immediately forgotten when she took the original buckle out from her handbag and placed it next to the new one for comparison. He interrupted.

'Don't tell me you've been running around with that buckle in your handbag for two days?'

No, of course not, she had mostly kept it in her pocket.

He had to restrain himself in order not to shout. 'You can't do that, woman. What were you thinking? It's evidence.'

Pauline took offence and stormed out. He shouted after her. To no avail.

The episode was witnessed by Arne Pedersen and a few hours later, it gave him an idea. The group of officers investigating Frode Otto's telephone records reported to him, and they had almost finished. Only one telephone number in the estate bailiff's contacts had taken a long time to identify. However, it turned out to be worth the wait. During the three years for which they had telephone records, Frode Otto had rung the number regularly, including every week before the first Saturday in odd months, though they had yet to establish why.

In addition, there had been activity between that number and the estate bailiff's mobile seven times in the period 19–24 March 2008 – four times, when the estate bailiff had called, and three times the other way. Each conversation had lasted more than ten minutes, but less than thirty. The first conversation had taken place when the unknown caller contacted Frode Otto on 19 March, at 11.33.

The officers were obviously very keen to know the caller's name, but unlike every other number they had checked, it proved difficult to obtain any information about this one. It was issued by the same provider as the one used by Frode Otto. However, NewTalkInTown refused to disclose the customer's identity without a warrant. There was a restrictive covenant in place, the company's head of security claimed, without being willing to explain what the easement covered. Indeed, he even refused to explain what an easement was.

Konrad Simonsen frowned; he hadn't come across this before. An *easement*? A *warrant*? What on earth was going on? He had emailed the Deputy Commissioner, perhaps she could help, but had yet to hear back from her. A more direct approach would be to call the number, of course, and Arne Pedersen had indeed done so several times, but had yet to get through – until a short while ago. By now he had been calling the number so often that he was expecting the number never to be answered. The voice wasn't Danish but Russian, as far as he could tell, certainly Slavic. It was a woman's. He switched to English and asked to whom he was speaking. His unknown conversational partner asked him the same question, this time in intelligible but stumbling Danish. There was something commanding in her voice, as if she was a person people usually obeyed. *Arne Pedersen from the Homicide Department and your name is . . . ?* She gave him her name without him being any the wiser. It was long and completely impossible to understand. Then she informed him with authority, but without irritation or indeed aggression, that he had to go through official channels if he wanted to speak further to her, and hung up.

He had recorded the conversation. He did so routinely when interviewing witnesses by telephone. It helped him if he made notes subsequently, and it was embarrassing to have to ring someone back because he couldn't remember what they had said. He called a colleague at the National Investigation Centre who was married to a Russian. He asked for his help and ten minutes later his colleague's wife called him on his landline. He played the recording on his mobile to her and she said:

'Вера Рождественская.'

Of course, how hard could it be? Then he asked her to spell the name, preferably slowly. She spelled it and added:

'It's not an uncommon Russian name, but try checking out the homepage of the Russian Embassy. I can't be sure, but I think you're in very fine company.'

He thanked her and followed her suggestion. On the homepage he found and played a three-minute video where a nice-looking woman in her early sixties spoke about the good relationship between Denmark and Russia. Her voice was easy to recognise, both in Danish and Russian. He exclaimed out loud.

'I don't bloody believe it!'

In the corridor between his and Konrad Simonsen's office, Arne Pedersen was then prompted by Konrad Simonsen shouting at Pauline Berg to a flash of inspiration. He stopped, smiled and made a short detour after Pauline in order to borrow her mobile. She handed it to him without asking any questions, apparently absorbed in something else. Konrad Simonsen and the Countess were both reading through their notes when Arne Pedersen entered. He wondered if the newlyweds were making a habit of reading notes together; he would often find them like this. He interrupted them.

'Listen, I've found this number, which we haven't been able to identify. I mean, I've discovered the owner of the number.'

They both put down their papers, this was much more interesting.

'You won't believe it, but I'm quite sure it belongs to the Russian Ambassador.'

He gave her name and managed to pronounce it correctly. Arne Pedersen had an ear for languages and, having heard it three times, he knew it now.

'The Russian Ambassador?'

'Yes, the Russian Ambassador, Simon.'

Arne Pedersen explained how he had found her.

'Wow! God only knows what Bepa was doing with someone like Frode Otto. However, this is highly sensitive and must be handled with great care.'

The Countess frowned at her husband.

'Bepa? Tell me, do you know her?'

'Not personally, but she used to be a chess player. It doesn't matter. How many people know about this, Arne?'

'Only the three of us, and Pauline, and she's handling it.'

'What do you mean?'

'The Ambassador is currently giving a speech in Industriens Hus, Pauline has gone there to arrest her.'

Konrad Simonsen shot up as if his office chair had exploded, propelling it backwards, and sending it crashing into the wall behind him.

'She has what? Are you completely out of your mind?'

'Didn't you hear the sirens? Pauline thought it was about time we taught those Russians a lesson.'

Arne Pedersen thought he had overegged his story at this point. But it would appear not. Konrad Simonsen was scrambling round his desk for something that could stop his officers from arresting the Ambassador. The Countess came to his rescue, pointing to his phone. He grabbed the handset and dialled Pauline Berg's number as quickly as he could. One second later a mobile in Arne Pedersen's inside pocket started ringing. He answered the call. *Hi, this is Arne Pedersen. I'm afraid Pauline Berg can't . . .* Konrad Simonsen stared at him for one short, mystified moment, then he threw down the handset and exclaimed in despair:

'Tell me it was a hoax. For God's sake, please let it be a joke.'

Arne Pedersen laughed so hard, he nearly fell off his chair. The Countess joined in when the penny dropped. A sheepish-looking Konrad Simonsen was left unable to decide whether he was relieved or furious.

Once Arne Pedersen had assured his boss that it was only the Pauline Berg story that was made up, Konrad Simonsen chased his staff out of his office, then phoned a friend who was a senior civil servant in the Foreign Ministry, and whom he had first met on a previous case. Unfortunately this man was abroad on business and unable to help. Konrad Simonsen was annoyed to hear it. Under normal circumstances this type of police business had to go through the Foreign Ministry protocol, which maintained relationships with foreign diplomatic representatives accredited to Denmark, but Simonsen knew from past experience that such requests could take a long time, sometimes months.

Instead he called another contact in the Prime Minister's office; his name was Helmer Hammer, and he reported directly to the Permanent Secretary. Simonsen hoped Helmer Hammer could pull a few strings to speed up the paperwork.

And indeed when Hammer heard what it was about, he asked the chief of the Homicide Department to meet him in the Foreign Ministry right away and not to do anything else in the meantime. The last point was emphatically reiterated. Helmer Hammer claimed he couldn't stress enough how important it was. In fact he could, because although Konrad Simonsen got the message he didn't follow the instructions completely and before he left Police Headquarters, he stopped by the Deputy Commissioner's office very briefly to inform her. In the corridor on his way out, he met the National Police Commissioner in the company of some bureaucrats from the Justice Ministry. The National Police Commissioner slapped him on the shoulder.

'How is the case going, Simon?'

He loved being informal, *Simon* rather than his title, followed by a matey slap. It was how the National Police Commissioner worked, especially when he had guests.

'Up and down.'

There was nothing else he could say. It was how he saw the investigation.

'Excellent, that's the way to go, Simon.'

Konrad Simonsen looked after them. One of the bureaucrats turned around and nodded graciously. Everyone was glad that everything was going so well.

CHAPTER 43

The Danish Foreign Ministry, a seven-storey glass-and-concrete monolith, is located on Asiatisk Plads in Copenhagen with the engineering tower on Knippelsbro Bridge as its nearest neighbour: architecture at its worst and its best, side by side. Konrad Simonsen walked from Police Headquarters, a trip that had to constitute that day's exercise.

Helmer Hammer had already arrived. He had borrowed an office and offered Konrad Simonsen coffee, but he was clearly in a hurry, so the introductory small talk wasn't particularly friendly, and they quickly turned to the real reason for the meeting. Konrad Simonsen methodically explained the situation, told him about Frode Otto and showed Helmer Hammer a printout of the estate bailiff's telephone records with any calls made or received by the Russian Ambassador circled in red.

Then he told him about Arne Pedersen's brief conversation with Bepa Rozhdestvenskaya and noticed how tiny beads of sweat formed around the man's nostrils when he heard about the call. Yet he didn't interrupt. When Simonsen had finished speaking, they reviewed everything carefully from start to finish at Helmer Hammer's insistence, something Konrad Simonsen found rather excessive, although he went along with it nevertheless.

'Very few Danes have that number.' Helmer Hammer said. 'I don't even have it myself. Or ever have had that sort of access.'

He made it sound like an accusation, as if the police had obtained the number without being entitled to it. And perhaps that was how he saw it. Konrad Simonsen stayed silent. Helmer Hammer continued.

'You need to be aware that regardless of whether or not Ambassador Rozhdestvenskaya is involved in your case, you have no chance of interviewing her, or even speaking to her, unless she herself agrees to it.

'Even if she has committed a crime, and I'm stressing that we're speaking here about a purely hypothetical and highly unlikely situation, even if it were the case, you have no right to confront her. That applies to you and indeed to all Danes, as it happens.'

Konrad Simonsen confirmed that he understood the situation. Helmer Hammer then explained the procedure. First he would make enquiries with his boss to see if he could contact the Ambassador about the case. If he were given permission, and that was by no means certain, he would speak to some people here in the Foreign Ministry, after which he would contact the Russian Embassy and ask if Mrs Rozhdestvenskaya would like to assist the Danish Police in this respect.

'Again: maybe she will, maybe she won't. That's entirely up to her.'

They went their separate ways with Helmer Hammer promising to keep him informed of any progress. It wasn't until he was heading back to the office that Konrad Simonsen began to question the nature of the meeting. He had never imagined that Helmer Hammer would involve himself personally, only that he would pull a few strings to get the ball rolling. However, Helmer Hammer had volunteered his help and had gone straight from the Prime Minister's office to the Foreign Ministry, which seemed remarkable. 'Very remarkable indeed,' Konrad Simonsen said out loud, and wondered whether it was simply his inherently suspicious nature that made him think that.

*

Two days later Konrad Simonsen and Helmer Hammer met again. They were in Kristianiagade outside the Russian Embassy on Østerbro in Copenhagen. Helmer Hammer pointed to the building.

'You're aware that the moment you step inside, we're on Russian territory. And I mean that literally. Legally speaking, it makes no difference whether you go to Moscow, Vladivostok or visit a Russian Embassy.'

Konrad Simonsen was already aware of this and confirmed it curtly; he was getting a little tired of being lectured to on his lack of authority in this case.

'And there will be no follow-up questions, so please bear that in mind. When Ambassador Rozhdestvenskaya has told us what she wants to tell us about the case, we say thank you and then we leave.'

'That's exactly what we're going to do.'

'This isn't an interview, is that clear?'

Konrad Simonsen sighed to himself and parroted:

'That's clear.'

Helmer Hammer eyed him suspiciously, clearly wondering whether the reply had been sarcastic, then he added:

'If Ambassador Rozhdestvenskaya wishes to speak in Russian, then I'll translate.'

'That's a good strategy.'

Konrad Simonsen's face was stiff with gravitas.

Entering the Embassy they underwent a very thorough and lengthy security check. They were then taken to the Ambassador's office on the third floor, where they were made to wait in an anteroom, before they were finally admitted to see Bepa Rozhdestvenskaya.

She was a petite woman, barely taller than 1.55 metres, though it was hard to tell as she was sitting behind an oversized mahogany desk that did nothing for her. She was expensively dressed in an international, slightly dull style, and welcomed the two men with just enough courtesy to avoid any impression of rudeness. She gestured with a slim hand towards a couple of chairs in front of her desk. Her guests were permitted to sit. Once they had done so, she zeroed in on Konrad Simonsen and, in Danish, said in a neutral tone:

'I want you to explain the case.'

Konrad Simonsen had prepared carefully, going through his presentation at home and putting his few papers in order, which was unnecessary because the case was straightforward enough. He explained briefly about Frode Otto, and showed her a photograph of the estate bailiff. She studied it closely without reacting, before nodding stiffly at him to signal that he could continue, which he did by placing a printout of a call log from Frode Otto's mobile phone provider in front of her. Her number had been highlighted with a yellow marker pen, Konrad Simonsen said superfluously:

'I would like to know what your connection with Frode Otto is.'

As with the picture, she scrutinised the printout in detail. Then she said:

'I have never seen or spoken to this man.'

It was an unequivocal reply, but also exceedingly unsatisfactory. Absolutely the worst possible outcome. And even worse, he only managed to pipe up a feeble 'But . . .' before Helmer Hammer slammed him down like a nail.

'Thank you so much for your reply, Your Excellency, and thank you for your time.'

The senior civil servant from the Prime Minister's office rose, the head of the Homicide Department stayed put. Bepa Rozhdestvenskaya furrowed her brow.

'Was there anything else, Mr Simonsen?' she asked coldly.

'Just a small thing, if you'll allow me.'

He turned his head a few degrees away from Helmer Hammer, aware that the bureaucrat's gaze was trying to laser him in half. Then he reached into his bag, took out a book and placed it on her desk.

'Please would you sign this?'

Bepa Rozhdestvenskaya didn't look at the book. Instead she studied him closely with a tiny smile on her lips, a small smile which gradually widened into a big one.

'You're interested in chess, Simon? Yes, my staff tell me you like being called Simon, rather than Konrad. It's unusual, I've never heard anyone do that before.'

Helmer Hammer sat down again. The Ambassador ordered tea.

CHAPTER 44

The Kingdom of Denmark had awoken from its winter hibernation and spring had taken a serious hold. March and April had been chillier than usual, but this May Friday was warm and pleasant.

White clouds drifted across a fresh, blue sky, and though there was still a risk of frost at night in the usual exposed areas, the Danes took to their gardens or sunned themselves in city courtyards. According to them Denmark was once more the best country in the world, inhabited by the best people in the world, with summer holidays and long nights not so far away now.

People are hornier in the spring, Karina Larsen claimed. Her turnover had risen by sixteen per cent in the last two weeks. She made this observation every spring, and every year she managed to make it sound as if it were a unique sociological insight.

'Well spotted, Mum. You would almost think it has rubbed off on the animals – they seem to be copulating with greater enthusiasm than in the winter.'

As usual Benedikte's irony went over Karina Larsen's head.

'But isn't that normal? Don't they usually?'

The two women were sitting on the terrace in the garden in Rungsted. It was eleven o'clock in the morning and several amateur sailors had set out to enjoy the day on the short, choppy waves of the Øresund. They were now scattered across the strait, easily visible with their bobbing, white sails.

Benedikte Lerche-Larsen had attended a lecture at Copenhagen Business School that morning before returning home. Karina Larsen had just got out of bed; she was in her dressing gown and enjoying the first cup of tea of the day, a blanket wrapped around her legs in order to stay warm. Benedikte Lerche-Larsen studied her; Karina had yet to apply make-up and the sunlight mercilessly exposed her. She thought that her mother was growing old, old and ugly.

'What did you want, Mum?'

Karina Larsen explained that a banking executive of some sort, who lived on Vedbæk Strandvej, wanted to buy one of her girls, in order to have her permanently to himself. He already acted as the girl's host family, so he wasn't just an ordinary client.

'I thought that perhaps you could drive over there and discuss it with him.'

Her mother always referred to the prostituted women as *hers*, and Benedikte Lerche-Larsen loathed it. If it really was essential to determine ownership, she could at least say *theirs*; they weren't her mother's sole property, God dammit. However, she also knew it was impossible to teach her mother new tricks. She had tried, for a time tenaciously, but had been forced to admit defeat. Possibly because her mother was quite simply too stupid; it would certainly seem so.

'So he's not going to rent her out himself, and become our competitor? Are we sure about that?'

'Yes, it's true love.'

'How old is he?'

'Fifty, would be my guess. Why? What does that have to do with anything?'

'Nothing, of course, I just wanted to know. But why don't you negotiate with him yourself? You don't normally leave that side of things to me.'

Karina Larsen squirmed on her chair, her embarrassment easy to read. Benedikte Lerche-Larsen pretty much guessed the answer before it came.

'I know him a bit from the old days.'

'Back when you used to turn tricks? Is he a former client?'

She loved it when the topic came up and had spoken in a loud voice. Her mother hushed her frantically.

'Be quiet, Benedikte. Mind the neighbours . . . this is a nice neighbourhood, you know.'

Karina Larsen's mobile rang. She answered it with a knowing look at her daughter. Then she straightened up in her garden chair with an 'Oh, no,' which she, unimaginatively, repeated soon afterwards. When she had finished the conversation, she looked upset.

'It's happened again. One of our girls has committed suicide. Havana, the one in Birkerød, she had been hoarding paracetamol.'

She waited for Benedikte Lerche-Larsen's reaction and, when none came, expanded on the misfortune.

'What do we do now? I've a hairdresser's appointment at two o'clock. Svend and I have a premiere to go to tonight and I can't possibly show up looking like this. How selfish of her . . . and I've just spent over nine hundred kroner on lingerie for her! We need to get a qualified replacement in place before tonight. The deputy chief executive of the local council is due to visit her, and we can't say no to a man like him.'

Karina wrung her hands in despair. Benedikte Lerche-Larsen got up; she didn't want to get involved if she could avoid it. Suicides invariably meant an awful lot of hassle and administrative problems, both for her mother and the girl's host family.

'Maybe he'll fancy her in her current state? It's not unknown. Why don't you ring him up and ask? Who knows? Today might be your lucky day.'

Karina gave the matter serious consideration as her daughter made a quick exit.

CHAPTER 45

'If we're to talk, I need to see you take off your shirt and vest and put them back on, then we'll go for a walk. This is not up for discussion.'

The man nodded, he understood completely: she was scared of hidden microphones, that he might be a police informant or whatever they were called. He was sitting on the sofa and next to him sat the girl this was all about. They were holding hands; she was smiling constantly, revealing bright, white teeth and empty, beautiful eyes. Benedikte Lerche-Larsen nodded.

The truth was she wasn't worried about hidden microphones. The police would never waste resources on the conversation they were about to have; the probability of a conviction was far too small and the sentencing guidelines would suggest only a fine. However, the trick she had learned from her mother was to make the demand in the first place. It was about psychology. If one party to a negotiation started by obeying orders, including an order of a relatively intrusive nature, it invariably affected the ongoing negotiation process. In short: she would have the upper hand.

They left the girl and went for a walk in his garden, which was of a sufficient size for this not to feel ridiculous.

'It's love, we've fallen in love. And I want to marry her, of course.'

Benedikte Lerche-Larsen congratulated him. It was always beautiful when this happened, and across age, race and culture, it could hardly be more romantic. He thanked her, seeming touched.

'So you're going to live in Nigeria?' she asked.

He stopped in his tracks.

Eh? No way, he wouldn't dream of it.

'So you've chosen Sweden, well, that's lovely too.'

Of course he wasn't moving to Sweden, why on earth would he want to do that? She explained to him: Denmark's firm but fair immigration policy, one of the most restrictive in Europe, made it pretty much impossible for his future wife to be granted leave to remain, let alone Danish citizenship. On the contrary, she would be sent home the moment her au pair permit expired, which was in approximately two months. In Sweden, however, they had a somewhat different view of their citizens' right to choose a spouse, an arrangement which many Danes took advantage of. Benedikte Lerche-Larsen said:

'Firm but fair hasn't really made much of an impact over in Sweden yet.'

She let him stew for a while. Not surprisingly, he started talking immigration policy, every Dane's favourite hobbyhorse. He was certainly in favour of border control, so the country's social coffers weren't depleted by hordes of greedy foreigners. She had to know that, of course he was. But this was different, he could support both of them, his girlfriend would never be a burden to the taxpayer. It wasn't fair. She cut through his whingeing.

'It's completely irrelevant whether she's a burden or an asset, she won't be allowed to stay. But there may be another option.'

He clung to the lifeline she had thrown him. She explained that her mother could apply for another temporary work and residence permit every eighteen months, when the old one expired. It would be issued legally, they weren't talking fraud here, but he mustn't ask any further questions. The man shook his head, he didn't care how it was done. She carried on.

'It'll cost you, of course, but it's nothing compared to the cost of moving, especially now, when house prices have plummeted. And then there's your lovely garden, it would be a shame to have to leave it.'

They negotiated a price. First a one-off payment for the girl, then a fee every time her papers needed renewing. He was a better negotiator than she had expected. Love might have made him blind, but not to numbers. At length, however, they agreed a price acceptable to them both. Benedikte Lerche-Larsen was a little annoyed. She would have liked to return home with a big win; now she would be coming back with a decent result, but not much more than that. He offered her a glass of white wine, and she accepted it reluctantly.

'Do you think I'm making a mistake in marrying her?' he asked.

Benedikte Lerche-Larsen considered this, uncertain of her reply. What did her opinion matter? Nevertheless, he had asked her. She ventured cautiously:

'If it doesn't work out, and your feelings go off the boil over time, then it might not be so practical. But you can always get divorced – marriage isn't for life.'

He could see that she had a point. If he tired of his girlfriend or just wanted to try something else, then of course it wasn't so convenient. Perhaps it was better just to live with her to begin with. They could always marry later.

'Tell me what else you can supply?'

'Everything, if you can afford it. Everything except white Western girls. Or underage, we don't bother with those. Otherwise you have a free choice: yellow, brown, black, everything in between, as well as white from practically all the new East European republics. But if you want to buy for personal consumption, you don't need us;

it's only if they need a "roll in the hay" first to be brought into line. Otherwise you can just shop on the internet.'

'I'm aware of that, but it's so easy to be conned. And where do you go to complain?'

He looked genuinely upset by the thought. Benedikte Lerche-Larsen got up, as did he.

'Why not white and Western?'

'Because the UK, Germany and the USA tend to get seriously pissed off if you abduct their citizens, and neither my mother nor anybody else I know wants the FBI coming after them. Besides, girls from those countries don't usually think it's a great treat to work in a Danish brothel, so they're likely to run away and find the nearest police station the moment they spy a chance.'

The man could see that, and appreciated it was the way things had to be. It didn't matter anyway, there were plenty of other girls to choose from. She confirmed that was indeed the case, and thought that she would leave now; he was starting to bore her. Yet she stopped in the doorway when he said:

'We might marry after all, we are in love.'

Benedikte Lerche-Larsen thought he was an idiot and said with a smile:

'It's so beautiful when that happens.'

'But there's another thing. I don't like those rumours about that girl in the lake. Was she one of yours?'

Benedikte spent another ten minutes convincing him that those rumours had absolutely nothing to do with her mother. Nothing at all!

CHAPTER 46

After Benedikte Lerche-Larsen had undergone her second and final punishment, she drove to Ishøj to see Henrik Krag. He had made coffee and they were sitting with it on the table in front of them.

'So, how did it go?' he asked. 'Why don't you tell me what you had to do?'

'All I had to do was take part in an audition. It was nothing special.'

'What kind of audition? Did you get through to the next round?'

She replied as casually as she could:

'It was just some sex stuff. It was OK. Now I can say I've tried that as well, even though it was actually pretty dull.'

Henrik Krag felt uncomfortably as if someone had punched his stomach and struggled to steady his voice:

'You auditioned for a porn movie? Is that what you're telling me?'

Benedikte Lerche-Larsen evaded his gaze, and shrugged.

'Wondering if I made it to the next round?'

She laughed in an affected manner, like an amateur actress, then suddenly sneered:

'It doesn't matter. What's the big deal? And besides, it wasn't really me.'

She hesitated over her words as she continued:

'. . . it was as if I weren't there. Not really . . . well, it's hard to explain. But it made it bearable at the time. Also now that it's over. Waking up with a hangover next to a man you should never have slept with, where it takes weeks to get over your sense of self-loathing, is much worse. I'll take an audition any time, much more straightforward.'

Henrik Krag asked in a monotone:

'But what happened?'

His stomach dreaded the answer, but not knowing was even worse.

'Well, what do you think happened? Do you want details? It's not important, it doesn't bother me. Tomorrow it'll be forgotten . . . over and gone. I've done my bit, and now it's your turn.'

She touched her ear quickly as if she had a headache. One eye narrowed as she pressed the palm of her hand hard against the ear, and repeated to herself:

'It doesn't bother me all. Not at all! Not at all!'

Then she started to slap her temples, Small, hard blows, silent-movie gestures.

He grabbed her wrist and locked her arm.

'What are you doing, you idiot? Let go of me!'

He held her until they both calmed down. A few tears trickled down her cheeks, and yet her voice was steady when she spoke again.

'I'll get through it. It's just a bit crap right now.'

He let go of her arm, and sat down on the coffee table facing her. She immediately snatched up his hand and clutched it in her lap as though she were drowning. He tried to be helpful.

'Don't you have a girlfriend you can call?'

She didn't reply immediately, and he could feel her shivering from time to time, as though she were cold. At length she said ironically, but without the usual sting in her voice:

'And what would I tell my girlfriend? That she can visit young-wannabes.sex.com.filthy and there she can look for horny little Louise, or whatever those bastards were going to market me as? It's bound to get a lot of likes among my friends. At least there's a chance no one will know it's me. They let me wear a half-mask. Always helps with your anonymity.'

'So no one will recognise you?'

She shook her head half-heartedly. He thought it might help a bit . . . make it a little easier to know that she was anonymous.

'I don't know, perhaps not. I want to go home and shower. I don't know why I came here . . . it's not like you can do anything, but . . . I didn't have anyone else.'

'I'm glad you came.'

She ignored him and repeated it again, as if she were talking to herself:

'I want to go home and shower.'

Yet she stayed where she was, and eventually she said quietly:

'Please don't despise me. I know you don't like what I did, and it isn't easy for you either, but I also did it for your sake. For our sakes.'

That set her shaking again. She squeezed his hand harder.

'I wish we had talked about it first. Then it never would have come to this. It would have been better to go to the cops and put our cards on the table,' he said.

'I can't bear the thought of you going to prison for twelve years. And what about me? My life would be ruined. My father would definitely throw me out. If he has to choose between me and his business, I don't stand a chance.'

'Why would he want to do that?'

'Because he would be put in an impossible position. As would my mother, but she's too thick to understand it. All our clients would run away screaming if the press linked him to the murder. Same with the poker players, not to mention Bjarne Fabricius, he would hate it, and I would be out in the cold immediately. And I would be more than lucky if that was all that happened to me.'

'What are you saying?'

'I'm saying there's big money and cynical people in this game. Surely you know that better than anyone? And if you and I become a sufficiently big liability – for instance, if we were the prime suspects in a murder investigation with direct links to my father's business – we would be the ones to take the hit. That's how it is, those are the terms. I didn't think I would have to explain that to you of all people.'

'No, I can see that now. I've never thought about it like that before.'

'The bottom line is, all we have is each other.'

It was a bottom line that Henrik Krag liked. Her doomsday scenario didn't upset him. Problems that might arise in the future weren't worth wasting energy on before they actually happened.

They played the order from their blackmailer, which Benedikte Lerche-Larsen had recorded on her mobile. She turned the volume to maximum, and the hated, synthetic voice filled the room. The first message was of little interest as it only told her to be ready with pen and paper in ten minutes. The second message related to her audition.

'You will take part in a porn movie, and you cannot tell Henrik. You will ring 70 80 10 01, the number for Danish spelled D a n i s h, emotional spelled E m o t i o n a l, Pictures spelled P i c t u r e s. Your audition must be uploaded to their homepage no later than Friday, you have one week.'

'Forget it, I won't do it.'

'Your choice. Have fun in Vestre Prison.'

'Why are you doing this, you pervert?'

There was no reply, the call was terminated. Henrik Krag said:

'Ida spells out words she doesn't recognise.'

'Yes, I had already guessed that.'

'What does it mean?'

'Danish Emotional Pictures, it's the company I . . . visited. I had to pay them to upload the film tonight. Two thousand kroner *and* they didn't even pay me my fee. I hate their guts, but compared to Ida, it's nothing. I'm going to kill him, if I ever find out who he is.'

It hadn't crossed Henrik's mind until now that Friday was today, but he decided not to ask why she had put it off to the last minute.

They tried their best to derive some information about their blackmailer from the recording, however tenuous, but as usual they got nowhere. Even their speculations were slow in coming. The earlier mood lingered for them both, and left little room for cold reasoning. Henrik Krag's jealousy was eating away at him, but now another feeling was intruding, new and forbidden, mixing with his jealousy in a cocktail that went against common sense.

As soon as she had gone, he sat down in front of his laptop: youngwannabes was easy to remember, but impossible to spell, and it was going to take him a lot of attempts.

CHAPTER 47

Konrad Simonsen had called a meeting to review the investigation. In addition to Simonsen himself, the participants consisted of just the Countess and Arne Pedersen, and the agenda was limited to a single item, because the investigation currently had only one lead to follow up, and if that proved useless, the case would have to be shelved.

The three officers were sitting around the conference table in Konrad Simonsen's office. He recounted yesterday's conversation with the Russian Ambassador. In the 1970s, Bepa Rozhdestvenskaya had taken part in the world chess championship for women. Twice she had reached the semi-final, where she was beaten by Nona Gaprindashvili, who later became the world champion, and her 1981 book on Queen's Indian Defence was even today . . .

Arne Pedersen yawned. He played chess himself, and was considerably more skilled than his boss, but he didn't share his fascination with the game. The Countess interrupted her husband:

'OK, we get it, Simon. And then what?'

'Well, Bepa convinced me that she was telling the truth. First she pointed out that a couple of the calls were made when she was taking part in meetings abroad, some in Moscow, some in Malmö. The latter, incidentally, is on public record. While she is abroad her Danish mobile is kept in her safe, though that particular bit of information is difficult for us to verify. And, yes, she made that observation herself when she saw the look on my face. But then she thought of something better. The whole Embassy, herself included, switched to a different mobile phone provider in December 2008. Purely to save money – they got a better offer. I have a copy of the Embassy's contract with the new provider, and if that information is correct, which I don't doubt for a minute that it is, then half the calls between Frode Otto and her can't possibly have taken place.'

'So the telephone records relating to that number have been falsified,' Arne Pedersen summarised.

Konrad Simonsen confirmed it. Yes, they must have been.

'If someone deliberately manipulated the data, they might have picked the number of the chess genius on purpose. Because she's impossible to check, I mean. After all, we very nearly didn't get the truth from her, and if we hadn't, we would have been left running around frustrated, imagining all sorts of international conspiracy theories.'

The Countess brought him down to earth with a curt, 'Quite!' Then she began:

'I'll call NewTalkInTown and ask for an explanation.'

Traditionally she dealt with telephone records, and she had said it as a matter of course, but when she saw Konrad Simonsen's sceptical expression, she added:

'Or?'

'Call them and explain the problem. Then tell them you'll pay them a visit. I'm inclined to agree with Arne, this reeks of someone deliberately sending us on a wild goose chase. Are you happy to go there without one of us for back-up?'

'Yes, I prefer to do that, though I'll probably take a couple of uniforms.'

This was one of the Countess's little tricks when she visited companies that specialised in information or knowhow; she would often bring along a patrol car and a couple of uniformed officers whose only purpose was to be seen standing outside the company's main entrance. She claimed it helped her be taken more seriously than if she turned up alone and that the arrangement reduced the waiting time to approximately zero. No one in the Homicide Department disagreed with her, but no one had copied her method, which they thought bordered on harassment and ill suited the sophistication they normally associated with her.

Konrad Simonsen remarked:

'This number change is all we have. I hope you find something so we can make progress.'

This wasn't like him. The statement was superfluous; she was perfectly aware of the current status of the investigation so his words could only be interpreted as pressure, the boss's order to try harder. Her reaction was arch. She replied with a smile:

'You could always go there yourself, if you prefer.'

Konrad Simonsen retracted his comment immediately: all three of them knew that she was undoubtedly best suited to this kind of work. Arne Pedersen, who sensed the shift in mood, asked tentatively:

'The spruce branches and the belt buckle didn't produce anything?'

Konrad Simonsen picked up the cue gratefully and spent a couple of minutes on his reply, although *no* and *no* would have sufficed.

'And what about the officer on vehicle inspection in Lynge?' the Countess asked.

'Won't be here until tomorrow, our first meeting was cancelled due to illness. But we shouldn't hold our breath.'

All that remained was Frode Otto and his mysterious confession as well as his refusal to talk about the burning down of the old hunting lodge and the construction of the new one. It had been passed on to Arne Pedersen, who had interviewed the estate bailiff three times. The Countess asked about the outcome, though she had already concluded that she would have been told something, had there been something to hear. Arne Pedersen said in a weary voice:

'I'm not getting anywhere with him.'

Konrad Simonsen heaved a sigh and asked them to leave. He had an unpleasant meeting in half an hour and wanted them out of the way in plenty of time. Besides, there was nothing more to talk about.

Pauline Berg refused to take a seat on the chair that Konrad Simonsen had shown her, replying, no, thank you, she was perfectly fine standing. He had already told himself not to get angry, and for once had taken on board some of the advice he had been given during the leadership courses he was forced to take part in from time to time. It was important to preserve everyone's dignity, it was important to make clear statements, it was important for the employee to have a chance to explain themselves, everything was terribly important . . . but no one had taught him what to do if the employee in question wanted to stand while he was sitting down. Could you force people to sit down? Konrad Simonsen could.

'Sit down when I tell you to sit, damnit!'

Cowed, Pauline Berg sat straight down, whereupon Konrad Simonsen got up and positioned himself by the window to cool down. He opened it to get a bit of fresh air. It opened inwards, a feature originally decided by the architect of Copenhagen Police Headquarters so that the strict order and symmetry of the facade would not be broken when viewed from the street.

'What am I going to do with you, Pauline? You don't give a damn about my orders, unless they suit you, and I can't sack or transfer you.'

It was the truth, and they both knew it. Pauline Berg's continued employment was guaranteed by the National Police Commissioner himself no less; he believed that the force, or the Homicide Department rather, bore its share of responsibility for the state she was in. That view wasn't without a kernel of truth. Besides, dismissing her would most likely generate negative press coverage; a fact which Konrad Simonsen was convinced was the real reason for the National Police Commissioner's humane attitude.

But whatever it was down to, the bottom line was that Pauline Berg was on an unusually long leash to do as she pleased. Which she took full advantage of. Most recently by trying to interview a forester from Halsnæs in the 'Juli-non-case', which Konrad Simonsen couldn't make her drop, and which regularly made him and the entire Homicide Department a laughing stock.

He told her this, as he had done before, and as usual she showed understanding for his *point of view*, as she irritatingly referred to it, but he also had to understand hers: she had made up her mind that the Juli investigation made sense. Maybe not to others, but definitely to her. And not many things in the world in which *she* was living did. In fact, her life was dreadful, dreadful and trivial at the same time, but she didn't expect him to understand. How could he, when he wasn't her? But the Juli case did make sense. Especially now, when it was brought into the open, and not ignored, condemned to a silent death, as she herself was being.

Konrad Simonsen thought that by this stage the warning had gone even worse than he had feared. If only she had screamed or shouted, or sulked as she usually did, but this . . . Seriously, what could he do? Storm out of his own office? Tell her to get lost, convince her she was wrong, help her with her non-case? He realised he had no idea how to finish the conversation.

'I have another meeting, but we'll discuss this some other time.'

'No, you don't, and yes, we will.'

She was still calm, self-assured and unwavering. He wondered if she was on medication.

CHAPTER 48

The telecommunications company NewTalkInTown had its headquarters in two yellow-brick buildings in Ballerup between Ring Road 4 and Herlev, an area popularly known as Denmark's Silicon Valley. The Countess parked in a visitor parking bay, and noted to her satisfaction that her patrol car had already arrived. Two uniformed officers were waiting for her alongside their vehicle in the street right next to the car park. She spent ten minutes talking to them, making sure to gesture regularly towards the building in front of them, where curious faces were already pressed against the windowpanes.

Outside the entrance to the main building a group of staff had clustered with their cigarettes. The flower beds to either side of the short flagstone path were littered with cigarette butts; dirty yellow filters at every stage of decay were scattered among vicious-looking firethorn bushes. A man was waiting a short distance from the smokers. He had arrived while she was talking to the officers, so it wasn't hard to guess that he must be her contact. Even from a distance she could sense his nerves. Yet again the performance with the uniformed officers had paid off, the Countess thought, on sparkling form as she introduced herself and shook his hand.

The man was in his early forties, of ordinary build as well as appearance, and his handshake was limp – it was like squeezing a fish. The Countess discreetly wiped her palm on her lower back. He introduced himself and stressed his title, he was the *chief programmer*. Then he took four pieces of paper stapled together from his inside pocket and handed them to her. His hand was shaking. The printout was headed THE CORRECTED DATA, written in a large red font. She flicked through them and saw that the papers consisted of a list of Frode Otto's mobile telephone calls. The list looked familiar except that the Ambassador's telephone number had been replaced by another one. She pointed to the new number:

'This mobile number, is it one of yours?'

'No, that's a Telia number. You need to speak to them if you want to know more.'

'Why was it wrong before?'

The man was sweating as he stuttered his answer.

'Someone changed the code in our printing program. But no one can prove who did it. It's impossible.'

'Are you sure about that?'

His voice rose a few octaves:

'You'll never be able to prove anything, ever!'

She said quietly:

'Then you leave me no choice. You have to come with me now to the station.'

He didn't react to her accusation, merely reiterated that she couldn't prove anything. She took him to her car and spent half an hour cajoling him, threatening him, even trying to appeal to his better judgement, but to no avail.

'You can't prove anything.'

He could barely utter the words, his voice was shaking so badly, yet he kept repeating this. It was like talking to a child. He was sweating and squirming, yet he stuck to his guns.

'You can't prove a thing, no way.'

A brief visit to the chief programmer's line manager didn't help her. The line manager refused, politely but vehemently, to join in any form of questioning of the employee. The Countess returned to Police Headquarters utterly frustrated.

The Hanehoved investigation was grinding to a halt. Konrad Simonsen interviewed the officer who, on 19 March 2008, had taken part in the vehicle check north of Lynge in Nordsjælland. The conversation was relaxed, he liked the man, and the officer tried his very best to remember more than he actually could, which was simply that he had seen an African woman in the back of a car. Possibly an expensive car, and possibly with two men in the front, but he couldn't be sure. His memory of that day was remarkable, something Konrad Simonsen began by asking him about. The officer's explanation was simple and credible. It was his wedding anniversary and purely by chance his wife had been out driving that day and been pulled over so that her car could be more closely examined, though not by him. Their car was an older model, and it had failed its inspection. Later he and his wife had discussed what a terrible way it was to celebrate their anniversary. He could provide no explanation as to why he remembered the African woman, though she obviously stood out due to the colour of her skin.

The officer's statement confirmed the date and the time of the killing, but otherwise wasn't much use, as he couldn't remember any further details. Showing him a reconstruction of the woman's face produced no results. It might be her, it might not, he simply didn't know.

Konrad Simonsen spent an hour with him before he gave up.

All that was left was the different telephone number the Countess had been given during her visit to NewTalkInTown, and a chief programmer and a rapist who both refused to share their knowledge with the police.

The telephone number was their best, if not their only, hope of progressing the case. It was a Telia mobile number and had formed part of a prepaid package deal sold via kiosks and petrol stations as far back as the spring of 2005. There was no information about the customer, of course, and Telia could provide no other information than that it had been topped up on a regular basis – roughly twice a month – usually with a hundred kroner at a time. The top-up cards had mostly been bought in the town of Roskilde, but it was impossible to trace by whom, let alone from which shop.

The Countess let herself into her office and locked the door, something she did only very rarely. Within the major telecommunications providers such as TDC and Telia, she had contacts who, from time to time, would get her information which, strictly speaking, the Homicide Department wasn't entitled to access. It usually required a certain amount of persuasion to convince her resources to deliver, and in this case it required a lot of persuasion. The man she spoke to protested vehemently.

'It means I have to search our whole database to see who was in contact with your number. It's not something you just do at the drop of a hat.'

The Countess understood, and was very grateful.

'And it's bloody well illegal!'

'I only need the names of the three people my number spoke to most frequently. That's all.'

That's all! It was plenty. She laughed and turned up the charm. He called back one hour later, grumpy and curt: only one person had cropped up. However, there had been daily contact, often two or three times a day. The Countess got the name and thanked him profusely. He hung up on her.

CHAPTER 49

It is a fact that hypochondriacs love reading doctors' advice columns in newspapers and that people with a fear of flying are regular viewers of TV programmes about plane crashes. So it was with Svend Lerche. His favourite hate figure was Helena Holt Andersen, a politician who had spent the past decade campaigning to introduce in Denmark a law, like the ones that had already been introduced in Norway and Sweden, that would ban paying for sex by criminalising the customers rather than the prostitutes. A law which, if passed, would utterly destroy Svend Lerche's lucrative business. No customers for Karina Larsen's African au pair girls meant no dirty money for the Poker Academy to launder, which in the best-case scenario would make him even more dependent on Bjarne Fabricius than he already was. In the worst-case scenario, he would have to shut up shop.

Helena Holt Andersen was taking part in a round-table discussion on the television debate programme *Deadline*. She had participated in such debates before, and every time she did, Svend Lerche would be ready and waiting in front of the television in a state of rising agitation. Karina Larsen reassured him:

'Don't worry about it, Svend. The Danes will always want to buy pussy, no politician can change that.'

Svend Lerche poured himself a whisky, his second in thirty minutes. He looked at his daughter, sitting in an armchair to his right, and pointed at the bottle. Benedikte Lerche-Larsen shook her head. Then he lectured his wife in a belligerent voice:

'It's not a question of what the Danes want, it's a question of what the government wants. That stupid cow will get her way in the end.'

'But they can't make a law if people are against it.'

Benedikte Lerche-Larsen took over from her father and said in honeyed tones:

'Oh, yes, Mother dear, they really can.'

She never missed an opportunity to observe her father when he was watching Helena Holt Andersen. She had come downstairs an hour earlier in order not to lose out on the fun, and her chair was strategically placed so that she could see both the television and Svend Lerche. He was perfectly aware that she was there only to savour his outrage, but he tolerated her presence nevertheless as she was a far better audience for his antagonism than his wife, who didn't understand even the most basic social mechanisms. Now he snapped at his daughter.

'What the hell are you going to do if that woman ever gets a majority?'

'A majority where?'

It was Karina Larsen airing her ignorance again; her husband and her daughter both ignored her. Shortly afterwards Benedikte Lerche-Larsen said:

'Our plan should be to buy a floating brothel, a luxury liner in international waters with a fixed schedule of speedboats from Copenhagen, Elsinore and Malmö.'

Karina Larsen swallowed the bait immediately. She burst out in excitement:

'What a brilliant idea, Svend, don't you think? That means we'll have a boat, I've always wanted a boat.'

'Well, that's agreed then. I'll request an opinion from the Faculty of Law regarding international legal issues. We can begin trading in a few weeks. Perhaps you should start shopping around for cheap life-jackets and a ship, Mum.'

'Stop that nonsense, Benedikte. I'm trying to watch this, look – there she is.'

And there she was. The programme had started with footage from an area described as Copenhagen's red-light district: a young woman in a tight miniskirt and high heels tottered up and down a rainy pavement as the viewers were fed statistics. There were three hundred thousand men in Denmark who regularly or often paid for sex. Denmark's neighbours, Norway and Sweden, had both made paying for sex a criminal offence. Every year traffickers made millions importing women from other parts of the world into Europe. More dull facts followed, all the stuff people pretty much knew already. Finally the teaser ended, and a camera zoomed in on Helena Holt Andersen, while the studio host opened a debate by stressing its importance in a professionally engaged tone of voice. Svend Lerche hissed:

'Arrogant, self-righteous cow.'

'Who is the other one, Svend? Is she another politician?'

'She represents your imported workers, Mum. She's a former hooker, just like you.'

When Benedikte Lerche-Larsen returned to her own flat, she called Bjarne Fabricius and gave him her weekly update. She concluded with her father's rage at the TV debate and Helena Holt Andersen, and chuckled while she told him about it. Bjarne Fabricius, however, didn't laugh. On the contrary, he asked in a cold voice:

'Is Svend losing his grip, is that what you're telling me?'

'Not at all. She just touched a nerve, she and the Revenue are his pet hates.'

'And what's he going to do about it?'

Benedikte Lerche-Larsen replied pensively:

'Nothing, I presume. What can he do?'

'Exactly what you say, nothing. Otherwise we have a situation. A serious situation, I expect him to understand that.'

'Of course. He's not stupid, just angry.'

Bjarne Fabricius reiterated his demands, and they went round in circles. The amusement of earlier had long since evaporated, and she had at least an hour's homework to do before tomorrow's lessons.

CHAPTER 50

Henrik Krag and his mates were watching football, a delayed broadcast of today's match at Anfield between Liverpool and Manchester United. A vital match if you were a supporter of one of the two clubs, which divided the four men neatly. The flat echoed with outbursts, cheers and sympathetic cries; at stake was the right to humiliate and mock the other two for the next six months, before the next clash between the two arch rivals. At half-time events on the field were discussed.

'I don't get why they have a fifteen-minute break when it's recorded. That's bloody stupid.'

'Shit, we were this close to scoring. Pass me a beer, will you?'

'Why the long face, Henrik, do you already know the final score? Did your crap team lose again?'

Henrik Krag denied this. Then he glanced at his beer supply, which had diminished considerably.

'How about one of you goes and gets some more beers? Or we'll run out.'

All three guests appreciated the gravity of the situation, and one of the group, who lived in the neighbouring block, got up. He soon returned with six beers and Benedikte Lerche-Larsen.

Henrik Krag was torn, but football won out. This became clear when the second half started and his friends' attention focused once more on the screen, as did his. However, his unexpected guest took her defeat on the chin, something that surprised him. The need to be the centre of attention was normally one of Benedikte Lerche-Larsen's more obvious characteristics. But not tonight it would appear. She stood still for a moment, looked around, then she shrugged her shoulders to signal that she knew when she was beaten, before unlacing her boots and kicking them off. From the coffee table she snatched a red and white scarf before flopping down on the sofa, where the seat vacated by the beer fetcher had yet to be occupied. She rested her head in Henrik Krag's lap, he put a scatter cushion under it and let her stay there. But during a pause in the game, he said in a low voice:

'I haven't received my task yet, if that's why you're here?'

She whispered back to him:

'I'm here because I want to be here, and I don't want to hear about your task until you've done it.'

'I'm not allowed to say anything?'

'No, and he'll probably tell you that. He said that to me the second time.'

'But no one'll ever know if I tell you.'

She shook her head firmly.

'Wake me up when you've finished your boring game.'

Then she folded the scarf and placed it over her head, cutting off any further communication.

The friends' traditional match post-mortem was suspended in light of Henrik Krag's latest arrival. The three friends restricted themselves to small talk and the winning team's two supporters refrained from major trash talk. Nor were there any crude remarks or telling grimaces. Henrik Krag removed the scarf from Benedikte Lerche-Larsen's face, and half-heartedly shook her a couple of times with no effect other than her clasping his hand, turning over onto her stomach and burying her face in the cushion. He let her sleep and at his request a friend fetched a duvet, which Henrik covered her with. The others said goodbye more with gestures than with words, and turned off the light as they left.

He sat quietly enjoying the moment, determined to stay awake. Perhaps he could stroke her hair later, carefully, very carefully, once he was absolutely sure that she was fast asleep. Or even better – smell her perfume, preferably on her neck, if he dared. His bold intentions made him close his eyes, and his hopes mixed with thoughts he couldn't control. Soon he too nodded off.

He woke up with a jolt when Benedikte turned onto her side, dragging his hand with her. She clutched it like a comforter and he could feel the warmth from her breast against his knuckles. A crescent moon hung at the top of his window and its faint light showed him the contours of her face. Carefully, he let his finger trace first her forehead, then her temple, her cheekbone, the bridge of her nose, her lips. And back again. Her breathing was deep; from time to time she wrinkled her nose and he would pause his stroking, but her unrest soon stopped. He thought how different she was from all the other girls he had ever known, and would probably ever know. Different, unobtainable, remote, and yet here she was lying next to him, alive and beautiful, how incredible it was. He reached out his hand to stroke her again, but she turned over onto her back at that same moment.

He froze when she pressed his palm against her breast, an anxious voice sounding the alarm inside him as adrenaline surged through his veins. He quickly closed his hand around two of her fingers, scared that she might wake up and think he was touching her while she was asleep. The thought made him blush and he almost apologised to her, but managed to stop himself in time.

Their thumbs accidentally brushed against one another, fingertip to fingertip; he removed his, only to find that hers followed. He did it again – with the same result. Wordless communication or random reactions? Tentatively he stretched out his forefinger, which was met by hers. His thumb, then his forefinger and also his little finger was answered. It was not until then that he saw it: the crinkling of a smile on her lips and around her closed eyes. His hand found courage. She helped him unbutton her blouse and remove her bra. Then he slid himself in beside her and felt how she arched her back, quivering at his hand's still hesitant journey, her Brazilian flanked by smooth shaven skin, neural paths exploding in his brain, soft warmth, moisture outside and in. Urgency as they clumsily fumbled to remove their clothing. He lay on top of her – their very first kiss, greedy, hungry – and then . . .

Then nothing!

Nothing except humiliating detumescence, an incomprehensible betrayal by his own body.

He sat up at her feet in black eternity, letting the cold punish him. Eventually she pulled him down next to her and shared her duvet with him. He muttered something, but her hand stopped his words and she patted his cheek softly. They lay like this for a long time, then she turned her head and whispered into his ear:

'When dreams come true, they can be hard to control.'

Her voice was tender, almost comforting.

She rose and got dressed; he stayed where he was, not caring about anything, including her leaving. Instead, though, she fetched a cushion and sat down. Their roles had been reversed, now his head was in her lap. For a while she stroked him affectionately, gently, as though he were a child. Finally she nudged him on the nose with her thumb. Then she spoke quietly.

'There's another explanation, Henrik. I can feel it. And don't blame yourself, it has happened before; it can be like this the first time between me and some men. Usually the ones who really care about me.'

He made no reply, and she continued speaking.

'When I was four or five years old, my father played a game with me. He lifted me up on our dining table and stood a short distance away, holding out his arms towards me. Then he told me to jump. He said he would definitely catch me, that there was nothing to be scared of, that he would take care of me. It was dangerous, it was a long way down, but eventually . . .'

He could feel her body tense and when the pause grew too long, asked cautiously:

'And what happened, did you jump?'

'*Never trust anyone, Benedikte, no matter who it is.* That's what he told me when I'd stopped crying. And he made me repeat it. *Never trust anyone, no matter who it is.* The next time it took even more persuasion before I decided that today must be a special day and he would catch me, as he'd promised. But I learned my lesson eventually. No matter what he tried to make me believe, I wouldn't jump. My mother praised me to the skies, he didn't.'

'What an arsehole! Are you scared of him?'

'Only in my dreams.'

There was another long silence, then she spoke again.

'I'm at one of those old-fashioned inns you find in the forest. People are sitting outdoors on benches enjoying the fine weather. Ordinary people, mostly peasants with their well-behaved children, boys in sailor suits, girls with red ribbons in their pigtails. The tables are decorated with simple blue-and-white gingham tablecloths, strings of coloured lights have been trailed across the yard for the evening and, outside the picket fence, a cart drawn by two shire horses rolls down the road. A black dog wags its tail. Everyone is having a nice time . . . the locals drink beer from large tankards, a couple of foreign tourists, who don't really fit in, drink wine.'

'You really remember your dreams, I'm impressed.'

'I've dreamed it many times and the start is always the best. A young man gets up to sing. He looks so blond and so right in his light-coloured cotton shirt, his leather belt tight around his waist, such white teeth . . . and he has a black scout scarf around his neck. His voice is loud and clear, he's singing from memory and it's as if he sings only to me, a wonderful, uplifting song about the future. And then this amazing thing happens – everyone is carried away by the situation, young and old, and one by one they stand up until everyone is singing in unison. Me too, I'm one of the first voices to join in. Now we're one big community. Even the stern-looking woman by my side, wearing a royal blue jacket and skirt and matching hat, has surrendered. Only an old, decrepit worker with glasses and wrinkles stays sitting down. It doesn't matter, he can barely raise his own tankard, we don't need him. The boy salutes his audience politely, as he sings the last notes, and people salute him back. I have a wonderful sense of calm all over, I believe that tomorrow belongs to me and everything looks bright.'

'That sounds like a nice dream, I wouldn't mind dreaming that.'

'It is a nice dream, until my father arrives, and he does that now. Suddenly, just as I'm feeling really good about everything, he arrives. In a terrifying disguise, his face made up all white with black eyebrows that end in a pointed triangle as though he has horns. Half devil and half clown. I hate clowns, you know. And he just sits there, smiling diabolically at me because he knows . . . he knows that I will fall and hurt myself. All my joy disappears, and my knees and elbows ache.'

Henrik Krag pushed himself up onto one elbow next to her.

'Is that why you're so toxic sometimes?'

'What do you mean? Am I?'

She sounded genuinely astonished.

'Yes.'

'I don't think I can bear to be betrayed. Jan told me so, and he has known me ever since I was a little girl. I think he was right.'

'Jan Podowski?'

'The very same.'

'Do you miss him?'

'I do sometimes. It's strange, him not being here. Wrong, almost.'

'I won't ever let you down.'

'Promise me.'

He repeated it.

The tears were rolling down her cheeks. One dripped from her chin and landed on Henrik Krag's hand. He sat up and carefully kissed her eyelids, first one, then her nose, then the other eyelid. She tasted of salt, expensive perfumed salt. Then he held her tight, and almost started crying himself, even though the whole thing was ridiculous.

CHAPTER 51

'We can't ostracise people with mental-health issues from society, just because it's more convenient for the rest of us. And I'm glad that senior management has taken the position it has. You and Simon can throw all your toys out of the pram, it won't make any difference, Pauline stays where she is. And thank God for that.'

The Countess emphasised her statement by hitting both palms lightly against the steering wheel, glancing sideways at Arne Pedersen, who was in the passenger seat. They had been bickering for most of the trip, not seriously, but enough for the mood between them to be strained. As usual the bone of contention was Pauline Berg. Arne Pedersen ended their discussion.

'I think we're nearly there.'

And indeed they were. Over the hill ahead they got an excellent view of their destination. The village of Karlslille consisted of eleven houses around a pond. In sunny weather it would probably be deemed scenic. At this very moment, however, it looked grim. Drizzle fell from a depressing grey sky.

At the bottom of the hill, the Countess turned right soon after the road sign bearing the name of the village, and shortly afterwards took another right before parking in front of a two-storey house, set back a little from the road. It was the former village school, red-brick, with '1903' carved in relief over the front door. The Countess got out of the car and surveyed the building. It had a dark grey slate roof. Ivy scaled the drainpipe on the gable end and reached across the gutter. From where she was standing, the back garden was, as far as she could see, very small compared to the size of the house, and enclosed by a sturdy fence. Arne Pedersen urged her on with a curt, 'Are you coming?' So she stayed a little longer than necessary to remind him that she wasn't someone you could boss around.

The woman who opened the door was beautiful. She was slim and of medium height, with a face that evoked ancient Greek statues. Her silver hair reached her shoulders and billowed around her. Her age was difficult to determine. The Countess guessed her to be around fifty, but she could be older. It took a few seconds for the officers to notice the milky membrane across her eyes. She was blind.

'Who is it?'

The voice was dark, a little rough and very obliging, and Arne Pedersen had time to think how remarkable that was, given her vulnerability, when another face appeared in the doorway. Both officers immediately took a step back, it was impossible not to.

The dog was enormous; it watched the officers with its heavy-lidded eyes, neither aggressive nor friendly.

The Countess introduced them.

'Are you Silje Esper?'

The woman confirmed this and agreed to talk to them, without however initially inviting them in.

'Do you have any ID? I would like to see that, please.'

She used the word 'see', and held out her hand. The Countess found her badge and a business card, which she placed in the woman's hand. She ran her fingertips over them and took her time, before returning the items.

'I've forgotten my ID. I apologise,' said Arne Pedersen.

The woman gave them a beautiful smile; it didn't matter, one badge would suffice. Then she opened the door and uttered a short and commanding *stay* to the dog. It instantly changed its demeanour and wagged its tail.

'Don't be scared of Mads, he won't hurt you. If he nudges you, just swat him across his nose.'

They followed her through a utility room and a kitchen-diner. Mads followed last and did indeed nudge Arne Pedersen in the back a couple of times. Or between my shoulder blades, as he would later tell it when they returned to the Homicide Department, but that really was an exaggeration. Even so, he felt no urge to swat Mads as the dog's owner had invited him to.

They entered the living room where Silje Esper offered them the sofa, while she herself sat down in an armchair opposite them. Mads settled down in a corner with his head between his paws and appeared to doze off. The Countess used the dog to open the conversation:

'Some pet you've got there. I've never seen a dog so big. What breed is he? I don't recognise it.'

'He's a cross between a Briard and a Great Dane, and you're right, he's remarkably big, but he's the nicest dog in the world. He looks after his pack, that's why he sometimes nudges people. He likes his pack to stay together, it's in his genes.'

Arne Pedersen asked tentatively:

'And what if you're not a member of his pack?'

The answer was blunt.

'If you're an enemy, I mean someone threatening his pack, he'll kill you if he can. But that's enough about Mads. I imagine you're here because of Philip.'

'What is Philip's surname?'

She answered Arne Pedersen after a slight hesitation. Philip Sander, that was his full name. But now it was their turn to talk.

The Countess explained how they had come across her telephone number through calls made to and from another number. She also briefly summarised the Hanehoved investigation as well as the burning of the hunting lodge and the building of the new one. Silje Esper listened without interruption. When the Countess had finished, she sat for a while staring into space. Neither of the officers interrupted her reverie, but Mads half opened one eye, as if he could sense tension in his pack.

'I've been expecting this conversation for many years, twelve, almost thirteen, to be exact.'

Her story was surprising. Philip Sander was her boyfriend, they had lived together for more than seven years, and she recognised the telephone number immediately as she had called it often. So far, so normal, but from then on their relationship was anything but.

'Philip lived two lives, which he kept completely separate. One here with me, and one I know nothing about. Right from our first meeting, which took place in a bank and is an awful story with a happy ending that I can tell you about another day, he made it clear that his job and what he did in general when he wasn't with me, wasn't something he wanted to share. *Two worlds, it's better this way.* I remember him saying that so clearly. That was in the beginning. Later I grew used to it, and then I stopped asking.'

The Countess said suspiciously:

'That sounds very . . . unusual.'

'It was unusual.'

'You say *was*, why the past tense? Doesn't Philip live here any more?'

'I think he's dead. Or in prison or in hospital, but sadly . . . I can feel that he's no longer here.'

The Countess had at least twenty questions, each more pressing than the others and almost impossible to articulate. Arne Pedersen beat her to it.

'How would you feel about coming with us to Police Headquarters in Copenhagen? We'll drive you back afterwards, obviously, but we have so many questions we would like to ask you.'

Silje Esper shook her head firmly. No, thank you. She didn't like strange places. However, they were free to come here as often as they liked, and she would be as helpful as she could, though it was bound to be difficult.

'What would be difficult?' the Countess asked.

'Finding out Philip's real name. I presume that's what you want to know.'

Konrad Simonsen was squabbling with his wife and Arne Pedersen. He was far from happy with the result of their trip to Karlslille. A dissatisfaction he shared with Klavs Arnold and Pauline Berg.

'Didn't you even find out when Philip Sander stopped coming home?'

Pauline Berg added:

'I don't believe her for a minute. Why didn't you just bring her in?'

The Countess came to Arne Pedersen's rescue, raising her voice, a rare occurrence. She lectured Pauline Berg:

'Because we can't just bring people in if they don't want to come and haven't done anything illegal. I would have thought they'd taught you that at the police academy.'

Then she turned to her husband.

'You can ask her yourself, when we go back. Because we will go back, of course we will, Arne and I have known that all along. Now, the pair of you, shut up and let us tell you what little we did find out.'

Malte Borup opened the door to the office, but hesitated in the doorway. He was ultra-sensitive to tension among those closest to Konrad Simonsen, and when he sensed things were out of kilter, he would disappear. Either into a computer program or physically, if he got the chance. The Countess encouraged him to stay with a brief 'Yes?' He quickly explained that of the seven men in Denmark aged between forty and sixty called Philip Sander, but at first sight there would not appear to be anyone who could be suspected of spending half their life in Karlslille. Nor had anyone of that name died in the last three years. He left and the detectives took the information on board; it was what they had been expecting, although not what they had been hoping for.

The intern's interruption had poured oil on troubled waters, and the Countess was allowed to summarise the few facts she had gathered.

Sander had lived with Silje Esper since 2002, but his postal address wasn't in Karlslille. Perhaps he had a bedsit somewhere or maybe just a PO box, his girlfriend didn't know. During their initial search of her house, they found several items belonging to him, but so far no personal papers. Silje Esper estimated Sander's age to be around fifty-five years, and she was fairly certain of that, but didn't know precisely how old her boyfriend was. Furthermore, he had grown up in Copenhagen, but again she didn't know precisely where. Likewise she knew that he had taken final school exams, but not at which college. She didn't think he'd had any higher education.

Klavs Arnold interrupted her irritably:

'What about his bloody job? She can't live with a man for—'

Arne Pedersen repaid the Countess's support from earlier.

'Shut up, Klavs, and let her talk.'

'Philip Sander has a job, presumably the same job he has had for the last seven years. But Silje Esper doesn't know where, only that it's relatively well-paid, and that his hours are often irregular. He doesn't own a car and tends to borrow hers when he goes to work in the morning. It explains why she has one, because she obviously can't drive it herself, but when he uses it, he parks at Roskilde Station and takes the train. He has two mobile phones, one for private use, that's the number we know, and one he uses for work only. She doesn't know the number of the latter, only that the SIM card is frequently replaced.'

The Countess paused, clearly thinking something through. Everyone looked at Simonsen, as would often happen when the group was divided. He grunted and scratched his temple with a knuckle.

'Silje Esper doesn't come across as a very curious person?'

The Countess answered.

'At the start of their relationship, she feared that her boyfriend might have another woman, perhaps even a whole family on the side. Back then she was both jealous and curious. But today she's convinced that isn't the case. She believes that the reason for the arrangement was because for all those years Philip Sander has wanted a place unknown to his employer. A sanctuary he can retire to on a daily as well as a permanent basis, should it become necessary. She also believes that he's involved in criminal activities, without being able to specify which ones or expand on her suspicion. The bottom line is that for many years she has supported the way he has organised his life. Largely by deliberately avoiding gaining knowledge about any part of her boyfriend's life that doesn't involve her.'

'You're saying he had a place to hide – you mean from us or from his colleagues?'

'Both, she thinks.'

Konrad Simonsen grunted again and repeated the same gesture as before, only with the other hand.

'But she's willing to work with us to find out his real identity?'

'So she says.'

'Do you believe her?'

'Yes.'

CHAPTER 52

Living in Denmark without the authorities knowing your name, your address or your job isn't easy. But not impossible.

It's an absolutely essential requirement that you don't receive government benefits of any kind. You have to be financially self-sufficient. If you have a job, you need to be paid in cash, and if you're living off your fortune, it must be kept in cash. Nor is it possible to own property or a vehicle.

Philip Sander fulfilled all these conditions. However, alongside his life in Karlslille with Silje Esper, he had his true identity, the one the police were looking for, so he couldn't be said to live completely off the grid.

The day after the Countess and Arne Pedersen's visit, Konrad Simonsen turned up at Silje Esper's house with a team of twelve officers, including the Countess.

The Homicide Department chief's irritation from yesterday had long since evaporated. Partly because he was sure he would discover Philip Sander's real identity fairly soon, and partly because he was delighted at finally having some real police work to do. He had tasked Arne Pedersen and Klavs Arnold with looking for Danish men in the relevant age group who had died, been admitted to hospital or sent to prison in recent months. Initially the two officers only had to come up with a rough estimate. Later, as a Plan B, this might become a line of inquiry to follow up. That left Pauline Berg at a loose end, but Konrad Simonsen had been unable to contact her; she didn't pick up her phone, nor had she turned up for work. A situation he was forced to accept, so that was what he did.

The plan was that the Countess would be in charge of the officers searching the property for any evidence that might reveal Philip Sander's real name. Konrad Simonsen himself would interview Silje Esper in order to form an impression of the woman, but also to get answers to the long list of questions he had brought with him.

As the Countess had predicted, Silje Esper was fully co-operative. She didn't mind her home being searched as long as the officers tidied up afterwards. That was a stroke of luck because Simonsen didn't have a warrant, nor in all likelihood would he have been able to get one. He promised that all of his staff would take care when carrying out the search, and on the Countess's instructions the officers were divided into pairs to comb the various rooms. Mads the dog helped the Countess keep the guests in check. He shuttled from room to room, checking everything was as it should be before continuing his inspection. The pack were scattered, but not under threat.

Konrad Simonsen and Silje Esper went outside to where the dog run was bounded by a two-metre high fence, recently painted red, apart from three to four metres where the old, peeling and grimy white paint still remained. The fence provided shelter. At the woman's recommendation, Konrad Simonsen opened his umbrella against the spitting rain, and they sat down on a couple of garden chairs next to a small table. He took out his Dictaphone and pressed Record.

Silje Esper's hearing was bat-like:

'What are you doing?'

Konrad Simonsen explained.

'You could have told me in advance.'

He apologised, she acknowledged this, and the interview began.

It was a long conversation, lasting almost two hours, but the result most certainly didn't match the effort invested. Konrad Simonsen learned very little actual information.

'You own a car, why?'

'Mostly for Philip's sake. But also for use at the weekends – we often drive to concerts, sometimes in Jutland, or on Funen.'

Fifteen minutes later.

'Does your boyfriend have friends, acquaintances or family that you know of?'

'No, not that I am aware of. I think he had a sister, but she has never been here.'

Nor did the blind woman know very much about her boyfriend's work.

'You suspect Philip Sander of being involved in criminal activities. Why?'

'He was paid his monthly salary in cash, that suggests something illegal. I don't know what, possibly smuggling of some sort.'

'Drugs, cigarettes, alcohol, bootleg goods, human trafficking?'

'Not drugs, I'm sure of that. Possibly alcohol. Like I said, he did drink heavily.'

'Does he have any convictions?'

'I don't know, but I don't think so.'

Konrad Simonsen took a break from the interview and when he resumed it, carried on asking for information that might lead to the identity of Philip Sander. But again there was nothing to be gained.

'Does your boyfriend have a Dankort or any kind of debit or credit card?'

'No. He deliberately avoided things like that. For example, he would always use my card to take books out of the library.'

'What about fines or other police contact while he drove your car?'

'Never. He was very careful to make sure something like that never happened. We have Brobizz transponders to pay for crossing the Storebælt and Øresund bridges, but they're both in my name.'

'You think that your boyfriend is dead. Why do you think that?'

'Because he hasn't come home, of course. And then it's a feeling I have. Besides, he lived a hard life, as I told you earlier.'

Silje Esper smiled apologetically, aware she wasn't being much help. Konrad Simonsen shook his head in frustration and tried again.

'Can you think of anywhere we might find a picture of him? Doesn't matter if it's new or old.'

'Definitely not, that was precisely one of the things he tried to avoid at all costs.'

By this point Konrad Simonsen's hopes of discovering anything of significance had plummeted considerably. He decided to change tack and take an interest in the woman rather than her boyfriend.

'Tell me about yourself. How do you manage on a day–to-day basis? Do you have help?'

'As little as possible, but the cleaner turns up Mondays and Thursdays, and meals are delivered by the council, ready for the microwave. They taste fine, by the way. I do my shopping by phone, and then it's delivered to my home. Of course, there are some problems, especially now that Philip is . . . gone. Would you like to hear about them?'

Konrad Simonsen shook his head, but checked himself.

'No, but please tell me about your personal finances. You have expensive things in your home. For example, I noticed a B&O television.'

She smiled at him.

'Yes, that's right. The television was mostly for Philip's sake, although I like listening to it from time to time, I enjoy current affairs. But my personal finances are in great shape, I have quite a lot of money in the bank. Not too much money, just enough.'

'Are you prepared to tell me how much?'

'More than four and a half million kroner, as well as some investments and shareholdings, but I don't know precisely how much they're worth.'

'That's a hefty sum.'

He didn't need to ask the question. She smiled again, modestly this time, and explained: she was a potter and had been one of the best-selling ones in Denmark for many years. She corrected herself: not just one of the best-selling, but *the* best-selling. She had specialised in studio pottery, which she had primarily sold to two buyers in Germany. A year ago she had stopped production and was now working only for the fun of it. But if he wanted to, he could go upstairs and visit her studio on the first floor.

'Today I mostly make mythical beasts as ornaments for gardens, and there's no money in that, but it doesn't matter as long as I enjoy making them. And I do. It's much more fun than making the same pot over and over again. Now it's more of a hobby than a job. I should have done it years ago.'

'Why didn't you?'

She paused before she replied.

'I think I was too greedy. When I finally started making money out of my pots, and believe me, there were many years when I didn't, well, somehow I couldn't get enough. It turned into a small industry, but that's not the point of pottery. It's a craft, it may even be an art, but it's definitely not an industry.'

The Countess opened the terrace door. It had been left ajar and was well oiled, yet Silje Esper immediately turned her head in that direction. The blind woman's hearing was particularly well developed. The Countess shook her head at Konrad Simonsen. They hadn't found anything that could lead them to Philip Sander's true identity. Simonsen threw up his hands in regret and asked Silje Esper his last few questions.

'Do you have children?'

'A daughter in Caen in northern France, I tend to visit her twice a year. Apart from that I have no other family. My father died a few years ago, he was a retired accountant. My mother has been dead for many years.'

'Have you always been blind?'

'No, I haven't. In 1996 I was in a car accident. It was near Næstved, and it wasn't my fault. To begin with I was bitter; it was a difficult time. But today I regard my blindness as a gift. If the accident hadn't happened, I would never have realised what hides inside the clay. It's hard to make others understand, but that's how it is. It's a gift.'

In the car going back to Copenhagen, Konrad Simonsen asked the Countess:

'What about fingerprints, didn't we find any of them either?'

'Yes, plenty of prints, but no identity papers.'

'Then we have to hope he's on our register. Otherwise we're none the wiser.'

She made no reply, none was needed. Instead she ventured:

'I just don't believe that she could have lived with a man for seven years without him at some point or other accidentally letting slip who he is or what he does for a living. Maybe not directly, but a tiny clue, possibly more, which can lead to . . .' She let the sentence hang in the air, but then added shortly afterwards: 'I just don't believe there was nothing.'

'That's how they would appear to have agreed to live.'

'Yes, they did. But no, it's not possible. If those prints don't produce a result, I'll go back and spend some time with her. After all, she's happy to co-operate. And I have another idea.'

She told him that she had seen busts of several different people in the blind woman's studio, and they were good likenesses. She corrected herself.

'I mean, they were lifelike. Seemed a true representation, if I can put it like that. I can't tell if the likenesses were any good, of course.'

'You want her to sculpt Philip Sander?'

'Precisely.'

'For what purpose?'

She explained: they could have Sander's face drawn or photographed and then show it to the commuters on trains departing from Roskilde Station around nine o'clock in the morning, the time he usually caught his train to work. Many commuters travelled at regular times, so it was likely that someone would recognise the man and know where he was going, or even what his name was.

When Konrad Simonsen looked sceptical, she added:

'If nothing else, it's far cheaper than tracking down all relatives of men in their fifties who have died in recent months. Because that really would send our budget into free fall.'

They drove on for a while. He wasn't convinced of the validity of her financial argument. And yet he decided to back it.

CHAPTER 53

The Countess spent three days with the blind potter and her dog. The two women got on well, and they covered many topics in their conversations, which the Countess, very deliberately, tried not to limit to matters pertaining only to Philip Sander. It meant that information about the man was gathered slowly, but gathered it was. For example, he had definitely been an alcoholic, obese and suffering from severe respiratory problems, for which he took medication. Several different types, every morning after coffee. He also used an inhaler; it was possible that he suffered from emphysema. The next day the Countess asked:

'Symbicort or Spiriva? Those are the capsules you inhale.'

Silje Esper shook her head, she didn't know.

'Amlodipine, Corodil – those are the most common drugs to reduce high blood pressure.'

'I don't know; those names are impossible to remember, though I think he actually did tell me. But some of the pills were pink, so he told me. And others were black. If that's any help.'

It wasn't much help, of course. And the same applied to Silje's story of how she had originally met her boyfriend. Nevertheless, the Countess listened with interest.

They had both been queueing inside Nordea Bank in Roskilde when she had dropped her Dankort debit card, which she had been holding in her hand. Philip Sander had picked it up in order to be helpful, but the dog she'd had at the time had bitten him. Silje laughed.

'That dog was crazy, it really was, and in the end it had to be put down. However, it was just as well that it did attack on this occasion or I would never have met Philip.'

The Countess made a note that Philip Sander might possibly have an account with Nordea Bank in Roskilde. Then she glanced at the dog, which was sleeping at her feet.

'That sounds serious, not to say dangerous.'

'Oh, no. My old dog was an Alsatian. Of course it was painful, Philip needed four stitches. But it was nothing compared to being attacked by Mads.'

Yet again the Countess marvelled at the woman's ability to sense what she was thinking, where she was looking and when. It was astonishing. She scratched Mads behind the ear. Truly astonishing.

Silje Esper embraced the idea of a bust of her boyfriend, and worked on it for more than five hours in her studio before she was satisfied. The Countess followed the creation, which was a fascinating process. In thirty minutes Silje Esper had shaped a face that seemed exceedingly lifelike, although she herself was far from pleased with it. She spent the following four hours on minor alterations that individually were barely noticeable, but together, as the time passed, made the clay face more and more convincing. There was something touching about the blind woman sitting at her work table, with her sightless eyes aimed at the ceiling, remembering her missing boyfriend, then tweaking his cheek, his neck, the root of his nose, with her clay-covered fingers ... everywhere, everything to perfection.

Meanwhile, the Countess made herself useful. She now moved around the woman's house with familiar ease: she prepared lunch in the kitchen downstairs for both of them, fetched fresh water for the clay or fed Mads from the sack of biscuits behind the door in the utility room. Finally Silje Esper said:

'I'm done.'

The Countess praised the result and called a photographer.

'I haven't shown you what he looks like to me, or he would have been completely different.'

'What do you mean?'

'That this task has been about craft, not art. Art isn't a recreation of reality, it's an interpretation of it.'

'How would you have made him, if you had *interpreted* him?'

She explained with her hands, as if holding up a scoop of sand and letting it trickle out between her fingers.

'More striving, like the way Chopin achieves brilliance for piano when the right hand plays only on the black keys. But Philip makes me sad, even though the clay wants something optimistic, something life-affirming. I miss him too much, I wouldn't be able to sculpt him properly, not yet.'

It was the first time that the Countess had heard her say that she missed her boyfriend. Silje Esper laughed, as usual aware of what the other woman was thinking.

'Yes, that's the way it is, but enough of that. Don't you think the two of us deserve a beer now? Or would you rather have some fresh coffee?'

It was rare for the Countess to drink beer twice in one week. Not because she objected to it, but because she preferred wine, and besides, she rarely drank.

The evening was light and mild. The few men from the village had gathered at the bench by the pond with a beer or two, to rehash today's events. It was a tradition in Karlslille in the summer months and a good tradition, if you asked the men – it was always time for a beer, and there was plenty to talk about. There was Skipper Thorkil's son, the lad had inherited his father's trawler and, imagine, had caught a WW2 mine in his nets last week. That old junk just kept turning up. The men nodded their agreement, although none of them had ever set foot on a fishing boat, let alone worked with nets. But it was a good story, as was the next one ... and the one after that. The Countess had to listen and react, laugh in the right places, look serious when it was the time for that. Her presence was received kindly, but she was firmly ignored. It was the men's way of showing her that she mustn't think people in Karlslille were impressed just because she was a Homicide investigator from Copenhagen.

There was rumbling in the distance. A bluish flash lit up the forest to the west, while the sky grew ominously dark, although the sun still illuminated the farms on the horizon and gave their contours a reddish, almost golden glow. The Countess cleared her throat during a lull in the conversation. She had done that earlier to no avail, but now she took another step into the circle of men, insistent, bordering on rude. The alternative was a good soaking. Her car was parked outside Silje Esper's house on the outskirts of the village, and the thunderstorm was fast approaching. The men fell silent. After all, they were intrigued, and they didn't want to finish their chat in the rain either.

Silje Esper worked the clay. She had a professional turntable with a wireless foot pedal and adjustable speeds of rotation, but it was hidden away in a corner in favour of an old-fashioned clay turntable, where her feet had to do the work with the treadle at the bottom. She was starting to shape the pot and her face was focused, as though she were listening to the clay. Admirable when you remembered she had made thousands of those pots and it had long since become routine. Nevertheless, she gave the process her full attention.

The Countess had walked around to the back of the house and entered through the French doors. The blind woman had suggested it: no need to ring the bell, not now she knew her way around. Mads got up when she entered the studio. His guest patted him, whereupon he returned to his corner and settled down, soothed by the monotonous sound of the spinning turntable. It was morning, and the Countess's sixth visit to Karlslille. Silje Esper greeted her.

'What terrible weather we had last night, did you get home all right?'

The Countess confirmed that she had, although she had had to pull over on the roadside for a few minutes, when the storm was at its worst. Without asking she helped herself to a cup of coffee from the Thermos flask on the table at the back of the room, and sat down on a chair. She kept her handbag on her lap.

'Are you working on my pot?'

'I am. It'll be ready the day after tomorrow, then you can take it home.'

'Is it the same kind you sold to Germany?'

'It's slightly smaller, but otherwise yes.'

'Remind me again how much you used to get for them?'

'Towards the end almost four thousand Euro each.'

'That's a lot of money.'

'They were sold as art in expensive shops all across northern Germany and in the Netherlands and Belgium.'

'Wow, that's incredible. And indeed it is a lie: you've added a zero. At least.'

Silje Esper let go of the clay and stopped moving her legs, the turntable slowed down before grinding to a halt. The blind woman turned to her guest with a face the Countess had never seen before. A hard, hateful expression had replaced the usual benign air. Silje snapped a short, incomprehensible order to her dog. Mads sprang up as if he had been given an electric shock and stood with his ears back and every muscle tensed. He focused on the Countess and growled, awaiting his next order. Silje Esper hissed:

'Who have you been talking to?'

'Your two German suppliers . . .'

Silje interrupted angrily.

'I mean, which of your colleagues have you been talking to? Wait, what was that noise? Answer me? What was it?'

'It was me releasing the safety catch on my pistol. If your dog takes even a tiny step towards me, I'll put three bullets in its head. And don't think for one moment that I'm working alone, no one in the police does that. All you'll gain from this is a dead dog and a charge of attempted murder, so if I were you, I would think very, very carefully right now.'

Silje Esper took her advice and reached the right conclusion. Her resigned 'Sit' to Mads settled the dog.

'Get him out of here and close the door.'

'How did you find out about me? Was it the money?'

'Partly that, but it was a number of things. Your neighbours didn't recognise the bust you made of your boyfriend, for example. There are other reasons, but we'll talk about them later. Now get that dog out of here.'

The blind woman slammed the door after the dog, and leaned wearily against the wall; she closed her eyes, her head turned upwards, theatrically. The Countess ignored it, and said coldly: 'Give me his name.'

'Jan, his name was Jan, and he's dead.'

'His surname, please!'

'Podowski. Jan Podowski.'

CHAPTER 54

I t was a spring like no other Henrik Krag had ever experienced. Everything was different, beautiful and hideous, wonderful and crazy, out of control like a runaway train, and he had no idea where he would end up. But he was happier than he had ever been. It was because of Benedikte Lerche-Larsen, pretty much everything was because of Benedikte Lerche-Larsen; he thought about her constantly and counted the days or the hours until their next meeting.

There's always next time, was what she had said that lovely, miserable night they had spent together. Since then the sentence had ballooned in his mind while he gradually pushed his humiliation to the back of it. *Next time* . . . It didn't matter so much that his first task was unpleasant. A task that must be got through as quickly as possible, and then forgotten. *Next time, next time* – better to think about that, and he could shout it out into the wind as loud as he wanted to; no one could hear him now while he drove.

Two days previously, Ida had called Henrik Krag to give him his first task:

Skovbrynet Station at the steps leading to the platform. I repeat Skovbrynet Station. A gang of hooligans hang out there, they bother people. You are to give them a thorough beating so they never show their faces there again. Wednesday or Thursday evening is best. You have one week.

Ida had repeated it, although there was no need, he had already understood. When she interrupted him explaining this, he shrugged. It couldn't be helped. He had hoped for a task like Benedikte Lerche-Larsen's, her first one obviously, some kind of volunteering or at least something where no one would get hurt. But it was not to be. He had no hope of negotiating with Ida.

He had checked out the place the same evening he got the message, and found it without any difficulties. Skovbrynet Station turned out to be a small station on the Farum line between Bagsværd and Værløse not far from Ring Road 4. The location wasn't bad, given the nature of his task: far from the nearest houses and well shielded by big concrete pillars, some supporting the railway bridge, others the Hillerød motorway, which crossed close by on an even higher bridge. There were no cameras, except on the platform itself, and in the just under thirty minutes he spent in the area, he counted only sixteen people entering or leaving the station. He didn't see the yobs Ida had referred to in her message, and he wondered why anyone would choose to hang out in such a deserted spot, yet at the same time he trusted that Ida knew what she was talking about. Before he went home, he memorised the train departures in both directions: 02, 22, 42 towards Farum, 03, 23, 43, going to Copenhagen, which was perfect and made 05, 25 and 45 good times to strike.

*

He had picked a complicated route going through Copenhagen, out via Strandvejen to Klampenborg, and then left through Lyngby and onwards to Ballerup on Ring Road 4. He had hoped it would give him time to adjust to his mission, prepare himself mentally, but it was not to be. He thought about Benedikte most of the journey, as usual. He slowed down his motorbike, slowly turned right at Bagsværd just before the lake, then took the first side road, where he stopped and parked.

He had a good look around and noted to his satisfaction that the road was deserted. He took out the baseball bat from his panniers and balanced it in his hand a few times, sensing the weight distribution and the striking power as though he were in a shop and considering buying. It was quite a few years since he had last used it. He unzipped his biker jacket halfway and stuck the bat inside to the left with the broader end tucked in his trousers and the handle diagonally to the right – in less than a second he could raise it to strike. Then he slipped his knuckle-duster onto his left hand, and walked with a confidence he didn't feel down the last short stretch to the station. His earlier thought came back to him: it was just a matter of getting it over with, that was all it was, nothing more.

Henrik Krag walked faster while thinking that he would soon be heading back, and that the youngsters deserved what he was about to do to them. They had been bothering people, that was what Ida had said, and she was probably right.

He knew the type, pissed halfwits, high on lighter fuel, morons shouting out after people, probably the elderly. No, not probably, definitely. Henrik Krag couldn't stand anyone being mean to old people. It made him angry. They should be left alone, not harassed, mocked or pushed about by a gang of noisy thugs. The thugs were about to get a well-deserved kicking as payback for all those old people they had terrified. He tried imagining his grandmother lying helpless in the street, crying, reaching out in vain for her stick. It was difficult, and the image disappeared when the road bent to the right and the station appeared in front of him. He heard laughter – high-pitched, bright girl's laughter. As he got a little closer, he stopped to take in the scene. Two boys were practising on their skateboards, a girl was sitting watching their efforts on the steps leading to the platform while another boy was sitting astride his moped. He, too, was watching the skateboarders. Four teenagers; Henrik Krag had feared there might be more. Now it was four, only four, and that wasn't too bad. Even if one of them was a girl. It could have been worse.

The element of surprise was entirely on Henrik Krag's side, and he made full use of it.

As soon as he was away from the concrete pillar, he pulled out his baseball bat. Five long strides brought him to the young men with the skateboards. He had already picked the bigger as his first opponent. With both hands and as much force as he could produce, he smashed the bat against the boy's collarbone and heard it snap. Then he lashed out at the boy's mate, small and weedy with unwashed blond hair and a back-to-front baseball cap. The bat broke the bone in his upper arm, and a well-aimed kick to his testicles floored him.

Another two paces and Henrik Krag was at the side of the stationary moped driver. He pushed him hard against the steps. The moped went over and the handlebars hit the girl's foot. All four of the teenagers were screaming, but none of them did anything constructive, let alone fight back. He tucked the bat into the back of his trousers. Then he looked at the boys and decided enough was enough. The girl, who was half standing, half sitting against the concrete wall, was screaming hysterically. He grabbed her by the hair and pulled her away from her whimpering friends and thought that the worst was yet to come. There was no point in dragging her round, he could just slap her where she was. He pushed her up against the wall and let go of her. She was terrified and sobbing.

'Please don't hit me!'

Don't talk to her, don't look at her, God dammit, you idiot, just do it. You don't know her, she could be anyone, it doesn't matter. She's the one who pushed your granny over.

The girl was blonde with a freckled face, a nose ring and a small, black rune of uncertain origin tattooed on her cheekbone near the hairline. Henrik Krag steeled himself and said:

'Close your eyes and count to twenty, and nothing will happen to you.'

She did as she was told. Counting out loud, as if to prove that she was obeying him, one, two, three, four . . .

He clenched his hand with the knuckle-duster, but couldn't go through with it. He satisfied himself by slapping her across the face with his other hand.

CHAPTER 55

On Thursday, 28 May Henrik Krag was given a small present by Benedikte Lerche-Larsen. It wasn't expensive or particularly imaginative, but she had taken the trouble of wrapping it up – an act he wouldn't normally associate with her, and for that reason it delighted him even more.

She picked him up from Ishøj Village at the car park behind the community hall where he had agreed to meet her at four o'clock. He got into the passenger seat. She handed him the present with a casual gesture as if it was no big deal and he was just one of many people to whom she gave things. Henrik Krag thanked her, surprised, and unwrapped it. It was a small plastic penguin, barely five centimetres tall, with a red heart on its white tummy and an egg at its feet. He held it up towards the light.

'That's really nice. But why did you give it to me?'

She shrugged her shoulders.

'It's nothing. Just a silly penguin. Would you like to drive?'

She was in her father's Audi and knew that he would jump at the chance. They swapped seats, Henrik by getting out, Benedikte by wriggling across to the passenger seat. As they drove out of the car park, she said gently:

'I'm glad you're here, Henrik.'

He didn't know what to say, not even when a little later she added: 'Her name is Pandora. The penguin, I mean. I've decided that.'

The village faded away in the rear-view mirror. There were now fields on both sides, some scattered farms, otherwise just a vast, green blanket. There wasn't much traffic, so they had the road to themselves. Then Henrik Krag remembered that he didn't actually know where they were going. When they had spoken that morning and he had given her the address, she had sounded enthusiastic: she had discovered something in the last few days, and she was excited about telling him, but she hadn't said what exactly she had found out. It was too complex to explain on the phone, she claimed, so he would have to wait.

He glanced at her. She sat with hands folded and her face turned to the window, apparently oblivious to him, and he thought maybe he should have expressed more appreciation of his penguin.

'Where are we going, by the way?'

'To your place.'

That made no sense. In that case, they might as well have met there. But he didn't say so. Perhaps she had simply wanted to pick him up, he could think of no other explanation.

'Please tell me what was so important? I'm really excited.'

'Yes, you are. Tell me, have you completed your first assignment?'

'Yes.'

'Was it tough?'

'I didn't think you wanted to know about it.'

'No, I don't. But was it?'

He hesitated.

'Not massively, but it wasn't nice either. Like you in the soup kitchen, I think you could say.'

'There's nothing wrong with that kitchen,' she said haughtily. 'It helps a lot of people who live a hard life. What about assignment number two, have you got it yet?'

'No, not yet. Why do you ask? Earlier you were adamant that you didn't want to know—'

She cut him off abruptly, but in a completely different tone of voice, more optimistic.

'I know what I said. I was just curious, forget it. Now, listen. I think I might know how to find the printer that printed the picture we were sent. Have you ever heard about the forensic printer-tracking program, also known as the yellow-dot marking technique?'

'I can't say that I have.'

'Me neither, until I went to a lecture last Monday. Does the CIA mean anything to you?'

Their backgrounds and experiences differed widely, he knew that better than anyone, and though he appreciated the way she would explain to him things about which he knew nothing, he was annoyed when she just assumed he was ignorant about subjects when he wasn't. He tried hard not to snap:

'Yes, of course. It's the American intelligence service.'

'That's correct, and now listen to this. I've been reading about it on the internet all day, and it turns out that we might be able to get a lot of data about the printer used for printing our picture. If we're very lucky, not just the type and serial number, but also when it was sold and to whom.'

'That sounds great. How?'

'What do you think I wanted to talk to you about? It was pure coincidence that I even heard about it. I was at a lecture on international law, where the lecturer – he's the one I called a nerd in my text message – told us, almost as an aside, how the Americans, that is the CIA, right back in the early 1980s, persuaded the leading laser printer manufacturers to secretly print almost invisible yellow dots on every piece of paper printed. The idea was to make life more difficult for criminals, but that's what the authorities always say when they want more information about their citizens.

'The manufacturers took up the suggestion, which is simply to repeat a faint pattern of tiny, yellow dots on every page that comes out of the printer. The dots will then be interpreted in a fifteen-by-eight-inch grid, where the pattern can be translated to the year, month, day, hour and minute that page was printed out, and – this is of most interest to us – the printer's unique serial number. I know it sounds like a conspiracy theory, but it's the truth.'

'It sounds like gobbledygook to me. I understood only half of it. Can you give me the super-short version?'

'Wait and see when we get back to yours. It'll be easier to understand then. I've bought everything we need.'

'Which is?'

'A powerful blue LED torch and a good magnifying glass. I've already tried it out and it works, but you have the picture we were sent and that's where it gets interesting, of course. Don't tell me you've thrown it out?'

She sounded panicky. He reassured her: the picture was back home in his cupboard.

About fifteen minutes later they entered his flat. Henrik Krag left his guest in the hallway and hurried to the living room where he quickly picked up the clothes scattered about the place – socks, shirts, a towel thrown across the television, underwear on the sofa. He chucked everything into the bedroom and carried yesterday's cups and plates to the kitchen. To begin with he thought she waiting outside to give him a chance to tidy up. But she wasn't. She called him to her. She had taken out the torch from her handbag, and swept its strong, blue light across the hangers, the small chest of drawers, a pair of worn-out trainers, and everything else he kept in the hall, which she claimed was the easiest room to black out. He didn't argue with her, and they got to work.

'The darker the better. Go and get your duvet, we'll put it along the bottom of the door, and then we need to cover the letterbox opening with newspaper. Do you have any sticky tape? You also need to turn off all the lights in the flat and close the blinds.'

He did as he was told while she continued to issue orders:

'Fetch the picture.'

He had put it in a plastic folder; she took it out and placed it, almost reverently, on the chest of drawers. It lay there ominously between them. He could tell from her movements that Benedikte Lerche-Larsen's infectious enthusiasm about her project had seeped away; she grew palpably less eager as the moment of truth arrived. She took out a palm-sized, rectangular magnifying glass from her handbag. Henrik Krag was intrigued.

'Where did you get that?'

'From a magnifying lamp. I had the good luck to find one in a vintage shop in Østerbro. The owner even helped me dismantle it.

Right, let's see if there's even something to magnify. Turn off the light.'

She switched on the torch and aimed it at the paper.

'We're looking for tiny, blue dots, and you need to look outside the image, on the white areas.'

'I thought you said the dots were yellow.'

'They are, but not in blue light, then they become blue and that makes them much easier to spot. That's the reason for the torch. They're easy to see. They're everywhere.'

'Not for me. I can't see anything.'

She turned on the light and explained:

'The pattern is repeated like a sheet of stamps, so now we need to isolate and highlight a single area. But it needs to be exact. So we'll do one each, first you, then me, and afterwards we'll compare them.'

'Do what?'

She had come prepared. Yet again she delved into her handbag and handed him a ballpoint pen and a squared A5 pad on which she had drawn a grid of fifteen-by-eight-inch square-lined.

'Look for seven dots in a column, that's the dividing line. And it's always there. Then look either side of it, left and right.'

She pointed, and gave him the magnifying glass.

Henrik Krag turned out to be surprisingly adept at spotting patterns. He finished his grid in less than a minute. Benedikte Lerche-Larsen was considerably slower finishing hers, but when they compared them, the results matched.

'What happens now?'

'Now you turn on your laptop. I've found a program called yellowDotSystem, where we can convert our pattern to a time it was printed and a unique printer number. Apart from the number, we'll also find the manufacturer of the printer, including the specific model. It's usually numbers and a couple of letters.'

'But how do we find the owner? I don't get that bit.'

'By using a hacker, and I have a handful of those among my poker players. Why don't you make us a cup of coffee in the meantime?'

Benedikte Lerche-Larsen sat at Henrik Krag's laptop. She half pushed the picture with the dotted grid under the keyboard, so only the information was visible. She opened his internet browser and typed 'y' into the search field. A drop-down menu of a list of hyperlinks of recently visited homepages starting with the letter 'y' appeared. Youngwannabes.com/audition/louise.html was number two. The mouse clicks followed swiftly and without hesitation; five clicks and she had a list of the laptop's temporary internet files, the telltale signs of what Henrik Krag had been up to online in recent weeks. She sorted the files, according to size and soon found what she was looking for. He had renamed it Bennedigte.flv. She double clicked and maximised Windows media player, but muted the sound. When Henrik Krag came back with her coffee, she was sitting at his dining table staring emptily into space, incredulous disappointment etched deep into her beautiful face.

He put the mug in front of her. She knocked it over. The hot liquid flooded the table and splashed onto the floor. Then she swept the mug aside, sending it crashing in pieces.

'What are you doing? Why are you being like that?'

She nodded at his laptop by way of reply. He cringed.

'Give me back my penguin, you bastard.'

CHAPTER 56

You couldn't tell from looking at Benedikte Lerche-Larsen that a few days ago, she had been deeply betrayed by Henrik Krag. If she felt bad, she didn't show it. And she had been like this for many, many years. *That girl is impossible to read. Who knows what's really going on in her mind?* Various teachers had said so ever since she started school, swapping concerned remarks, convinced that her closed mind was a negative trait. Since then she had developed and polished her appearance to near perfection, ably aided, of course, by her beauty. Some people – usually men she had turned down – thought she was nothing but her appearance, a decorative but empty shell. Others believed that her introversion, her hype and stage persona, as they liked to call it, reached well beyond vanity and should definitely be viewed as a psychological defence mechanism. This view somehow made her more human, possibly even attainable, so it was definitely the theory with the greatest number of supporters. Only two people knew the truth, one of whom was dead and the other was herself – and she wasn't saying anything.

On Saturday, 30 May Benedikte Lerche-Larsen had a lie-in, and it was past ten in the morning before she stepped out into her parents' garden, dressed in old clothes and smiling at the sun. She wore a pair of worn Italian loafers, jeans and a lumberjack shirt, not an outfit she would normally be seen dead in, but for the next hour she wanted to cut the grass.

Manual work, whether in the garden or elsewhere, wasn't usually her thing, and she avoided it whenever she could, which was pretty much always. But lawn mowing was the exception. She enjoyed walking around and around in regular patterns, trailing a band of freshly cut grass behind her. Raking up the cuttings afterwards, let alone pulling out dandelions or other weeds, she couldn't be bothered with, but the mowing itself was another matter. She had a standing agreement with the gardener that he was only allowed to cut the grass when she told him to.

She started the lawnmower, but hadn't managed even two rounds before she was stopped by Jimmy Heeger, the man Svend Lerche had recently hired to replace Jan Podowski. He was in his thirties, well built, with gel in his hair and a flashy dress sense that made him look like a cheap movie gangster. Benedikte Lerche-Larsen couldn't stand him. Firstly, because she hadn't been involved in hiring him; her father had interviewed him on his own, even though she was the one who had found the man's name on Jan Podowski's computer. Secondly, because he spoke to her arrogantly, almost as if he were her superior, which pissed her off no end because he wasn't, he wasn't even her equal. He bent down and turned off the lawnmower.

'You can do that later. We can't hear what we're saying.'

He pointed to the open window of her father's study. She didn't deign to reply, merely shook her head – did he really think she would take someone like him seriously? She bent down to restart the lawnmower. But to her astonishment, he pulled her upright with a firm grip on her upper arm, showing no respect, as if she were some schoolgirl.

'Listen, didn't you hear what I said?'

Jimmy Heeger was angry; he was quite obviously a man with a short fuse and a big ego, a bad combination. He shook her before he let her go. Then he encroached severely on her personal space by shoving his face right up close to hers. His hair gel smelled sharp, cheap and unpleasant. She smiled sweetly at him, scratched her cheekbone, then jabbed her finger straight into his eye, quick and hard. Her finger went in as though she had pricked a balloon without puncturing it. The man howled in pain and clutched his eye; she patted him on his cheek, and said almost cheerfully:

'Yap, yap, yap . . . You can bark, but don't bite.'

Then she restarted the lawnmower and carried on mowing, knowing full well she was unlikely to complete many more rounds before her father would appear.

Benedikte Lerche-Larsen beat her father to it; she was on the offensive and fuming.

'You and I have our disagreements, I know that. But I'm your daughter no matter how we look at it, and it's completely unacceptable that an employee attacks me physically. What the hell were you thinking? This isn't just about my authority, it's very much about yours also.'

'Keep your voice down, think of the neighbours! There's no need to involve the whole street.'

He had dragged her down to the terrace, and he too had grabbed her by the arm, but that was somehow different, and she accepted it.

The sun was bright and hot and there was a light, shifting breeze from the south. Svend Lerche struggled to put up the parasol; he loathed direct sunlight. The parasol continued to play up. Benedikte Lerche-Larsen seized the moment to reinforce her point of view.

'If you can't control your underlings, I'll find somewhere else to live. Either that or I want a bodyguard, someone who can teach our staff to keep their hands off me.'

Svend Lerche finally succeeded with the parasol; he sat down in the shade and took control of his anger. Partly because nothing good would come from arguing with her, and partly because he had to admit she had a point. He could see that now, but hadn't been able to do so earlier when he had reacted purely to her attack on his new man.

'I think he needs a trip to Casualty. Did you have to poke him in the eye? Was there no other way?'

By way of reply she peeled her shirt over her head revealing her bra, a silky number with French lace around the triangular cups. Her father protested, outraged: 'What the hell do you think you're doing? Get dressed at once.' She ignored him and showed him the red marks on her upper arm, where she had been held and shaken. They didn't look terribly serious, but they were there, that couldn't be denied. She said in a low and lethal voice:

'Make sure that never happens again, Svend.'

He mulled it over. When she was younger, she could wrap him round her little finger, make impossible demands and threats she didn't, couldn't or wouldn't be able to carry out. Only a year ago she would have insisted that Jimmy Heeger be sacked, but she had grown smarter, much smarter. There was no denying it. As it happened, he too was very unhappy with the new man, who had quickly shown himself to be unnecessarily brutal and cruel, something Svend had been in the process of telling him when they were interrupted by the lawnmower.

'OK, Benedikte. It won't happen again, I promise. Now put on your clothes, I don't want to sit here with you looking like that.'

'Then go away, *I* didn't drag *you* down here.'

Despite her words, she did put her shirt back on. When she had done so, and after a period of reflection, Svend Lerche said:

'Maybe you moving out isn't such a bad idea after all. Your mother and I have talked about it possibly being better for you.'

She concealed her astonishment; pretty much everyone except her father wouldn't even have noticed it. She was silent for a few seconds and then matter-of-factly addressed the air, as though she wasn't speaking to him at all.

'Mum has an IQ as high as the room temperature, and she doesn't give a toss about anyone but herself.' She turned her head abruptly and caught his eye. 'Neither do you, Svend, you're just better at pretending that you do.'

'I want to help you buy something decent. I'm presuming you'll want to move into Copenhagen.'

She ignored him and carried on her own sharp analysis.

'But you're scared shitless that I might quit. Because you would then be forced either to cut down your business considerably or let major areas drift.'

He swung around and answered her with the same cold, distanced air she had adopted.

'You're overselling it, I'm not scared shitless, as you put it. But you're right, your work is of great importance, it would be foolish to deny that. On the other hand, I trust your greed, your love of money. In this area you're so wonderfully banal and predictable.'

She nodded to herself. *Yes, indeed I am, indeed I am.* Balance, equilibrium, guarded neutrality, the rest was nothing but words – words that changed nothing when push came to shove. She said:

'I'll think about it, it might not be a bad idea.'

'Fine, but don't take too long.'

It sounded fair: don't take too long. She went back to the lawnmower and had made up her mind before finishing the next round.

CHAPTER 57

The cogs in the police machine whirred into action, and they did so effectively. Once the investigation knew Jan Podowski's name, his life was revealed in a matter of days. It was a simple question of resources and Konrad Simonsen could allocate enough. His investigation, which had seemed hopeless to him, had taken an extremely positive turn, and like an old circus horse smelling sawdust, he was starting to trust that he would have a result in the not-too-distant future. The same applied to his staff. Not that they discussed this openly, that would be tempting fate, but the mood in the Homicide Department was clearly optimistic.

The pieces in the puzzle that made up Jan Podowski's life had pretty much fallen into place except for an ugly and significant hole in the records of the man's activities in the last ten years, but it would eventually be filled in, Konrad Simonsen had every confidence.

Jan Podowski was born in 1955 in Copenhagen. After leaving school at the age of sixteen, he was apprenticed to a cabinet maker, and qualified almost five years later in 1975. Then he worked for three years at Claus Pedersen Furniture Makers in Frederiksberg where he assembled and varnished designer dining chairs. He left the factory in 1978 after one of his colleagues had a serious accident. Klavs Arnold explained in his presentation to Konrad Simonsen:

'His mate had removed the shield on his saw in order to cut a concealed slot. Then the sheet flipped and his hand was severed at the wrist. After that experience Jan Podowski was out of there. He thought there had to be easier and less risky ways of making money. We can say with some certainty that he chose crime.'

'Excellent, let's move on.'

Klavs Arnold leafed through his papers laboriously; it took some time, but finally he found what he was looking for.

'The poor man only got thirteen thousand kroner in compensation.'

Arne Pedersen sighed, though he often agreed with his boss that the Jutlander could be long-winded. The presentation continued: in the 1980s Jan Podowski had worked as a driver, often for criminal ringleaders. Alongside this, he had also worked as a bouncer for Copenhagen nightclubs where, on several occasions, he had been charged with selling illegal substances, but the charges had been dropped every time. For a long period he had also worked as a stagehand at the legendary Madame Arthur, Copenhagen's wildest nightclub in the 1980s, the home of gay men, drag queens, transvestites and everyone who liked to party hard, until AIDS eviscerated the place at the end of the decade. In the 1990s, he was involved in the illegal importation of bootleg goods and the smuggling of cigarettes. He was also suspected of robbing trucks and of ram-raid robberies, but without ever ending up behind bars. He had either been lucky or clever or possibly both.

Arne Pedersen had taken over from Klavs Arnold.

'Where do we have our information from?' Konrad Simonsen asked.

'Informants, but it has been independently verified. Many people in the Copenhagen, and for a time also the Odense, underworld remember him clearly. He was well liked, incidentally, if that's in any way useful to us. A man whose work you could trust – that was his reputation.'

'What about addresses, girlfriends, finances?'

'We know all of that: do you want me to read it out loud? There's nothing very interesting.'

There was no need. Instead Konrad Simonsen said:

'But we lose him towards the end of the 1990s.'

It was a statement rather than a question; Arne Pedersen confirmed it:

'His last known address is a bedsit in Brannersvej in Charlottenlund. He moved out in 1996, and since then hasn't been listed at any other address. There can be no doubt that he tried putting up barriers between his working life and his private life, as well as disappearing from public registers. He has paid no tax since 1994. In 2002 he sells his car and closes all his bank accounts, he receives no state benefits and lives in Karlslille under the name Philip Sander . . . yes, he did a thorough job. But we still don't know why, and we still don't know what the last job he did was.'

Konrad Simonsen was hopeful.

'We'll find out, it's only a matter of time. How about children, family, anything like that?'

'No children that we know of, but two sisters he never sees. One lives in Belgium, by the way.'

'So his blind girlfriend is right when she claims not to know what his job was?'

Arne Pedersen had his doubts about that, so that question had to be left open for the time being. But he had no doubt at all that the Countess would uncover the answer to that question and many more.

CHAPTER 58

The break-up with Benedikte Lerche-Larsen hit Henrik Krag like a kick to the stomach.

It was a vacuum, a sub-pressure, sucking him in, eating him up, driving him to despair whenever he thought about it, which he did many times every day. He rang her constantly, especially in the weekend after the break-up, but she didn't pick up when he called, and he could have saved himself his tortuous text messages – he received no replies. Even so he carried on, spelling his way through the words on his computer, where he could have his message read out loud: *I'm sorry, Benedikte. I love you, Benedikte. I'm so sorry, Benedikte. I can't live without you, Benedikte.* Ironically, Ida read them for him. Afterwards each letter would have to be transferred to his mobile, checked and double-checked, before he felt confident it was all spelled correctly and he could finally hit send. But all to no avail.

Several times he tried using another phone, mobiles belonging to colleagues or friends, but no luck there either. *Benedikte, please don't hang up . . .* He never got any further before she hung up, her voice as she said her name fading in his mind far too quickly.

He drank more beers in the evenings than were good for him, but they didn't soothe his longing in the slightest; in fact they almost made it worse. Even so, he would often buy a six-pack on his way home from work, more recently two. He avoided his friends.

Nights were better, more honest in a strange way; they made no promises they couldn't keep. He wouldn't have called her at night, even if things had been the way they used to be; at night she slept. He hoped. Familiar jealousy pierced him from all sides, and painful images formed in his brain. Sleep was chased away. Benedikte with another man, Benedikte naked, uninhibited, groaning, sweaty . . . just like the footage he couldn't help viewing, which was the author of his misfortune, and which he still, still, *still* couldn't help looking at – it was beyond belief. Why did he do it? He was an idiot that was why, he couldn't see through anything, understand anything . . . but not even his traditional escape mechanism worked. He sat up in bed and punched the wall, the pain shooting up to his elbow, and he reached out for another beer. On Monday morning he called in sick.

Monday evening they had been due to meet at his flat, and he hoped sincerely that she would still turn up. Four days had passed since she had stormed out in anger. He spent the whole day trying to convince himself that as she hadn't cancelled and in view of their important, shared project, she would turn up after all. Of course she would. How could she not? He listened to noises on the stairwell, peered out of the window for her car; she didn't come.

Early Tuesday morning he drove to Solrød Strand; he couldn't sleep. Nor could he stand being at home. On the way there he thought that if he was stopped and breathalysed, he would lose his licence. He also realised that he no longer cared.

He walked on the beach. The sun was blurred and foggy, still low on the horizon, and the few boulders cast long, pale shadows across the sand. If they were in his way, he kicked them aside in an impotent, destructive rage. Yet another day that just had to be endured. He spat at a squashed milk carton the sea had washed up. And missed.

Later, when he felt relatively sober, he drove home, parked his motorbike and went to the kiosk where he bought a carton of Prince cigarettes, a bottle of whisky and a crate of beer. Then he went to see his mother. She opened the door in her nightdress and was pleased to see the whisky and the cigarettes. She fetched glasses, they drank. *Tell me, how are you doing, Henrik?* She refilled their glasses. He opened two beers. *I'm good, Mum, I'm good.* She turned on the television; she liked it droning on in the background. And suddenly – he barely knew whether he had been there an hour or three by then – she had a rare moment of clarity. As a cigarette dangled from the corner of her mouth, with the glass she had just refilled in her hand, her laser-cutter voice that had caused such him embarrassment since he was a child, said:

'Bloody fight for her, you coward. Don't just go around feeling sorry for yourself.'

He didn't remember even telling her about Benedikte Lerche-Larsen. Maybe he hadn't, perhaps she had guessed, it was easy to underestimate her.

'How can I fight when she's not there?' he said despairingly.

'Is she dead or has she left the country?'

OK, so it had been a guess. 'No, Mum, she's not dead.' He opened another beer, his fifth, and thought wearily that perhaps it would be better if she were. It would certainly be easier.

'Then if you want her, you'll have to find her. It's either that or drink yourself to death like me.'

His mother laughed, a surprisingly attractive sound, not the kind of laughter you would expect from her. It took a little while before he realised that she was right. He tipped the rest of his beer into a potted plant. She smiled when she saw it, then she drained her glass.

CHAPTER 59

After the incident with the dog, the relationship between the Countess and Silje Esper soured. The Countess had no doubt that, given the opportunity, the blind woman would have ordered her dog to kill her had she thought she could gain anything from it. The Countess had to mobilise all her experience in order to carry out subsequent interviews in a professional manner.

She discussed the case at length with Konrad Simonsen, and decided that she would interview Silje Esper in her house in Karlslille, rather than at the police station, which – in view of the situation – would have been more appropriate. However, the fact that Silje Esper was blind weighed heavily on the decision. It was quite simply easier to interview her in her own home. Furthermore, the Countess wasn't interested in an official recording, at least not for the time being. There were things she would rather not have on the record. Despite this, the logistics of their conversations, compared to their earlier talks, had changed considerably. The Countess now arrived with two officers. One was a dog handler who together with Silje Esper contained Mads in his van before the Countess even got out of her car, a procedure she adhered to, without fail, despite the blind woman repeatedly assuring her that her dog posed no threat to anyone.

However, putting the tension to one side, the Countess's interviews brought results. They came slowly, but they were crucial. The woman's own life had also been scrutinised under a microscope at headquarters, once it had become clear that she had been lying to the police.

When the Countess resumed interviewing her, she began with the relationship between Silje Esper and Jan Podowski.

'You have a brain-damaged son, who is cared for at Sankt Eliza Pflegewohnen in Rinteln in Germany. Is he the son of Jan Podowski?'

Silje Esper nodded; the Countess reminded her of the Dictaphone and asked her to speak up. Yes, that was correct, Frederik was Jan's son.

'Go on.'

Silje Esper and Jan Podowski had had a brief affair back in 1986 when she was married and lived in Middelfart. She became pregnant while she and her husband were undergoing fertility tests at Odense University Hospital, tests that concluded her husband's sperm quality was too poor for him to father children. The marriage had collapsed, she had moved to Copenhagen, where she lived with her son for a number of years in the Vesterbro area. The Countess interjected:

'You didn't contact Jan Podowski?'

'No.'

'Why not?'

'Initially because I thought Jan might not be Frederik's father. But later, there was no doubt, I could tell from looking at Frederik. By then I had grown used to living on my own . . . without a man around, I mean. It wasn't until later, after the accident, that Jan contacted me. He already knew that he was Frederik's father, or rather, he had guessed. He told me that he had been keeping an eye on me and Frederik from time to time, without us knowing.'

In 1996 Silje Esper crashed her car with her son and a friend of his in the back. It happened on Ballerup Boulevard, and she had been mildly intoxicated and speeding. The consequences of the accident were tragic: Silje Esper was blinded, her son severely brain-damaged, and his friend was killed. Jan Podowski had contacted her while she was a patient at Herlev Hospital, worried about his son and . . . Silje Esper smiled a sad smile, which didn't reach her blind eyes . . . *Yes, he was also worried about me.*

On her return to Police Headquarters, the Countess reported back to the others in the Homicide Department.

'They found a residential care home in Germany for Frederik Esper. He reacts to light, sound and pain, but he's unable to communicate or move in a co-ordinated manner. He can't recognise anyone, and can only grunt when, for example, he's in discomfort. He's strapped to a wheelchair all day, he's doubly incontinent and is fed through a tube. Sankt Eliza is a very good place for people suffering from such conditions as Frederik's, but it's also very expensive. Approximately three thousand Euro a month, of which the Danish state pays about half, but even after that it was much more than Silje Esper could afford.'

Klavs Arnold voiced everyone's thoughts:

'But not for Jan Podowski?'

'No, not for Jan Podowski. His work brought him into contact with large sums of money . . . yes, I'm quoting Silje Esper here. When he met her for the second time, if I can put it like that, he was already siphoning off a little extra for himself whenever the opportunity arose, but once he had a family to provide for, he systemised his skimming. Silje Esper claims she doesn't know the name of his employer, and I believe her. However, she does know how much he stole, and it was a considerable amount, roughly fifty thousand kroner per week.'

Arne Pedersen whistled.

'And she has no idea what he did for a living?' Konrad Simonsen asked.

'She had her suspicions. Brothels and illegal gambling, she thought. But she stresses that she's merely speculating. Apart from a few indiscretions from Jan Podowski over the years, there was nothing concrete. She can't recall a single episode where he told her anything directly.'

'Is that all? Given how long the two of them lived together, it sounds highly unlikely that she knows absolutely nothing about Jan Podowski's work.'

It was the tenth time, at least, the Countess had heard this statement, not to mention all the times she had thought or said it herself. But the fact was that it *was* the case, whether or not anyone believed it; or at least it was for now. She planned on another trip to Karlslille during the week; there were still loose ends to tie up. And there were two more pieces of information she had yet to tell them, and these might be significant.

'The man Jan Podowski worked for had three cars, one of which one was an Audi R8 and another a white Porsche. It's not a bad starting point; there can't be many people in Denmark who own two such cars at the same time. And there's another interesting fact. Jan Podowski worked regularly on his computer on something he referred to as his *pension pot*. He didn't want to tell Silje exactly what it was, but he saved the results on a USB stick, which he kept hidden, she's sure about that. Only she doesn't know where.'

Konrad Simonsen grunted contentedly, the bit about the cars was especially pleasing. He asked Arne Pedersen to follow up that line of enquiry, adding:

'It sounds as if we need another search, do you think Silje Esper will allow it? If not, we'll need a warrant.'

The Countess thought she would agree to it, and Konrad Simonsen made a brief note on the pad in front of him. He told them to carry out the search first thing Monday, and for the Countess to lead it. She nodded, then he asked:

'So they came up with the pottery scam? Tell us about it.'

The Countess began. Jan Podowski and Silje Esper had a big problem: all the money Jan Podowski made was in cash and illegal. It constituted a considerable risk as far as the Revenue was concerned, but more importantly it stopped them from making legitimate savings arrangements so that Frederik Esper could stay where he was for the rest of his life. Before she was blinded, Silje Esper taught pottery at evening classes and other venues, anywhere she could find work. After the accident the couple bought the house in Karlslille, renovated it, and Silje Esper set up pottery production in her studio. Her pottery skills had survived her blinding and many of the items she made were indeed sold, but definitely not at the prices she had told them her fictitious German buyers had paid. The result was, of course, that she – once the taxman had taken his share – was able to build up an apparently legitimate fortune, or rather some savings that could see the light of day.

The Countess had finished, but Arne Pedersen queried something which, to him, seemed baffling.

'Why did Jan Podowski live a double life? I mean, why did he invent Philip Sander? As far as I can see, he wouldn't need to do that in order to launder the money.'

'No, not immediately, and perhaps not at all. Silje Esper thinks it was primarily so that he had an escape route, not from the authorities, but from his employer, if he was caught with his hand in the till one day. If that were to happen, he could quietly retire as Philip Sander and enjoy his life in Karlslille. Oh, by the way, there's one thing I forgot to tell you.'

Konrad Simonsen, and he was possibly the only one, could tell that she had forgotten nothing, but deliberately left it till the end.

'I've promised Silje Esper not to broadcast her German pottery arrangement. There's no need for the state to know about her son's money, and I assume you all agree.'

'No, I definitely do not.'

It was Klavs Arnold speaking; the three others looked at him in surprise. The Countess said slowly, in a hostile tone, without hiding her astonishment:

'You don't?'

'Definitely not. Everyone thinks the state is some big monster eating our money, but who do you think pays for the care of all the other traffic accident victims in the same condition as Frederik Esper, who haven't got the benefit of a private luxury care home?'

The Countess asked sharply:

'And you've never accepted a bit of cash in hand for all those extra jobs you did when you lived in Esbjerg?'

'And what gives you the right to bend the rules whenever it suits you?' Klavs Arnold retorted.

It was a minefield. Arne Pedersen got busy looking out of the window; no one should expect him to join in. The Countess and Klavs Arnold sat poised, like two fighting cockerels between rounds. Konrad Simonsen raised his voice and asked in an ominous tone that clearly indicated he would like to see some discipline in the ranks: 'Did you tell Silje Esper that we would be willing to overlook her fortune if she helped us?'

The question was naturally addressed to the Countess.

'Not as directly as that, but it was implied.'

Her reply was fluid, to put it mildly; this could mean anything, something that Klavs Arnold was quick to point out. But he fell quiet and awaited his boss's verdict. After a period of consideration, which was purely for show, Konrad Simonsen announced:

'We're not the Revenue, and it's essential that we can be flexible when we need to be. We'll forget about the money, Klavs.'

Klavs Arnold made no reply.

Konrad Simonsen repeated his statement, while looking straight at the Jutlander. That did the trick. Klavs Arnold echoed irritably:

'We'll forget about the money, Simon.'

CHAPTER 60

The Countess's theory that few people in Denmark owned both an Audi R8 *and* a Porsche turned out to be right. There were only two, of whom one was a sausage producer who lived in Herning in Jutland so Jan Podowski could not have worked for him. Besides, his Porsche was light blue. Arne Pedersen informed Konrad Simonsen that the other man lived in Rungsted.

'His name is Svend Lerche, he trained as an engineer, he's in his early fifties, and is now the CEO and joint owner of something called the Poker Academy.'

'And what does that do? It sounds a bit dodgy.'

'It seems legit. Lerche hires a number of people who play poker online on his behalf. I've checked with the Revenue and they say everything is in order. Accounts, employment contracts, it would appear to be a legal business. He has a restraining order against him sought by a member of staff at a tax office, someone he threatened about a year ago; apart from that he's clean.'

'So no illegal gambling?'

'Poker isn't gambling, it's only the legislation that defines it as such. In the long run poker success is about skill and nothing else. Even so Silje Esper might still have thought it was illegal gambling.'

Konrad Simonsen wanted to know the address; Arne Pedersen walked back to his office, a little annoyed, and found it on his computer. He had been on his way home to start the weekend, and besides, how many people called Svend Lerche could possibly live in Rungsted? Simon could easily have looked it up himself. When Arne came back, he handed his boss the address.

'Can't it wait until Monday?'

The Countess, who had just entered her husband's office, agreed. However, Konrad Simonsen was of the opinion that he could find the time to visit on Sunday morning. It was worth a try. In response to his quizzical look, Arne Pedersen paused. He didn't have the time, unfortunately, but that was just how it was. He had promised to take his twins to a football tournament, and it would eat up all of his weekend. His boss accepted this; he might send a couple of other officers, he said. The Countess and Arne Pedersen exchanged a quick smile; it was obvious to them that would never happen.

'By the way, as you are here . . .' the Countess addressed Arne Pedersen '. . . it'll just be you and me and a couple of officers on Monday. I've cancelled everyone else. Silje Esper called an hour ago to tell me something interesting she had remembered. Once, when Jan Podowski was working on his pension pot, by which I mean his

USB stick, she could smell paint. So perhaps all we have to do is check any paint tins in the shed. That's a traditional hiding place.'

CHAPTER 61

It took Henrik Krag four days to pluck up the courage to follow his mother's advice to contact Benedikte Lerche-Larsen. He did so on a Saturday, which was dull from the moment dawn broke. The sky merged into a uniform grey mass, the sun was nowhere to be seen. The only mitigating circumstance in the gloom was the mild temperature, and at least there was no wind.

Henrik Krag studied the house, and looked up again at the windows of Benedikte Lerche-Larsen's first-floor flat. He felt exactly what he was: a stranger, unwelcome. It was nine in the morning, and he had yet to observe any activity. Not even on the ground floor where her parents lived, and where he had often been inside when he was an employee. He had never been upstairs; today would be his first time. First and possibly only time, if she even let him in that is, he thought, and immediately reminded himself that he had nothing to lose. Things between them couldn't get worse than they already were, and the last nine days had been pure hell. Rather finish it for good, so that he could get on with his life. He had repeated this exchange with himself several times. Even so he hesitated on the pavement where he was standing, clutching his bouquet of flowers.

He had forgotten that you could smell the Øresund from here. But now he remembered it. Not that it made him feel any better. He braced himself, marched the few steps towards the gate and then came to a standstill. If she had a visitor, it would be even worse; the thought was unbearable. Or if Svend Lerche chased him away.

Perhaps he would be better off going home and forgetting all about it.

He didn't make up his mind until he saw her curtains part and a middle finger being held up for a few seconds.

When he reached the house, she had already opened the front door to her flat. He entered carefully, his pulse racing as if he had run a hundred-metre sprint. He found her in the living room, where she waited in silence. A quick look around her flat gave an intimidating impression of class, style and a lot of money. As he had expected. He walked up to her, unable to help himself. It was clumsy: his hand on her upper arm, on her shoulder, then on her back while he was holding her flowers in the other. She didn't react, just stood there, putting up with his intimacy without any expression like a statue.

Tentatively he took a step back and offered her the flowers. She tossed them aside with an indifferent gesture. They landed on the bottom shelf of the bookcase, the cellophane wrapping crackling briefly in protest. She turned slightly, so she was facing him directly, and folded her arms across her chest. Her gaze was blisteringly cold, direct and confrontational, barely restrained anger in her voice, ominous like kettledrums in a symphony. She stressed every word.

'Your touch is disgusting. Besides, I'm tired of your body, I know your muscles inside out, and there's nothing more to discover about you. I'm done with you for good. Not even your stupidity surprises me any more.'

The insult hit hard. Henrik Krag's face reddened. He couldn't think of a suitable reply. Benedikte Lerche-Larsen continued:

'Why did you watch my movie?'

He bowed his head and flung out his hands. She repeated the question in a higher pitch and added:

'I want to know why, tell me or get out.'

At least he was honest, but it was hard going. The words came in embarrassed half statements mixed with long, awkward pauses and interspersed with pleading looks at her to understand without him having to elaborate. In vain – she showed no mercy, and he stuttered on, red-faced, stammering and humiliated, until at last she cut him off.

'And what did you think was so wonderful to look at? The bit where I lie on my stomach like a boned chicken, while the camera devours every skinfold, every hair follicle, even the tiniest drop seeping out of me? Oh, yes, I've watched it myself, but in contrast to you, the shame nearly made me throw up. It's the worst thing I've ever experienced. Or so I thought until I found out that you'd been salivating over the performance. That was even worse. So is that the kind of thing you get off on, Henrik?'

He shook his head silently. She continued roasting him.

'Look at me, and don't stand there like a beaten dog. Does it turn you on, knowing the whole world can look inside me? Answer me!'

Before he had time to say something, she added, her voice saccharine and vicious at the same time:

'Stroke of luck you turning up today, Henrik. Because tomorrow my boyfriend and I are going to Milan, and we'll be there for a few weeks or five. We can send you a postcard, a really intimate one, the kind you like.'

Rejected, contemptible, wretched, soiled. Henrik Krag loathed himself, and hoped she would throw him out since he couldn't leave of his own accord. But then suddenly – it was the last thing he had imagined – her arms were around him.

'Don't say anything.'

The request was welcome; he had a lump in his throat, and didn't know if he even could. They stood like this for a long time, until she broke the silence.

'I made up the bit about the holiday and the boyfriend.'

Again they stood for a long time. Silently she freed herself, almost. She held onto his forearms.

'What took you so long, you coward? I've missed you so much.'

He told her about his mother; honesty was his best policy. She laughed, but not scornfully.

'Do I get a kiss? Or do you have to ring your mum first to . . .'

He smothered her words with his lips.

The flowers were picked up and put in water; she poured him juice from a jug on her dining table. She had already put out two glasses; he hadn't noticed that until now. She smiled, when she saw him wondering about it, and then she asked:

'Any news from Ida?'

'Yes, she called the day before yesterday. She was pleased with my first task, and I'll get my second one on Monday.'

'How can Ida know how you carried out your first task?'

He took the newspaper page from his inside pocket and unfolded it.

'It was on the front page of *Bagsværd Bladet* last Wednesday.'

The headline was *Four youngsters brutally attacked at Skovbrynet Station*. She skimmed the article.

'Where did you get the newspaper?'

'Gladsaxe Library.'

'Do you want me to read it to you?'

He shook his head. What was the point? Then she looked at her watch. He knew what it meant, but right now he could handle anything, including her not having any more time for him.

'Are you nervous? About the next task, I mean.'

'A bit, it's bound to be worse. But I'm trying not to think about it, and so far that seems to be working. There have been so many other . . . I mean, with you and everything.'

'Are you allowed to tell me about it?'

'I haven't been told yet.'

'I prefer not to know what it is until it's over. Possibly not at all.'

'Why not?'

'I'm scared, I think. Also because somehow it's harder when you're not the one doing it. I mean, if you had been told about my . . . second task, I don't think I would have been able to go through with it.'

'That might have been for the best.'

'If I can do it, so can you.'

She sounded a touch sharp, and he quickly added:

'I'll do my bit, you can be sure of that. But does it mean that we can't see each other until it's over? It could be a long time.'

It didn't. Benedikte Lerche-Larsen flicked through her diary.

'Tonight is absolutely impossible, and I'm on duty today. I simply have to study tomorrow, and Monday and Tuesday are also . . .'

She shook her head in resignation. Henrik Krag asked with interest:

'What kind of duty?'

'I promised to do a couple of day shifts at the soup kitchen. It's not a permanent thing, they're just really short of people at the moment.'

It was rare for her to blush.

'Are you surprised? You know I liked it there. I've already told you.'

He didn't reply, instead he said: 'I've missed you.'

'Me too. Why don't you come back early tomorrow morning, and we can bathe together?'

'Bathe? You mean in the sea?'

'No, are you mad? Don't you have a shower in the morning?'

'Yes, of course.'

'So do I. And perhaps you could pick up some fresh rolls on your way. If you get here early, we could have two or three hours together. That gives us enough time to look for a flat.'

He was speechless; he just stared at her, not sure if he had heard her right. She kissed him briefly.

'Can you be here at seven?'

He could.

CHAPTER 62

Benedikte Lerche-Larsen received Henrik Krag in a diaphanous negligee of silk and chiffon, under which she was naked, having neglected to put on any underwear. In the living room, as he waved the bakery bag containing the fresh rolls, she posed for him. Just briefly, almost in jest, in profile against the light from the window, and with practised bashfulness: a downcast gaze as if she didn't dare meet his eyes, her shoulder pulled up so it covered her chin, a protective forearm across her breasts, modest yet coy. *Aren't I beautiful?* or *Catch me if you can* – his choice, both were true. Then she laughed, a touch self-consciously, and he got his kiss, a long kiss, with her soft arms around his neck. She removed his hand.

'Patience, breakfast first.'

She gestured to the dining table, which was already set. Then she freed herself, took the bag and sat down.

'OK, I can't really blame you for staring. My timing is bad. But I have found some flats I want you to look at first. Hold on.'

She got up and disappeared into another room. When she came back, she had put on a dressing gown and was holding her MacBook. Together they looked at flats for sale in Copenhagen, expensive flats. She talked, compared one to the other. The one on Amerika Plads was modern with underfloor heating and two bathrooms, but only had two bedrooms and that was possibly not enough. The flat on Christianshavn, however, now that was on two floors and the terrace was great with a view of the canal; the question was, of course, whether the neighbourhood was a little too lively, she thought one might tire of that eventually. As usual he didn't know what to say. The all-important question, whether he would be moving with her, he didn't dare ask. It was not until she commented on a flat with basement storage and said, 'You could keep your motorbike there in winter,' that it was clear he hadn't been mistaken. He asked cautiously:

'You mean I'm moving in with you? That we'll be living together?'

'Yes.'

No more than that, *yes*, as if it were the most natural thing in the world. It was utterly overwhelming. And insane. He had a thousand questions and didn't manage to ask a single one of them.

It was a wonderful breakfast and, for a time, he completely forgot their promised shower. Slowly he began to comment on the flats, and they discussed them amicably for a little while. At length they agreed on two, and he promised to go home, look them up on his computer and think about them. Later they would view them. She said:

'I'll send you the addresses, so all you have to do is click on the link.'

The implication: so he wouldn't have to try spelling them. He thanked her, it was nice of her.

'When do you think we'll be moving?'

'Soon, four weeks max, preferably sooner. When you have completed your last task, and we can put all that crap behind us, hopefully. I also need to sort out a few things with my father. But soon. What do you think?'

He said that as far as he was concerned they could move in tomorrow. And that he couldn't understand why she wanted to live with him. The truth was he was scared that she might be having him on. She grabbed his hand across the table.

'You don't have to worry on that account, Henrik. I don't. Now let's go and have that shower.'

She was controlled in her passion, and at no point during their lovemaking did she let go completely. Most of the time she kept her arms around his neck as though she would fall into a void if she didn't. She moaned into his ear, short gasps, which she bit in half so they would not take control of her. When they happened to turn so that the spray from the shower hit her face directly, she pulled away. Afterwards they soaped each other, gently and slowly. When the shower was over, she took out a couple of towels from a cupboard. She smiled, trailed her fingers across his face, patted his cheek. Then suddenly she stopped, listened and opened the big bathroom window, which until then had only been ajar. They both looked down. The French doors into her parents' flat were now open.

She was patient with him, caressing him, and using her mouth. When he was ready again, she turned around, rested her forearms on the windowsill, thrust her groin backwards and pushed him into her. In contrast to earlier, this time her groaning was uninhibited, as loud as she could manage, like a tennis player on overtime. Then suddenly she stopped and pulled away from him. He heard the garden gate.

'Shit!'

'What is it, Benedikte?'

'We have visitors, that's what it is.'

Henrik Krag stood next to her, leaned forwards and looked out.

'Who is it?'

'I don't know their names.'

'But?'

'But one is a Homicide chief from Copenhagen.'

CHAPTER 63

The Countess accompanied Konrad Simonsen to Rungsted on Sunday morning. It was a short drive from their home in Søllerød and besides, the more she thought about Svend Lerche, the more he intrigued her. A company that hired poker players to play online? Now it could be entirely legitimate, of course, but there were lots of reasons why it might not be. You didn't have to be a financial crime expert to suspect that.

She parked her car behind a motorbike, a Harley-Davidson, an impressive piece of engineering. Looking at the clock on the dashboard, she said:

'A quarter to ten on a Sunday morning, it's a bit early, isn't it?'

Konrad Simonsen, who was in the passenger seat, struggling with his seatbelt, grinned.

'For a routine question that could easily be dealt with by a phone call tomorrow, it's completely unreasonable.'

They got out of the car without commenting further on the situation. Though they had both been with the police for more years than they cared to remember, they still from time to time derived quiet satisfaction from showing the wealthy, the elite, the successful, that despite their powerful connections or their riches, they had to defer to a police badge and the name of the Homicide Department. It was good to live in a country where everyone was equal before the law, and it did those who lived on the sunny side of society no harm to be reminded that ultimately they occupied the same world as everyone else. There were limits to this harassment, but they lay well beyond being woken up a little early on a Sunday morning.

They stopped in front of the gate and took time to study the house. The Countess commented like an estate agent: 'Between twenty to twenty-five million kroner, even after the collapse of the property market. If it was mortgaged to the hilt a couple of years ago, I'm sure the collapse would make Svend Lerche technically insolvent.'

Konrad Simonsen didn't comment, but asked:

'What's that noise . . . it sounds like someone . . .?'

He chuckled softly; the Countess listened too and shared in the joke.

'Someone's clearly awake by the sound of it. Shall we?'

She pointed to the gate, and they entered. The noise stopped when they had walked a few steps up the garden path.

Konrad Simonsen had his warrant card ready when Svend Lerche opened the door. He held it up and snapped it shut immediately.

'Are you Svend Lerche?' the Countess asked.

'I am, yes. What's this about?'

The man's face was inscrutable, neither relaxed nor nervous, but something else again, something the officers rarely experienced. With that absence of expression and body language, it became clear after only five seconds – he was a true poker player. Konrad Simonsen said:

'We would like to talk to you, would you mind letting us in?'

Svend Lerche's reply came half a second too late to be a casual response.

'Why don't we sit outside on the terrace. After all, it's such a lovely day.'

It was obvious to the two officers that the poker CEO had no wish to co-operate. His attitude was closed, reserved, negative.

When the three of them had sat down on garden chairs on the terrace, Konrad Simonsen took out a picture of Jan Podowski from his inside pocket and unfolded it in a leisurely manner. The picture was grainy and of poor quality, copied from a driver's licence which had been issued more than fifteen years ago, but it was all they had been able to find. He placed the picture on the garden table in front of Svend Lerche.

'Jan Podowski, we have some questions about your former employee.'

The officers held their breath as they waited for the reply; it could go either way, but it was clear that Svend Lerche knew Jan Podowski, he barely looked at the picture. Finally, the poker boss made up his mind and shook his head vehemently.

'I know no Jan Podowski, and I've never seen that man before.'

'Don't lie to us.'

The Countess sounded irritated rather than angry. Her tone said: *Listen, let's not waste each other's time, it doesn't benefit any of us.* Konrad Simonsen thought this was the moment the man would get up and tell them he would only continue this conversation in the presence of his lawyer. Two seconds later Svend Lerche responded predictably true to form, although with a slight variation:

'I see no point in talking to you when you don't believe anything I say. You can see yourselves out.'

Konrad Simonsen stood up and held out his hand.

'That was certainly a short conversation. But goodbye for now, Mr Lerche, we'll meet again sooner than you think, and I'm already looking forward to it. Meanwhile, I wish you well.'

Svend Lerche wondered briefly whether to return the handshake, then decided to ignore it.

CHAPTER 64

Silje Esper hadn't had a good death. She had been taped to a chair in her living room, and her fingertips – and the toes of her left foot – crushed. Probably with a hand vice, pliers would not have been able to do this. Her left eye had been gouged out. And then she had been strangled. Her face was turned up to the ceiling, mouth wide open in a silent scream, and her remaining blind eye bulged from its socket. There was blood everywhere – on the floor, on her clothes, in her hair. The Countess shook her head sadly.

'Dear God.'

She held Arne Pedersen back when he made to move closer. He said:

'I just want to see if some of the stains on her clothes are paint, they look like it from here.'

So did the Countess and she let him go. Arne Pedersen walked up close to the dead woman and leaned forward to check. He confirmed it, yes, it was paint, red paint on her sleeve in between all the blood. The Countess said:

'You make the call; I'll go and check on our colleague.'

They had arrived a few minutes earlier to discover an officer bent double outside the front door, throwing up in the flower bed to the left of the steps. The police had been contacted by Social Services when a carer who had turned up to clean for the blind woman had looked through the window. The Countess and Arne Pedersen had entered the house despite the officer's warning.

The Countess helped the officer into his car, but told him not to go anywhere. Arne Pedersen joined her shortly afterwards.

'Her dog is dead in the kitchen, two shots to the head, and in the shed someone has tipped the contents of a tin of red paint over the floor.'

'Only red?'

'So it would appear, but I didn't go inside to check, the technicians will have a fit if I do. Anyway, the entire circus is on its way. Melsing himself is turning up.'

'What about Simon?'

'He'll be here in three-quarters of an hour. It would seem we're not the only ones looking for that USB stick, don't you think?'

The Countess agreed, yes, she thought so too.

'She couldn't tell them anything except about the smell of paint, poor woman. And yet they carried on all the same.'

Monday proved to be a long day, and it was after five in the afternoon before they were able to leave Karlslille. They would have to await further information from the autopsy report, and the result of forensic investigations as well as their own police work, interviewing the neighbours, the public and so on. Konrad Simonsen managed to extract only one piece of information from Kurt Melsing, the head of Forensic Services, and its implication was chilling. Fairly soon after Melsing had arrived at the crime scene, the Homicide chief insisted on speaking to him. Konrad Simonsen ushered him out of the house, so they wouldn't have an audience and asked in a low voice, dreading the answer:

'I know that this isn't your department, Kurt, but you've seen many more bodies than the rest of us put together. Was she killed before or after yesterday morning, are you able to tell me anything about that? I really need to know. Otherwise I wouldn't have dragged you out here.'

'Why don't you ask the doctor?'

'I have, but she's new, and refuses to say anything until she gets the body on the slab.'

'Well, that could take twenty-four hours at least. But I can, totally off the record, tell you that the death occurred before yesterday morning. Quite definitely. Friday evening would be my estimate, but definitely before Sunday.'

Konrad Simonsen slammed his fist into the palm of his hand in anger. Yesterday morning he had visited poker boss Svend Lerche and shown him a picture of Jan Podowski. He had been working on the theory that the visit could have been what triggered off the woman's death but this news from the head of Forensic Services had ended that theory.

Kurt Melsing wasn't a stupid man; he could join the dots. His manner was quiet, and you had to know him extremely well to see that he was almost as upset as Konrad Simonsen.

'And the only people who knew where this woman lived and that Jan Podowski's USB stick might be hidden somewhere in her house . . .'

Melsing didn't need to complete his sentence. Konrad Simonsen finished it for him:

'. . . are police officers.'

CHAPTER 65

The National Police Press Office had been set up in record time. Just under three years ago the National Police Commissioner had decided that in addition to a communications consultant, he also needed a press officer. The other top executives, to whom he compared himself, all had one of those, so a press officer was duly hired. It went without saying that this was unnecessary, but then again it wasn't the end of the world either. At least not initially. But in no time at all one press officer had turned into three, and the original staff member had to be promoted to chief press officer. A year later those three had turned into seven and been given their own offices as well as their own oval in the organisational chart where they were shown to be reporting directly to the National Police Commissioner. By now there were nine employees and they were all working flat out, so more press officers were expected to be hired in the near future.

Konrad Simonsen's own attitude to press briefings had always been ambivalent. On the one hand he acknowledged their usefulness, when, for example, an investigation could benefit from help from the public. On the other hand, he fundamentally disliked them, and often despised crime reporters, whom he – with very few exceptions – regarded as idle and ignorant.

His feeling about the National Police Press Office were equally mixed: most of the time it suited him that others dealt with the media, sparing him the trouble; whenever he did want to speak to the press, he would consistently ignore the new rules that all *external communication*, as it was called in the shiny, new internal folder, must go through the National Police Press Office. The chief press officer would consequently call him and blow his top, while emphasising his own many areas of responsibility. Konrad Simonsen honestly couldn't care less, something he would also tell the man, which enraged him even more, and that was the end of it. There was never any follow-up.

*

The murder of Silje Esper caused a stir in the media, and a press conference was arranged for Tuesday morning at ten o'clock at Police Headquarters, but unfortunately not in the National Police Press Office's new offices, which were still being renovated. The chief press officer was annoyed. If only the murder had happened a week later, then . . . but alas, the offices would have to be baptised on another occasion.

At nine-thirty, a fuming deputy chief press officer turned up in Konrad Simonsen's office. The Homicide chief was sitting behind his desk and glanced up from his papers as the woman practically fell into his office, showing every sign of stress in her pretty, tele-genic face. No one could tell from looking at him that he had been expecting her for the last half hour. The deputy chief press officer's voice was shrill.

'What's this I hear that you won't be attending the press conference?'

'I prioritise my time, and I have the utmost confidence in dele-gating that type of briefings to you, the professionals. Also, it says in one of your folders that . . . hang on . . .'

He found the leaflet, which happened to be lying to hand on his desk, and flicked through it. She interrupted him with a hiss:

'I'm perfectly aware of the contents of our folders, but what on earth do you think *we* can tell the press? Are you aware that they're already lining up their cameras?'

He answered her as accurately as possible.

'I haven't thought about your first question, and no, I didn't know about the cameras.'

'But this is sabotage; you're working directly against us.'

'Not in the least, I'm only following your rules. You write your-selves . . .'

He flicked through the booklet again; she gave up. Her attitude changed and she became more contrite.

'Please will you help us? We don't know anything about the Karlslille murder.'

'Of course I will. Take a look at these, then you'll know exactly what happened.'

He handed her a stack of photographs. She paled at the first, turned over to the next picture, paled even more and suppressed a gulp. The photographs slipped from her hand and onto the floor.

Konrad Simonsen was at her side in a moment. 'Come on, put your head between your knees, and if you need to be sick, then be sick.' He grabbed her shoulders and pressed her head down, while he kicked away the pictures in her immediate field of vision. Slowly she regained control of herself. Meanwhile, one of the photographs caught his attention. It showed the dog run outside Silje Esper's back entrance, which until now had been of little interest to him.

The deputy press chief sat down on a chair; she was upset, but not so much that she couldn't speak. 'Thank you. I'm sorry.'

He picked up the photographs.

'Shut up, please. I promise to help you, but right now you need to . . . well, just shut up.'

She did as he had asked her. He stared vacantly at the window for a few seconds, then he called Arne Pedersen, who appeared in his office almost immediately. Simonsen gave his orders absent-mindedly, his attention elsewhere.

'Go and help out with that press conference, Arne. And take the Countess with you, if you like.'

'She's in Karlslille heading the search for that USB stick.'

It was as if Konrad Simonsen didn't understand the message, replying, 'Yes, she is, that's great.' A strange, misplaced reply.

'I'm going out for a couple of hours.'

Arne Pedersen, who knew his boss and recognised when he needed time on his own, promised to handle the press conference. Konrad Simonsen wasn't even listening.

The Countess was pleasantly surprised to see her husband in Silje Esper's studio, where she was busy giving orders to three men. She finished her instructions, but waited until the officers had left the room before she asked:

'I thought you weren't supposed to be here until the afternoon?'

He confirmed, yes, it was what they had agreed, but . . . he didn't elaborate. Instead he asked:

'Have you come across a stool or something similar around the house?'

'There is a small stepladder in the kitchen.'

'Please could you keep your men away from the dog run for five minutes?'

The wooden fence around the dog run was roughly two metres high. It consisted of nine posts, of which two were corner posts, and two were placed as close to the house as the foundations would allow. Between the posts, two rows of horizontal beams had been fixed, one at a height of 1.8 metres, and one just thirty centimetres from the ground. Planks had been nailed vertically to the horizontal beams. Ninety per cent of the wooden fence had been painted red, and that had happened recently. It was the unfinished paintwork that had caught Konrad Simonsen's eye when he glanced at the picture in his office an hour ago. Having stared intensely at the fence for a minute or two, he decided that he would have picked one of the two posts nearest the house, of which one was unpainted. He put up the stepladder next to the other one and climbed it.

The black USB stick had been wedged into the space between the post, the horizontal beam and the first plank. He fished it out with a little difficulty, using his pen, before wrapping it in his handkerchief and stuffing it in his pocket.

In the living room four officers were working diligently. The Countess was sitting on a chair at the dining table, but got up when he entered. He whispered to her:

'I've found it.'

She patted his upper arm without saying anything.

'But carry on looking for it as you otherwise would have done.'

'Of course we will.'

'I'll go and see Melsing and get him to check it for fingerprints, but I won't log it with an evidence number. Not now, but possibly later. This is about keeping our mouths shut.'

She couldn't agree more and quietly asked him if he had informed the Department for Public Prosecution about their presumed leak. He had; he had spoken to the deputy director, who would form a small group of competent colleagues to investigate the matter. It was standard procedure, but in contrast to what the public tended to believe, being questioned by such a committee was absolutely no joke. On the contrary, internal matters were pursued both consistently and zealously.

There was nothing more to discuss and she gave him a quick kiss goodbye. As he left, she watched his back and thought that at times he was a brilliant head of investigation. She also thought that she loved him, and that he was growing old. That although he now – in contrast to earlier years – took regular exercise, there was something laboured, something weary, about his gait that used not to be there.

However, someone else watched Konrad Simonsen as he left, and he didn't think that the chief was ageing. It was the mole, the man who had told Svend Lerche about the search.

He was squatting on his haunches, looking through some braille books in his hunt for the USB stick, something he dearly hoped would not be found or else that he would be the person to find it. Last Friday afternoon he had been assigned to take part in the search, which was scheduled for Monday. Rumours were already spreading by that point that they were going to Karlslille to look for a USB stick. That was bad news for him, as he had a very unpleasant suspicion about the contents of the stick and was only too familiar with the man whose picture was being circulated by the Homicide Department. He didn't know the name Jan Podowski, but he had met the man on several occasions and spoken to him on the phone even more frequently in order to buy himself a night with one of the lovely African women who worked as maids in Nordsjælland.

On his way home from work that day he had called the number he usually rang and insisted on being put through to the boss, without knowing who the boss was. After some discussion, he was told to hang up and wait. Soon afterwards he was called by a woman who introduced herself as *Mrs Larsen*. He had told her what was in the offing, and given her the address of the house in Karlslille, while crossing his fingers that the USB stick hadn't been found already. He had never in his wildest imagination thought that his tip-off would lead to the blind woman's murder. But what was done could not be undone, he couldn't change that, and he was now very, very scared of the man who had just left the living room.

CHAPTER 66

Konrad Simonsen took the USB stick to Malte Borup.

After being hired just under three years ago, the student intern had been moved around several times, but in the last two years he had shared an office with Pauline Berg. The two of them got on well – Malte Borup tended to get on well with pretty much everybody – and neither of them seemed to mind that space in the office was at a premium when they were both there. Besides they were rarely there at the same time, but they were both there this Tuesday lunchtime when their boss entered. Without making small talk, he said:

'Two things. One: under no circumstances mention this USB stick to anyone. It's vital that you don't.'

Pauline Berg promised him to keep her mouth shut, not one word would pass her lips, even in her sleep. Konrad Simonsen grunted and continued.

'Two: Malte, it's locked. I need some sort of password, I think. Can you read it without one? I mean, unlock it or whatever the term is.'

Malte Borup glanced fleetingly at the USB stick. Yes, he could probably do that. He held out his hand.

'I'll need about half an hour, so if you have something you want to do in the meantime ...'

The intern hated people looking over his shoulder when he was trying to work. When he first started this would have been a problem, as he would never have dared to speak to his boss so bluntly. Today he had grown more courageous. Konrad Simonsen promised to go to the canteen and have his lunch. It wasn't a great sacrifice to make.

When, sated and content, he came back to Pauline Berg and Malte Borup about forty minutes later, they were both seated behind the intern's computer, gazing at the screen. Pauline Berg with curiosity, Malte Borup with his head turned, half looking at the screen, half peering to the side. Konrad Simonsen looked with them: two naked people. A middle-aged white man thrusting in and out of a young African woman. From time to time he would turn his bloated, red face to the camera; the woman stared at the ceiling, scratched her cheek and looked bored. The quality of the film was poor, the people moved in jerks, above and beyond what the situation required. Malte Borup explained.

'This is an access file, it means it's a database. It's full of men with black girls. The entries are listed according to the men's data, that is to say, their name, title, picture, and then one or more film clips associated with them. The women have no surnames, only first names such as Iben, Frida, Carmen and so on.' He paused the film. 'We have muted the volume, if you want it on, you need to . . .'

Konrad Simonsen interrupted him:

'That won't be necessary. Do you know how many entries, i.e. men, we're talking about?'

'Just under six hundred, but we've only watched a few of them, obviously.'

Pauline Berg pointed to the screen where the man had been caught with his mouth open, as if he were about to eat the woman's face. She said dryly:

'I never did like him much as a TV presenter.'

At Konrad Simonsen's request, Malte Borup printed out a list with the names and titles of the five hundred and ninety-one men on the database. He arranged the names in three columns and reduced the font size, but still the printout took up four pages. Then he followed his boss to his office, and showed him how to operate the database. It wasn't difficult. When the intern had left, Konrad Simonsen skimmed the names on the printout. Sometimes he would emit a small noise of recognition or an affirmative snort as if to say that he wasn't surprised. The names weren't listed alphabetically, and he had reached the second to last column on the final page, when he froze and sat looking perturbed. Then he scrolled through the data on his computer, as Malte Borup had shown him, to confirm that no mistake had been made.

He called the intern, who immediately came to his office. Once he was inside, Konrad Simonsen locked his door, something he didn't remember ever doing before. Malte Borup looked rather alarmed, as if he had been taken hostage.

'Can you delete an entry from the database? And I mean remove it so that no trace of it remains?'

CHAPTER 67

Konrad Simonsen left the day-to-day management of the investigation into the murder of Silje Esper to Arne Pedersen, but he was present in the big conference room when his second-in-command reviewed the current status of the investigation and delegated tasks to his fellow officers. Konrad Simonsen noticed how Arne Pedersen was far more willing than he was to let individual officers voice their concerns or suggestions. It was time-consuming, and in most cases a waste of time, but Simonsen never intervened, merely listened, and on the two occasions when Arne Pedersen asked him if he thought this or that, he simply returned the ball with a brief, *that's up to you*.

On their way out of the room, he said to Arne Pedersen:

'We'll meet in my office at six. There are some issues you have yet to be briefed on. You'll also give me a super-condensed review of the state of your Silje Esper murder.'

Arne Pedersen noticed the small *your*, which placed the responsibility for the investigation squarely on his shoulders. His boss was notorious for delegating, and then being unable to let go when push came to shove, but not, it would appear, in this case. This suited Pedersen fine and made him feel a little proud. It also made him a very busy man.

'Yesterday I thought this was a professional killing, but now I'm almost convinced that it wasn't.'

'Killings rarely are, but save your powder until six o'clock. I'll see you later.'

The inner circle had gathered around the conference table in Konrad Simonsen's office: the Countess, Pauline Berg, Klavs Arnold and Arne Pedersen waited excitedly for their boss to begin, which he did by showing them the USB stick and explaining its contents. He finished off:

'. . . but it's obviously important that we keep in mind all the time that the six hundred clients haven't done anything illegal, unless we can prove that some of the women were under eighteen. And even if we can, then we're talking about minor offences punishable by fines, as none of the women is a minor, if you get my drift.'

His audience did. Klavs Arnold said darkly:

'These men bought and paid for sex, that's entirely legitimate and above board. How lucky for them that they didn't get caught buying a suspiciously cheap B&O TV, then we could get them for buying stolen property, because they ought to have known that the price couldn't be right. But even the most dim-witted man must have known that those women wouldn't willingly submit to this unless . . .'

He couldn't think of a suitable image and muttered grimly that this didn't bear thinking about, but he already knew that.

No one disagreed with the Jutlander, and all five of them wished that the politicians would get their act together and ban sex for money, and more importantly criminalise the customers rather than the women. Such legislation would undoubtedly have its downsides, but none that cancelled out the definite benefit of crushing the market for sex trafficking in Denmark. Besides, men's entitlement to buy sex from imported foreign women wasn't a right enshrined in the Danish constitution. Konrad Simonsen said:

'Pauline and Klavs, you'll be joined by a craniologist tomorrow. She's on loan from Melsing, and is the only one apart from him who knows that we're in possession of Jan Podowski's database. Find somewhere you can work undisturbed, and then compare the images we have of the victim from the Hanehoved investigation with the prostitutes in the database. I had a brief go at it myself, and it's an extremely difficult job, but the craniologist is convinced it can be done. It will just take time.

'I would also like you to take a good look at the venues where the activities are taking place. As far as I've been able to establish, each woman has her own room, but I want to know where. You may not be able to find this out, the information on the footage is very limited, but try anyway.'

He paused. Presumably to draw breath before issuing new orders, Klavs Arnold thought. The Countess took over without having been asked; Konrad Simonsen looked at her in surprise, and wondered whether he had accidentally given her a sign that she had misinterpreted.

'We keep our mouths shut about that database. I've asked Malte to make two copies, so currently we have three, but no one must make any further copies without Simon's express permission. We suspect one of our own of having leaked information to the wrong people, and thus they are directly or indirectly responsible for Silje Esper's death. Or – and we can't yet rule this out completely – they might have committed the murder and torture in Karlslille themselves.'

Arne Pedersen asked:

'Is there any link between the customers and us? I mean, to the Homicide Department or to Vestegnens police, whose staff I borrowed?'

Konrad Simonsen seized the opportunity to get back to his agenda. He held up his hand. 'There might well be, but that's not for you to investigate. The deputy director of the Department for Public Prosecution will handle that; a special committee has been set up. And that's your only restriction, Arne. So if at any point you start to suspect that the killer comes from our own ranks, I will take over. And please note that I say *suspect*, not *find indicative evidence*.'

Arne Pedersen accepted this. Konrad Simonsen then handed over to him for a brief – he stressed the word – update on the Karlslille murder investigation.

*

Arne Pedersen complied with his boss's wish for brevity. He had plenty of other things to do, and wasn't interested in a lengthy meeting. So he spoke exclusively about matters that were important but not yet common knowledge. He didn't impose any chronological order; he left that to his audience.

The preliminary forensic investigations suggested one killer, who was not, as had been initially presumed, professional in the slightest when it came to killing, whatever that meant. On the contrary, he seemed borderline desperate. He had tortured the blind woman for at least three hours *after* he had crushed her first finger even though she had presumably already given him all the information she had on her dead boyfriend's USB stick, namely that it smelled of paint. She didn't know any more, yet he had crushed her remaining nine fingers, as well as five toes, and gouged out one eye before he had given up and strangled her. He had smothered her screams with a cloth from the kitchen, and had poured water over her to rouse her when she had passed out from the pain. He appeared to have taken out the cloth when he wanted to interrogate her in between the torture sessions. The result was that he had left excellent DNA evidence on the material, while his hair and a certain number of fibres had been found at the crime scene. The Countess burst out with a short 'Brilliant' when she heard the last part – a sentiment they all shared. Klavs Arnold seized the natural pause to interject a question:

'He shot the dog, but strangled the woman? Do you think that he's a sadist?'

Arne Pedersen shook his head; he didn't think so, more desperate. And perhaps he was angry with the woman because his mission had failed, but it was too early . . . Konrad Simonsen cut him off:

'No details, we can read about them later. Tell them about the hand vice, and then we'll stop. Or rather, the Countess and I will leave. The rest of you are, of course, welcome to stay and carry on talking, if you like.'

Arne Pedersen had no wish to do so; he stated briefly that the hand vice had probably been bought for the purpose and its make could be identified by forensic investigators from imprints on the dead woman's nails, after which the meeting was closed.

CHAPTER 68

Konrad Simonsen was in an excellent mood as he and the Countess walked along the pavement.

Copenhagen and the gentle summer suited one another, and the pair of them took their time. She asked him, 'By the way, where are we going?'

'Three streets away.'

Then he told her that he had removed an entry from Jan Podowski's database. She accepted his decision immediately without knowing the background. It was one of the things he liked about her: she trusted him. His action could be viewed in an unfortunate light – as tampering with evidence, for example. He took out a piece of paper from his inside pocket and gave it to her; she unfolded it, glanced briefly at it, then quickly folded it again and gave it back to him.

'Are we about to meet him?'

'Yes.'

'Where?'

They walked behind Ved Glyptoteket and he pointed in the direction of Tietgensgade; he thought they could find a place behind Tivoli where they could have a beer or a soft drink. She stopped.

'Why did you bring me?'

She was puzzled. Normally his judgement was so assured when it came to witnesses, but here it would appear to have failed him completely. He carried on walking a few steps before he realised that she hadn't followed him. He stopped and went back to her.

'I'm sorry, what did you say?'

'I said, why have you brought me?'

He explained that he didn't like keeping secrets from her, especially when there was no need. She smiled. That sounded lovely, but it was only a half truth. It was also about him wanting to share the moral responsibility for his decision. Wanting her acceptance that he had done the right thing by deleting their friend from the database.

And she did understand; she would probably have done the same herself. But now that he'd had her support, she had no further role to play. Indeed her continued presence was a really bad idea.

'Mind you don't put pressure on him, Simon. He will never tolerate that in any way. And as you yourself highlighted not that long ago: he hasn't done anything illegal. I'll see you tonight, I'll cook supper, but if the two of you want to eat out, that's fine with me, just call to let me know.'

She kissed him. For a moment he stood there, almost like a bashful schoolboy. *Are you leaving?* And finally the penny dropped. *Yes, of course. Of course you are.*

Konrad Simonsen sat down on a bench with his back to Tivoli; behind him he could hear joyful squeals from visitors to the amusement park, in front of him lay Ny Carlsberg Glyptotek, the beautiful museum on Dantes Plads. A young couple, closely entwined, nearly bumped into him. The young man apologised, the girl patted his arm and sent him a beaming smile. There was a happy smell of popcorn and love about the city. He waited ten minutes, then Helmer Hammer arrived.

'Your conversation with Ambassador Rozhdestvenskaya, how glorious, Simon. That story has been round practically every department on Slotsholmen, and everyone is laughing at me. Even my boss finds it hilarious. But tell me, how are your lovely wife and Anna Mia?'

It took ten minutes of conversation before Helmer Hammer asked:

'Right, so tell me, what can I do for you this time?'

'Perhaps you could tell me why you handled the meeting with the Ambassador yourself? It must have caused no end of bureaucratic complications for you, and it would have been far easier for you to send a diplomat from the Foreign Ministry to accompany me. All you had to do was pick up the phone.'

Helmer Hammer didn't reply, Konrad Simonsen carried on:

'However, it did give you plenty of opportunity to stress that under no circumstances must I ask Bepa any follow-up questions.'

Helmer Hammer said quietly:

'What do you want, Simon?'

Konrad Simonsen told him about Jan Podowski, his database, and how he had tampered with it. He left the two pictures in his inside pocket where they were.

Helmer Hammer sat staring inscrutably at the pavement for a while.

'It was a birthday present, I was given two vouchers, but used only one, and I shouldn't even have done that. And, yes, I'm glad that you removed me from the database, I wouldn't want to be found there. But . . .'

Konrad Simonsen waited patiently for the rest.

'I'll help you, Simon, I don't see that I have any real choice. But you're on thin ice here. I hope you're aware of it.'

'No, I'm not. I would never dream of putting pressure on you, directly or indirectly. But I would rather speak to one co-operative witness than squeeze the truth out of twenty unwilling ones. Besides, I have good reason to proceed with caution. After a lifetime in the police, I've heard and seen more . . . unusual and private situations than you can imagine. And this is nothing.'

Helmer Hammer said falteringly, 'No, I don't suppose it is, when you put it like that.' A little later, he added: 'Ask away, and I'll see if I can answer you.'

'Good. You can start by telling me about the vouchers you got, and why you only used one?'

Helmer Hammer explained: he had received two home-made, plastic laminated cards the size of a credit card; on one side there was a smiley, a number, five digits as far as he could recall, and the name of the girl, but only her first name, no surname. On the back was an address and brief instructions: walk around the house, down the basement steps and ring the bell. He had been received by a woman, he had given her his card and . . . well, Simonsen knew the rest.

'Where did the woman live?'

'In Taarbæk, I don't remember the address off the top of my head, but if I were to drive there again, I can definitely find it. Would you like me to do that?'

'Perhaps. You didn't use the other voucher, you say?'

'I threw it away, and I left after several hours with the woman I visited, although I could have spent the night with her. But it seemed wrong, and she was also very young, I'm afraid to say. I should have left the moment I saw her.'

Konrad Simonsen made no attempt to reassure him.

'Yes, you should have, but you didn't. Your friend, the one who gave you the voucher, would it be possible for me to speak to him?'

'It was a woman. She and her husband have . . . an African woman staying with them. But that wasn't where I was invited. I don't wish to report or protect her. However, I think I can find you a witness who is better informed than I am. If you'll excuse me for two minutes.'

Helmer Hammer got up, walked away and made a call on his mobile. He returned soon afterwards.

'You'll have an email with a name and a meeting place by the time you get home. He knows how the system works . . . *the system*, those were his words. Five thousand kroner for a night, it was more than I would have guessed. The list you have, it must be of the great and the good, if I can put it like that.'

Konrad Simonsen was perfectly aware that Hammer was fishing and he deflected the question. 'Yes, it probably is,' he replied, the implication being that he hadn't noticed that particular detail.

'Let's find somewhere we can have a beer, I could do with one now. We can go in there.'

Helmer Hammer tossed his head in the direction of Tivoli. Konrad Simonsen had no wish to drink beer with him, not right now, perhaps some other time. The truth was that he was disappointed in his contact and friend, though he had no right to be. He had imposed his own standards on Helmer Hammer, and they had been violated. He replied unenthusiastically:

'Yes, let's.'

They joined the queue. Helmer Hammer asked cautiously, almost mournfully:

'The African girl who died, was she the one I slept with?'

'I don't know, I didn't watch for very long.'

'So I'll never know?'

Konrad Simonsen shrugged. Perhaps he would . . . well, he could if he wanted to. Helmer Hammer changed the subject and his tone of voice became more business-like, but Konrad Simonsen could still hear that it was forced.

'There's one other thing.'

'Yes?'

'If I were you, I would start with the Integration Ministry and take a good look at the unit that issues au pair permits.'

'That sounds like a very good tip-off, thank you.'

'I can get you a discreet appointment and help your investigation proceed a little more smoothly. I'm good at that sort of thing – but you already know that.'

'Yes, I do, but I'll manage on my own, it's better that way.'

The pause between them grew somewhat awkward. They bought their tickets and entered the Tivoli Gardens. Helmer Hammer said, 'Yes, I suppose it is.' And a little later, he added: 'That business about the au pairs is something that only just crossed my mind. You have to believe me.'

'Of course I believe you,' Konrad Simonsen replied, knowing he was lying.

CHAPTER 69

Pauline Berg was sitting on her balcony on the sixth floor in Rødovre. She was comfortable, it was a pleasant morning, already warm, and everything predicted a lovely day. She was precariously balanced on the ledge at the edge of the balcony. When she became uncomfortable, she would shift slightly forwards or backwards to ease the pressure. Otherwise, everything was as it should be; below her, trains headed for Brøndbyøster Station. She liked the red local trains, they were always there, and there was something reassuring about their familiarity. She waved to one of them. She didn't quite know why she was sitting where she was sitting; it was just the way it was this Monday morning. However, she did know that for the first time in a long, long time she had a sense of being in control of her own life. It was welcome; she ought to sit here more often.

Her Sunday had been dreadful, as so many days were for her. She had worked together with Klavs Arnold and the craniologist; hard work, but also productive. They had eliminated forty-seven of the fifty-one African women in the database. None of them was the African murder victim, and now only four possible candidates remained: Jade, Jessica, Kaya and Kiki. They warranted further investigation, but with a little bit of luck, they would have narrowed it down to just one in the next day or two. Then suddenly, just before they were about to go home, Pauline Berg had developed a dreadful suspicion. The three of them were sitting behind the same computer, a large workstation with two screens, which the craniologist had had moved from her office and set up temporarily in the Homicide Department. Pauline Berg pushed herself forward without explanation and took over the keyboard from Klavs Arnold. He moved to the side, somewhat mystified, and watched her search for a name he didn't recognise. She repeated the search three times, then she got up, spat at the screen and marched out of the room without explaining her absurd behaviour. The Jutlander told the craniologist that his colleague didn't always feel well. Then he fetched a piece of kitchen towel and wiped away her saliva.

Pauline Berg had reached Gammel Strand and got on a canal boat trip. She did this regularly. In the old days she would go to Copenhagen Central Railway Station and get a magazine and a cup of coffee, something she had now replaced with a canal boat trip. She could sit at the back of the boat, crying, usually without anyone noticing her. Yesterday she had got off at Langelinie, walked up to Esplanaden and onwards to Store Kongensgade where she picked a random café and found a random man whom she brought home. He had left a short while ago, and now she was sitting here. She realised she had already forgotten his name, and giggled uncontrollably.

Pauline Berg's front door had been forced open. Konrad Simonsen and Arne Pedersen entered without ringing the bell. In her living room a dozen people were standing or sitting, the balcony door was open, and an older female officer from Gladsaxe police, whom Konrad Simonsen knew well, was in the doorway talking to Pauline. He could see her through the living-room window, the wind tearing at her hair, her back and her face in profile, turned to the officer.

The sense that this was wrong crossed his mind, though a stronger word would have been more suitable, but his immediate thought was that this was wrong. He could feel adrenaline surging in him. Perhaps it was not until now that he truly understood the seriousness of the situation. He took two deep breaths and his pulse settled. But not by much. Then he said with forced calm to Arne Pedersen:

'Get those people out. You yourself will be the last to leave.'

He stepped up to the sergeant from Gladsaxe and placed a hand on her shoulder. 'I'll deal with her from now on, Gudrun.'

When Pauline Berg noticed him, she briefly looked away, and he wondered whether he could lunge forward and grab her before she had time to react. Then she turned her head again, and the moment was gone. He had brought one of her dining chairs with him, and now he placed it right outside the balcony door. He thought it would look less confrontational if he sat down.

'Don't get too close, Simon.'

He made no reply, not even when Pauline informed him a little later, giggling:

'Wait, now I remember, his name was Tom.'

Konrad Simonsen said quietly:

'I spoke to Klavs on my way here. You know I deleted a name from Jan Podowski's database.'

It wasn't until then that they made proper eye contact. She asked:

'Are you worried?'

'Yes, very.'

'Why? You usually get what you want.'

She said it as if it had nothing to do with her, merely a statement of fact. As she was sitting there on the ledge talking to him anyway, she spoke again, now slightly more engaged with him.

'And the same goes for your fine friends, they always come out all right in the end too. But if I carry around a belt buckle, you scream at me.'

He had decided to tell the truth, come what may.

'When you were trapped in that bunker, I traded your life for someone else's. Very few people know that, and now you're one of them.'

Initially she didn't accept this shift in conversation, but giggled again.

'I survived, Jeanette didn't. Nor did Juli, she didn't survive either. But you don't want me to find her killer.'

Jeanette had been killed in the bunker in which Pauline Berg had been imprisoned. Juli was the protagonist in her non-existent murder investigation.

He felt stumped by this and unhelpfully reflected that a professional would have done much better, a trauma counsellor or Pauline Berg's own psychiatrist. What on earth could he do, if he couldn't make proper contact with her, then what? He didn't know. Suddenly she shouted angrily:

'Tell me about that bloody trade. I want to know what happened.'

It was a very long account, but Konrad Simonsen took his time and included all of the details. He wanted to be sure that she understood what he told her. When he had finished, she asked quietly:

'So I owe my life to that Helmer Hammer guy?'

'No, *I* owe your life to that Helmer Hammer guy.'

'Why haven't you told me this before?'

'Because I would rather forget it.'

She nodded sympathetically, it was how she felt about most things these days. Then she looked down for far, far too long. Konrad Simonsen noticed that his temples were throbbing, but he said nothing. Finally she raised her head and looked at him.

'I'm scared, Simon. Everything is turning ugly. Please would you come over and hold me?'

In the car park outside the high-rise apartment block he handed Pauline Berg over to the Countess, who would take her to the psychiatric emergency unit at Glostrup Hospital. It was what the ambulance driver had suggested; Arne Pedersen had discussed it with him. Konrad Simonsen was exhausted, and asked the first officer he saw to drive him home.

CHAPTER 70

The Ministry for Refugees, Immigration and Integration, commonly known as the Integration Ministry, was one of the newer Danish official bodies. It was set up in 2001 for the purpose of facilitating the integration of new arrivals into Danish society, and since its inauguration, and under successive ministers, it had become a political football and the source of several scandals. The Au Pair Office was a subsection of the Immigration Unit, and was housed in Ryesgade in Østerbro, which was where Klavs Arnold drove on Monday afternoon, stepping in to replace his boss, who had gone home after the incident with Pauline Berg earlier that day.

In reception the Jutlander was met by a middle-aged man who made no attempt to hide his irritation at not being sent the head of the Homicide Department as the Ministry had been promised. This man was a permanent undersecretary, and he was clearly nervous. Klavs Arnold apologised for the absence of Konrad Simonsen, but offered no explanation. It was none of his business, as he informed the Permanent Undersecretary when asked directly. And no, cancelling the meeting and postponing it until a time when the Homicide chief would be available wasn't a better option.

The Ministry had been advised of the reason for the meeting in advance and had had time to carry out its own quick investigation. This was because last Friday, Konrad Simonsen had had had second thoughts and taken up Helmer Hammer on his offer to pull strings so the Integration Ministry would be more willing to co-operate with the police. And with him, Klavs Arnold thought, as he was ushered to a conference room where no less than nine people were waiting for him. Soft drinks and biscuits had been set out, and in front of an empty chair at one end of the table, a notepad with the ministerial logo and two needle-sharp pencils had been neatly arranged. He was asked to take a seat.

The moment the Jutlander had sat down, a man in his fifties sitting at the opposite end of the table opened the meeting. Klavs

Arnold missed his title and did not care, but this was clearly the top dog in the room. He announced in smoothly modulated tones that unfortunately there had been some irregularities in the Au Pair Office and as a result, the Ministry intended to carry out a quick but thorough investigation of the matter and pass on any findings to the police. Klavs Arnold was here to provide some input into this investigation, he was told. The Jutlander replied with a brief 'I see,' and the man moved quickly on, because this was only one of two points on today's agenda. The other was that the Ministry and the police should reach an agreement not to inform the public until this investigation had been concluded. 'We obviously can't avoid a scandal, but it's critical that we control the timing. Going public with this right now would be highly inconvenient. Extremely inconvenient. I cannot stress this too strongly.'

Klavs Arnold had plenty of time to study the people around the table, and it was clear to him that the two women sitting at the end next to the top dog were the cause of these irregularities. Their eyes were empty, defeated; one had recently been crying. He was surprised they were even present at the meeting, and he was also shocked that they were female. Men would have been his guess. He wondered how much money they had made on the side.

The top dog had finished, silence ensued and everyone's eyes turned to Klavs Arnold. He pressed one of the pencils against his notepad until it snapped, and observed how the abrupt, sharp sound rippled through those present. Then he snapped the other pencil in half and asked the air, not addressing the question to anyone in particular:

'And how long would it be before I got that report?'

A couple of the men discussed this briefly, then they agreed on a few weeks, one month maximum.

Klavs Arnold got up and positioned himself so that he faced the two women. He pointed at them with one of the broken pencils.

'The two of you are up to your necks in it, but I'm guessing you already know that.'

One of them peered up at him, but was too scared to look him in the eye. She nodded. The other one was crying openly now.

'Let me give you two pieces of good advice. Number one: make sure you own up to everything, absolutely everything, don't hide a thing. Then, if you're lucky, the judge might knock a few months off your prison sentence. Number two: get yourselves a couple of good lawyers as soon as possible, because the gentlemen around this table definitely don't have your best interests at heart.'

Both of them looked at him like drowning people who have just been thrown a lifeline. He dismissed protests from the top dog next to them by raising his hand, then said quietly:

'I presume money changed hands?'

They nodded, red-faced. Yes, money had changed hands.

'And what about your superiors? Did they take a cut or get a free shag from time to time to look the other way?'

The statement hit home; several of the men squirmed uncomfortably on their chairs. The top dog practically screamed: 'That's enough, Sergeant Arnold, or whatever your name is.'

Klavs Arnold, however, shouted even louder; an incoherent roar to make the man shut up. And it worked. The Jutlander pointed at him and said slowly:

'Application forms, residence permits, names and addresses of host families, the names of the women, their nationalities, passport numbers – I want copies of everything. Secondly: the bribes. How much, how were they paid and by whom, as well as procedures, requests, telephone conversations, all emails relating to that . . . everything, including anything I've forgotten, and you'll have that ready for me at twelve noon tomorrow.'

The man shook his head angrily and said icily:

'I'll be speaking to your superiors. It's quite obvious that we have a problem here.'

Klavs Arnold exaggerated his Jutland accent, which seemed the right thing to do in this situation.

'You're right, but I'm not the problem, my wife is. I'm telling you that once she gets the bit between her teeth, there's no stopping her. Once we've put the kids to bed, Stella will spend all night thinking up questions for your minister, even if I assure her that you and I will sort it out on the quiet. So you see, I can't come home with anything less than what I've just suggested.'

It took a couple of seconds before the chairman linked the name Stella to the surname Arnold, then his face went bright red, but he managed to stutter:

'Less than twenty-four hours? That's impossible. I need two days.'

Klavs Arnold was feeling generous:

'Then we'll say ten o'clock Wednesday morning and not an hour later. Right, I had better be on my way. After all, you've got work to do. Enjoy.'

He left.

CHAPTER 71

When the Countess took Pauline Berg to the psychiatric emergency ward at Glostrup Hospital, she was prepared to stay there for as long as necessary, but a nurse, whom Pauline already knew and clearly trusted, soon arrived. The Countess's presence was rendered superfluous; she left after half an hour with a promise to come back that same evening.

On her way to her car, she decided she would drive past Ballerup and pay the chief programmer at NewTalkInTown another visit. But first she called the CEO of the telecommunications company, to tell her about the most recent development in the case, and to make sure that her witness was at work. When she arrived, the CEO was outside the entrance to the company, smoking; she was alone. The Countess would have put her down as a non-smoker, she looked like a health freak who detested tobacco, but appearances could clearly be deceiving. They shook hands, and the woman explained she herself had spoken to the programmer.

'He has a tendency to overreact, if pressed too hard.'

She sounded apologetic, but the Countess appreciated her assistance and was just happy that she could get the information she needed without even having to step inside the building. She left with a brief: 'Thank you for your co-operation.'

Halfway through the week, the Hanehoved case took a new turn. Klavs Arnold had spent a couple of hours on Wednesday afternoon familiarising himself with the fat file he had received from the Integration Ministry. It was clear that a woman called Karina Larsen controlled the system of African au pair girls turned prostitutes. She would appear to be a high-class madam for the gin and tonic belt, with a grand house in Rungsted and ... and then a loud bell started to ring. He found the woman's address, checked another report, and result! He went to see Konrad Simonsen.

'The Poker Academy and the au pair girls are connected, is that what you're telling me?'

'Karina Larsen is married to Svend Lerche; both businesses are run from their home in Rungsted. I wonder if *his* business launders *her* money.'

Konrad Simonsen whistled. Yes, that made sense.

He and the Deputy Commissioner had just visited the National Police Commissioner to ask for more resources, which they had been granted. Now they would have to go back for even more.

Konrad Simonsen restructured his team. He set up a Data group to expose the Poker Academy, including monitoring the players online. An Au Pair group to investigate the fraudulent au pair applications and the trafficking of African women. A Host family group prepared charges against host families, and finally a Logistics group was created to co-ordinate everyone's work and make sure resources were used most efficiently.

It was also the responsibility of the Logistics group to ensure that important information was shared between the groups. Backed by the National Police Commissioner, he was allowed to borrow skilled and experienced senior officers from Vestegnens and Nordsjællands police forces. They headed the Data and Au Pair groups, while Konrad Simonsen himself handled Logistics. He also replaced Arne Pedersen with Klavs Arnold, who now took charge of the Karlslille murder investigation, which meant

Arne Pedersen could assume responsibility for the Host family group.

Everyone worked hard, and the police force's already heavily burdened overtime expenditure grew considerably. Konrad Simonsen couldn't care less. For him, this was purely about getting results and filling the holes in his investigation, and slowly it was happening. Svend Lerche's poker scam was quickly identified by a statistician on loan from the University of Copenhagen. He explained, in a didactic manner, to a large group of officers gathered in Lecture Hall B at Police Headquarters:

'Each poker player plays twice for three hours in the evening and night, once for himself and once for the Poker Academy. The trick is that it's not until afterwards that they decide which half the poker player played for himself and which was for the Academy. Imagine that the game isn't poker, but heads or tails, played with a coin twice. That gives us four options . . .'

Arne Pedersen looked at the chart the statistician was showing them on an overhead projector, then gave up. He looked around and realised he wasn't the only one. He leaned nearer to Konrad Simonsen, who was sitting next to him.

'Do you get it? I bet you do?'

'If you buy a lottery ticket and you're allowed to decide on the Sunday whether your ticket applies to Wednesday's or last Saturday's draw, then you double your chances of winning. But explaining that in court will be hell. Especially when a skilled defence lawyer gets the chance to obfuscate it, then no one has a hope of understanding. I hope this won't be trial by jury.'

'When are you going home today?'

'Late, I guess. The Countess and I are interviewing someone, and afterwards there are many other things I need to get my head around. Why?'

'Because we've narrowed it down to just the one woman, Jessica, and I hope to have a name for you in a matter of hours.'

'Her real name?'

'Yes.'

Arne Pedersen turned to the front and tried to concentrate on the lecture, but it was way too late – the lecturer had added amounts and percentages to his review, and was talking about distributions, whatever they were.

Pedersen asked his boss:

'Why bother with interviews yourself? You're already ridiculously busy.'

Simonsen deflected the implied criticism, saying there were some things you had to do for yourself.

CHAPTER 72

Chamberlain Adam Blixen-Agerskjold was sweating profusely and feeling thoroughly ill at ease. His lawyer looked worried as she studied him, then asked the Homicide investigator sharply: 'Is that the only reason you've dragged my client in here? He's done nothing illegal. Are you going to charge him?'

Konrad Simonsen ignored her and spoke directly to the Chamberlain.

'Jan Podowski ran a business within a business. He provided young African escorts for weekend trips for wealthy men like you. He charged twenty thousand kroner and had plenty of customers, which surprises me, but some people clearly have more money than sense. Jan Podowski would hand over ten thousand kroner to Karina Larsen, who would think she was being paid for two normal visits. But you didn't pay twenty thousand, did you?'

The lawyer intervened again, insisting that nothing illegal had happened, and the very least they could expect was a bit of courtesy to be shown to her client. The Countess ignored the lawyer as well, and continued.

'You knew exactly what went on in your hunting lodge.'

Konrad Simonsen completed her sentence:

'Assaults on young women who were unwilling to be abused. Do you also know what happened there on the nineteenth of March last year?'

The lawyer objected for the umpteenth time. Konrad Simonsen thundered:

'Answer me, damn you!'

It was no use; the Chamberlain continued to sit in silence, staring into the air with a miserable expression on his face. The self-pitying look was sickening, Konrad Simonsen thought as he continued his onslaught. He placed three carefully selected and very graphic pictures in front of the man; the lawyer blushed and looked away. The Countess picked up the conversation.

'But you didn't restrict yourself to weekends . . . you also had fun during weekdays. Incidentally, did Lenette know about your hobby? Your grandmother must be so proud of you, Adam. It's a blessing she no longer understands what's going on.'

'Now that's enough! I've never heard the like . . .'

It was the lawyer speaking again, but it made no difference. Adam Blixen-Agerskjold said, quietly but clearly:

'It was an accident, and I don't know how it happened.'

With some difficulty the lawyer managed to get his attention. She whispered in his ear. She appeared to have to repeat her instructions before the Chamberlain said, in a ridiculously formal voice:

'I won't say anything until you stop the video recording.'

Konrad Simonsen got up and turned off the camera, which was set up behind them.

'Who beat her up?'

'Jan, and he had a helper, he always did. But I don't know who.'

'No one else?'

'No, no one else.'

'How do you know that?'

'There never was.'

'Never, you say. Were women often assaulted in your lodge?'

'Not often, three to four times a year at the most, as far as I know.'

As was so often the case the Chamberlain's confessions, perhaps self-recriminations would be more appropriate, constituted an anti-climax that was unpleasant for both Konrad Simonsen and the Countess to witness. They felt no triumph, rather revulsion – revulsion at this man, and also at their job.

Adam Blixen-Agerskjold had had, as they already knew, his share of the African women in recompense for turning a blind eye to events in his hunting lodge. However, he claimed, in a voice bordering on hysteria, he'd known nothing about Frode Otto's rapes, and they had come as a shock to him. The police officers believed him. He had got to know the programmer from NewTalkInTown when the man and his parents spent their vacation in one of the estate's holiday cabins. The man had later written some customised software for the estate's operations. In return, by way of payment, Adam Blixen-Agerskjold had invited him to a weekend in Paris, with escorts. Later, the man had been given Jan Podowski's work number and had bought himself an African woman whenever he could afford it and had the time and the inclination.

'Was it a coincidence that he was working for the mobile phone provider also used by Frode Otto?'

It wasn't. The Chamberlain told them how the programmer always carried the documentation for introductory offers in his bag. Frode Otto had let himself be persuaded. When the police came too close to the estate bailiff, the Chamberlain had contacted the programmer and asked him to falsify his phone records as they related to Jan Podowski. The Countess asked why.

'I worked out that at some point you would check Frode Otto's calls. But that was before I knew what he had done. I assure you, I would never have agreed to cover for a rapist.'

'Only for a murderer?'

The Chamberlain said miserably:

'It was an accident.'

'Do you know why Frode Otto confessed to the rapes, but refused to talk about the au pairs?'

'No, I've no idea.'

'Did you know where Jan Podowski lived?'

'No.'

'Does Frode Otto know?'

'I would think so. They were friends.'

'Who did Jan Podowski work for?'

'Karina Larsen and Svend Lerche, a couple from Klampenborg, I think.'

They carried on for a while without it producing much more in the way of results. When Konrad Simonsen finally finished, Adam Blixen-Agerskjold asked in a tired voice:

'What's going to happen to me?'

'Absolutely nothing,' his lawyer replied. 'You might be charged, but you're under no obligation to incriminate yourself, and they have nothing on which they can convict you. At some point the charges will be dropped.'

Sadly that was the truth.

CHAPTER 73

Konrad Simonsen spent an hour he didn't have decorating his office with pictures of all of Jessica's customers as recorded in Jan Podowski's database. He knew by now that they were just a drop in the ocean; it had become clear that the database contained only the names of customers who were rich, famous or both. Jan Podowski had presumably planned to blackmail them to add to his retirement fund, but as they now knew, he never made it that far. Malte Borup produced the printouts, and underneath each face he had written the person's name and position in big letters: Hans Tage Smidt, CEO; Peter Ertmann, first violinist; Niels Sværte, head teacher – Konrad Simonsen cheered every time he neatly stuck a piece of paper to the wall. There were fifty-four pictures, so it took some time. He had borrowed a ladder from the cleaners and at the very top he had placed the picture of the victim whose real name was still unknown.

This changed about ten minutes after he had finished the wall, when Arne Pedersen entered. His deputy studied the wall in detail.

'Impressive, Simon. You know a thing or two about rogues' galleries.'

'So, do you have her real name?'

Arne Pedersen handed his boss a piece of paper. He had compared the passport photos from the Au Pair Office to the women on the USB stick and now knew their real names and nationalities. Konrad Simonsen read it and said hesitantly:

'Ifunanya Siasia . . . that's a beautiful name. Please give this list to Malte.'

'Yes, boss. And how about her description? May I suggest, "Nigerian, aged sixteen"?'

Konrad Simonsen nodded gravely, it was a good suggestion. A damned good suggestion.

CHAPTER 74

Henrik Krag could smell lilacs. Lilacs and rum. He knew where the scent of rum was coming from, but he couldn't see lilacs anywhere.

He looked around: a big Japanese cherry tree immediately to his left, a hedge teeming with yellow flowers, whose name he didn't know, but no lilacs. He had stopped without knowing why, maybe it was those sodding lilacs or maybe his body was objecting to his task and wanted to slow him down. His legs started to wobble, not as badly as when he had got up an hour ago, but no less irritating, not to say worrying.

He took out the bottle of rum, held it up to a street light and could see that he had drunk less than a third of it. So he took a big swig, followed by another somewhat smaller one, and heat spread through him and steadied his knees. It was a balancing act: it was about reaching the point where he could still do what he needed to do, but not be afraid. Or maybe it wasn't about fear, maybe it was because the rum chased away reality and made everything bearable. It enabled him to focus on one thing at a time, not to look back, not to think ahead, just do what needed doing right now. He walked on, turned right; the next road on his left would take him to his destination. His watch told him it was 1.55 a.m.

Vallensbæk Village lies between the Holbæk and the Køge Bugt motorways, and Henrik Krag knew the area well. It wasn't far from where he lived, and he had cycled there tonight, his bicycle being less conspicuous than his motorbike. He had left the bike behind a bus shelter a kilometre away and thought that when he next saw it all this would be over. He had already broken his task into stages; the bike ride was the first, and the walk to the house was the second. The two easiest, true, but at least they were done now, and every little helped.

It was a square, red-brick house, neither big nor small, that almost bordered the road. It had a semi-basement and a raised ground floor, a mansard roof and wide black-painted windows; an ordinary house, a Goldilocks house, was how he would describe it. Alongside the house was a paved driveway almost completely taken up by a truck, which Ida had told him about. The truck was facing the road and backed up to the house wall with great precision, ready to leave in the early hours when its owner would drive to the vegetable market.

There was just enough room for him to squeeze his way between it and the wall of the neighbouring house. He waited for a while between the wall and the cabin of the truck, methodically scanning the windows in the houses across the road. There were no lights on in any of them, nor any signs of activity. He went back onto the road to inspect the house he would be entering, but were there no signs of life in there; everyone was asleep. He sidled up the driveway and past the truck. He stopped twice to listen, but only his own footsteps broke the silence; they seemed far too loud to him. He knew it was a trick of the mind, he was wearing trainers with rubber soles, but even so he started to tread carefully, slowly.

Behind the house there was a small yard between a workshop of some kind and a back entrance to the house. Brick steps led up to the kitchen door, while others led down to the semi-basement. A blue Suzuki was parked in the yard. He checked the windows of the house for signs of life again and, finding none, walked down the steps and tried the door. It was locked, as he had expected it to be. He went back up and squatted down in front of one of the two semi-basement windows. It was roughly fifty centimetres in height, one metre wide and it was ajar; he slipped in his hand and checked that he could pull up the hasp. Then he took his torch, shone it through the windowpane and saw three removal crates stacked on top of each other, and a pool table with two cues lying across the surface. Right, he thought, that was the third stage. He turned off the torch, put it back in his inside pocket and swapped it for the bottle of rum.

The next task had to be executed quickly. He couldn't be sure that someone might not wake up in the neighbouring houses and glance out of the window. It was a question of speed now; there was no more time to waste looking around.

He returned to the front of the house. An ornamental chain was suspended from a row of half-metre-high posts, dug into the ground at fifty-centimetre intervals. The chain was rustically rusty, presumably the intention. He tore it away from the first post; it was easy, fixed with only one staple to the crumbling wood, a child could have done it. As quickly as he could, he moved along the posts, freeing the chain from each of them, wrapping it around his shoulder as he progressed. It was heavier than he had expected, but not so heavy that it was a problem; he could easily carry it. When he had finished, he slipped into the shadows in his old spot next to the truck and studied the windows in the houses across the road again. As before: no one in sight.

He suppressed the urge to have another swig of rum and proceeded directly to the next stage, unwrapping the chain and putting it on the ground by the front wheel of the truck that was closest to the house wall. He reached one end as far in between the wheel and the neighbouring wall as he could. Then he walked around the truck, lay down on his stomach and crawled underneath it. With some difficulty he grabbed hold of the end of the chain and carefully pulled it along as he reversed out. He rolled over, turned on his torch, found a strut on the chassis frame, wound the end of the chain around it and managed to tie five knots before it ran out.

When he was free of the truck, he allowed himself some rum, but only two little sips, plus another for luck. Then he went back to the front wheel to pick up the other end of the chain and trailed it along the foundations of the house until he reached the light-well of the semi-basement window facing the drive where the curtains were closed. Quietly, one metre at a time, he let the rest of the chain slip into the light-well, there was plenty of it, plenty ... he prayed for rain, heavy rain, it would lessen the pain.

CHAPTER 75

Getting through the half-open semi-basement window at the back, which opened upwards and outwards, proved no obstacle for Henrik Krag. He wiggled through on his stomach, legs first, with his rucksack in front of him. Once inside, he pulled the rucksack on his back again, and briefly turned on his torch, before turning it off and then walking softly through the room, edging his way around an old television set and opening a door to a passage.

The door's brass handle squeaked loudly no matter how careful he was. He opened the door just enough to be able to slip through and took forever to close it again. Once he was at the bottom of the stairs, he disabled the lock to the semi-basement door, which faced the steps he had walked down earlier, while checking if the door was locked. Now he had a quick way out, should it become necessary, which he hoped it wouldn't. If everything went according to plan, the idea was to leave as quietly as he had arrived.

He waited until his eyes had adjusted to the darkness, then he followed the passage, which turned left after a few metres, and ended at a white-painted door. He shone his torch into a laundry room with a washing machine, tumble dryer and a clothes horse with things drying on it. He walked on, then he took a couple of deep breaths, carefully pushed down the handle and opened the white-painted door, stepped inside and closed the door behind him.

Henrik Krag's heart was racing, his pulse galloping, and his temples throbbing. It took him a few seconds to realise that he could see perfectly well. He hadn't factored that in. A little light crept under the curtain – not much, but enough to see by. He sat down on a nearby chair, which stood opposite a desk with a pair of trousers lying on it that he shoved onto the floor. Then he took a big gulp of rum, which was very much needed.

The couple on the bed were asleep, the young man on his back with his mouth open, his breathing calm and steady. The young woman lay on the other side of him with her face turned towards his shoulder. Her hair was flowing around her and she was snoring, a small, fine sound, which would occasionally turn into a grunt and break off, only to start up a few seconds later.

Henrik took off his rucksack, slipped on his knuckle-duster and took out the knife. It was his biggest kitchen knife, and its primary purpose was to induce fear and hopefully to make them shut up. If he had to resort to violence, it wouldn't be the knife, he vowed to himself. The knuckle-duster, yes, the knife, no. He studied the young man for a while; he was of slim build and presented no physical challenge. All that remained was what Henrik had always regarded as his biggest problem: they mustn't scream. Neither of them.

He pulled a balaclava over his head, flicked on the light switch and reached their heads in two steps, brandishing the knife. His eyes adapted more quickly to the light than he had expected. *Lie very still, be quiet, don't make a sound, and nothing will happen.* Still they panicked, the boy squealed, Henrik hit him. *Shut up! Make another sound and you're dead.* Then the girl clasped her hands over her ears and started trembling hysterically, so he hit her too. Neither of them screamed, they merely whimpered.

'Stay where you are,' he snarled angrily. 'And shut up! Just lie still, God dammit. Close your eyes, and if one of you opens them again, I'll cut the other one's throat.'

They both squeezed them shut, reaching for one another exactly as they were supposed to.

'I'm going to pull the duvet over your heads, and you'll stay calm the whole time.'

The girl gasped and clung to her boyfriend. Henrik Krag added:

'No, not that. Nothing of that sort will happen to you … to either of you.'

He pulled it up and over them, stuffing the end between the mattress and the headboard, so they couldn't see anything. They were naked and both tried pulling the duvet back to cover their groins, stretching it as far as possible. His earlier assurances had had no effect. He found a blanket on an armchair next to the window, unfolded it and covered them with it, so that only their feet and calves were visible. The girl had wet herself, he could see a dark stain but smell nothing, oddly enough. They began to relax a little, he could see. Good. He turned off the light, and tried to work out how many stages he had now covered, but couldn't remember. Then he drew the curtains and opened the semi-basement window. It tipped upwards and outwards just like the one he had climbed through earlier; it was the same type, only painted white. He lifted the coiled chain he'd left in the light-well and closed the window over it. Then he dragged the chain across the floor and placed it on the bed by their feet. From his rucksack, he took out a roll of gaffer tape.

The waiting was terrible. He nearly fell asleep sitting on the chair, so had to stand up. From time to time he would fling aside a corner of the duvet and repeat his order for them to lie still, but apart from that he had nothing else to do. After all the rum, he needed to pee. What an idiot he was, he should have gone earlier. He held it in and suffered. At regular intervals he checked his watch. It wasn't even 2.30 a.m. Time passed slowly, more slowly than he could ever remember it passing. Finally he heard activity upstairs: footsteps moving about above, then a gurgling of pipes somewhere, then footsteps again.

The person upstairs chose to leave by the kitchen door, as Henrik Krag had hoped. Otherwise he would have walked all the way along the posts and couldn't have failed to have noticed the missing chain.

Whether he would also have worked out where it was now seemed less likely, but could definitely not be ruled out.

However, he had chosen the kitchen door, and now Henrik Krag could stop worrying. He heard the door of the truck slam shut and soon afterwards the sound of the powerful engine starting up, mixed with music. The chain stirred, rattled, but didn't tighten, the shadow of the truck from the street light slowly travelled past the window, and then . . . suddenly the two young people were yanked out of the window much, much faster than he had expected. They left their screams behind them, despite the gaffer tape, and Henrik Krag threw up. He couldn't help it. He did so again outside in the yard, and realised that the police would now be able to trace him.

Then he panicked and ran.

CHAPTER 76

Svend Lerche rang his daughter's doorbell with some hesitation. Two quick presses. After all, it was only seven in the morning, but he thought he had heard her moving inside. Benedikte Lerche-Larsen opened the door and, when she saw who it was, turned on her heel and marched straight back inside the flat, but left the door open. Svend Lerche followed her and sat down at the dining table; she emerged from the kitchen, put a cup of coffee in front of him, still without saying anything, then sat down on the opposite side of the table with her own cup.

'Is this going to take long, Svend? Because if it is, then I need to make a few phone calls first.'

He shook his head.

'Tell me, are you ill?' she asked. 'You don't look too good.'

Svend Lerche looked what he was – a troubled man, a man who hadn't slept all night. He dismissed her question with a wave of his hand. *So-so*, it was meant to indicate.

'Your flat has been sorted; I'll bring up the papers for you as soon as I get them, this afternoon at the latest. And I bought the place in such a way that you won't get into trouble in the event of my death. We can review the paperwork tonight, if you have time.'

Henrik Krag and she had finally opted for a loft apartment on Gråbrødre Torv in central Copenhagen.

'Why are you being so nice to me? It's not like you. And what kind of trouble might you be having?'

Svend Lerche ignored her rudeness and partly deflected the question.

'It's Jimmy Heeger, the new man, the one whose eye you poked out. He's no longer with us, I've sacked him.'

'Because?'

'Well, you were right, he didn't fit in, and he's screwed up big time. Don't ask any more questions, it's not something you need to know about. But other things have happened, and if it's a pattern, I mean, if it's all connected, it's . . . very worrying.'

He explained. Karina Larsen's contacts in the Integration Ministry were no longer taking her calls; there was an inexplicable drop of more than twenty per cent in client numbers for their Nigerian staff and more than a thirty-five per cent decrease compared to last year's turnover at the same time. Which couldn't be explained by a random, statistical fluctuation, if she knew what he meant. She nodded, somewhat exasperated, it was he who had bottle-fed her probability calculations. He continued: six poker players and three host families had opted out of the programme, without warning, in the very same week.

She let him finish, fetched him another cup of coffee, but none for herself, and drew the conclusion for him.

'So I'm not getting any time off work? Is that what you're trying to say?'

He confirmed it, he needed her more than ever, and she accepted that. Tentatively, as if uttering the words was hard for him, he added:

'We may be forced to shut down for a while, put everything on the backburner. Your mother and I may . . . go away on holiday.'

Benedikte Lerche-Larsen nodded; she understood completely what he was saying.

'You don't think it's a coincidence?'

'Unfortunately not, I think we're being watched.'

'What does Bjarne say? Does he agree we should shut everything down?'

'It's by no means certain that's how it'll end.'

'So what you're telling me is, you haven't spoken to him?'

Her father failed to answer, nor was it necessary. Instead he asked: 'What are you doing today?'

'Buying myself a car, going for a walk with Henrik, going to the university, helping Karina with—'

As she counted things off on her fingers, he interrupted her.

'OK, I get it. Let me ask in another way: what can you cancel?'

'Everything except Henrik.'

He smiled for the first time that morning.

'You've taken quite a shine to him, haven't you? Don't forget to take a coat if you're going for a walk. They say it's going to rain.'

She got up without replying. Henrik Krag was none of his business.

'I'll be down in your office in half an hour.'

CHAPTER 77

Every time Helena Holt Andersen visited Viborg the town seemed increasingly alien to her.

It was where she was born, had gone to school and college, and she had lived here half the time she attended university.

But that was a long time ago now, the town had changed and so had she. Today she felt more at home in Copenhagen, possibly because she now had children of her own, and they had grown up in the capital. It was hard to pinpoint what made you belong to one place rather than another, and yet it was often a matter of huge importance. Despite her diminishing sense of belonging, she had continued to represent her old constituency, although she had had many opportunities to replace it with one closer to the capital, which – and this was the crucial part – was an equally safe seat.

It was the centenary of the local party branch. She was the main speaker this morning – and tonight as well. She looked around and met smiling faces, but also many she didn't recognise. Clearly she had no excuse for declining the invitation when she was asked, and at the time – more than six months ago – she had also wanted to attend. Unfortunately the centenary now clashed with frantic negotiations within the area of social care in which she was her party's spokeswoman, making it tricky for her to be away from Folketinget right now, and her fellow party members had dropped many heavy hints about her cancelling her trip to Jutland. Which might explain why she hadn't done so.

The guests were singing. She sang along as she took out her speech and placed it beside her plate. She was due to speak next, but she had to pick the right moment to start – people should also have time to enjoy their food. And their drink; a bottle of bitters was making the rounds. She passed it on with a brief shake of her head. At the same time she tried telling herself that she ought to be sensible and give the speech she had prepared.

In theory she had had free range when it came to picking the topic. The party chairman's suggestions were wide and varied. *The current political situation. Or something about the future, something you can build on, Helena, you choose.* Something you can build on ... God help us all! Nevertheless, it was what she told her secretary. *Please write something about the future we can build on, visions and, well, you know what I mean.* Which she had done, and the result lay ready on the table. Easy, uncontroversial, an assured success – if she could pull herself together for fifteen minutes and deliver it. Helena was a good public speaker; it was one of her strengths, possibly her greatest. And now all she had to do was give her damn speech, nothing more.

The problem was that last night she'd happened to flick through a copy of *Viborg Folkeblad* and had stumbled across an article written by the local branch chairman. Headline: *There'll always be hookers.* Subheading: *Why we shouldn't ban sex for money.*

Hookers . . . how she hated that word. Hookers, monkeys, pakis, retards – those words all represented the same thing, the natural right of the stronger to linguistically denigrate the weaker. In the article the branch chairman had echoed all the usual ridiculous objections to a ban, arguments which didn't bear closer scrutiny, but which were nevertheless repeated over and over, as if the debate never moved forwards, but had to start at the beginning every single time.

If you banned selling sex for money, prostitutes would become even more vulnerable, relegated to shady backstreet brothels. Many sex workers – another expression she hated – were absolutely fine with their profession and would not have chosen another. Disabled people should also have the opportunity to have sex. A ban would be impossible to enforce. She shook her head and tried yet again to dismiss her thoughts, again in vain.

It was ultimately about power. Men's power over women, although in rare instances rich women's power over poor men. The power to have a sexual relationship where the buyer didn't have to deal with the seller, their humiliation, their degradation – and the countless cases she knew from the Copenhagen prostitution scene where women were subjected to indescribably awful things – all of this the buyer could shrug off. It wasn't his problem. After all, he had paid.

It was eight years since she had embraced this cause. It was a lost cause, her Achilles heel, if she wanted to rise in the political firmament, but it was a cause for which she burned. Back then she had the support of exactly two of her colleagues, and had become a target for personal attacks that more than hinted that her views were about her having issues with her own sexuality. She had achieved a lot since then; a party congress decision opposing sex for money was no longer the stuff of fantasy. But, more importantly, she was taken seriously; the powers that be had been challenged, albeit they were still far from vanquished. The local branch chairman's moronic article was proof of that. Besides, it was obviously aimed directly at her, though he had not, of course, mentioned her by name. He didn't have the guts, the coward.

She took a sip of juice, got up, crossed to the middle of the floor where she focused on the chairman. Then she began to speak in a loud, clear voice:

'The happy hooker is a myth . . .'

CHAPTER 78

The officer who entered the room was in uniform. Even so, no one took any notice of him; everyone was looking at Helena Holt Andersen.

She gesticulated, fingers synchronising with her voice almost as if she were performing her own sign language. Her gaze shifted from audience member to audience member, convincing, confronting, conscious of her effect on pretty much every single person there. She spoke quickly with three, sometimes four, points intertwined, but at the same time with a brilliant command of language, which meant that she brought her arguments elegantly home . . . a display of intelligence, which was attractive in itself, without at any point coming across as manic or excessive. However, neither of those factors explained her well-deserved reputation for getting through to people. It was based on something much simpler: she believed what she said with every fibre of her being, and she was honestly committed to the people she championed.

The police officer debated whether to let her finish her speech or interrupt her but concluded he had no choice. The information he had been given over the phone about the attack in Vallensbæk was too distressing to wait.

The young man and woman had been dragged through a semi-basement window and down to the end of a residential road. Here the truck had stopped for a passenger car, a taxi, which had turned down the road just as the truck was leaving. Despite their serious injuries, the couple tried to get up and away, only to be pulled back down and knocked over a second later and swung around the corner. Here one of the young man's eyes had been ripped out by a loose wire fence. The young woman's head was smashed against a road sign and then another as she was dragged across the central reservation. The next hundred metres were down a straight road and the truck had accelerated.

There was no doubt that the couple would have died except that the taxi driver spotted them as he turned into the road, and reacted with impressive speed. Ignoring the protests from his astonished customer, who had seen nothing, he spun the car one hundred and eighty degrees, hit the accelerator and raced as fast as he could down the wrong side of road before cutting in front of the truck and blocking it.

The truck driver slammed on the brakes and got out furiously; the taxi driver dragged him to the back of his vehicle, where he collapsed when he saw what he had done to his own daughter. The taxi driver called an ambulance while a nurse, who had been woken up by the noise, came running out into the road in her nightdress and administered first aid.

The officer could see the fear in the politician's eyes; she was a mother first and foremost. He broke the news as sensitively as he could.

'Your son has been in an accident. He'll survive, but one eye is badly damaged.'

Helena Holt Andersen left with the officer, dazed, unable to take in the information. A few people clapped but were hushed by the others. The chairman rushed after the officer and the politician; his face was grave, but inside he was cheering.

Helena Holt Andersen was right: it was all about power, and the exercise of power was ruthless.

CHAPTER 79

'It's as if Svend has found some way of disciplining me my whole life, a way to mould me into what he wanted me to be. Later, when I learned to put up with it – or possibly even fight back – he would just think of something else.'

Benedikte Lerche-Larsen's father had been her pet subject in recent days. Henrik Krag listened and interjected brief, suitable remarks from time to time. They were walking together through the forest, trying to keep as straight a line as possible. He thought that even when they went for a walk, she dressed well. She wore camel-coloured suede brogues, black jeans, a white silk shirt and an emerald green tweed jacket.

She had suggested that they took the direct route through the forest from the main road rather than walk down the country lane and around the hunting lodge. *I don't need to see that blasted place again.* Henrik Krag agreed, but for him that applied to everywhere in that cursed forest, including the lake they were currently heading towards. He had a hangover after this morning's terrible . . . incident, and had taken a few pills, though they had yet to make much difference. They crawled under an upended tree, she waited for him on the other side and snuggled up to him, resting her head against his chest, which made it difficult for them to walk. The rain had held off. It was cloudy above the spruces, but it wasn't cold.

'As a child – not long after I'd started school – I would often dream that I was dead. I would lie there, a little girl tossed among lots of other bodies in my red coat, and I would be the only thing you could see on the pile. All the other dead people were anonymous, pale, black and white, gone somehow, as they ought to be. But I stood out and I wanted to adjust my coat so it would cover my legs better, but I couldn't. I *had* to, my father shouted at me, but it was impossible. He threatened to kill me if I didn't look decent. Kill me *again*, I mean, I was already dead. It was ridiculous and at the same time so frightening, you can't imagine. *Kill me again.*' She threw back her head dramatically. 'Isn't that crazy?' Henrik Krag responded without paying her much attention, he had enough problems of his own. She didn't seem to notice his lack of interest, and carried on.

'I always had to look decent, respectable, take care of all my things, always know where they were, stay on top of everything that was mine. After I became a grown-up that has mostly been money. Not only, but mostly. I've been thinking, Henrik, maybe I could get an ordinary job and perhaps we could manage on less?'

'Says the girl who has just bought a flat for four million kroner in cash.'

He caught a glimpse of her disappointment before she covered it up with a smile. He apologised, genuinely sorry, and hugged her, trying to tell her how much he loved her, although he struggled to find the right words. The embrace also made him feel better. It was easy to imagine they were the only two people left in the world, or that they were far removed from all their problems out here in the forest. He thought that whatever happened . . . whatever happened to him that is, not to her, nothing must happen to her . . . then it would all have been worth it.

They stood like this for a while before she snapped out of her reverie. As if she could read his thoughts, she said:

'Something good is about to happen, Henrik. And in the long run I'm sure we'll be all right – I know we will. We have our whole lives in front of us and we have each other. That's no bad thing, we must never forget that.'

He tried to kiss her, it was the only response he could think of. She put her hand on his chest and gently pushed him away.

'No, don't interrupt me. I'm nervous, that's why I'm rambling like this. But even so I still have to know. Was that you in Karlslille – Jan's girlfriend?'

His mouth felt dry, knowing what her next question would be.

'No.'

'I'm so glad about that, but then it must have been you this morning, the two teenagers in Vallensbæk?'

'I didn't think . . .'

She interrupted him softly.

'Was it, Henrik?'

He nodded.

CHAPTER 80

Henrik Krag and Benedikte Lerche-Larsen were lost; by now they should be near the lake and the deciduous part of the forest. They split up in order to search more efficiently, but kept within sight of one another. Perhaps it was just as well. He needed privacy to compose himself; it had been easier when she didn't know anything about this morning. When *no one* knew anything. But it didn't take long before she came back to him, took his hand and pointed. He followed her.

'What's the good news? You said earlier that you had some good news.'

She squeezed his hand a little harder; they could see the lake diagonally in front of them.

'So I have but I'm starting to get a bad feeling about this trip. We should have come here ages ago. I know we've both been scared to come back, but putting it off was a mistake.'

She pointed to the deer stand, which had just come into view. They could see across to the other side of the lake, to where they had carried the body of the Nigerian girl into the water. It wasn't a great distance, shorter than Henrik Krag remembered. He stood still. Now it was his turn to ask a question.

'There's something I need to know. I haven't dared ask it before. Why me, Benedikte? And why so quickly? Two weeks ago, I was walking up and down some stupid beach missing you like crazy, today we're a couple about to move in together. Don't get me wrong, I'm happy about it – happier than I think I've ever been – but I don't understand it.'

She replied matter-of-factly:

'Because we're alike. You don't think so, but we are. And because you love me, it makes me feel safe.'

He blurted it out because he knew he would never dare ask otherwise. 'Do you love me?'

She stood for a long time without looking him in the eye, and eventually she replied.

'Now don't get upset, Henrik, but I don't think I can really love anyone. It's not about you, sadly. It's just the way it is. But perhaps I can learn, perhaps you can teach me. Who knows?'

She caressed his cheek, and he couldn't decide whether that was good or bad. She continued:

'Right, do you want the good news? I think we could do with some.'

He would.

'You're going to be a dad.'

The deer stand was nearly five metres high, but it was made of pressure-treated timber and looked solid enough. Benedikte Lerche-Larsen was the first to scale the ladder. When she had climbed a few steps, Henrik Krag ran his hand up the inside of her thigh; she turned to look down at him. *Hands off, you fool.* He didn't do it because he wanted her, he always did, but more to prove to himself that he could, that he was allowed. He grinned and smacked her calf, then waited until she was at the top before following.

When he joined her, she was looking shocked. The picture they had received from Ida was lying in her lap from where it had slipped out of her hands. He took it, looked across the lake, compared the two and reached the same conclusion that she had:

it hadn't been taken from up here, it couldn't have been, it was obvious once you sat here. All this time they had been thinking this must be what had happened. A bird-lover with a camera zoom. But it was impossible, the angles were all wrong. He felt his old fear return.

'So what do we do now?'

She didn't reply. Instead she climbed down with a grim expression on her face. He picked up the picture and rushed after her.

There was a post at the spot where they had lugged the Nigerian girl into the water. It hadn't been there before, as far as Henrik Krag could recall. He wondered if it had been put there because of her, and concluded that it must have been.

Benedikte Lerche-Larsen squatted down with the photograph in her hands; she peered up the slope and would occasionally move a little closer or further away from the lake. He was standing behind her, looking at the picture. It was clear that the angles were right. Nevertheless, she kept shifting position before suddenly taking the picture out of its plastic folder and tearing it into tiny pieces. Not angry, slowly, almost lazily.

'Jan Podowski.'

She shook her head and pressed her hands over her ears.

'Jan Podowski . . . and your dad.'

She screamed. Shut up! He was to shut his big mouth, she just wanted to go home. She flung aside the last fragments of paper. She wanted to go home, it was the only thing she wanted to do, go home. Now. He held her, she shook off his arm, but by now he was starting to know her and he persisted. *All right, Benedikte, then let's go home.* When they had walked a few steps, she said:

'The picture is gone, I'll never think about it again.'

She was crying, and he gently dried her cheeks with the back of his fingers. Yes, the photograph was gone, but he could vividly recall the yellow dot pattern, and in his flat he had several photocopies of instructions from when he had worked for Svend Lerche. He would examine and compare them. He had to, for her sake . . . and for the sake of their child. He lifted up his head and nodded towards the sky. Yes, that was what he was going to do.

CHAPTER 81

Bertha Steenholt, the Public Prosecutor, lived up to her nickname as she stood in Konrad Simonsen's office, lightly clenched fists resting on her solid hips while she carefully studied the portraits on the Homicide chief's wall.

She's the size of a primeval cow, Konrad Simonsen thought, and acknowledged in the same moment that he wasn't entirely sure what such a creature looked like. He had positioned himself diagonally behind her, ready to answer her questions; he couldn't help smiling stiffly although there was nothing much to smile about. He felt like a bellboy with a guest with no luggage. He ought to sit down rather than stand about uselessly and probably get on her nerves, though he was trying to be helpful. In her place he would have felt irritated, he thought, and yet he stayed where he was, shifting his weight from foot to foot. It was a habit he had acquired many years ago as a young officer on guard duty, and which had now come back to him, though he couldn't think why.

There was a knock on the door and the Countess entered; she greeted the Public Prosecutor and was rewarded with a short, nasal sound and vague outburst, which could mean anything from *hello* to *don't disturb me*. The Countess lined up to look at the pictures as well. Now three of them stood in silence. Behind Bertha Steenholt's broad back Konrad Simonsen turned his frozen smile on the Countess. When he had heard the knock, he had assumed that it would be the Deputy Commissioner, who had an uncanny ability to turn up in the wake of the Public Prosecutor. Almost as if she were constantly lying in wait around the corners of the Homicide Department's corridor, in order to 'accidentally' bump into her whenever the opportunity arose: *Oh, my, are you here? Oh, how lovely*. But today her vigilance appeared to have let her down. For now.

Bertha Steenholt raised her head and nodded briefly at the female portrait at the very top.

'I gather that's the nignog?'

It was impossible to say where Konrad Simonsen found the courage, but possibly it was the stirrings of a minor rebellion because he had been standing in attendance for so long and felt the urge to claim a little independence. Whatever the reason, he took a step forward, looked her in the eye and said, more sharply than was necessary:

'Ifunanya Siasia. In here we call her Ifunanya Siasia!'

He stressed the words *in here* clearly, almost aggressively. The big woman frowned, then she looked up again at the picture of the young Nigerian woman and said in a conciliatory tone:

'Yes, fair enough. Ifunanya Siasia was her name and Ifunanya Siasia is what we'll call her. I apologise.' Then she asked in her professional voice, 'Right, where are we? What's the current state of the Hanehoved investigation? I gather it has turned into a major inquiry in record time.'

The current state of the Hanehoved investigation . . . Konrad Simonsen recognised his own turn of phrase.

'I've just sent you a lengthy memo about precisely the current state of my investigation.'

'Yes, and I'm here because I can't be bothered to read thirty-five pages when I can get you to give me the highlights in fifteen minutes.'

The Countess grinned, this was proper plain speaking; she suggested they all sat down, which was met with approval. As they settled around Konrad Simonsen's conference table, Bertha Steenholt expanded on the reason for her visit.

'I'm also here because I've heard about your rogues' gallery and I wanted to see it. While we're on the subject, Simon – why are they on your wall? I assume none of them is anything other than peripherally involved in your investigation?' She gave him time to confirm her assumption, before she continued. 'Good, because I hope you know that they haven't broken any laws – at least, none that I can prove.'

It was the Countess who provided the answer. The clients of the African girl were on display because they deserved it. To be put in the stocks, that was why. And also because it was outrageous that none of them could be held responsible for Ifunanya Siasia's life and fate, although each and every one of them shared in the responsibility for her death.

The Public Prosecutor slammed a massive fist on the table, shaking it; she agreed with them, they shouldn't think otherwise, but she wasn't going to tilt at windmills. She made this admission with regret, and also when she added that she genuinely believed the Homicide Department's time was better spent on people who could potentially be convicted, rather than those who couldn't. It was an irrefutable argument, which also served as Konrad Simonsen's cue to update her about his case seeing as she wouldn't take the trouble to read his memo. He cleared his throat and began.

'We're close to tracking down the henchmen, or the employees, if you like, of Karina Larsen and Svend Lerche. Including those who used to work for them, but don't do now, which is just as significant. One of them took part in the murder of Ifunanya Siasia on the nineteenth of March 2008 in Hanehoved Forest, together with Jan Podowski, who you already know about. I don't think it'll be long before we know the identity of his accomplice. A couple of weeks, maximum, would be my guess. Whether we also manage to find enough evidence to convict him – only time will tell.'

'And the other murder, the blind woman in Karlslille, how is that going?'

'It's part of the same investigation if the killer is also on the couple's payroll, and he might very well be. Again I think uncovering that too is only a matter of time. And here we do have excellent DNA evidence, so it'll be difficult for the killer to talk his way out of that.'

'Might it be the same killer?'

'Easily, but we're not able to prove that for the time being.'

She accepted that and he moved on.

'Then there's the scam with the prostituted au pairs. Here we have made significant progress.'

Konrad Simonsen spent the next ten minutes explaining how Karina Larsen's customers bought access to her prostitutes. The customer first needed to register with her, and she only accepted them if they came recommended by two existing customers. Once registered, you could get access to a woman by buying a card that usually cost five thousand kroner. There were two types of cards, green and red; one gave access to a specific woman, the other a free choice.

Once you had bought a card of any colour, you logged in to Karina Larsen's homepage using the unique card number, where you could view a list of women available and book the time you wanted. These cards could be bought in a variety of ways, of which the simplest was to visit the Skovridderkroen Restaurant in Klampenborg any night between six and seven, where one of Karina Larsen's staff would be waiting to sell them. Payment was always in cash, and the au pairs made sure to get the card back when the men visited them. A range of discounts and special offers was available to regular clients. Would she like him to explain those? The Public Prosecutor shook her head.

'How did you get this information?'

'From clients. Several are very keen to co-operate if we promise to keep their names out of the media. They weren't difficult to track down. We also have quite a few of these cards as some men bought five or ten at a time. These are currently being examined by Forensic Services.'

'For fingerprints?'

'Amongst other things, yes.'

Konrad Simonsen then briefed her on the host families and the staff from the Integration Ministry who had taken bribes to approve the au pair applications. He went on to summarise the poker players and the activities of the Poker Academy. The Public Prosecutor didn't interrupt. When he had finished, it was the Countess who asked the next question, which took them both aback.

'When do we strike?'

Konrad Simonsen and Bertha Steenholt turned to her in surprise. Then the Public Prosecutor repeated, 'Yes, when do you?'

This was already a major dilemma for Konrad Simonsen and he had absolutely no need to have it so directly exposed in front of Bertha Steenholt. He looked at the Countess. *Thank you, darling wife, I could have done without that.* She responded with a beaming smile. He waffled: it was difficult to say, there were many factors to take into account, some were for, others counted against. The Public Prosecutor pounced immediately; this was exactly the kind of talk you could not get away with in front of her.

'You can save that rubbish for the airhead. Tell me the truth!'

This was a reference to the Deputy Commissioner.

Konrad Simonsen thought that it wasn't complete rubbish. In complex cases like this one, knowing when to draw the line and decide that the police had watched the suspects for long enough was invariably a problem. If you went in too early, you risked not having enough evidence for a trial, and if you kept the surveillance going for too long, there was a danger that it would be discovered and the culprits could get away.

'The Data group dealing with the poker players say they need at least another month; the Host family group dealing with the host families would also like more time; the Au pair group would like us to strike now, today rather than tomorrow. It'll be a compromise, I guess.'

'You guess? I thought you were in charge?'

'Not entirely. There are so many resources involved that I can't ignore the wider cost implications. And if I decide to do so, senior management will undoubtedly want to teach me a lesson.'

Bertha Steenholt scratched her upper lip with her thumb and forefinger, while mulling this over.

'Today is Wednesday; let's say another ten to twelve days, so that'll make it Monday, the sixth of July when you bang up anyone who needs banging up. Or the Tuesday, if that suits you better, but no later than that. What do you say?'

Konrad Simonsen said it sounded fair. She promised to get their agreement confirmed with his bosses and then got up with a remark about having somewhere to be. On her way out, she stopped again in front of the men's photographs on the wall. It was obvious that they fascinated her. The Countess said:

'Yes, it's a shame. They'll go free, only to find other women to ruin.'

Bertha Steenholt didn't comment on that, instead she said:

'Don't expect miracles – procuring and economic crimes are lengthy and complicated cases. And if the prostitutes and the clients don't want to testify, and they rarely do, it usually ends in virtually nothing. That is to say, with a very light punishment or even none at all. And that's the good option. I'm afraid that's the truth.'

The two police officers knew that only too well, as Konrad Simonsen said on behalf of both of them. The Public Prosecutor responded but they couldn't hear what she said, she was still staring at the men as if struggling to tear herself away. She said pensively: 'I know several of them.'

The Countess replied quietly:

'I don't care. Responsibility, ethics, morality or common decency don't apply to them. They've paid to escape all of that, and with the blessing of society. So I don't care if you do know them.'

Big Bertha broke into one of her rare smiles. She looked as if she had spied a particularly delicious piece of meat on her plate.

'I don't care either.'

CHAPTER 82

The Countess had a well-developed system of those to whom she owed a favour, and those from whom she could expect one, and she knew the balance of this mental bookkeeping exactly. In recent years she had expanded her system to include her husband. So if Konrad Simonsen had done someone a favour, she regarded herself as entitled to collect one in return from that person, should the need arise.

It was the way things worked when you shared your household finances with someone, she thought. And there could be no doubt that Konrad Simonsen had done Helmer Hammer a massive favour by removing him from Jan Podowski's database. Even if paying for sex were legal, it would look very bad if Helmer Hammer's name appeared on such a list, circulated internally at Police Headquarters. She called him privately and asked him outright.

'Tell me, don't you owe us a massive favour after what Simon did for you last week?'

Helmer Hammer made no attempt to wriggle out of it; it was impossible to deny.

'Are you free to speak?'

No, not really, but they could meet at ten o'clock, if she was prepared to drive to Copenhagen. He mentioned a restaurant that stayed open until midnight. She promised to be there, although it wasn't terribly convenient.

Three hours later they sat each with a glass of white wine in a discreet corner of a nearly deserted dining room. Apart from an elderly couple at the other end who were finishing their dessert, there was no one in sight.

'You look tired.' The Countess sounded almost concerned.

Helmer Hammer slumped another centimetre. It was part of his image never to look tired, but this past week had been unusually hectic, even by his standards. At first he merely nodded, but then elaborated in a flat voice.

'Yes, I could do with a few days off, not to mention a lovely, long holiday. But the best I can hope for right now is a decent night's sleep. So let's talk fast, then I can go home and hit the sack. What do you want me to do? Because I agree that I owe you.'

'Perhaps I should start by telling you that you never had the pleasure of meeting the Nigerian girl who was killed in Hanehoved Forest. I gather Simon promised you this information.'

Helmer Hammer thanked her and looked relieved; he briefly flashed her his normal obliging smile, which the Countess thought it was nice to see.

'I want two things. Number one: I have the name and a picture of a young Nigerian woman about whom I want to know as much as possible. How she got to Denmark, what happened to her in Nigeria, where she grew up, her background, possible education, family and so on. I've written down my questions and I imagine that, with your unique contacts, you can get our embassy in Lagos to assist me. I have enclosed twenty thousand dollars to cover any expenses incurred, and if there's any money left over, I want the embassy to give it to her family – if she has any, that is. Otherwise they can find some deserving charity to give it to. I don't want any receipts, only results, and ideally quickly. Do you think you can manage that?'

Helmer Hammer nodded:

'The capital of Nigeria is called Abuja, not Lagos, and Denmark has no embassy in that country, only in Ghana, and that's some distance away. But the Swedes have an embassy in Abuja, as far as I recall, and I wonder ... Yes, you can rely on me. I'm not sure if your money will be needed, but perhaps it'll speed things up, seeing it's a matter of urgency. I'll take it, and then we'll have to see.'

He took her envelope and put it in his inside pocket.

'That was your first request, what was the other?'

'Three residence permits.'

He shook his head. No, it was out of the question. Even for him. Especially for him. It was far, far too ... politically sensitive. The Countess argued that she had good reason to ask. If the investigation was to have any hope of convicting the ringleaders, it was essential that some of the African prostitutes were prepared to give evidence, and a basic premise for their co-operation was that they would be granted leave to stay. He insisted that it couldn't be done.

'So we're happy to let those women be abused for months, while official Denmark closes its eyes, but to grant three of them leave to stay is way beyond our abilities. Have I understood you correctly?'

'Yes, I'm afraid so.'

'Quite right. Just imagine if millions of young African women suddenly choose to come here, to be degraded and exploited, in order that later they would be given leave to stay in our wonderful country ... Is that the thinking behind this insanity?'

'Pretty much.'

'OK, can you get me just one?'

He finished his wine and sat for a while mulling it over, then he said tentatively:

'Possibly, I'm not making any promises. I will try, but then we're even.'

The Countess thought that they really weren't, and that he had given her nothing except what common decency should allow. But common decency had become a rare and expensive commodity in the Kingdom of Denmark this past decade. She didn't say that, however, and it irritated her all the way home to Søllerød.

CHAPTER 83

Forensic investigators found a match between the DNA collected from Silje Esper's living room and one of the cards that had been bought as an entry pass to Karina Larsen's prostitutes. This provided Klavs Arnold with his big breakthrough in the investigation into the murder of the blind woman. And it wasn't just that: there was also a nice thumbprint on the card that matched one in the police database. The Jutlander cheered and made a beeline for his boss's office.

In there he found Arne Pedersen in a meeting with two colleagues the Jutlander didn't know. He interrupted them, joyfully announcing his news, and finished with the name.

'Jimmy Heeger, aged thirty-six, with an extensive criminal record. Stabbings, assault, beatings, burglaries, two robberies, handling stolen goods – a thoroughly unpleasant piece of work. I can't wait to get that bastard. I hope they lock him up for good.'

Arne Pedersen and his guests shared Klavs Arnold's joy; you had to look long and hard for a killing as sadistic as the one in Karlslille.

'Do you know where he lives?' Arne Pedersen asked.

'So far, I know nothing except what I've told you. I just had to share the news with someone.'

'Call Simon. If he doesn't answer his mobile, then find out where he is. And if he's in a meeting, then drag him out of it.'

Two hours later Klavs Arnold knew a lot more about Jimmy Heeger. The man had the background of a classic offender: his parents had split up, he came from an abusive home where he was brought up by an illiterate mother with a series of ever-changing boyfriends, had had major issues at school, then youth institutions, open as well as closed, and several suspended sentences, until the trap finally shut in 1994, when he served three years for the armed robbery of a petrol station and actual bodily harm. From then on there was no let up, one crime after another.

Jimmy Heeger used to live in the area around Valby Langgade Station and Akacieparken. At one point he had rented a flat there, but he had been evicted eighteen months ago. That was his last known address. Klavs Arnold dispatched his colleagues to find the man or get further information on him. Soon he was able to add the designations *obsessed with weapons* and *potentially dangerous* to the description of his alleged killer. He also learned that Jimmy Heeger had tried to join the biker gang Hell's Angels but they, however, wanted nothing to do with him. The reason was given to the police by an informant with close links to the organisation: *he's a psycho*. Something that was becoming increasingly clear to Klavs Arnold. He called home and told his wife he would have to work late; he didn't know for how long, but probably all night.

Later that evening a couple of officers got the tip-off they had all been waiting for. Jimmy Heeger was hiding out with his half-sister in Tårnby on the island of Amager. An ex-girlfriend, high on drugs and furious because he owed her money, had snitched on him. Two plainclothes officers on loan from Vestegnens police had told her they were from the Danish lottery service and that Jimmy Heeger had won a major prize; they claimed they had been looking for him all day, and there was three hundred kroner in it for her in return for information. She swallowed their ridiculous story, snatched the three banknotes and gave them an address, not far from the motorway to Copenhagen Airport. They called Police Headquarters immediately; the woman had seemed credible, despite being high. Klavs Arnold dispatched them to Tårnby, with instructions to watch the address, but not to carry out an arrest. The man was dangerous, possibly armed, and they were under orders not to take any chances.

Jimmy Heeger was in the bar, which was where he had spent most of his time since Svend Lerche had sacked him following his fatal trip to Karlslille. Fortunately he had been given a handsome sum of money as a *severance payment*, as the upper-class idiot had called it, as if Jimmy didn't realise it was in return for him staying far away from Rungsted for now and for all eternity.

He drank routinely, without joy; drinking had long since become a habit, a way to distance himself from things. He was drunk, but didn't really feel it. Just now he had told everyone in the bar who could be bothered to listen to him that he was no lamb you could lead to the slaughter. He didn't say who would want to slaughter him, but one look at his red, moist eyes stopped his audience from asking. That made him belligerent and he aggressively repeated his statement, people edging away from him as he did so. He ordered another beer and thought about the events in Karlslille, as he had already done many times when the alcohol didn't seem to work.

It had gone haywire, spun totally out of control, an absurd short-circuiting in his brain that he didn't think was his responsibility. It was as if a secret window he didn't even know existed had opened for some terrible but also wonderful hours. Once he started with the hand vice, he couldn't stop. He had enjoyed her screams, her pain and, not least, his own power. Afterwards it wasn't something he was proud of; the truth was he would rather not think about it. But that was difficult, not to say impossible. The thrill of instilling terror continued to give him a buzz, and he felt a strong urge to try it again.

The officers in the Ford Ka parked in a car park diagonally across from number 11 Bredagerstien, discussed briefly if they – despite their orders – should get out and arrest Jimmy Heeger when clearly intoxicated, but not catatonically so, he staggered along the pavement opposite them at about two o'clock in the morning. They chose not to, though they could probably have apprehended him without any difficulty. Instead they rang Klavs Arnold and just said: 'He's here.'

Klavs Arnold was dozing behind his desk, but was instantly awake when he got the message. He immediately contacted Konrad Simonsen, as he had been told to do. It took a while before the Homicide chief picked up the phone. When he did, the Jutlander repeated what the officers had said to him:

'He's there. Number eleven Bredagerstien in Tårnby, he has just walked up to the flat.'

To the Jutlander's annoyance, Konrad Simonsen's orders were:

'Send in the SWAT team and stay out of their way, Klavs. Leave the young ones to do their job, they're trained for it. I'll be there in an hour, but I won't take over, you're doing fine.'

Klavs Arnold did as he was told. He arranged with the head of the SWAT team that five a.m. would be a suitable time to strike. It gave the officer plenty of time to gather the men he needed and they could expect Jimmy Heeger to be fast asleep by then.

CHAPTER 84

Right from the start the head of the SWAT team made no attempt to hide that this was his operation.

He greeted the Jutlander a little curtly and asked him to wait, telling him they would bring him his prisoner in fifteen minutes. There were four cars and eleven men, all experts in the job they were about to undertake. Each was armed with the standard police pistol, a Heckler & Koch USP 9-millimetre, and each and every one exuded confidence and calm. The team had assembled a hundred metres down the street from Jimmy Heeger's sister's flat. It was on the first floor above a pizzeria, and an external wooden staircase led up to the flat's front door. The head of operations had obtained a floor plan of the flat which, in addition to a bathroom and a kitchen, consisted of one bedroom and a living room with a balcony overlooking a lawn behind the building. He had explained his plan to his crew and they had reviewed it earlier, and did so again, one more time before it was done for real. Then they marched quickly down the street towards their target.

Klavs Arnold followed discreetly and joined the two men due to take up position below the flat's balcony. He heard a loud crash as the front door was bashed in soon afterwards.

The noise woke Jimmy Heeger; he leaped from the sofa where he had been sleeping, realising what was about to happen, but aware that the door to the living room would be much harder to break down than the front door. His sister's boyfriend had mounted eight solid hammock hooks into the frame on either side of the door, so that a nylon net could be stretched tightly across the hooks when the living-room door was closed. The net provided an effective obstacle against unwanted guests entering in a hurry, which gave his sister enough time to call the police whenever her ex-husband tried to break in because he felt like giving her another beating. Which he often did. When Jimmy Heeger had returned a few hours ago, he had put the net back up. Better safe than sorry. Then he had flopped onto the sofa and fallen asleep.

As soon as the killer was woken by the sound of the front door being forced open, he snatched his rolls of money from a compartment in his rucksack, which was lying next to the sofa, and stuffed them into his pocket. Then he found his pistol, which was also in the rucksack, a 22-calibre with a silencer, the same weapon he had used in Karlslille on Silje Esper's dog. Then he pulled on his shoes, ran out the balcony door and jumped over the railings.

Jimmy Heeger's feet hit the shoulder of one of the officers on the ground. The man had moved under the balcony so he wasn't immediately visible from the living-room window of the flat. Everything happened so quickly and it was such bad luck that no one could reasonably reproach the officer, who was definitely vigilant. Yet he stumbled and fell onto the grass. Something that Jimmy Heeger, who landed with remarkable agility pretty much on his feet, didn't. He sprang up with his pistol in his hand, and pointed it down at the fallen man's head, ready to liquidate him.

Klavs Arnold fired three shots at Jimmy Heeger, two in the back between his shoulder blades, the last and final one to the back of his head.

The prostrate officer staggered to his feet, and looked down at the wounded man, his body convulsing in spasms that soon subsided. Then he said matter-of-factly:

'Someone's in trouble.'

CHAPTER 85

Benedikte Lerche-Larsen was sitting in Klosterstræde in her brand-new silver Citroën C5, near her newly acquired flat, waiting impatiently for Henrik Krag, who had been allowed to leave work early and was on his way home.

It was twelve-thirty, the sun was shining generously and the neighbourhood was surprisingly quiet, as if the lunch-time customers for the area's many restaurants couldn't cope with the heat and had decided to stay at home. A bee buzzed past, zigzagging down the street, looking for a flower pot or a balcony trough. She waved it away through the open car window. *You're not coming in here.* A car alarm howled continuously a few blocks away. She barely registered it, but seemed troubled as she sat there, looking first one way, then another, as if she could speed up her boyfriend's arrival.

She had called him twice to find out where he was, but both times in vain. *Hi, this is Henrik, I'm afraid I can't* . . . She had ended the calls with an angry push of her thumb and concluded it probably meant he was on his way. It might well be a positive sign, but it only seemed to add to her impatience, and she inwardly urged him on, *Come on, Henrik, God dammit*, or *Get a move on*. From time to time she would wipe the sweat from her brow with the back of her hand, cursing the sun. What she needed was a packet of Kleenex, but she rummaged through her handbag without success.

At last she heard the deep growl of a motorbike, and shortly afterwards he turned into the street. She reached her hand out of the window and caught his attention. He drove up alongside her, took off his crash helmet and asked in surprise:

'Why are you dressed up, are you going somewhere?'

She was wearing a simple lavender silk blouse and a tight pencil skirt in two layers, the inner layer white silk and the outer almost transparent ivory lace. Around her neck she wore a heavy string of pearls, which matched her drop earrings. She answered only part of his question:

'We're going somewhere. Park your motorbike and jump in.'

When he got in the car, he took a closer look at her.

'You look upset, is everything all right?'

'Not really, let me drive for a while, I just need a moment.'

'Where are we going?'

She caught him looking at her lovingly, began to feel more energised and said, 'Henrik, just enjoy the weather.'

She drove down Østerbrogade and when she turned off down Ryvangs Allé, she was her old self again.

'Svend and Karina have left Rungsted and gone underground, or whatever you'd call it. They didn't bother clearing up after themselves – I mean, shut down the hookers and the poker players. Bjarne Fabricius has gone mental, although he's trying not to sound as if he has. Svend and Karina both feature in the Wanted section on the homepage of the Copenhagen Police. Svend has written to me using an email address only he and I know, and I'm meeting him at six o'clock. They're leaving the country and I've promised to help them.'

Henrik Krag was pragmatic about the news and not particularly troubled.

'What does that mean for us?'

'I don't know yet, perhaps that's just as well, but there's more.'

He ignored her and said:

'I don't get why you want to help that bastard after what he did to you . . . to us, and to me.'

She retorted, 'Bjarne is coming round tonight at nine o'clock. It'll be an inclusive session for us all.'

'You mean me as well?'

'Yes, you as well. Do you still think I don't care what happens to you?'

Her voice was soft; it made him happy. Normally she would say something like this in a sharp, distancing tone. He sounded serene when he said:

'I know I have to pay for what I've done, one way or another. I've known it for a long time, but I still wouldn't change a thing. Not even if I could. Even though I've done things I shouldn't have.'

They drove a few kilometres in silence, each pondering their fate, before Benedikte Lerche-Larsen said: 'I thought you were all about living in the here and now?'

'Yes, whenever that's possible. I mostly try that when I don't want to think too much.'

'Right, then let's do that for a few hours.'

'OK, works for me. Is that why you won't tell me where we're going?'

'Exactly.'

She stopped in Vangede Bygade outside a florist and took a thousand-kroner note from her purse. She gave it to him.

'Go and buy me an incredibly gorgeous bouquet.'

'Me? I don't know anything about flowers. Which ones do you want me to get?'

'Ask for the cleverest, Henrik. The cleverest they have.'

He hesitated. *But I don't think* . . . She could still do this to him, but it was rare for her to resort to it now, and when she did, it was with a teasing sweetness that didn't truly mock him. She tilted her head and flashed him a small smile. He gave her the finger and grinned at himself. How stupid could you get?

He came back with a beautiful bouquet of white lilies and pink roses and explained superfluously, 'The florist helped me.'

'Haven't you guessed it yet?'

He hadn't, were they about to visit someone?

'You're such an idiot.'

'Yes, I am.'

Five minutes later they reached their destination. It was a yellow-brick house that looked like any other, the only exception being the five empty parking spaces in the road outside. Benedikte Lerche-Larsen parked in the central bay, then got out and grabbed a plastic bag from the boot, then opened the front door. Henrik Krag rushed after her without having time to spell his way through the sign to the left of the door.

They were warmly welcomed by a woman in her early seventies with a beautifully wrinkled face and bright, friendly eyes.

'Benedikte! What a lovely surprise. How are you?'

They embraced each other as the woman asked:

'And who is this handsome young man?'

'He's my boyfriend, Granny, and we want you to marry us. Now . . . immediately.'

Henrik Krag dropped the bridal bouquet.

Benedikte Lerche-Larsen's grandmother ushered them to an office where a gangly woman in her thirties was typing on a keyboard. She introduced herself as the parish clerk, shook hands with Benedikte Lerche-Larsen and Henrik Krag and then carried on with her work, as if to indicate that they were not to mind her, she didn't see or hear anything. The Lutheran minister shook her head.

'That's you to a T, my darling girl. Always in a rush, never looking back. But marriage is a serious decision, and you need to have a very good reason before I'm willing to marry you in haste.'

'What's the best reason, Granny? We'll go for that.'

'The best reason is acute, life-threatening illness, and you both look the picture of health to me.'

'It's because I love him, and if we're married, I can't be forced to testify against him. As things are at the moment, that's a real possibility, and that would be wrong. You shouldn't be forced to testify against someone you love.'

It grew silent, even quieter than before, Henrik Krag thought; then he realised that the parish clerk had stopped typing. The minister thought long and hard. After what seemed like an eternity, she addressed Henrik Krag.

'Beauty deceives and Loveliness is a thing of Vanity, as Blicher writes. Do you love her, my young friend? I mean truly, behind her beautiful exterior?'

Henrik Krag had no doubt about this. Yes, he did. The parish clerk said:

'I can have an advance approval from the council and the papers ready in half an hour. They can post the marriage certificate later. What should I give as the reason?'

'Acute, life-threatening illness. I've been tricked by that once before, now I can flip the coin the other way,' said the minister.

She pointed to Benedikte Lerche-Larsen.

'I agree, my darling girl, it's wrong to testify against someone you love, your reason isn't silly at all. But I think my bishop would prefer the one about the illness, and I'm going to ring him now. What's in the bag?'

Benedikte Lerche-Larsen replied:

'Champagne and wedding rings, and a box of chocolates for the pair of you. May I use your cloakroom to freshen up?'

CHAPTER 86

Benedikte Lerche-Larsen and her father met at Lake Furesøen in the car park outside Næsseslottet, Frédéric de Coninck's elegant late-eighteenth-century country house. The weather was just as beautiful and sunny as it had been all day, but neither of them was tempted to go for a stroll in the magnificent park. Benedikte got into her father's car; he had come in the Audi R8, his favourite.

You didn't need to be a psychologist to spot that Svend Lerche was a man under extreme pressure. He looked terrible. His eyes were shadowed black from lack of sleep and worries he couldn't handle, and his voice sounded rusty, as if he had been smoking. They greeted each other, neither heartily nor in a hostile manner, perhaps business-like would be the appropriate word. Benedikte said, and it was part question and part statement:

'Mum and you have left Rungsted?'

Svend Lerche confirmed this and added that they wouldn't be coming back in the near future, which even he could hear meant never, ever. He handed his daughter a fat envelope and explained that it contained the papers to give her power of attorney over the house, its contents, his two other cars, the holiday home in Dronningmølle, along with several other assets. She should, however, expect to fight the fraud squad for them, so he had included the names of two lawyers, esteemed senior partners, who had already been paid, she needn't worry on that account. He reeled off a number of other practical items and referred constantly to his envelope. Benedikte Lerche-Larsen restricted herself to nodding in the right places or replying monosyllabically; there was no reason for a lengthy debate. When Svend Lerche eventually fell silent, she asked:

'I gather you haven't spoken to Bjarne Fabricius yet? Even though your entire business is up the creek.'

'No, I haven't spoken to him.'

'He called me. He's not a happy man, Dad, and he's looking for you, I think, although he never said so outright. If I were you, I'd make sure he keeps looking.'

Svend Lerche snarled:

'What do you think we're trying to do here?'

'The police would also like to talk to you, I gather. You made the four o'clock news. Not to mention the tabloids, but I imagine you've already seen them.'

'Tell me, are you enjoying this?'

'A bit, yes. Where are you staying now?'

'You don't need to know that. Have you planned a route for us like I asked you to, so we can get out of the country?'

Svend's excuse for asking this was that he had no internet or any other sources of information where he was, but they both knew that was a lie. Not least because he had sent her an email. The truth was that he was brilliant at sitting in his office working out poker statistics, but he was like a lost child if he ever had to move outside his set routine. His planning talent didn't stretch that far; Benedikte Lerche-Larsen was only too aware of it and the fact her mother was so dumb, she could throw herself on the ground and miss.

'Do you have passports in names other than your own?'

He nodded, they did. As long as they could get to London or Paris, they could make their own onward arrangements. Where he didn't say, nor had she expected him to.

'And you have money? Otherwise I have some.'

He had lots, but it was nice of her. She unfolded a map.

'You need to avoid the Øresund and the Storebælt bridges, unless you're travelling by train. But I'm guessing you're not. In which case, I would strongly recommend that we swap cars.'

Svend Lerche accepted this, he had been expecting it. She went through the route in detail.

'Drive via Roskilde, Holbæk and Vig until you get to Sjællands Odde, but stick to minor roads, avoid the major ones. Take the fast ferry from Odden to Aarhus, the last one leaves at nine in the evening, and you'll be in Aarhus roughly one hour later, by which time it'll have started to get dark.

'Then drive via Viborg and Skive, taking the smaller roads, cross the Sallingsund Bridge to Mors and drive diagonally across the island until the Vildsund Bridge and onwards to Thy, where you need to aim for Thisted. The rest of the route is complicated, but I've highlighted it on a map for you, and I've booked a small holiday apartment in a discreet, almost-deserted location near a village called Vigsø by Tannis Bay.

'The farmer knows you'll be arriving late and he won't ask any questions, he'll just give you your key. Don't use the Satnav. I don't know if the police can trace it or if it was automatically registered to my car when I bought it. Stay in the apartment until the following afternoon when your host will drive you to Hanstholm. There you'll buy two tickets for the Bergen ferry; it departs at six-thirty and you'll be in Norway the next day. Take a taxi to the airport and a plane to London, there are several daily departures. *Bon voyage*!'

He thanked her and sounded as if he meant it.

'Don't worry about us; once we get to London, we'll be fine. We've been planning this for years. I'll write to you as soon as we are where we want to be.'

'I'm not worried.'

There was nothing more to say, even so he stayed in the car as if he wanted a conclusion of some kind. He said in a strange, wistful voice:

'It was Jimmy Heeger, that lunatic, and what he did in Karlslille that caused this. I should have listened to you and had you with me when I interviewed him, then maybe it would never have happened.'

She gave him the keys to her car, adding, 'Love to Mum, Dad.'

CHAPTER 87

'That was the easier of the conversations.'

Benedikte Lerche-Larsen had mentioned it twice already.

'Yes, so you keep saying. Are you nervous?'

'Absolutely, and you should be too. What's the time?'

Henrik Krag laughed. 'You're wearing a watch, Benedikte.' He wasn't nervous, only a little excited. So many wonderful things had happened in the past week for him. He was going to be a dad, he had moved in with her, they had been married, and Ida, or as it turned out, Svend Lerche, wouldn't torment them any longer.

Perhaps the cops would nick him, they probably would, they usually did, but he would still have Benedikte and when he got out of jail, they could live together like any normal family. He was also entitled to conjugal visits – the Danish prison service wasn't inhumane, and that would give him something to look forward to.

And Bjarne Fabricius? Well, they would just have to wait and see. Henrik ran his thumb back and forth across his wedding band, a simple gold ring with three small diamonds, discreet, not ostentatious, exactly the one he would have picked if he had been able to afford it. Who would have thought he would ever wear a ring like this and have a wife like Benedikte?

'How did you know the ring would fit me?'

The doorbell rang. She jumped up. '*He's here now.*'

The newlyweds had managed to assemble their dining table, and Benedikte had prepared modest refreshments of cold mineral water, a jug of iced tea, a bowl of peanuts and some glasses. She had also put her bridal bouquet on display on the table, but at one end, so people could see one another. The rest of the flat was one big mess of removal boxes and stacked furniture; it would take them weeks to unpack.

It was plain to see that Bjarne Fabricius was in no mood for anything other than business. His greeting was reserved and though he clearly noticed the rings on their fingers and could probably guess what had happened, he made no comment. He sat down at the end of the table, ignored the beverages but grabbed a small handful of peanuts, while the newlyweds took seats either side of him.

'One single lie and it's over,' he warned.

Benedikte smiled at him, looking relaxed and natural, which was an incredible performance given how nervous she really was.

'Why would we lie to you, Bjarne? What would we get out of that?'

Bjarne Fabricius, however, refused to be placated, and said icily:

'Yes, what would you?' He pointed at Henrik Krag. 'Tell me about that business with your blackmailer, or whatever we call him.'

Henrik Krag glanced sideways at his wife for permission without realising that she must have been the one who had told their guest about the blackmailer in the first place. Bjarne Fabricius slammed the palm of his hand against the table so the glasses clattered. '*Watch it!*' he said. Benedikte Lerche-Larsen wasn't in control here, he was, *so start talking*.

Calmly and systematically Henrik Krag gave a rather fine presentation, which included everything; the photograph they'd been sent, the money they'd had to pay, the calls from the synthetic voice, their four tasks as he called them, and how they had finally worked out that Svend Lerche was behind it all. Bjarne Fabricius listened without interruption, and neither of them could tell from looking at him what he was thinking. When Henrik Krag had finished, he wanted only one point clarified.

'Those kids at Skovbrynet Station, what was the point of that?'

Henrik Krag didn't know, he had only done what he had been told to do. Benedikte Lerche-Larsen was hesitant, she didn't want to interrupt without permission: 'I know.'

Bjarne Fabricius granted it. 'Tell me.'

'One of the kids who was beaten up is the son of the Revenue officer Svend was barred from contacting.'

Bjarne Fabricius slapped his head with the palm of his hand, but didn't comment on Svend Lerche's lunacy in any other way. He turned to Benedikte.

'And the idiocy relating to Jan's widow? Do you know anything about that?'

'My father claims it was a mistake. That moron Heeger would appear to have gone berserk. And I think that Svend is telling the truth, it didn't happen with his blessing. It's out of character for him; he wanted Jan's USB stick, that was all.'

'But he didn't get it?'

'No, he didn't. I think the cops have it, but I'm just guessing.'

'You say it's out of character, but it's wholly in his character to send his own daughter to a porn audition, not to mention that crap with the kids and the truck . . .'

'That was personal, it was about feelings, that's different.'

She sounded almost as if she were defending her father and wasn't upset in the least when she said:

'Some people have a love-hate relationship with their parents; I've always had a hate-hate relationship with mine.'

Bjarne Fabricius poured himself a glass of iced tea, and they could see that he was mulling things over.

'The question is, what the hell do I do with the pair of you? Do you have any ideas?'

The latter was spoken ironically, but Henrik Krag missed this and said:

'I think I'm going to prison, but I don't really mind. It wipes the slate clean, then I can start over when I get out.'

That was how he viewed it. When you had done your time, you were cleansed of your guilt, you had paid the price and could start over. That their guest didn't think in those terms and that Henrik Krag's punishment, should Bjarne Fabricius pick one for him, would be of a more permanent nature, he hadn't grasped. Benedikte Lerche-Larsen had, however, and she fought for her husband.

'The girl from Vallensbæk is in Rigshospitalet's trauma unit, but she'll live. My guess is that Henrik will get six or seven years, eight if he's unlucky. And once he has confessed the investigation will go quiet, so there will be nothing that can hurt you. And I can rebuild your . . . our business, you know I can. Even better than before.'

'You can and you will. But how long do you think Henrik will hold out during an interview? The very political system has been challenged. That's normally called terrorism, and there are several nasty laws in place to deal with that kind of thing, which give the police significantly extended powers. The gloves are well and truly off, I can promise you that.'

Bjarne Fabricius spoke to her as though her husband weren't present. Then he had an idea. He turned to Henrik Krag again and said slowly:

'If you lie to me now, Henrik, you won't live to see tomorrow, it's that simple. So tell me, was Benedikte present when you and Jan killed that black whore in Hanehoved Forest?'

Time quivered. Benedikte Lerche-Larsen could feel an uncontrollable tic develop near her right eye, but sat frozen in her seat, unable to do anything about it. Bjarne Fabricius leaned across the table menacingly and narrowed his steel-grey eyes. At length Henrik Krag said:

'No, she wasn't.'

'And you're not lying to me?'

'No, I'm not lying to you. Only Jan and I were there.'

Bjarne Fabricius laughed, gave Henrik Krag a hearty slap on his shoulder and said in a conciliatory tone: 'I've got to give it to you, my friend, you've got guts. You had the courage to lie, I didn't think you had the balls for that. But I already know she was there, she told me a long time ago, as did Jan. On the other hand, perhaps the cops won't have such an easy ride with you as I first thought.'

It was at that moment, that very moment, that Henrik Krag saved his own life. He refused to let himself be carried along by the laughter.

'No, she wasn't! Benedikte wasn't there.'

Bjarne Fabricius folded his hands behind his head, scratching his neck with his thumb while thinking it over again.

'All right, Benedikte, he's all yours.'

Benedikte Lerche-Larsen relaxed, collapsing as if the air had seeped out of her. Henrik Krag asked her, still confused:

'Is this good?'

She and Bjarne Fabricius exchanged glances and both of them couldn't resist smiling faintly despite the seriousness of the moment. The initiates indulging the novice. It was Bjarne Fabricius who answered.

'Yes, that's good.'

To claim that the mood then lightened would be an exaggeration, but for a while it was a little less tense. Bjarne Fabricius took time to comment on the flowers: he liked the lilies, found the roses to be anaemic, gene-manipulated rubbish unlikely to survive outside the greenhouse. He was offered a glass of red wine; Benedikte Lerche-Larsen had brought a good bottle in anticipation of his visit. He declined, then changed his mind and accepted one after all. Henrik Krag found a glass in a box and used a screw and a pair of pliers to open the bottle. Benedikte was annoyed with herself, she should have organised a corkscrew in advance.

Bjarne Fabricius, however, continued to ask difficult questions.

'Why didn't you come to me about those four lunatic tasks?'

'I was afraid you would solve the problem by eliminating us,' she replied.

It was plain speaking, the way he liked it, and he had a sudden understanding of her position. He sipped his wine and praised it.

'You have two days.'

'Four. Today is our wedding day, the others can be your present to us.'

He agreed and told her that such a smile was irresistible. Who could say no to her? He certainly couldn't. Henrik Krag asked:

'Four days until what?'

Again it was Bjarne Fabricius who gave him his answer.

'Four days until you find a police station and turn yourself in – that is if you haven't been picked up already, which I think is a real possibility. When I leave today, you'll be coming with me; you need to speak to a lawyer, and he needs to practise some things with you. Including forgetting all about the blackmail, it's too complicated. Svend paid you for the tasks, end of story, much simpler that way. Where would you hide money, if you had been given some by Svend?'

Henrik Krag didn't hesitate.

'With my mum, she lives in Ishøj.'

'Fine. I have a couple of wads that I know Svend has touched. Take them to her tomorrow. But I'll charge them to you later, Benedikte.'

She replied, a little anxiously:

'Of course, but a lawyer at ten o'clock at night?'

'My lawyers are there whenever I need them. And don't be nervous, you'll get him back early tomorrow morning. I don't lie when there's no need.'

Playtime was over. Bjarne Fabricius drained his glass and looked at Benedikte Lerche-Larsen, then shook his head as she made to refill his glass.

'So, Benedikte, the balance needs to be restored, equilibrium is important. In order to get, you have to give. Did Svend like the route I had planned for him?'

She nodded, the tears starting to well up. It wasn't that easy after all. He went on:

'Do you have the times for me?'

She handed him a note. He thanked her and added:

'Please don't cry. Wait until I've gone, I hate women sobbing. Besides tears age you, and that would be a shame. I like it that you're young.'

CHAPTER 88

The two men Bjarne Fabricius had sent to Jutland worked all night, and no one could say that they came easily by their money.

Initially, they waited impatiently in the yard for half an hour in front of the farmhouse they had borrowed. Although the day had been roasting hot, the night was chilly and they were both freezing. They could have gone inside where it was warm and just kept an eye on the gravel road leading up to the deserted farm – it wouldn't be difficult to spot a set of headlights – but they were professional and had also factored in that their guests might be driving with the just the side lights. So they endured the cold.

When the car finally arrived, one of them greeted the driver with a friendly 'Welcome to Thy', while the other stepped out from the darkness and shot the couple in the back of their heads, first the man, then the woman. Then they got down to work.

The two victims were undressed and their clothes gathered up, while their bodies were put into two strong plastic bags normally used for recycling cans. The car, a brand-new Citroën C5, was driven behind the house where it was doused in petrol and torched, along with the clothes, which had been left on the back seat. They waited until it had burned out, poured water over it to cool it down and began systematically to cut it up with a laser cutter and an angle grinder; reliable tools, the best on the market.

After two hours of hard graft, the car had been cut down into suitably small pieces, apart from the engine block, where only the serial number was removed. They loaded the metal scraps onto a small lorry and drove to Hanstholm harbour. The fisherman asked no questions, he had been paid generously not to. The two men carried their load onto the cutter and a couple of hours later it was dumped in the North Sea at a depth of five hundred metres in the waters known as the Jutland Reef.

A shame really, it had been an excellent car.

*

Viewed from the North Sea, Hanherred is a gloomy and inhospitable landscape. Once you have fought your way to the top of one of the grey sand dunes that line the beach, the view is desolate. From Bulbjerg in the west to Hanstholm in the east, along the crescent coastline and as far as the eye can see, the landscape is bleak. The dunes lie close together, one on top of the other, some large and craggy, others small and oppressive, but all of them scarred by black heather or dirty yellow lyme grass, which the wind would appear to have long since whipped the life out of. Here, in the midst of this barren area, far from everything and everyone, and half-hidden behind a sandy ridge to the east, lies Lodbo church.

The church was built in the twelfth century and consists of two conjoined buildings, stark-looking inside as well as out, with a deep piety that reflects the location in which it was built. The cemetery encircles the church and is surrounded by a stone wall as tall as a man, with a cast-iron gate set in the northern end. It is small yet the graves lie scattered, clustered in threes or fours, as though the congregation isn't able to fill out the space.

The gravedigger helped the monosyllabic foreigner carry the two bodies. He had dug the grave needed a metre deeper than necessary, so the two dead bodies would be in fine company underneath their legitimate owner; a former county councillor whose parents were buried in the adjacent grave.

Svend Lerche and Karina Larsen had lived most of their lives in luxury while exploiting others and inflicting incalculable damage on many people. And yet they had a good, if rather premature death; they never knew what happened: one moment they were here, the next they were gone. Who wouldn't want that? Now they were laid to rest together in a cemetery they didn't know existed, in a grave paid for with money earned for them by their prostitutes.

Once the bodies had been dumped in the grave, the gravedigger started shovelling soil onto them. He had been well paid and wouldn't talk to anyone, and besides, it wasn't the first time he had been party to an additional funeral. It had happened before, but never with two bodies. The Pole folded his hands and said a prayer in his mother tongue while he bowed his head and looked into the grave. He was a Catholic and respected death.

CHAPTER 89

Konrad Simonsen was depressed; no one had seen Karina Larsen and Svend Lerche since Tuesday. Today was Friday, and it was as if the ground had swallowed them up. He had issued Wanted notices for the couple across Denmark, and also Europe via Interpol, but with no luck – for now. Their daughter, however – he couldn't remember her name off the top of his head – was driving around in one of Svend Lerche's three luxury cars, while her own, newly acquired Citroën C5 was missing. Or rather missing in the sense that the police didn't know where it was.

It was an obvious deduction that she had swapped cars with her father, and Konrad Simonsen had demanded that video footage for the last few days from the Storebælt and Øresund bridges be examined, but that hadn't led to anything either. He thought that ultimately he wouldn't know when his work was done. Deep down he had never believed he would get a result, although he had always hoped.

Arne Pedersen was dispatched to the daughter's home to interview her, but the officer could have saved himself the trouble. She had stubbornly refused to utter a sound until her lawyer was present, so Arne Pedersen had had to wait for an hour on the stairs outside her front door; it was out of the question he was allowed in. When the lawyer did finally turn up, he had arrogantly informed Arne Pedersen that his client didn't wish to answer questions relating to her parents. And under the current circumstances that should be interpreted in the broadest possible sense, the lawyer said, without explaining any further. Unfortunately it was – Konrad Simonsen remembered her name: Benedikte, Benedikte Lerche-Larsen, that was it – unfortunately that was Benedikte Lerche-Larsen's right. According to the law, she couldn't be compelled to testify against her parents. Arne Pedersen had no choice but to leave empty-handed and could report nothing on his return to Police Headquarters other than that she was incredibly good-looking:

'I'm telling you, Simon, she's gorgeous.'

Konrad Simonsen was standing by the window in his office – his usual spot whenever the world turned against him – staring down into a street that gasped in the heat. Life had pretty much come to a standstill in protest at being treated in this Mediterranean fashion. Adding to his troubles was the fact that the African au pair girls were quietly leaving the country one by one, without him being able to do anything about it. He couldn't legally detain them, and what would be the point? Forcing them to give evidence was obviously impossible, though essential if the host families were to be prosecuted for anything other than minor offences. But none of the women wanted to help the police; they were too frightened, and probably for good reason.

However, there was one exception in the form of a young Nigerian woman who had married her host, an older banking executive from Vedbæk. The Countess was currently working on getting a permanent residence permit for the woman, a permit Helmer Hammer had paved the way for, though how the Countess had talked him into that Konrad Simonsen couldn't imagine. But the woman refused to say anything until she got her residence permit, something with which Konrad Simonsen could fully sympathise. He had insisted on round-the-clock personal protection for her, knowing full well that the traffickers who had imported her into the country would stop at nothing to protect their business.

But even so, the truth was that his investigation was crumbling by the hour without him being able to do anything other than stand by the window feeling sorry for himself. However, on that account at least he was doing really well, he thought bitterly, and took the few steps back to his desk after which he called Pauline Berg. He knew that she had been discharged from hospital yesterday, and he invited her out for ice cream. She was pleased, she sounded happy when she answered her phone, which was a relief, and they arranged to meet in Rødovre Centrum Shopping Centre, which was easy for her to get to, and where he hoped it might be a little cooler.

CHAPTER 90

Henrik Krag had a pleasant feeling of serenity when on Friday, 26 June, fifteen months after his fatal trip to Hanehoved Forest, he drove slowly across the pavement and parked his motorbike right outside Halmtorvet police station in Copenhagen.

He placed his crash helmet on the saddle and thought, without regret, that it would be a long time before his next ride. He smiled at an older man who commented on his parking by pointing at a sign to the left of the entrance. 'This is the dumbest place you can park illegally, mate.' The man was right, but it made no difference to Henrik Krag, not in the situation he was in.

He had insisted on saying goodbye to Benedikte in their flat. She had offered to accompany him all the way to the station, but he didn't want that, which she accepted. They had made love and afterwards she had cried – it was just like it was supposed to be, exactly like that. Then suddenly she said in wonder, sounding like a little girl, between sobs:

'I'm going to miss you. I can feel that.' The next moment she added tentatively: 'If you miss someone, does it mean you're in love? You must know, Henrik, does it?'

She so very much wanted to be in love with him, and it was by no means the only occasion when she had asked him such a question. It was endearing, but also encouraging for him. Here he was the expert and she the novice, and he would laugh at her, pat her indulgently on her cheek or maybe kiss both of her ignorant eyes. *Yes, perhaps, perhaps you are.* And when his answer made her sad because she had thought it otherwise, had hoped for more, he would teach her:

'When it happens, you'll feel it. Then you won't be in any doubt.'

Sexual desire was sexual desire, and he was crazy about her. He was crazy about her body, he loved it when she lay moaning underneath him, but most of all he was crazy about her beauty; it was so perfect and so complete that the first times they had been together, he had been frightened he might destroy it. It was terrifying and arousing at the same time, an intoxicating feeling he didn't share with her, it was his secret. He was also a little worried that it might be morally wrong. However, possibly right from the start, his desire for her had turned into love. She had given him something he thought he would never get from her: equality. Respect for him as the person he was. And briefly she had let him into a world that he knew existed, of course he did, but which he had never imagined someone like him could ever be a part of. Not because it was a better world than the one he knew, far from it, but it was different, unobtainable, he had been convinced of that for a long time, and now it turned out that it wasn't. Not with her.

He straightened up, took in his surroundings with an open gaze and walked with his head held high into the police station. Utterly sure of his purpose.

CHAPTER 91

Pauline Berg and Konrad Simonsen were eating ice cream – fattening and delightfully, nutritiously wrong – in a café outside a bakery in Rødovre Centrum Shopping Centre. She looked good, Simonsen reflected, thinking that the same could not be said about him; he felt like he had been dragged through a hedge backwards. Pauline said cheerfully:

'I don't want to talk about the hospital, OK?'

'Absolutely OK, hospitals don't exactly feature in my top ten conversational topics.'

She smiled, they had a deal. Then she sniffed her ice cream suspiciously. 'I think it's off!' He smelled his own, but could find nothing wrong, yet she insisted, holding out her ice cream: 'Go on, smell it.' And when he did so, trusting her, she thrust her hand forwards, so his nose was buried in it. She roared with laughter like a teenager being tickled.

'Haven't you ever seen that one, Simon? It's the oldest trick in the book.'

He laughed along with her, while he wiped his nose with the napkin she had had the foresight to bring with her from the counter. It was liberating to see her so happy, though as usual she came out with impulsive remarks or brought up private subjects.

'I've decided not to pick up random men any more.'

'And I've decided to turn a deaf ear to things I don't want to know about.'

He knew her too well and it took more than a small provocation like that to shake him. Even when she said: 'I've written my resignation, you'll have it in the next few days . . .'

. . . he would parry with, 'Excellent, but it's going straight in the bin.' There was no way she would be allowed to leave them. He thought that he would speak to the Countess about finding a new role for Pauline that she would enjoy. There had to be something they could do.

He was halfway through his ice cream when he got a call. He promised to be at Police Headquarters in half an hour; as soon as he had slipped his mobile back into his breast pocket, he got up.

'Well, you know this better than most. I have to go back, one of the guys involved in the murder of Ifunanya Siasia has just turned himself in.'

She got up along with him without any show of irritation. As he said, she knew better than anyone how things were. It had been great that he had made some time for her. They passed the bin and she chucked in the rest of her cone.

'I didn't want that rancid ice cream anyway. Come on, I'll walk you to your car.'

CHAPTER 92

Henrik Krag was transferred from Halmtorvet police station to Copenhagen Police Headquarters; his first interview lasted about two hours and went well, from the perspective of the police.

The interview was carried out by Konrad Simonsen and Arne Pedersen and in addition to Henrik Krag, an old lawyer from one of the city's most expensive legal firms was present. The lawyer, however, threw no obstacles in the way of the interview; on the contrary, on several occasions he helped the police get his client to remember when he was asked a question to which he didn't have an immediate answer. But not so that he directly worked against Henrik Krag, just helped things run smoothly.

The young man's account of the death of Ifunanya Siasia pretty much matched what the Homicide Department already knew. Krag explained how, on Wednesday, 19 March 2008, he and Jan Podowski had driven to the hunting lodge in Hanehoved Forest with the Nigerian girl, to punish her for not giving her clients a good time. The girl was undressed, tied to a stake, a form of torture known as the macaw's perch, and was then hoisted with a rope looped over one of the lodge's cross-beams. The plan was for Henrik Krag to beat the girl with a truncheon brought along for the purpose, but before that happened, the knot tying the rope to the wood-burning stove had loosened and she had crashed to the floor and broken her neck. The two men had carried the body down to the lake, which Jan Podowski already knew about, after which they had picked up the milestone from the road and transported it through the forest on a litter made from a couple of spruce branches they had found behind the hunting lodge. They had tied the girl to the stone and the branches with the same rope they had hoisted her up with, and then they had carried her as far out into the lake as they could, before letting her go. Before leaving Hanehoved Forest, they had poured petrol from a canister in their car over the hunting lodge and burned it down to eliminate potential evidence. On the way back Jan Podowski had told Henrik Krag that he could no longer work for Karina Larsen, that he had been sacked, and he had been given nine thousand kroner in compensation, money that Jan Podowski had had in his wallet.

Henrik Krag's story was simple and straightforward. Konrad Simonsen and Arne Pedersen went through it with him step by step, twice, and concluded that it sounded credible, except for the point about him not having beaten Ifunanya Siasia before she fell down. They pressed him, Arne Pedersen tough, Konrad Simonsen persuasive, and apart from a single, 'Hang on, let's calm down a bit, young man,' directed at Arne Pedersen, the lawyer didn't intervene. After ten minutes of this Henrik Krag admitted that, yes, he had hit her, which was why she had fallen down. He added:

'But we didn't mean to kill her.'

The lawyer supported his client: killing the woman on purpose would have made no business sense. The two police officers agreed that it would not.

After a short break, Henrik Krag was interviewed about his employment with Svend Lerche and Karina Larsen, and in this respect, he was also extremely co-operative. Among other things, he gave them details about the system for the purchase of prostitutes, which the couple had developed; he would make an excellent witness against them, if and when they were found. For example, on several occasions he had witnessed how host families were paid in cash at the end of the month. However, he knew nothing about the Poker Academy, nor did he know the couple's current whereabouts.

On only one occasion, at the very end of the interview, did Henrik Krag surprise the police officers. That happened when he announced that he was married to Benedikte Lerche-Larsen, Svend Lerche and Karina Larsen's daughter. This opened the door to a long list of other questions, but they would deal with these later. Henrik Krag would now be brought before a judge and would be remanded in custody in solitary confinement for four weeks, so he wasn't going anywhere soon, giving them plenty more chances to talk to him. Konrad Simonsen had one further question.

'Does the name Bjarne Fabricius mean anything to you?'

The lawyer burst out with an astonished, 'Why drag him into this?' But he wasn't; Henrik Krag shook his head.

'No, I don't know him. I dealt mostly with Jan . . . I mean Jan Podowski.'

Arne Pedersen looked at Konrad Simonsen; surely that was enough for today? And yes, it was. Konrad Simonsen ended the interview. Or so he thought. But the lawyer said wearily: 'There is another charge.'

Henrik Krag explained.

'It was me who tied the two kids to the truck in Vallensbæk Village last Friday morning.'

CHAPTER 93

The Hanehoved murder investigation could now be regarded as solved. So Konrad Simonsen announced – not without a certain amount of pride – to the Countess, Arne Pedersen and Klavs Arnold at his final briefing meeting. The Countess and Arne Pedersen smiled; it was a fine result of which they could be justly proud. Yet Klavs Arnold didn't join in the celebratory mood. 'For me personally, it's a case I'd rather forget.'

An awkward silence ensued until Konrad Simonsen apologised.

'I'm sorry about my tone, Klavs. It was inappropriate. We all know that you've paid a high price.'

The Jutlander accepted the apology and evaded his colleague's questions. He would get over shooting Jimmy Heeger in time, but there was still no reason to rejoice. Konrad Simonsen continued, more formally, this time.

It had now been established that Henrik Krag had also committed the crime in Vallensbæk Village, DNA tests proved it. He had further confessed to an attack on four young people at Skovbrynet Station in Bagsværd on the evening of Wednesday, 27 May. Those two crimes had been planned and paid for by Svend Lerche, though after Henrik Krag had ceased formally working for him. Police had found part of the payment hidden at the back of the kitchen cupboard in the home of Henrik Krag's mother, exactly where Henrik Krag had told them the money would be. The notes could be traced back to Svend Lerche and had been sent to Henrik Krag through the post. However, the two men's communication couldn't be traced. Henrik Krag's instructions were to call Svend Lerche from a public telephone booth on a number he unfortunately had thrown away after his last task, as he had been scared of discovery and didn't want to be a part of this activity any longer.

Svend Lerche's motives appeared to be a personal vendetta against the politician Helena Holt Andersen for her campaign against prostitution, and against an officer from the Revenue, whom he had threatened on previous occasions. Svend Lerche had punished both of them by hurting their children.

So far, so bad. But there were still unexplained questions, and they increasingly centred around Henrik Krag's wife, Benedikte Lerche-Larsen.

'Why did Henrik Krag sell his motorbike, only for Benedikte Lerche-Larsen to buy back the same bike the following week?' Konrad Simonsen asked. 'And what did he do with the money, we're talking about almost sixty thousand kroner, once he had paid off his bank loan? This is presuming we don't believe his story that he gave it to a friend whose name he has forgotten.'

The Countess backed up her husband:

'Why were Benedikte Lerche-Larsen and Henrik Krag married in haste by her grandmother in Vangede? Henrik Krag claims it was so that she couldn't be forced to testify against him, but that makes no sense because he has already confessed to his crimes. However,

342

it makes a great deal of sense if this was really about *him* not being able to testify against *her*.'

Arne Pedersen said:

'And the biggest mystery of them all: what's a loaded, stunning-looking, upper-class girl from Rungsted doing with an illiterate loser from Ishøj?'

This became too much for the Countess, but she was alone in her opinion as Konrad Simonsen and Klavs Arnold both thought that Arne Pedersen had hit the nail on the head.

They had many more questions, and there was much to indicate that Benedikte Lerche-Larsen had held a significantly more prominent position in her parents' business than they had previously believed. Klavs Arnold asked Konrad Simonsen:

'Is he refusing to talk about her?'

In addition to the official interviews, Konrad Simonsen had visited Henrik Krag in Vestre Prison several evenings in a row in an attempt to get to know the young man. The lawyer wasn't present during these conversations, as Konrad Simonsen had convinced Henrik Krag that they weren't interviews, just chats in order for him to better understand the background to the events. Henrik Krag had accepted this, seemingly happy for the break in his monotonous day. However, he had made it a condition that he wasn't recorded, which the Homicide chief found reasonable. Konrad Simonsen said:

'Oh, no, you can't shut him up. He adores her. He's proud of her, but if I ask about anything that might compromise her in the slightest, he clams up like an oyster. And he's incredibly skilled at knowing exactly when to keep his mouth shut.'

The Countess said:

'We can't be sure that we'll ever know all the answers to our outstanding questions.'

She had spoken to her husband at home and already knew how fruitless Konrad Simonsen's efforts had been.

What remained was a long list of potential charges and possible convictions of people who, in various ways, had been involved in Svend Lerche's and Karina Larsen's business. And here things didn't look good.

The long list shrank every single day. None of the many clients of the African prostitutes that the police had contacted were willing to testify in court, so only two of the host families could be prosecuted, of which one was the family of the banker from Vedbæk, whose young wife filed for divorce and declared herself more than willing to testify against her future ex-husband the moment she was granted a residence permit.

The other was a couple from Gammel Holte, where the husband had been stupid enough to keep records of the income he got from his au pair girl, a set of accounts his wife had snatched and handed over to the police after a major fight. The couple had since separated.

Added to that, the Public Prosecutor for Financial Crime, aka the fraud squad, had given up trying to get its hands on Svend Lerche's and Karina Larsen's assets, comprising of their holiday home, their house in Rungsted and three expensive cars. Charges against the couple in absentia were dropped. The chances of a conviction after a protracted and expensive court case were quite simply too small. The court subsequently suspended the freezing of the couple's assets, and ownership of these was transferred to their daughter, who had incontestable documentation for her authority in this respect. The bottom line was that only six potentially successful prosecutions in the case remained: Henrik Krag, two women from the Integration Ministry and possibly three people who had provided homes for two au pairs. It wasn't much, some might even deem it a failure and a waste of taxpayers' money, but this was where the National Police Commissioner's Press Office proved its worth.

In a brilliant campaign, they convinced the public that police had spared no expense in order to solve the case of the poor Nigerian girl who had been killed and thrown into the lake in Hanehoved Forest. The story featured all over the media, the Danes loved such stories: here in Denmark, all murders were treated equally, regardless of cost or skin colour, as it said in a tabloid newspaper. The National Police Commissioner was happy and praised Konrad Simonsen, who objected.

'But we haven't closed the case yet.'

'No, but go on and do that, Simon. You have my permission. Brilliant work.'

CHAPTER 94

The home of Public Prosecutor Bertha Steenholt and her daughter was exactly as sinister and forbidding as the Countess had been told it would be: a monstrosity of a house with a beautiful copper-roofed turret on one side, no less. It lay set back from the street in the Humlebyen area of Frederiksberg, the overgrown garden, practically a jungle, enclosed by a tall fence. After she had let herself in at the gate, the Countess looked curiously through the undergrowth at the house. All that was missing was a moat and drawbridge, or even better, a barge with a hunchbacked ferryman and then the picture would be complete, she thought, and nearly jumped out of her skin when a cat sitting nearby on a crumbling stack of logs snarled at her.

Bertha Steenholt received her in a much friendlier manner than the Countess had feared would be the case, and though she didn't have an appointment, she was invited into a dining room with a high ceiling, where Bertha and her daughter were having a late supper. The Public Prosecutor fetched cutlery and a plate without asking, insisting that the Countess should taste her daughter's ragoût as it was delicious. She wasn't asked the reason for her visit; that had to wait until after supper. The Countess thought, *I'm a dead woman*, and then ate to her heart's content. She hadn't had time to have dinner yet, and the Public Prosecutor was right, the food really was delicious. It wasn't until the daughter had cleared the table and Bertha Steenholt had lit a cigar that she said:

'Not many people visit me privately to discuss business. I must say, I'm looking forward to this.'

It was the moment of truth for the Countess and she launched herself into it, quoting from memory: 'Anyone who has intercourse using violence, or threats of violence, is guilty of rape and liable to imprisonment of up to eight years. Violence also includes rendering the victim in a state where they are unable to resist the act.'

'Section two hundred and sixteen of the Penal Code, the rape section. Why are you reeling that off?'

'Because of her.'

The Countess took out seven A5 photographs from her bag, which she had gone to the trouble of laminating. She handed them to Bertha Steenholt, who studied each one carefully. The pictures all showed Ifunanya Siasia in everyday situations and at different ages. Her first day at school where, grinning proudly from ear to ear, she posed with her satchel on her back in her new blue and white uniform. A picture of her feeding her baby brother, who had food smeared all over his face and was turning his head away as she approached with the spoon. Her tenth birthday when she and her brother had both been given bicycles that her father and uncle had fixed up. Several pictures of the everyday, the ordinary.

'She lived in a village in the Yenagoa province and attended a Catholic school three kilometres from her home. Everyone liked her, her parents loved her, as parents always do, her teachers praised her, she was especially good at English and Maths.'

Bertha Steenholt wasn't unmoved. 'Oh, dear God,' she murmured. The Countess didn't comment on the outburst, but continued talking.

'On the fifth of June two thousand and seven Ifunanya Siasia was offered a lift to school in a car driven by a former schoolmate. He anaesthetised her with ether and drove her to Lagos almost five hundred kilometres from her home. Here he sold her to a brothel, where she was beaten and raped repeatedly until she learned to welcome the brothel customers. At that point she was, according to her parents, fifteen years old, although her passport fraudulently lists her as older. After six months, she was sold on and trafficked to Europe, initially to Madrid and later to Copenhagen. In Denmark, she worked first in a massage parlour in Skælskør, then she was bought by Karina Larsen and became an au pair and prostitute in Gammel Holte. All entirely of her own free will, of course.'

The Public Prosecutor said in a low voice:

'If you're hoping I can get the men on Simon's wall convicted of rape, you're very much mistaken. I can't get them convicted of anything, and you know it. If I didn't know you better, I would think you were wasting my time.'

'I might be. But is it legally possible to interpret their actions as rape? I mean: the girl was under duress and the men knew it. Or

346

they must have known that there was a very big chance that she was. They're all educated and must have heard of human trafficking unless they're deaf *and* blind. And yet they had sex with her.'

The big woman thought about it carefully. The smoke from her cigar wafted around her; the cat meowed in the garden, sounding like a troubled child.

'It would be hell to prove, but yes, I suppose I could try.'

'What would happen if you had them arrested and charged with rape?'

'What would happen? Why, they would be released again, of course. I would be overruled by the Director of Public Prosecutions or the Justice Ministry, and quite rightly so.'

'I meant what would happen to you?'

'To me?' the Public Prosecutor replied in surprise. 'Nothing, I guess. Admittedly, it's an offence to bring charges that I know won't stand up in court, but . . .'

Her daughter, who was sitting in an armchair at the other end of the room, interrupted them:

'Then I promise to defend you, Mother. I would love the chance.'

Bertha Steenholt shook her head; it would hardly come to that.

'Ultimately I would just be reprimanded, that is if anyone can be bothered, given that I retire in three months . . .'

She stopped and smiled like a wolf smelling meat. The Countess gave her time to savour the idea, but the Public Prosecutor soon shot down the unspoken suggestion.

'It won't work. The moment the officers tasked with the arrests start talking about what's going on, the Director of Public Prosecution will issue counter orders.'

The Countess replied, quietly and without theatricality. Even so, both women felt that the air in the room practically quivered with intensity.

'You give written orders for the arrests to me and I'll find fifty officers who won't say a word until those men are at Police Headquarters.'

'Fifty officers! Tell me, how many of the men do you plan to arrest?'

This was easily answered.

'All of them.'

CHAPTER 95

Benedikte Lerche-Larsen's interview was postponed twice; her lawyer called Konrad Simonsen to inform him that she was unable to attend and they would have to reschedule. When the interview finally took place on the morning of Tuesday, 30 June, it descended into pure farce.

Benedikte Lerche-Larsen arrived at Police Headquarters in tailor-made, navy blue silk trousers with pleats and a simple white shirt. An Hermés Birkin bag in the fashion house's signature gold colour dangled from her arm. She looked like a million dollars, and not a million dollars that was in any way intimidated at being interviewed. Her lawyer was a man in his mid-thirties, impeccably dressed and dry as a bone. He announced to Konrad Simonsen and the Countess, just as he had previously told Arne Pedersen, that Benedikte Lerche-Larsen would say nothing about matters pertaining to her parents or her husband. And in the current circumstances this applied in the broadest possible terms. He savoured his choice of words and Arne Pedersen, who was sitting behind the one-way mirror observing the interview, grinned. Konrad Simonsen was sorely tempted to slap the lawyer. Instead he began the interview by recording the formalities for the benefit of the videotape before asking Benedikte Lerche-Larsen his first question.

'Henrik Krag, your husband, tells us that he turned himself in on your suggestion. Why did you encourage him to do that?'

The lawyer said that Benedikte Lerche-Larsen wouldn't answer that. It related to her husband and, as mentioned in his earlier statement, she could not be compelled to testify against him, neither in court, nor to the police.

'Then tell us if you have heard anything from your father or your mother.'

The Countess asked the question this time but the lawyer gave her the same spiel.

They tried another seven questions and in response to every one, the lawyer chanted his mantra, editing it to fit the occasion. Even when the Countess asked the witness if it was correct that she studied at Copenhagen Business School, she was told by the lawyer that Benedikte Lerche-Larsen wouldn't be answering that question. The Countess asked irritably:

'How does that in any way relate to her parents or her husband?'

'I will explain that in court, should it become relevant.'

It was hopeless. Konrad Simonsen asked sarcastically:

'What do you think about the weather we've been having recently?'

The lawyer replied, deadpan, that he found the question irrelevant, and if it were an expression of some kind of misplaced humour, he would strongly recommend that the police kept this kind of thing internal.

Konrad Simonsen threw in the towel and ended the interview.

Benedikte Lerche-Larsen left Police Headquarters. During the interview she had not said a single word, and all that Konrad Simonsen gained from the non-conversation was that he had to agree with Arne Pedersen: the interviewee – or rather the non-interviewee – was seriously attractive.

The evening turned out to be another disappointment for Konrad Simonsen. It started with a call from the chairman of the committee set up by the deputy director of the Department of Public Prosecution to identify the source of the leak within the police force of the planned search of Silje Esper's house. The group had just finished its meeting, and had decided to suspend its work because although it had a prime suspect, it was unable to secure any evidence, and thought it was impossible to make further progress. Konrad Simonsen expressed his appreciation for the call, and concealed his irritation.

Later, he and Arne Pedersen had driven to Elsinore Chess Club, which was to be visited by chess genius Vladimir Kramnik, no less, as part of its anniversary celebrations. Simonsen had booked his friend and subordinate in plenty of time to take part in a simultaneous chess tournament, and was looking forward to watching how Pedersen would do against the master. However, when they arrived, the master had fallen ill and was in his hotel room with a temperature, and that evening's games had had to be cancelled. Simonsen drove home to Søllerød, feeling thoroughly annoyed. Then, however, something quite remarkable happened.

As he was taking off his shoes in the hallway, the door to the living room opened and out stepped Anni Staal, a crime reporter from *Dagbladet*. Anni Staal was formerly an object of hatred for him, though it had diminished slightly after she had helped him, albeit involuntarily, in a major investigation. She greeted him amicably on her way to the toilet. His jaw dropped. Anni Staal here? In his home! He marched into the living room, but stopped and stood gawping like an idiot. Around the coffee table, in an exuberant mood, sat the Countess, Stella Arnold, the Deputy Commissioner and Bertha Steenholt. The three guests greeted him and then the Countess said:

'This is a closed meeting, Simon.'

CHAPTER 96

Bertha Steenholt's exit from a long working life in the legal profession became the stuff of legend as she left with a bang that echoed for a long time afterwards and successfully secured her reputation.

It happened on Tuesday, 7 July at Police Headquarters in Copenhagen, more specifically in the newly renovated offices of the National Police Commissioner's Press Office on the ground floor, to the right of the building's main entrance. The rooms were still empty, but the walls were freshly painted in the new colours of the police force, an optimistic spring green, a competent steel blue and an extrovert egg-yolk yellow. The floors had also been sanded down and varnished, though just with ordinary varnish, which did nothing to promote the force's new values. However, the press officers had yet to move into their new home, and the Countess had, ably assisted by the National Police Commissioner's secretary, been given permission to borrow the offices for the first two days of the week.

The previous day she had discreetly equipped the place with the few items she would need, namely a workstation with a computer at one end of the larger room and a few props in a smaller, adjacent one; she had also decorated the walls in both rooms. Nothing else was needed. The Deputy Commissioner had helped with the decoration. It wasn't in the original plan that she would have an active involvement with events, but she couldn't help herself and had sneaked in.

When the two women had finished their work, they took a few minutes to study the result, pleased with their efforts. All the way around the previously dull, soon to be 'communication-facilitating' walls were now pinned pictures of Ifunanya Siasia, enlarged from the family photographs the Countess had obtained thanks to Helmer Hammer.

She had had the pictures Photoshopped by a graphic designer who had done an excellent job by consistently highlighting Ifunanya Siasia's face in every picture, letting it stand out sharp and in full colour, while the rest of the picture was in muted, slightly blurred greyscale. The graphic manipulation made the pictures intriguing, and as a spectator you now lingered a little longer on them than strictly necessary, possibly even asking yourself – a little uncomfortably – what does that girl want from me?

With a confident eye and true to form, the Deputy Commissioner had chosen to set this month's record in poor fashion choices: a far too short silk dress with elbow-length black sleeves and a white front patterned with black polka dots. She looked like an overgrown, spotty penguin, and the Countess thought that her terrible dress sense, combined with her often overfamiliar, flowery personality meant that you couldn't help but warm to her. She was entirely her own woman and good for her. The respect seemed to go both ways. On her way out of the door, the Deputy Commissioner commented:

'I wouldn't have thought it of you, Countess ... I mean you taking social issues as seriously as you do. After all, you lack for nothing, why trouble yourself with other people's misfortune?'

The statement took the Countess by surprise, and she didn't know how to reply.

'I don't always feel like this.'

It was the best she could come up with, but the Deputy Commissioner was satisfied. Sometimes is better than never. She smiled her pretty smile. The Countess felt like throwing the penguin a herring.

The Countess dispatched her pairs of officers. All wore uniforms and drove an ordinary patrol cars and each pair was assigned one person to arrest. They had prepared on the quiet, and all had a good idea of where they could contact their suspect, in most cases their place of work. Across Copenhagen and Nordsjælland, men of all ages, all successful and in important positions, were arrested, handcuffed and taken away in police cars. Often to the astonishment and disbelief of colleagues and employees.

Knud Arvidsen, the time is 11.37 , and I'm arresting you for sexual assault. Loud and clear so that Mr Arvidsen could be in no doubt as to the seriousness of the situation, then without further discussion, the shocked man was turned around, his arms pulled behind his back, handcuffs clicked in place and then off with their catch, a firm grip on the prisoner's upper arm. Questions or protests, and there were usually plenty of those, remained unanswered, this wasn't a debating society, and the prisoner would be allowed one phone call once he reached Police Headquarters.

The officers, service-minded as they were, would also refer the man to the website of the National Police Force, where he could read the replies to frequently asked questions, along with lots of other interesting information.

Of the fifty-four customers who, according to Jan Podowski's database, had paid for sex with Ifunanya Siasia, forty-three were arrested. Two of the men, a member of the Folketinget and a

Swedish diplomat, the Countess and Bertha Steenholt had already decided to disregard. They had no wish to provoke a diplomatic or a constitutional incident.

A further six men were on holiday, two could not be found, and one had that same morning been admitted to hospital with acute appendicitis, so the officers would have to do without him too. The rest were taken to Police Headquarters, where they were herded into the Countess's borrowed offices in the press centre. Here they were allowed to make their statutory telephone call.

Most of the men were incandescent with rage; they protested vociferously and threatened the police with everything from million-kroner law suits against the state to complaints filed with every possible department, the Ombudsman and the Justice Minister being amongst the most popular. A handful stood out from the crowd by being more or less frightened and cowed, and one treated the whole thing as a joke, laughing out loud and behaving with exaggerated civility towards the officers, until a female sergeant from Vanløse pulled him aside, pinched his arm hard and told him to behave himself.

As the men arrived and had their handcuffs removed so they could make their telephone call, they were lined up on the floor in the manner the officers sometimes used when mass arresting protesters. They sat sandwiched in between the person sitting in front and the person sitting behind, while they waited to be booked in. They were processed with irritating lethargy by an older sergeant, who sat at a desk at the end of the room and with a two-finger typing style laboriously entered their details into his computer, after which he would gather up their personal possessions in a designated storage bag, meticulously list the contents and the name of the prisoner once again, obtain a signature and continue with the taking of fingerprints. Later he would take two mugshots – one in profile and one full face – with an old-fashioned Polaroid camera. Finally he would confiscate their belts, ties and shoelaces, which were also logged before being put into a separate bag. The latter was for the benefit of the prisoner, so that he could do no harm to himself, the sergeant explained amicably. How on earth you could hang yourself with a shoelace when you were sitting on the floor surrounded by twenty officers, he could not explain, but there was no need to get worked up, after all, the shoelaces would be returned in due course. *And now, please would you go and sit down at the back of the queue so I can get started on the next one?* Two officers stepped up to remove the prisoner should he prove unwilling to leave of his own accord. *And do remember to pull up your trousers.*

The men suffered, shouting out from time to time, and constantly complained, but overall they were surprisingly obedient. The officers present agreed that they had experienced far more challenging behaviour from other prisoners. The only hint of a collective rebellion arose when *Dagbladet*'s crime reporter Anni Staal arrived with a photographer. She had – she later insisted – a long-standing agreement with Bertha Steenholt to observe her at work for a day, to get pictures and background material for a feature about the Public Prosecutor's retirement later that year. And how on earth could it be her problem – she practically screamed at her editor-in-chief – that some old lecher from *Dagbladet*'s board of directors happened to have got himself arrested on that very same day? And she would really like to know, and here she jabbed a finger directly against the forehead of the editor-in-chief, if he was hinting that she shouldn't write her front-page scoop for that very reason, because then she was absolutely sure that *Dagbladet*'s free and independent journalists . . . here the editor-in-chief stopped her nervously by holding up his hands. *No, God dammit, Anni, of course we'll run the story.*

The upheaval among the prisoners that began when the press turned up was successfully quelled by the officers, who didn't need to do much more than take a few steps towards the men sitting on the floor. So the photographer got their pictures and Anni Staal her interviews. *Oh, hello, Mr Olesen – you are Torsten Olesen, the famous financier, aren't you? Tell me, is this the first time you've been arrested for rape?*

When the prisoners had finally all been logged on the sergeant's computer and fingerprinted and had their mugshots taken, Bertha Steenholt made her entrance. She held a stack of papers in her hand, which without comment she distributed to every single prisoner. The Countess had had Malte Borup working overtime, and the intern had produced a small dossier for each man with clear pictures of his physical encounter with Ifunanya Siasia. When Bertha Steenholt had finished handing these out, she thundered in a voice that reached every corner of the room that she had distributed evidence to all of them, so they could see for themselves that there was a reason why they had been arrested.

One of the men protested, 'There's no legal basis for your charge,' but was immediately cowed by her authoritative: 'Quiet! We'll get to that later.' Then Bertha Steenholt took her time recounting for them Ifunanya Siasia's life and tragic fate, regularly referring to one or more of the pictures on the wall. Despite hardly any of the men looking at them, she soon got into her stride. Her next point was the legal aspect, and here she made no attempt to hide that what she was undertaking was a test case, which would hopefully extend the application of the sexual assault legislation. There could be little doubt that the case would ultimately end up in the Supreme Court, and she had decided that the time had come for her to try and see if she could get a conviction based on the probability, bordering on certainty, that they all knew Ifunanya Siasia was under duress when they had sex with her.

And in that respect Bertha Steenholt could inform everyone present that none, *none* of the very best experts in the Justice Ministry, had disputed her assessment. The Public Prosecutor took her time, she was thorough, but when she was done, the men were quiet. There could be no doubt: she had scared the living daylights out of every single one of them.

The next and final point had been carefully choreographed between the Countess and Bertha Steenholt. A female officer arrived with a dog and initially waited at the back of the room, but then the devil got into the animal; it strained on its leash towards the row of sitting men, barking fiercely and loudly. It was a Labrador and it wasn't particularly aggressive despite its performance, so none of the men felt very scared. Most ignored it; they felt they had more important things to worry about. Bertha Steenholt, however, was furious with the animal, it had interrupted her speech, although she had almost finished. She commanded angrily: 'Get that dog out of here now, so I can hear myself speak.'

The dog fell silent, but the Countess interrupted her with a 'But . . . but . . .' Bertha Steenholt made no attempt to hide her irritation.

'What do you want this time?'

'It's a sniffer dog.'

There could be no doubt: one or more of the prisoners was in possession of banned substances. And at Police Headquarters, of all places! This was totally unacceptable. The Public Prosecutor tried the carrot.

'Would the man in possession of cannabis make himself known immediately?'

But the criminal held firm, and so there was no other way. A thorough, physical examination of every prisoner would just have to be carried out. Luckily there was a police surgeon in the building, in the department next door, as it happened, and he was willing to offer his expertise, he really didn't mind. The examinations would be carried out in the adjacent room with suitable respect for each man's modesty. Bertha Steenholt apologised. Such examinations were obviously never pleasant, but based on the police's legitimate suspicion it was, according to section this, that and the other, entirely legal and unfortunately pressingly urgent to . . . The men's names were called and they were taken individually to see the doctor.

It took a long time before the performance ended. The five women who had met in Konrad Simonsen's living room had been very creative. The action had been carefully chosen to take place on a day where the National Police Commissioner was attending a conference in Aalborg, and the Assistant Commissioner was on holiday in Norway. The result was that the many telephone calls that came in, especially from the Justice Ministry, were put through to the Deputy Commissioner, but she was happy to reassure the agitated civil servants that it must be a baseless rumour; she had never ordered a mass arrest for rape, and she had personally visited every possible location where she could imagine such a group of men might be held and had not found the slightest trace of any such activity. Perhaps it was another police force, she couldn't comment on that, but it wasn't hers.

Eventually the telephone calls subsided; the Justice Minister had received a tip-off. Rumour had it that, politically speaking, it would be career suicide to intervene in what was going on, if indeed anything was, and soon the lowest clerk knew that they were unlikely to advance up the ladder if they poked their nose into what was happening. The result was that the many outraged lawyers who rang the Ministry were passed from pillar to post, as no one wanted to take responsibility for the conversation.

Only one person could effectively put a stop to this abuse of power, and that was the Director of Public Prosecutions. He had taken a day off to do some gardening and sort out his flowerbeds, but was eventually forced to concede that he had to leave his home in Snekkersten and drive to Copenhagen. But he had barely driven one kilometre before he was stopped by a police patrol car for speeding. He was furious, he had been four kilometres above the permitted speed limit, what overzealousness in their job! And not only that, his car was then inspected from top to bottom, even though it was leased and in superb condition. But there was nothing he could do about it.

CHAPTER 97

Benedikte Lerche-Larsen stretched out on the bed, then rolled her shoulders a couple of times, first one way then the other, before interlocking her fingers behind her head. She was naked, her body sweaty, and felt in need of a shower. Bjarne Fabricius lay by her side resting on one elbow, while he tickled her nipple with his fingertip. There was nothing sexual in his touch, he was distracted, lost in his own thoughts and hardly aware of what he was doing. She freed one of her hands and removed his finger, which was irritating her. It appeared to bring him back to the present. He caught her eye, evaluating her as if it were the first time he had seen her.

'This is a one-off, it won't happen again.'

She tried to match his tone of voice.

'If you say so.'

'I say so.'

He didn't elaborate, nor had she expected him to. She sat up, as did he.

'I have a suitcase of money that belongs to you. I don't know how much, but it's quite a lot.'

'From Svend and Karina?'

He confirmed that, yes, it was from them. She asked him cautiously:

'Will you tell me if it was quick?'

'I will, and yes, it was. They never knew what happened to them, but don't ask me again.'

She accepted this, and what more was there to know? She made a quick decision.

'I think you should keep the money. You've lost a great deal recently, and it's partly because of me.'

The smile he gave her never reached his eyes.

'You're a clever girl, Benedikte. That's a deal. And while we're on the subject, how long do you think it will be before we're up and running, according to your new model?'

'I intend to present a detailed plan to you next week. There will be things you'll need to decide.'

'Fine, but could you give me an idea of it now?'

Benedikte Lerche-Larsen quickly went through the main points. Four to five ordinary brothels, preferably in the provinces where competition was less intense. Billing once a month where the 'hosts' would pay them a fixed amount, and what money they made above and beyond that was theirs to keep. No involvement in the operation from his or her side, ideally; a monthly payment to be made to a Caribbean account from which money would be transferred to international poker players. She swung her legs over the edge of the bed and continued talking:

'The only restrictions are: no children, no unnecessary violence, and the girls will be bought through you. How quickly and how many can you deliver?'

'As many and as quickly as necessary. Expected profits?'

'You'll have to wait for that, it would be irresponsible of me to pluck a figure out of the air before I have the full picture. But, in no more than six months, at least the same as you used to get from Svend – and please note, all of that money would be laundered. And that's a conservative figure, I don't want to make promises I can't keep.'

He was about to praise her for her cleverness once more, but stopped himself. Business over and done with, he asked:

'Are you going to take a shower?'

'Yes, will you be joining me? Or does that come under your comment about this being a one-off?'

He laughed, no, it didn't. That wouldn't apply until tomorrow morning.

CHAPTER 98

At the height of the summer of 2009, Benedikte Lerche-Larsen's departure, on her parents' behalf, from the beautiful three-storey house with a view of the Øresund, was undramatic. The neighbours watched the event with excitement, twitching hand-embroidered kitchen curtains or glancing quickly over privet hedges, and saw the young woman walk out through the garden having locked up behind her.

Once outside on the pavement, she carefully closed the wrought-iron gate and glanced back at the house, which had been the scene of hectic activity that whole morning as its contents had been cleared and driven away in large removal vans. None of the neighbours knew to where. She walked at a leisurely pace up to the Volvo that had arrived half an hour ago. The car's tinted windows were open. Everyone craned their necks to catch a first glimpse of the new owners of the house. Rumours had spread like wildfire. The estate agent, a local firm from Usserød, had sold the house to a retired couple from Horsens. He was a former sales director in the meat industry, and she was – and here the estate agent had smiled mischievously – well, she was his wife.

The meat salesman got out of the car and his wife followed suit. Benedikte Lerche-Larsen handed him the keys and handshakes were exchanged, while a dachshund with a slipped disc, belonging to a high-ranking barrister, barked angrily. It had spent enough time sniffing the same lamppost and was ready to move on. The neighbourhood's verdict was positive. At first sight, the couple seemed like decent people. Judging by their clothes, possibly a little provincial, but that would hopefully pass in time. Besides, anything was better than Benedikte Lerche-Larsen and her parents. Even a hippy commune would have been preferable to that.

The street's hidden audience divided its attention when Benedikte Lerche-Larsen, smiling and courteous as always, said goodbye to the couple, but rather than get into her car, or rather her father's car, started chatting to a man who had appeared by her side. Some turned to focus on the new arrivals, others continued to follow the young woman's departure.

The man who had turned up so unexpectedly was about sixty, a little chubby, tall and with a slightly stooping posture. A few recognised him from the television as a senior police officer of some kind; most insisted he was a reporter, probably from one of the more popular tabloids, as his charcoal grey suit could easily be identified, despite the distance, as having been bought off the peg. As if the road hadn't already had its fair share of that type.

Konrad Simonsen looked around uncomfortably. He felt he was being watched. Benedikte Lerche-Larsen read his mind. She looked around.

'Yes, it's like living in a goldfish bowl. I imagine my dear neighbours want to be absolutely sure I have gone for good.'

'Can you blame them?'

She gave a light shrug.

'I didn't think the two of us would meet again. Incidentally, you don't look at all well, are you ill?'

'That's none of your business.'

'No, I don't suppose it is and ultimately I don't care. Are you here to arrest me?'

There was no hint of fear in her voice. She knew the answer.

'No, sadly not.'

'Then why are you here?'

'To tie up loose ends. Call it curiosity, if you like.'

Her short, ironic burst of laughter was predictable.

'How stupid do you think I am?'

'Bright enough to express yourself in hypothetical phrases, which will prove nothing if I'm wearing a wire ... which, by the way, I'm not.'

'I shouldn't even be talking to you. You have five minutes, then I'm leaving. I have things to do.'

Konrad Simonsen had calculated that she would be intrigued if he turned up for an informal chat, and he would appear to have been right.

'I've spent many evenings with your husband, and I must say, he really does care about you. He sends his love, by the way.'

Both statements were lies, he didn't send his love, and *many evenings* was a huge exaggeration. His conversations with Henrik Krag had provided very little information, and Simonsen had stopped going; they weren't worth his time. Nonetheless, a couple of minor details had further strengthened his suspicion that Benedikte Lerche-Larsen was much more heavily involved in the Hanehoved crime and its many offshoots than had been revealed. But how and to what extent he didn't know, and probably never would.

'You must have a very special body.'

'Thank you.'

'Please excuse me for discussing your personal life, but I know that the first time you slept with Henrik Krag was Sunday the seventh of June, and only twelve days later you announced you were pregnant. I've checked with an expert, and it's just about feasible, but I don't think you're even a little bit pregnant, Benedikte.'

She wasn't in the least surprised to hear this, and quickly flipped the situation:

'Perhaps I should take another test to be absolutely sure. That's a really good idea, thank you so much.'

'And then there's another interesting thing about you: when you dream about your father, which according to Henrik, you often do, your dreams always have a remarkable similarity to famous film scenes. Don't you have the imagination to come up with your own dreams?'

She laughed. *Is that the best you can do?* There was nothing forced about her laughter, she really was enjoying herself, and Konrad Simonsen felt humiliated. He considered telling her that she was a bitch, which he was entirely convinced of. But he didn't. Instead he said slowly:

'I'll be keeping an eye on you from now on, Benedikte. I'll keep coming back to check what you're up to, see if the relationship between you and your husband changes over time so that he might want to tell me more about you than he's currently willing to do.'

That didn't shake her either.

'You're welcome, then perhaps we might meet again.'

'I hope so.'

'Yes, I'm sure you do. You and so many other men.'

She smiled, this time icily, then turned around and walked to her car.

CHAPTER 99

Benedikte Lerche-Larsen drove to the car park in Rudersdal where she had seen her father for the last time. She got out of her Audi R8, strolled leisurely past Næsseslottet and picked a path at random in the romantic country park without knowing whether or not it was a public right of way. It was sunny, but not unpleasantly hot, and to her right grey rain clouds were gathering, though it was hard to decide if they were drifting in her direction. The wind played lazily with her dress, which felt nice.

She tried as honestly as possible to evaluate her own role in the events of the last few months.

It had taken time, but it hadn't been difficult to produce the picture of her and Henrik Krag in Hanehoved Forest carrying the stone between them. She had waited until the anniversary of the hooker's death and then gone to the same spot, wearing the tracksuit she had worn on her first visit. With the remote control timer on her camera she had taken countless pictures of herself posed as though she were carrying the spruce branch with the stone. The milestone itself had been depicted in several newspapers, from which she had scanned it. Henrik's hands and arms she had found in an advertisement. The rest was sheer hard Photoshopping, and the result had been good. When she had finished, she had reduced the picture to a coarse mobile-phone format, and then enlarged it to the final photograph, which she sent to herself, along with the front page of *Poker Player* and a letter. Unless you were an expert, and Henrik Krag most definitely wasn't, it was impossible to see that it was a forgery.

The other major technical challenge was the synthetic voice that Henrik had called Ida. The majority of the messages, which she claimed to have recorded with herself as the recipient, were easy to produce and it was even easier to call Henrik and let Ida give him his tasks.

But the very first exchanges at Jægersborg Library, where she'd needed to talk to Ida in front of Henrik, they were difficult. Technically it wasn't a challenge; it was only a question of getting the telephone card in her computer to call her at a given time and play the two sound files she had already recorded with Ida. But it was incredibly difficult to time the conversation, so that it sounded natural. She had practised many, many times, before she mastered it, and would never forget the four sentences, even if she lived to be a hundred:

'State your name again, your first name and your surname.'
'Benedikte.' *Wait, wait. And then*: 'Lerche-Larsen.'

'Why is there an echo?'

Wait for a long time, pretend to be thinking about it, then: 'There are two of us on speakerphone.'

The rest was a matter of Henrik becoming so strongly attached to her that he reached the point where he would do anything for her. Things that would fatally undermine her father and thus her mother in Bjarne's eyes, until he saw no other option than to eliminate them. But Henrik had been easy, and she had played her role so successfully that for a time it had become a part of her, so much so that she had really enjoyed her time with him. Except for her own two tasks, which were obviously unpleasant, but necessary.

She had also been lucky, she was happy to admit that. Take Jimmy Heeger, for example. Now she might have been the one to tell her father that the man's name was listed as a potential employee on Jan Podowski's computer, and she might have undertaken a massive piece of research reading printouts of previous offences to find the biggest psychopath she could, but she had never dreamed for one moment that he would actually kill Jan's widow.

However, not everything had gone according to plan. She had expected Bjarne to also eliminate Henrik, but that hadn't happened. The irony was that it was possibly because she herself had fought so fiercely for him, but by then she had had no choice. If Bjarne Fabricius had had even the slightest suspicion that she might have been happy to see the back of her husband, it could very easily have proved fatal to her. There was no room for any kind of double-dealing, she had had to give Henrik everything she had, and that, combined with his enormous loyalty to her, had been enough to save him. On the other hand, he was fine where he was, and unlikely to present much of a problem, at least not for many years.

Then there were her errors, because she had made a few of those and she had to acknowledge them if she wanted to do better next time. Her pregnancy announcement had been a mistake, it was badly timed. Of course she would have to tell Henrik that she had miscarried. She had planned to do so all along . . . how terrible, suddenly there was blood everywhere, etc. . . . but with Simonsen in the wings, that would be more difficult and not as straightforward as she had imagined.

It had also been a mistake to leave some of the research into the politician Helena Holt Andersen's son and his girlfriend to a random poker player. Perhaps the biggest mistake she had made. By now the poker player must have guessed what his information had been used for, given the press coverage of the attack on the two young people in Vallensbæk. And if he had contacted the police – although he had been strongly advised not to do so – things could have gone very wrong for her. Especially while her father was alive. Fortunately, that hadn't happened, but she certainly couldn't take the credit for that. She had been so incredibly tired and simply hadn't had the time to do everything herself, but it was a poor excuse, which had again resulted from poor planning.

Sleeping with Bjarne had been her final mistake. She should definitely not have done so, or rather, she should have waited months at least. As it was, she had now been unfaithful to Henrik and it was vital not to upset Bjarne's view of her and Henrik's love. Besides, the encounter had proved to be a waste of time, not that it mattered. She had hoped that her openness – she smiled – would rub off on their business relationship, but that hadn't happened, not at all.

She sat down on a bench and studied the ashes of a bonfire directly in front of her on the far side of the path, before a beautiful rainbow across Lake Furesøen caught her attention. She checked that she had remembered everything. She thought she had. Perhaps there were a couple of missed details, but they would probably come back to her some other day and if not, they couldn't be that important. Overall it was an excellent result: she had gambled with high stakes, the way she loved to do, she had won, which she loved even more, and now she had money, power and freedom, which she loved most of all.

She got up again although she had just sat down, unable to make up her mind, a touch restless. She would grant herself the rest of the day off, she had earned it. She began to walk back to her car with a wonderful feeling of having the world at her feet.

A NOTE ON THE TYPE

The text of this book is set in Adobe Caslon, named after the English punch-cutter and type-founder William Caslon I (1692–1766). Caslon's rather old-fashioned types were modelled on seventeenth-century Dutch designs, but found wide acceptance throughout the English-speaking world for much of the eighteenth century until replaced by newer types towards the end of the century. Used in 1776 to print the Declaration of Independence, they were revived in the nineteenth century and have been popular ever since, particularly amongst fine printers. There are several digital versions, of which Carol Twombly's Adobe Caslon is one.

THE GIRL IN THE ICE

The second in the international bestselling five-part Konrad Simonsen series, a chilling tale from the authors of *The Hanging*

Under the heartless vault of the Greenland's arctic sky the body of a girl is discovered. Half-naked and tied up, buried hundreds of miles from any signs of life, she has lain alone, hidden in the ice cap, for twenty-five years.

When Detective Chief Superintendent Konrad Simonsen is flown in to investigate this horrific murder, it triggers a dark memory. As Simonsen's team work to discover evidence that has long since been buried, they unearth truths that certain people would rather stayed forgotten. But the pressure is on as it becomes clear that the killer chooses victims who all look unsettlingly similar, a similarity that may be used to the investigators' advantage, just so long as they can keep the suspect in their sights ...

'The best Danish crime fiction in years'
LARS KEPLER

ORDER YOUR COPY:

BY PHONE: +44 (0) 1256 302 699; **BY EMAIL:** DIRECT@MACMILLAN.CO.UK
DELIVERY IS USUALLY 3–5 WORKING DAYS. FREE POSTAGE AND PACKAGING FOR ORDERS OVER £20.
ONLINE: WWW.BLOOMSBURY.COM/BOOKSHOP
PRICES AND AVAILABILITY SUBJECT TO CHANGE WITHOUT NOTICE.

WWW.BLOOMSBURY.COM/AUTHOR/LOTTE–HAMMER

B L O O M S B U R Y

THE VANISHED

Not all secrets stay buried

A man is found dead at the bottom of his apartment stairs. His death appears to have been a tragic accident.

But, when Detective Superintendent Konrad Simonsen discovers images of a long-missing girl plastering the walls of the man's attic, the case takes a sinister turn. The homicide team at the Copenhagen Police Force is forced to delve deep into a disturbing past, dragging up skeletons that would sooner be forgotten.

'Delicately crafted and supremely atmospheric'
DAILY MAIL

ORDER YOUR COPY:

BY PHONE: +44 (0) 1256 302 699; BY EMAIL: DIRECT@MACMILLAN.CO.UK
DELIVERY IS USUALLY 3–5 WORKING DAYS. FREE POSTAGE AND PACKAGING FOR ORDERS OVER £20.
ONLINE: WWW.BLOOMSBURY.COM/BOOKSHOP
PRICES AND AVAILABILITY SUBJECT TO CHANGE WITHOUT NOTICE.

WWW.BLOOMSBURY.COM/AUTHOR/LOTTE–HAMMER

BLOOMSBURY

THE NIGHT FERRY

The chilling fifth book in the Konrad Simonsen series

Sixteen children and four adults are killed in a devastating boat crash in Copenhagen. Detective Chief Superintendent Konrad Simonsen is called in, only to discover that this was no accident and that one of the passengers has a very personal connection to the homicide team.

Reeling from this revelation and not knowing who to trust, Simonsen follows a trail that eventually leads him to Bosnia and a legacy of criminal misconduct. All evidence points towards one shady figure: a high-ranking army specialist with a suspicious past. But the more Simonsen digs, the further the truth slips from his grasp.

'Terrific ... A rattle-paced, twisty thriller. I can't wait for the next in the series'
SAGA

ORDER YOUR COPY:

BY PHONE: +44 (0) 1256 302 699; BY EMAIL: DIRECT@MACMILLAN.CO.UK
DELIVERY IS USUALLY 3–5 WORKING DAYS. FREE POSTAGE AND PACKAGING FOR ORDERS OVER £20.
ONLINE: WWW.BLOOMSBURY.COM/BOOKSHOP
PRICES AND AVAILABILITY SUBJECT TO CHANGE WITHOUT NOTICE.

WWW.BLOOMSBURY.COM/AUTHOR/LOTTE-HAMMER

BLOOMSBURY